# Jimmy Jones' Puzzles

## The Mystery of Blackhill Estate

Bogumil Kaczynski

authorHOUSE®

AuthorHouse™
1663 Liberty Drive
Bloomington, IN 47403
www.authorhouse.com
Phone: 1-800-839-8640

©2011 Bogumil Kaczynski. All rights reserved.

No part of this book may be reproduced, stored in a retrieval system, or transmitted by any means without the written permission of the author.

First published by AuthorHouse    1/11/2011

ISBN: 978-1-4567-7245-1 (sc)

Printed in the United States of America

Any people depicted in stock imagery provided by Thinkstock are models, and such images are being used for illustrative purposes only. Certain stock imagery © Thinkstock.

This book is printed on acid-free paper.

Because of the dynamic nature of the Internet, any Web addresses or links contained in this book may have changed since publication and may no longer be valid. The views expressed in this work are solely those of the author and do not necessarily reflect the views of the publisher, and the publisher hereby disclaims any responsibility for them.

In the memory of Czarek Olszewski

"**S**hall we go through the park?" suggested Vanessa.
"What, now? When it's dark?"...
"You heard about the ghost in the old mansion and you're afraid" Vanessa teased.

"I'm not scared" Ronnie shrugged" The only thing is that it's dark and you can easily stray off the path and fall into the bushes or worse, into the stream. I think we should take the road, and although it takes longer we will get home without any trouble. And for the record I've not heard about a ghost haunting the old mansion, it's just little kids trying to scare people. You don't believe in ghosts, do you? "

"I don't know, maybe, and you don't?" Vanessa looked at Ronnie "Well...?"

"No, a serious person doesn't believe in things like ghosts" he answered.

Vanessa laughed "And you are this serious person then?"

"I am "he replied patiently "I want to be a doctor so I need to have a mature way of looking at things" he continued.

"Well, I want to be a famous actress when I grow up" she said.

"Yes, I know, I know... "Ronnie muttered under his breath as he turned onto the path leading through the park.

"So now you want to go through the park?" Vanessa asked, stopping.

" Well, yes, I'll prove to you that there are no such things as ghosts and that it is a silly story that people have made up" Ronnie replied.

Vanessa stood in the middle of the path, shivering. Ronnie grabbed her hand, pulling her towards the park.

"If you're scared of something, you need to face it to overcome your fear, anyone will tell you that. Come on"

It was only 6 pm but being October, it was already dark and the overcast skies only added to the gloom of the evening. Ronnie and Vanessa were on their way home from rehearsals for the school's Christmas play. They had a four mile walk from school and taking a shortcut through the park would mean taking off about a mile off their journey. The park, as they called it wasn't really a park but part of Blackhill Estate. The Blackhills were once rich and had owned a lot of land, but the last in line, Lord David, had not taken care of the estate and eventually had to sell it. It was bought by Mr. Doughty who was an antique enthusiast. He was usually away from the estate, travelling around the country, buying antique furniture and paintings for his new home. He kept mostly to himself and did not get involved in community life so there were rumours circulating that he was a bit strange. He took care of the house, but didn't fuss with the garden so with time it had become a bit overgrown and untidy. The locals had made a path through the estates' gardens, providing them with a shortcut that was commonly used in the summer, less often in winter.

Mr. Doughty had passed away recently and there was speculation amongst the locals, adults and children alike about the future of the estate. Mr. Doughty had no family or relatives and there had been rumours that he had passed the entire estate onto the National Heritage Society with a request that they turn it into a museum. No one had any idea why an old country mansion would make a good museum, so everyone waited to see what will happen.

Vanessa and Ronnie started down the path.

"My dad would like the mansion to be turned into a museum" said Ronnie "We would get tourists and our town would be a bit livelier. But the mansion has been sealed off and he is worried that nothing will come of it."

Vanessa sighed "A museum is a great idea, but if it were a real haunted mansion that would be even better, it would attract ghost hunters and our town would be famous. That would be great"

"Is that why you mentioned about the supposed ghost?" asked Ronnie.

"Yeah, and if it isn't real than we can make one up. I would be up for it" said Vanessa "Or play the role of someone who has seen it to make it more convincing" She looked at Ronnie " I can use the role as practice before I go to drama school" . She stopped suddenly in the middle of the path, grabbed Ronnie's hand and with a frightened look on her face she stuttered out" I saw him... he was horrible, I'm terrified, the scull had an eerie glow... help me" and she burst into tears.

Ronnie winced and looked at her "You are joking, aren't you?" he asked worryingly.

"Of course I am" Vanessa laughed "I was only acting, silly" she looked her normal self again. She gave him a pat on the back. "Well, it would be harder to convince people that there is a ghost here, a real one" said Ronnie, trying to ignore the fact that he had actually fallen for her trick.

"You're right" said Vanessa "But it's definitely worth trying" and after a slight pause she added "It's so scary in the park tonight."

Ronnie shook his head, not sure whether she actually meant that or whether it was another trick. He didn't want to fall for it again. The park wasn't a very pleasant place to be at this time and on a winter's evening. There was no light along the way and it was so dark they had to hold onto one another so one of them wouldn't stray off the path and end up in the bushes. They knew the way as they had used the shortcut during the summer every day, but everything looks different in the dark.

They had reached the hedgerow which separated the park from the front lawn of the mansion. It wasn't much further from here. They only needed to cut over the lawn, follow the path on the other side through the park, cross the bridge over the river and then back onto the road. From there it was only a few minutes to their houses.

After a few yards, the darkness brightened a little. They had walked onto the lawn in front of the mansion. The wind was strong and the evening was cold, and by now it had started to rain. Vanessa stepped a bit closer to Ronnie.

"Wasn't he afraid to live here all by himself?" she whispered to Ronnie.

"I'm sure he got used to it" said Ronnie" Anyway, he was mostly away hunting for his antiques"

"Besides he had the caretaker Dave staying in one of the outbuildings, see that is him there where the light is lit" added Ronnie.

She saw a little window in a distance with the light on and felt better. A dark and unlit mansion seemed very frightening and scary to her, but the light in the nearby caretaker's house was giving little life to the dark scenery.

"What about him, is he not afraid?" she asked.

"Who, caretaker Dave? You're still on about that?" asked Ronnie.

"Well, I'm scared of him, he looks so .... Odd" Vanessa hesitated.

"Not a big deal" said Ronnie "He's just weird, that's all, same as Mr Doughty was. Now stop being silly."

"Shush" said Vanessa and squeezed Ronnie's hand even harder.

But he did not hear anything but the wind howls that were overcoming all other sounds around them. -What is she on about? - He wondered. And then he understood. He saw a light on the first floor of the mansion. It was flashing in the room above the main entrance .There was a row of ten big sash windows and huge balcony supported by six pillars. Light flashed on the right side, then moved slowly all the way to the left and disappeared.

"But, the mansion has been sealed off by the officials "said Ronnie with an uncertain tone in his voice.

"Yyyeess" said Vanessa. She was trembling all over and this time it was for real.

"Thieves! Someone has broken in!" shouted Ronnie. He took Vanessa by her hand dragged towards the building where caretaker was staying. "We have to tell Dave."

"That wasn't thieves, it was a ghost" she said, clearly frightened.

"Hey mister, mister, thieves!" shouted Ronnie.

They stopped outside the door and it opened almost instantly. A big figure emerged from the doorway. He had a big bushy beard, small hump on his back and longish grey hair.

"What's the problem?" He grumbled, looking at them. Ronnie explained quickly about the lights they had seen in one of the windows of the old mansion. He was standing there listening in dismay to Ronnie's story. When they finished he went back in, took his torch and went outside. The children followed him around the building as he checked all of the doors, windows and shutters. There was no sign of a break-in .Only then he looked at them and said "You must have imagined it kids" his voice was bitter and chilling. But Ronnie and Vanessa clearly saw light and movement inside, and didn't understand why he didn't believe them.

"Maybe it was ghosts "whispered Vanessa.

Dave looked at her carefully then he glanced at the mansion and said "That's where the library is" he said slowly" That is where Mr. Doughty spent most of his time when he was at home" he added, deep in thought.

"And what do you think?" asked Vanessa

"Maybe he's still there" said the caretaker giving them a strange look. Vanessa felt a shiver down her back.

"There are no such things as ghosts "said Ronnie. But he was not so sure of it now. He was standing in the middle of dark, scary park. He remembered the light that they had both seen, a light that shouldn't have been there because the mansion was sealed off and there was no way for anyone to get inside .They were both confused and little bit shaken .Dave put the torch close to his face and said with a scary voice "So it was all a dream, now go home ".Turned torch off and disappeared into the darkness of the park. Ronnie and Vanessa held their hands and started to run, ignoring the bushes and brunches in their way. A little bit out breath they stopped when they reached the main road. They spotted the small B&B in the distance and felt more at ease.

"You wanted a ghost and now you have one" said Ronnie to Vanessa with a bit of anger in his voice, as if she was to blame for what had just happened. They did not speak for the rest of the journey home, only once they looked back at the big, old, scary park looming in the darkness.

# CHAPTER 1

At the beginning of November, I had been called to see my superior, who was now the director of the culture and arts department for National Heritage Society. Their office was located in central London, just around the corner from Tottenham Court Road tube station.

After graduating university I had been working in various museums all over the country, gaining experience and knowledge, but a few years ago I had been transferred to work within the offices of the National Heritage Society. My job at the offices did not have an official title to it. Of course it didn't mean that I didn't do anything, on the contrary. I was assigned on special cases and my work was varied and interesting. I was assigned to difficult and delicate cases, investigating illegal trade of antiques, paintings, searching for museums' lost or stolen collections and searching for lost treasures. I often worked closely with the police, antique dealers and experts. Of course I had a lot of 'cold cases' which I did not manage to solve, but I did have a lot of successes in my work and my last assignment had been just that. I couldn't wait to debrief to my supervisor, Mr. Simpson and see what new case was waiting for me.

As I sat down, I looked around. There was a few people waiting to see Mr. Simpson as usual, and his secretary asked me to wait because he wanted to see me urgently and would fit me in between his appointments. I looked around at the other people waiting to see Mr. Simpson but did not know any of them. Next to me a couple was talking loudly and I couldn't help but overhear their conversation. I looked over at them without being too obvious. A man in his early twenties was sprawled in one of the big chairs, wearing a baggy black jumper, tight black jeans. His hair was shoulder length and a bit of a mess. Next to him was a young woman, about the same age as him, but she seemed to care more about her appearance as her blonde hair was neatly tied back in a bun and she was wearing a well cut skirt suit. Her make-up was very delicate, enhancing her natural beauty.

"... that post should be assigned to someone young, energetic, straight out of university" she continued the conversation" but I will bet you that neither me nor you will get it."

"I know exactly what you mean" he agreed" They probably have a curator assigned, someone from here who has been stuck in a dusty office for the past fifteen years, has forgotten everything they learnt at university and has ancient working methods. A post like that should be assigned to someone young and dynamic whose ideas will bring visitors in, not scare them away."

"I know, I bet he got the position because of friends in high places if you know what I mean" She sighed.

"Do you know who it is?" he asked.

"No, but someone told me about this guy. Apparently he barely graduated, and his first curatorship was secured with help of friends in high places. Then, with a little help from his friends again, he got a job at Society headquarters, but because he is no good, he has been given the position of curator so they won't have to worry about him anymore. Some people get everything handed to them on a platter, not like us, we have to work our way to the top" she finished angrily.

"Is he old?" he asked

"In his mid thirties, why?" she asked looking at him.

"Well, maybe you can charm him, get married and have an easy way to the top" he said with a cheeky grin on his face.

"I'm sure he isn't even nice looking" she said, giving him an angry look.

At this point I stopped paying attention as Mr. Simpson's secretary said that he was ready to see me.

I went in and sat down. I couldn't wait for my new case and the adventures it would bring.

Mr. Simpson looked at me and with a small smile playing on his lips asked me "Have you ever heard of John Doughty?"

I looked at him" Umm, no, I haven't, should I have?" I asked.

"Well, no, not really, I am not surprised that you haven't. He wasn't well known, an antique enthusiast, he used to have an antique bookstore in Kensington. He made a bit of money and decided to leave London. He moved up north, he bought the old estate that was once owned by the Blackhills in Cromdale. He spent a lot of time travelling and antique hunting; his dream was to restore the mansion to what it was in its high time. He also spent a lot of his time researching the freemasons; this passion had started back in the day when he owned the bookshop. He accumulated a lot of interesting first editions as well as furniture and paintings from the period when the mansion was built. Now, James, You don't know why I am telling you all of this, do you?"

"No, I don't Sir, but I would like to find out" I said

"Well, Mr. Doughty had passed away recently. He had no family or relatives." Mr. Simpson explained "He has left the entire estate and its contents to the Society, under the condition that it will be turned into a museum. We have looked into the matter and it is feasible. You still don't know what I'm getting at do you?" He looked at me.

"No I don't Sir" I replied, intrigued.

"The mansion has been sealed off. This was over two months ago. The museum needs to be ready for the grand opening before the summer so we can maximise visitor numbers. We need to check the inventory of the mansions, see what treasures Sir Doughty had collected over the years and what the best way forward for the museum is. For that I need someone who has vast knowledge and who will be the curator for the new museum. And that someone is you my dear James" he looked at me, smiling.

I jumped to my feet.

"What? Me? You must be kidding!" I was surprised and shocked "I wouldn't know where to start; I am good at solving cases, not organising and running a museum...

"Sit back down James, please. Here is all the information you need, you have been assigned to the post and that's final." He handed me a small file "I'm telling you that you are the right person for the job."

I slumped in the chair. His word was final. No new adventure waiting for me. I couldn't believe it.

Whilst I sat dismayed in the big chair, Mr. Simpson asked his secretary to call in Miss Lucy Crane and Mr. William Brown. He turned his attention back to me "These young people will be your colleagues in the next few weeks and they will help you with all the work required for the new museum. They are fresh out of university and I am sure that working alongside you will give them a good start in their careers."

My worst fears were confirmed as my new colleagues entered his office- it was the young pair which had been in the waiting area, complaining about the hardship of students entering the workplace. And I turned out to be the old boring guy who had gotten where he was through good connections.

"Miss Crane, Mr. Brown, I would like to introduce you to the curator of the museum you will help to create, Mr. Jones" Mr. Simpson said.

They both looked at me thoughtfully as we shook hands. They did not catch onto the fact that I had heard their conversation in the waiting room. I could tell that they weren't impressed at their future superior.

"So" Mr. Simpson spoke, breaking the somewhat awkward silence" When should I expect you to arrive in Cromdale and start?"

I looked at him and despite the fact I wanted to find a way out of this new venture, I said

"As soon as possible" I looked at my new co-workers, Lucy and Billy (William seemed too serious of a name for him).

"Excuse me?" Young Mr. Brown looked shocked "You can't do that, I have a million things to sort out before I can leave London" He looked at Lucy for support. She looked as surprised as he was.

Mr. Simpson seemed not to take notice of the pair and looked at me "Good, then. That's what I like to see, straight to the point as always, Jones."

"You can't do that; I need to pack and everything..." Lucy's voice trailed off and she looked angry.

"Lucy, Billy, I think three hours will be enough to pack and get any matters sorted out. My car is parked outside, I will meet you there and we can drive down today. The sooner we get there the better. If either of you is unable to sort your things out within the next three hours, then there is a train that you can get tomorrow. It leaves at 5 am, but there is a two mile walk from the station to the mansion. Tomorrow will be our first day at the new placement. "I decided.

"All is well then" Mr. Simpson looked pleased "I can see that these young people will have a good start under your watchful eye. I'm sure the three of you will get on like a house on fire"

'I'm sure we will- I thought to myself. I looked at them" Should I wait for you two or will you be coming on the train tomorrow?" I asked.

"I will be here in three hours" Lucy said.

"Yep, me too, not a big fan of walking" Billy admitted.

The pair left the room and I could tell they were not pleased. I spent a few more minutes talking a few things over with Mr. Simpson. I went home, packed some things for the stay in Cromdale and drove back to

Tottenham Court Road and found a parking spot, which was a bit of a mission. I looked at my watch as I put money in the meter and decided to have a quick wander around the shops as I was a few minutes early.

I returned to my car right on time and sat and waited. After a few minutes I saw Lucy walking towards me with a big suitcase. She scanned the cars and spotted me. As she approached my car she looked at it with a curious look on her pretty face. I opened the door and greeted her.

"Hi" she answered back." Wow, isn't your car a bit old?" she asked.

"Well, I have had it for some years but it's in great shape" I answered, thinking that it was a bit of an odd comment.

"My dad says that any car over five years old should be taken to the scrap yard. Technology is constantly improving and is extremely important for safety and comfort in cars." She added in a know-it-all tone. "And this car looks like its well past its prime"

I couldn't believe her arrogance. "Well, it's a good car and gets me from A to B. That's all I need"

I answered and decided not to discuss the matter further. She got in the back and we sat in silence whilst we waited for Bill.

I looked at my watch again. It was now quarter past two. I decided to give Billy a few more minutes and then we would set off. I didn't want to get stuck in rush hour traffic and it was a good few hours to Cromdale once we got out of London. We sat in silence for another ten minutes.

"It seems the Mr. Brown will not be joining us today and will come on the train tomorrow." I said as I put the key in the ignition. "Time to go if we are going to beat the traffic."

"Please wait a few more minutes. He will be here. Billy does not like walking and he always had trouble waking up for his morning lectures. Not an early riser if you know what I mean…Can I call you Jimmy?" she asked.

"James is fine. Only my friends call me Jimmy" I answered, waiting to see what her reaction would be.

She looked shocked. "I didn't realise things would be on such a formal basis in such a small team" she said eventually. "Anyway, he was late for his lectures, but he was always there." She added.

"Well punctuality is a good quality to have. Maybe we should just go. It will teach Billy a lesson about the importance of punctuality." I said, turning the key in the ignition. I saw the look on her face in the rear view mirror. I had a strange sense of satisfaction. I was not impressed that they both had formed an unflattering opinion without even knowing me. Well, I guess I would have to teach them a lesson.

"Right" I said, looking at her reflection in the mirror" We are obviously going to have to keep an eye on the punctuality issue. Working hours will be from eight in the morning to five in the afternoon with an hour lunch break. Any lateness will not be tolerated and will have to be worked past five."

"You are joking right?" she gasped "I thought that within such a small team we would have a flexible and pleasant working environment..."

"I didn't get to where I am today by being nice. A bit of discipline and knowing people in the right places goes a long way..." I interrupted her midsentence, but couldn't continue as I saw Billy approaching with a small suitcase. He spotted me in the car and picked his pace up a bit. He looked closely at the car as he reached it and opened the door.

"Hi all" he said with a big grin and his face." Nice car although maybe a bit on the old side" he added as he settled himself into the passenger seat. "What's the top speed? I love driving fast."

"Don't get too excited Bill, I'll be surprised if it manages more than forty miles per hour" she laughed.

"I can assure you that it can mange quicker than that." I muttered under my breath as I joined the traffic.

As we went through London, making our way to the M25 I thought about what lay ahead. I did not have a good feeling about it. My new colleagues were fresh out of university and had no experience in the type of project we were undertaking. I thought again about how I managed to get myself onto this mess- I am not cut out for this- I thought to myself- What was Mr. Simpson thinking?- as we came off the M25 and onto the M1, finally on route for Cromdale.

As we arrived in Cromdale it was very late into the night and it was raining to make things worse. We could hear the wind howling and the waves crashing against the shore in the distance. We drove through the gates of the estate and along the gravelled drive. I could see a faint light in a window of the outhouse where the caretaker lived but everything else was dark. I shuddered. The place did not seem welcoming at all. I was tired and wanted to go to bed. We finally reached the end of the drive and saw the mansion- our new home, at least for the next few weeks. It looked dark, empty, and lifeless.

I woke Lucy and Bill and we got our things. They looked at the house and then at each other. I don't think they liked what they saw. We went to the front door and I opened it.

"This is just perfect" Bill muttered under his breath, as I turned on the lights.

We had a quick look around the ground floor and then we went upstairs. The house was much cluttered, and at first glance, nothing of great value was visible.

"Right, I think we are all tired so let's find suitable rooms that each of us can use and we can see what we are dealing with in the morning". I said, trying my best not to yawn.

We had chosen three rooms off a small corridor on the ground floor and said good night to each other. I jumped into my bed and as I drifted off to sleep I wondered what tomorrow would bring.

I woke up in the middle of the night and gazed round, unsure at first of where I was. After a few seconds I remembered I was in Cromdale and was settling myself back to sleep when I heard a soft thud. 'That's probably what woke me up' I thought to myself. I lay still, listening. 'It was probably just the wind' I decided. As I closed my eyes I heard the sound again. This time it was louder and sounded a bit like footsteps. It was coming from upstairs.

There were just three of us in the mansion, Lucy and Bill were sleeping in the rooms next to mine, and sounds were coming from upstairs. I got up from my bed checked my watch. It was well after two in the morning. I sat up and listened, maybe I had imagined it, and after all I had a long day behind me. Just as I decided that I had imagined it I heard it again. This time it definitely sounded like footsteps of at least two people, walking around upstairs. 'Are my colleagues exploring at this time of night?' I thought to myself. I got out of bed and grabbed my torch. 'What on earth are they doing?' I went into the corridor and knocked lightly on Billy's door. There was no answer. 'Are they playing a joke on me? We will just see about that' I thought to myself as I headed for the stairs.

As I went up the stairs, I tried to remember the layout of the first floor and decided the sound came from the library. I quietly approached the door and listened again. I heard a door creak. I pushed the library door open and fumbled for the light switch. The library was empty. There was nobody there. I went through to the study and switched on the lights. Empty. 'Strange' I thought, switched all the lights off and made my way back downstairs.

As I reached my room, I saw Lucy peeking out of her room

"What's going on?" she asked in a sleepy voice.

"Nothing, I thought I heard footsteps upstairs" I shrugged, feeling a bit silly.

"Did you find anything?" she asked, looking a bit concerned.

"No, I think I must have imagined it. Go back to bed" I said.

"Well, it's an old house, maybe it's haunted" she smiled "I am going back to bed" she said and closed her door. I thought I should probably do the same, but I just wanted to check something first. I waited for a few seconds and then quietly opened the door to Bills room. There he was, fast asleep. I closed his door and went back to my room. As I lay in bed, I knew it wasn't Bill and Lucy playing tricks on me. I heard footsteps in the library. But how could it be, it wasn't any of us. Maybe it was just my imagination, I was spending my first night in an old house and simply wasn't used to the sounds I heard, it could have been the wind, or the water in the pipes or something else, it had to be because I didn't believe in ghosts. I fell into a light sleep, still unsure about what woke me up in the first place.

# CHAPTER 2

The next morning I woke up around twenty past nine; I was late because of my night adventure. I couldn't believe it, after my lecture to Lucy yesterday, it was me who was late. I got dressed quickly, and went to the kitchen, where I could hear Lucy pottering about.

"Good morning "I said, as I came in.

"Morning ,I am making some breakfast, if you want to go and wash up and grab Bill it will be ready in few minutes" she said. Without saying anything I went back to my room to grab towel and my toothbrush. As I was leaving the bathroom I could see Bill walking into the kitchen, so I dropped my things off in my room followed him into the kitchen. We sat around the table eating our breakfast in silence. I wondered if she had told Bill about what happened at night.

"All right you two" Lucy said as she got up from the table" breakfast was my treat but we need to sort out a permanent arrangement for meal times, and since you're the boss" she pointed at me" I think it's up to you to sort that out"

I shrugged. I was somewhat surprised at the situation we were in. Mr. Simpson sent us here with nothing else but the keys and instructed us to see what we could do to get things going and set up a museum. I had no idea where to start; I had never done anything like this before in all the years I had worked for him. The place was a mess, it had obviously not been cleaned for a while, and there was no phone, no internet. We were left on our own to deal with everything. As far as I knew this is not how it worked normally. What was Mr. Simpson thinking, sending me and two young graduates here? I didn't know so I decided to make the most out of the situation.

"I think we should start by having a good look around this house first, see what we have and then check out the local area" I said.

"The kitchen is well equipped, so we are ok here, we just need supplies. I suggest you boys start cleaning the place because the dust is horrific, figure out how to get the boiler working because it's freezing and I think all of us would like to have a hot shower rather than a cold one. I have found a bunch of keys which should have a use for something, but I haven't figured that out yet. I will go to the local town and get some basics for us so we have something for breakfast every day." Lucy said. "As you can see I did not sleep in" she added looking at me.

"Well, you didn't go off on escapades during the night and looking for ghosts" Bill said laughing.

So I guessed she had told him and they were having a laugh at my expense.

I shrugged my shoulders "I never said it was a ghost, I heard something though" I tried to explain.

"Right" Lucy said with a cheeky smile "You boys get the boiler going, I'm off" she left the kitchen to get ready to go out. I looked at Bill "Don't worry, it's only a joke" he said, still smiling. "I don't believe in ghosts either". He looked at me "I will go and find the boiler, most likely it's in the basement, one of the keys Lucy found should work" he grabbed the keys she left on the kitchen table and headed for the basement door.

I decided to take a quick look outside. The weather was better than last night, it was a bright morning and the wind had eased a bit but was still fairly strong. As I went onto the gravelled drive I could hear the waves crashing in the distance, the sea was not that far away. The mansion was surrounded by grassy areas and flower beds which now of course were empty, and further away from the house there were shrubs and trees. It was a big 'garden' and looked like it had seen better days; some of the shrubs needed trimming and some of the grass areas were overgrown. I could see the roof of the caretaker's house and thought I should go and see him, but that could wait till later. I started walking down one of the paths leading into the park when I saw an older man come out of the little house and he started walking hurriedly towards me. I didn't like the look of him, he seemed a bit scruffy, but I waited for him to catch up to me.

"Hello" he said in a raspy voice, and coughed "I'm Dave "he introduced himself "I am the caretaker, or at least I was until Mr. Doughty passed away. I took care of the grounds, did odd jobs around the house for him.

You must be the guy the National Trust sent?" he asked, looking closely at me.

"Yes, my name is James, but people call me Jimmy. We arrived yesterday, but I thought it was too late in the night to bother you." I said.

"That's fine; I saw you arrive and guessed it was you. I don't get many visitors here anymore. If you need any help with anything let me know." He gazed into the distance, and then he looked at me again. I waited patiently, he looked like he wanted to tell me something, but wasn't sure whether he could. "I had worked all those years for Mr. Doughty and now I will get chucked out of my little house. I think it's a good idea to have the mansion turned into a museum, but he said I could stay on as caretaker, but apparently that will not happen." He said in an upset voice. "So if I can do anything to stay on, I will, you just let me know." He looked at me again.

"That's very kind of you, thank you. At the moment we are just settling in, but if I need anything I'll let you know" I smiled, hoping that it would reassure him.

He nodded and said "Not to worry then, you know where to find me". He reached out with his right hand for a handshake, so I shook his hand. He mumbled something under his breath, turned around and walked back towards his house. I thought he was a bit odd, but didn't really give it much thought. It was time to go back, I had left Bill by himself and there was a lot of work to be done. I wanted to take a good look around the grounds but it would have to wait for another day, there were more important things to be done today. I made my way back to the house.

As I went in Bill came out of the kitchen looking rather pleased with himself. "Well, got the boiler working, so we should be nice and cosy soon" he said. "That's good then" I answered and thought about the tedious task of cleaning that was awaiting us. "Let's get to work then and clean this place up a bit."

"Well, we don't have a TV but there is a computer upstairs" Bill said" do you think we have the internet connected?" he asked. I laughed" we don't have the phone line connected so my guess would be no. Our mobiles won't even be of much use to us here, the network coverage is really bad. We should be glad the gas and electricity are on".

Bill looked a bit shocked

"What are we going to do for fun here?" he asked.

"We didn't come here for fun" I said "We are here to organise a museum. And the sooner we do it, the sooner we go back to London." I explained to him, not exactly happy with the situation myself.

"You can go back to London at the weekends" I tried to cheer him up.

"The train takes six hours. It is hardly worth it." He replied with an unhappy look on his face. "And to make things worse, I didn't bring my mobile phone charger with me" he added.

"Well, I've got mine with me so you can use that if you need to. We are not in the middle of nowhere, the town is a couple of miles away, and Edinburgh is just under an hours' drive. It's not as bad as you think." I said, looking at him. Bill shrugged "I guess" he replied, unconvincingly.

"Right now lets' get this place cleaned up. I think the library would be a good place to use for our working room, so we can start in there. And I'll take a quick look at that computer, it should be of some use to us I hope" I said "where are all the bits we need for the cleaning?" I asked.

"Lucy said there is a utility room off the kitchen and it's all in there, the dusters, the vacuum cleaner and stuff." He said as he headed towards the kitchen."Come and give me a hand"

I followed Bill, we got all the things we needed and headed upstairs. We started by uncovering the furniture and even though it was pretty cold, we opened the windows in the library and the study to let in some fresh air. We started the cleaning when Lucy returned.

"Hi guys, how are you getting on?" she asked cheerfully.

"What are you so happy about?" asked Bill in a grumpy voice, clearly not enjoying himself.

"Well, I managed to buy a few things and met a few of the locals" she replied "I see you are off to a good start. I managed to sort out the meal situation; there is a small local restaurant where we can go for lunch every day. The prices are reasonable and the owner is most keen to have a museum here. We can also go for a fancy evening meal if we want" she let out a small giggle.

"Well, that's settled then, we will go into town for lunch and we can have more time for work in that case" I decided, glad that at least one thing was sorted. "Now let's finish setting up our working headquarters and we can get on with what we came here to do".

"Sir, yes Sir" Bill answered jokingly. We spent the next hour or so finishing off the household tasks, cleaning and unpacking. When we finished we gathered in the library and sat around the large table there.

"So, where do we start then?" Bill asked, settling himself into one of the chairs.

"Mr. Simpson has given me an inventory of all items in possession by Mr. Doughty, so we can check that it is all here" I answered, opening the file which I had brought with me from London. "But we will need to make a more specific one ourselves so we can identify the value of the pieces Mr. Doughty had managed to collect over the years. I know he had a few quite valuable pieces of furniture and paintings as well as many book."

"Of course it's all here. Why wouldn't it be? Hasn't the mansion been locked up?" Lucy asked looking at me.

"Well yes, but we need to know what we have and we need to check it ourselves and not rely on someone else's work." I replied.

Lucy opened her mouth to say something but Bill interrupted her

"I think we should take a look at that computer, I'll bet it has everything we need and will save us some time; it'll be time for lunch soon". He got up from his chair and went towards the door leading to the study. Lucy and I followed him. It was a good idea, and it would give us an idea of what Mr. Doughty was like. It wasn't very polite looking at someone's personal things but it could really help us. Lucy sat in front of the computer and switched it on. As we waited for it to come on, I had a quick look through the papers on the desk. Nothing of importance was there, just a few bills and letters from antique collectors, offering to buy some of Mr. Doughty's pieces. I wondered what his response was to these, but I figured it would all be on the pc.

"Well, here we are then" Lucy said as she settled herself more comfortably into the chair. "Just the usual then, a few pictures, letters, lists of antique dealers, stuff like that, nothing much really."

"What's that file there?" I pointed.

"Well, this one has a password on it, I have no idea what it is" Lucy answered. "We can't take a look at it without the password."

"I wonder what is in the file if he put a password on it." I wondered "Is there a way that we can try to figure it out?" I asked, looking at my colleagues.

"Doesn't the file you got from Mr. Simpson mention anything about it?" Bill asked. "Take a look".

I scanned through the file; there was no mention of the computer in it at all.

"Looks like we have a mystery on our hands" Lucy laughed "The mystery of the secret file"

"It must have been something important if he put a password on it" I said. "But what can we do to open it?"

"There is a password suggestion icon, let's see what it says" Lucy said and clicked on it "The key is the symbol of beginnings" she read "What on earth does that mean?" she asked looking at me and Bill.

"Well, what symbol is it? That is pretty vague" Bill said.

I agreed with him. How were we to try and figure it out if we didn't even know what field it referred to?

"Maybe if we found out a bit more about Mr. Doughty that might help us along. Any ideas?" I asked.

"The owner of the restaurant said he knew him, maybe he will know something?" Lucy suggested. I looked at my watch and it was 12.30. "I think it's time for lunch anyway, we can see if we find anything out when we get there".

"That is a very good idea" said Bill "I am starving, and a walk after all that work will be nice" he said and went downstairs to get ready. Lucy followed him but I stayed in the study for a few minutes. As I turned the computer off I wondered why it wasn't included in the inventory. All other items seemed to be there, excluding the domestic things, even the telephone set which was sitting on the desk was listed, so why not the computer? The encrypted file on the computer was bothering me as well and I was determined to find out what the password was so I could have a look at it. As far as I knew, Mr. Doughty didn't have any relatives, which is why his home was being turned into the museum, it was his last will. So the only people that would know anything at all about him were the locals and I didn't know if they would be any help. The only other person that knew him well is the caretaker, but I didn't feel it was a good idea to ask him about it. Something was not right about him and I wasn't sure what. I made my way downstairs to find Bill and Lucy waiting for me by the front door.

"Maybe we could drive? " Bill asked "It is quite a long walk from what Lucy said"

"The drive would take longer than walking; we would have to go around the whole park, onto the A1 again and then back towards town. It's not worth it, and also I think we can all clear our heads so we can figure out that password." I replied, putting on my coat and scarf.

Lucy looked at me "Is it really necessary for us to figure the password out? We have the inventory and his list of valuables, maybe its love letters or something and we are prying into his personal business." She said. "The computer is not listed in the inventory, maybe we should leave it alone".

"I think it's important. If you are not up to the challenge I will figure it out on my own" I said and opened the door. "Now let's get going".

We locked the door and let Lucy lead the way. I looked again at the park, the trees and wondered why Mr. Doughty left everything to the National Trust, why he wanted his home turned into a museum. He did have pieces of historical value but why the mansion? Did it have some sort of history behind it? I decided to find out. There were over tree thousand books in his library; maybe there was some relating to the mansions history. I looked over at Lucy. She was walking, deep in thought. " I am going to check the books later on today, make sure that they are all there, it will be a good place to start I think." I said, catching up to her and Bill.

"Why would there be any missing?" Bill asked. "Everything is there like it should be yes?" he asked.

"There is a lot to check through and it needs to be done, will you help?" I asked him

"Only during working hours, at five o'clock my working day finishes and I need to relax." He replied.

I looked at Lucy, "Will you give me a hand?" I asked.

"Sure, I thought there may be a couple of books about the history of the mansion within the collection and I would like to learn more about it" she replied smiling at me.

"Great, that is the exact reason why I wanted to have a look at his books" I said to her, glad that at least she would help.

We reached the edge of the park and went out on to the main road. We crossed the bridge over the river and caught our first glimpse of the town. It looked pretty small; in the distance we could see the church spire, a few houses and a B&B.

"That is where the restaurant is" Lucy said pointing at the B&B. "There isn't that much here, a pub, a post office and a local shop. It must be great during the summer, the sea is very close" she explained. We made our way towards the B&B. The restaurant was located in a large conservatory at the back of the main building and it had sea views. Further down the street was a community hall. Bill spotted the notice board and went over to have a look. Lucy and I waited for him to return before we went into the restaurant.

"They have a movie night every Thursday on the big screen, and since its Thursday today, I think I will come and watch it." He said as he joined us.

"Well I am glad "I said "Maybe it won't be so bad for you over here after all" I added sarcastically. Lucy giggled quietly and went into the restaurant. It wasn't very big but nicely decorated and had a cosy feel to it. We grabbed a menu and sat at one of the tables. There weren't a lot of people, just a couple sitting at one table and a young family at another. We ordered our food and each of us stared off into the distance. Our food arrived and we ate in silence. A couple of tables away, a young woman sat eating alone. She was pretty, with long blonde hair and lovely blue eyes. She kept glancing at us and Bill finally asked

"Do you mind if I ask her to join us? I don't think she is enjoying her meal eating on her own".

Lucy gave him a strange look "What a gentleman you are Bill, go ahead, unless you mind?" she asked me.

"No it's fine by me" I said and Bill got up and asked the young woman to join us.

"Hello" she said as she sat down "My name is Susannah" she smiled. Bill introduced himself, then Lucy and me. "Are you the people that have come here to set up the museum at that old mansion?" she asked.

"Yes" I answered, thinking that our arrival must have been big news in such a small community.

"It will be good for the village. It is a little boring here to be honest. I am here as sickness cover at the bank for a few weeks, but I regret it a bit, there isn't much to do here at this time of year." She shrugged" So when I heard that the mansion is haunted I wanted to meet you to see if there is a chance of coming to have a look and see if I can see the ghost. That would give me something exciting to talk about when I got back to my branch". She said looking at me." Do you think it would be possible to arrange that? Or would I have to wait for the grand opening, but I may not be here by then and then I will have nothing exciting to talk about" she added unhappily.

I looked at my colleagues and then at her "I think it would be possible for you to come and visit us, but not yet. We only arrived last night and haven't quite settled in yet. Once we have done that I think it would be fine" I said, smiling at her. Lucy rolled her eyes at me and asked "So how do you know the mansion is haunted then?"

"It was the restaurants' owners' son that told me about the ghost. He and his friend, Vanessa, were coming back from their school's Christmas play rehearsal when they saw the ghost. They normally take a short cut through the park and one evening they saw lights in the first floor windows even though the mansion was sealed shut. It has to be a ghost, isn't that right?" she said looking at me."That's what the locals say anyway"

"Well, I am sure we can sort something out so you will have something to talk about when you return from your placement. But in a few days, at the moment we are still settling in." I said, smiling.

"I am staying at the B&B so I have all my meals here, I guess I will see you tomorrow then?" she said. "If you excuse me I have got to go now, but it was great meeting all of you" she got up from the table and got ready to leave. "Yes, we will be here for lunch tomorrow, we will see you then" said Bill. We said our goodbyes and we also left after paying our bill.

As we walked back home to get back to work, Lucy was very quiet so I chatted to Billy.

"If we put our heads together I am sure that we can arrange a ghost for Susannah" I said.

"She is definitely worth the effort" he chuckled. "What did you have in mind? Maybe you can sit with her on the sofa in the drawing room and I can walk about in the room above, making a racket?" He suggested. "That's lame, I think she should see the ghost that would be more convincing" I said. "What dress up in a sheet and yell 'BOO!'" he laughed "That is good for scaring children"

"I don't understand how you two can joke about this. Don't you think that there is something going on at the mansion?" Lucy interrupted.

"What? I don't believe in ghosts" I said.

"Well something did wake you up last night, and those kids did see lights in the mansion when it was locked up, so what was it?" Lucy asked, looking at Bill and me. "Something is going on, we should find out what." She said in a determined voice.

I laughed "You do believe in ghosts"

"Oh, dear, she will now try to solve the mystery of the haunted mansion" Bill laughed with me. "That will be a first"

Lucy looked at us, upset "Fine you two can joke about it all you want, but you were sure you hadn't imagined the noises last night, and now the kids' story" she shook her head.

Maybe it all was a coincidence or was there something going on at the mansion? I had nothing to go on so I would just have to wait and see if anything else would happen. Right now it was just a story two local kids had spread around and there was no proof for it. Lucy was simply reading into everything a little bit too much.

"We still have a lot of work to do so let's just get back and get on with it. Let's not take children's tales too seriously" I said looking at Lucy.

She didn't say anything, just picked up her pace and we carried on walking in silence. When we got back, I went to the library and took a look at the computer. There was a file which listed all the books in the collection and I checked if there were any books of interest to me. I found three titles which should be of use to me and I started to check the books. Lucy and Bill went to finish cleaning their rooms and to unpack. I was counting through the volumes when Lucy popped her head through the door. "Tea is ready" and went back downstairs. I looked at my watch. It was five minutes past 5. I didn't even realise when the time had passed. I went downstairs and joined Lucy and Bill in the kitchen. Lucy had made some sandwiches for everyone and Bill was already tucking into one. I poured myself some tea.

"How far did you get?" Lucy asked "I am sorry I haven't been up to help you but we needed the place clean. Billy helped me out a bit" she smiled.

"Well, I am about halfway through." I said, grabbing another sandwich.

"I'll will go up and carry on after we eat" she said. "What are you going to do Bill?"

"I am going to watch that movie in the village" it starts at seven, so I have plenty of time to get ready. Are you going to work overtime or are you coming with me?" he asked.

"I think I will give it a miss" I said.

"Same" Lucy added.

"Suit yourselves" he shrugged his shoulders.

We finished our meal and Lucy and I went back to the library, Bill got ready and left to go and watch the movie. I sat in one of the big armchairs and waited for Lucy to finish the book count.

"I got three thousand, eight hundred and seventy five. How many should we have?" she asked.

"Three thousand, eight hundred and seventy nine." I replied.

"That's four missing then" she said.

I got up from the chair "These are the four missing books" I said and gave her a piece of paper with for titles written on it.

"How can you possibly know that? You couldn't have gone through every title in that space of time, it would take a week to do that" she said, surprised.

"Simple, they are the books I wanted to take a look at and they aren't here" I replied.

She looked at the titles " ' A brief history of the Blackhill family', ' Cromdale and the importance of Blackhill Estate', 'Origins of Blackhill Estate' and the last one I see was written by Mr. Doughty 'The Freemasons influence in Scotland'." She looked at me "I didn't know he published a book?" she said. "As far as I know it hasn't been published, Mr. Simpson told me it was a manuscript. " I replied.

"But three of them are about the mansion and the estate" she said.

"Maybe the one he wrote is as well, the question is, where is it?" I asked.

We went into the study and had a good rummage through the desk. We didn't find anything.

"Do you think that it may be on that password protected file on the pc?" Lucy asked.

"That is a good point, but there should still be a copy if it had been catalogued with the other books. Let's carry on looking" we had another good look but didn't find anything. It was well after ten when we gave up. The manuscript was not there. I decided to give Mr. Simpson a ring in the morning and that was all I could do. Bill returned from his movie night and joined us in the library. Once again we sat around the big table. We told Bill about the missing manuscript.

"Maybe he gave it to a solicitor for safe keeping or something, I wouldn't worry about it." He said "and the other books he could have borrowed to someone and they simple didn't give them back". That made sense so I decided to give the matter a rest. We sat in silence, each with our own thoughts, when Lucy said suddenly "Did you hear that?" We listened. Bang. We all heard it "There it is again" she said in a frightened voice. Bang, we heard it again. It was pitch black outside and the wind had picked up again. We run down the stairs and I opened the front door. "There is no body there" I said. We heard the bang again. I went outside to have a look. It was one of the shutters; it wasn't secured properly and kept banging against the wall in the wind. I secured it and went back inside. "I think we all had a long day and we need some rest. Goodnight" I said and made my way to my bedroom. "Goodnight" mumbled Lucy and Bill and they disappeared in their rooms. As I settled in bed, I could hear Lucy walking around, the floorboards in her room creaking, but eventually everything fell silent. Finally I fell asleep, tired from the previous two days. As I was drifting off to sleep, I heard a loud bang upstairs. I jumped out of my bed and out into the corridor. Lucy and Bill opened their doors almost simultaneously.

"It came from the library, follow me!" I shouted and headed for the stairs.

Bill and Lucy ran after me. I flung the library door open and switched on the light.

"My books!" Lucy shouted.

Sprawled on the floor were four or five books.

"I had picked them up to have a read before I went to bed and forgot to take them with me when we went downstairs." She said, picking them up.

"So what knocked them over? Did you leave them on the floor?" I asked.

"No…" she said slowly "I left them on the edge of the table" she said and put the books down on the table. "Like this" she demonstrated. The books were sticking out over the edge of the table.

"It's as if someone has walked into them in the dark and knocked them off the table" Bill said out loud exactly what I was thinking.

"Stop scaring me" Lucy said in a frightened voice.

"Well we know it wasn't a ghost, they can walk through walls" I said as I tried to lighten the mood

"Stop it, you're making fun of me" Lucy was clearly upset.

"Well, maybe I do believe in ghosts" I said.

I shrugged my shoulders and didn't say anything and as we stood there trying to make sense of the situation, something strange happened. A grinding noise came from the direction of the big grandfather clock that was standing in the corner and the glass covering the dial cracked in two. Right there, in front of our eyes. But none of us approached it, no one had even moved. All three of us stood there, staring at the clock.

"What on earth…?" Lucy gasped.

Both of them looked petrified and I realised it was up to me to calm them down.

"Nothing to be alarmed about, don't worry. The house has been empty and cold for a long time, now that the heating has been on all day, the glass expanded and cracked, that's all" I said.

"What about the books then?" Bill asked.

"Lucy, maybe you put them down differently and they eventually fell off. It is nothing to worry about" I tried to sound reassuring. They looked at me, thinking about my explanation of what had happened.

"Maybe you're right, let's go to bed" Lucy said and headed downstairs, Bill and I followed. We went to our bedrooms, and as I fell asleep, I wondered what tomorrow would bring

# CHAPTER 3

The next few weeks were quite uneventful in the mansion. Every day we would check through the things Mr. Doughty had collected over the years. He had quite a few paintings by famous artists, antique furniture pieces dating back to the eighteenth century so we had to value and authenticate them as we went along. Everything we checked was in place, nothing was missing but the four books from the library which made the whole thing even more suspicious. We had no luck with opening the computer file either. I had spoken with Mr. Simpson about it but it didn't help. He didn't know Mr. Doughty personally and he suggested we contact his solicitor. I was planning on doing that anyway as I wanted to get a hold of Mr. Doughty's manuscript. I was worried that the only copy was missing and that we would get the blame for losing it. It was still here when the inventory was done and no one had been inside since then, except for us. The books must have been there as well. Although it sounded crazy even to me; the only explanation I could think of is that someone must have taken them away after the inventory was done but before we arrived. But I knew, and was sure that no one had entered the mansion before us. The front and back doors were locked and sealed and were intact when we had arrived and the windows couldn't be opened form outside. This and many other unexplainable things I had come across in the mansion within my first few weeks were bothering and worrying me.

One morning I woke up and the house was freezing cold. I got out of bed to check the radiator. It was cold. 'Great,' I thought to myself 'that is all we need'. I got dressed quickly and decided to take a quick look at the boiler, maybe the pilot light had gone off or something like that and I could fix it. I looked at my watch; it was only half past seven. I went down to the basement to take a look. It seemed to be on and working fine. I headed upstairs and into the kitchen. I had no idea what the problem was. As I put the kettle on to make some tea, Bill came into the kitchen.

"Good morning" he said as he sat down at the table "Why is it so cold today?" he asked me.

"I don't know, I had a look at the boiler, but everything seems fine, I am not a plumber, you know. I will maybe ask Dave, the caretaker, to take a look, he did say he did jobs around the house, so he might know what the problem is" I answered.

"The sooner, the better," Billy said, shivering.

"Morning all," Lucy said, as she entered the kitchen. "I guess we have a problem with the heating?" she asked as she poured herself some tea.

"Morning," I replied "Yes, I will see if Dave can fix it"

"That's a good idea" she said "He did offer his help after all".

We ate breakfast and I went to see if Dave was able to help us with our heating problem. He said he would be right over and that it was simple but time consuming to resolve. He went down into the basement and I put on an extra sweater on and joined my colleagues. We had finished with everything upstairs and we were half done with the ground floor. There wasn't anything really special in the mansion, and it would probably just end up a small museum that reflected the way of life in the region over the last two hundred years. It wasn't anything great and that too kept bothering me. I didn't want my museum to be like so many other ones you could find up and down the country. I went to the kitchen to get a drink of water when I heard a quiet banging sound coming from upstairs. 'Great now the ghosts were bothering us during the day as well' I thought to myself jokingly. I decided to sneak upstairs and finally come to the bottom of it. I was tired of the atmosphere that we had, bangs heard during the night, doors left open when they should be closed. I went quietly up the stairs and stopped to listen. I heard it again, a quiet banging, like the sound of a hammer. It was coming from the library. I went towards the door and pushed it, hoping it wouldn't creak as it opened. I peeked inside the room. I couldn't see anyone. Then I heard the sound again, it was coming from behind one of the big armchairs standing next to the fireplace. I walked up to the fire place and found Dave on his knees, with a hammer, banging gently on the skirting board.

"What are you doing?" I asked, giving him a fright. He had not heard me come into the room.

"I was in here checking the radiator when I heard a scratching sound.

I am just checking to see if everything is ok here, the last thing we need are mice" he explained in his raspy voice "They like to go into the warmth at this time of year and if something isn't done quickly, we could end up infested with them" he carried on talking quickly, looking closely at me. He sounded and looked like he was checking whether I had 'bought' his story. I nodded and smiled at him "Well, it's nice to see that you still care about the place. Thanks but we spend most evenings in here and we haven't heard any scratching or rustling sounds." I replied, hoping that he would think that I did believe his story. "How are you getting on with getting the heating going?" I asked.

"Well, I just have a couple of radiators to check downstairs, and that should be it, I will be able to put it on again for you" he replied, satisfied that his explanation had worked. It was obvious to me that he did not hear mice, but I would find out soon enough what he was doing.

"That is great; do you think you will be finished before we go to lunch?" I asked.

"Oh, yes, should be another twenty minutes at most" he said and went out of the room.

He was an odd fellow and his behaviour was strange to say the least. At least he was some help though. I decided that we should go for lunch as soon as he had the heating on. Even though we were all wearing an extra layer and had our coats on we were freezing. A brisk walk into town would warm us up, as would lunch. By the time we got back, the house would be warm and we could carry on with our work. Finally Dave got the heating on and we were ready to go to lunch. Bill and Lucy were glad that we had gone a bit earlier and we walked quicker than usual. We arrived at the restaurant a bit too early so we decided to have a cup of coffee before lunch. As we sat around a table, I looked around to see if Susannah was in the restaurant. I couldn't see her anywhere, and thought it was probably still a bit too early for her to be on her lunch break. As we sat drinking our coffee, a man in this late thirty's approached our table. With him was a young boy, around eleven or twelve.

"Hello," he said as he got to our table "I was hoping to catch you in here. My name is Bob; I am the owner of this restaurant and the B&B. I am so glad that something is being done in the mansion, it will be good for the community." He said, smiling. We all introduced ourselves and he shook our hands in turn. "You are doing a great job in there I am sure. It will benefit our little town having a museum."

"It will help that it is haunted." added the young boy.

"Oh, so you're the one who saw the ghost in the mansion." I smiled at him.

Bob started laughing "Well, you know what the kids are like, making things up".

The boy put on a serious look on and said "We did see a light on in the mansion on the second floor even though it was locked and all the doors were sealed. Vanessa was there with me and she saw it as well. She thinks that we should spread the word about the ghosts, and then we will get more visitors. Haunted castles and mansions are more attractive".

"I agree" I replied, smiling "Such an old mansion must be haunted, it just wouldn't be right if it wasn't. And the more ghosts it has the better."

"Will this never end?" Bill said, clearly not in the mood for jokes. "Can we talk about something else please?"

"I am afraid that Billy here is not too keen on ghosts" I laughed. "He doesn't like unexplained situations"

"Funny you should say that, we did have a few of those around the time Mr. Doughty passed away." Bob said.

"Really? What do you mean?" I asked, curious of what he meant.

"If you're going to tell me that he died in mysterious circumstances then I am moving to another table" Bill said, grabbing his coffee cup.

"Oh, it was nothing of the sort. He was an older man; he suffered a stroke which partially paralysed him. A few hours later he suffered another one which put an end to his life, unfortunately." Bob explained.

"So where is the mystery then?" I asked, intrigued.

"Well, the day that all this happened, Dave, the caretaker, came here and told me what was going on, so I called the doctor and we both made our way to the estate. The doctor could see that it was serious and an ambulance would be no good to the old guy so we stayed with him. This was quite early in the morning, but around noon a chap arrived and wanted to speak with poor Mr. Doughty. Even though I told him that he was practically on his death bed, he wouldn't take no for an answer and insisted on seeing Mr. Doughty. The doctor said to let him in, what harm could he do? So we did. The chap tried speaking to Mr. Doughty, but by then it was too late, he was partially paralysed after all. But he obviously had something important to get across because he got a bit of paper and a pen. He didn't want us to know what this important matter was so instead of writing, he drew a symbol. Mr. Doughty drew another one, as if he gave him an answer but the chap had no idea what it meant, he just shrugged. So Mr. Doughty looked at me and the doctor and wrote- make a museum, where the snakes meet, and the crown- this was all he managed, he couldn't write anymore. He died shortly after, and the chap that came to see him left, not very happy at all" Bob paused, thinking.

"So what happened to the piece of paper then?" I asked, even more intrigued.

"Because Mr. Doughty had not left an official will, it was understood that the last thing he wrote was his dying wish if you like. He had no family at all, the poor fellow, so it wasn't contested in court and here you three are" Bob smiled at us.

"And do you remember the symbols that he wrote, him and the guy that came to see him?" I asked, thinking about the unopened file on the pc. It asked for the name of a symbol, maybe if I knew what symbol Mr. Doughty had used I could figure out at least where it came from and I could decipher the password and open the file.

"Yes, of course, you don't forget things like that" Bob said, and drew the symbols for me on a napkin. I looked closely at them and smiled to myself. This made things a lot easier for me. But there was one more thing I had to know "So what about the strange words he wrote on the bit of paper for you and the doctor? What did you do about that?" I asked.

"Well, the first part, like I said was treated as his last wish, his will. The bit about the snakes and the crown, well, the court ruled it as gibberish" he laughed, somewhat uncomfortably "considering he had a serious stroke and died not long after, maybe they were right. I have no idea what he meant, and if he actually meant anything by it." He added.

"That's a very convenient explanation" Lucy shrugged.

"Do you know what he meant by those words then?" Bob asked.

"No..." she replied

"What about you?" he asked me "any ideas? Or was it just gibberish then? You have to admit it is a bit of a mystery"

"It sure is" I agreed" It's worth having a think about it. Did you know him well? Mr. Doughty I mean? I am having trouble finding someone who could tell me a bit about him." I looked at Bob.

"I have lived here for a long time; Mr. Doughty was always away, looking for antiquities to add to his collection. It was only in the past few years that he spent a lot more time at the mansion that I got to know him. I wouldn't say I knew him well, he came to my house for dinner a few times, and I went to see him at his house. We were acquaintances I suppose" Bob said " You know, we had different interests, he was passionate about history, antiques and so on, I am afraid I did not share his interests."

"What was he like, his personality?" I asked.

"He was the kind of person that gets on well with everyone, but doesn't have any real close friends, if you know what I mean. He was a bit of an odd fellow, absolutely loved his mansion and its contents" Bob chuckled quietly to himself "I think he had a bit of a grudge against the Historical Society for not publishing his book and not taking him seriously as a historian."

"So he didn't have any close friends then?" I asked.

"As far as I know he didn't. He didn't have any visitors in the few years he spent at home, no one came to see him; a bit sad really. But in the last few months he seemed different, more confident..."

"Really..." I muttered under my breath.

" He said to me one time, ' Bob, you just wait and see, I will finally be known as a great historian, the folks at the Historical Society will be green with envy when I go public with my discovery'. I asked him what he discovered, but he didn't tell me; instead he asked me not to tell anyone about our conversation." he continued.

"So you don't know anything else about this discovery?" Bill asked, curiously.

"No, nothing at all. But he must have discovered something, because in the past few months he had quite a lot of visitors, and the chap who came to see him on the day he died had been here three or four times before that." Bob answered.

"He found a treasure" whispered the young boy "He found a treasure at the old mansion, didn't he?" he asked his father.

I smiled at him "Sorry to disappoint you, but I don't think he found a treasure. From what your father says he was a historian, not a treasure hunter. He would have been more thrilled if he discovered a play written by Shakespeare that no one previously had known about, not if he found gold or precious stones, it was a historical discovery, I think."

"And he could have made a discovery like that in the old mansion?" asked the boy, not convinced.

"Of course" I replied "A few years ago, a painting by a famous artist had been discovered in someone's attic, it needed to be confirmed by experts, but none-the-less, and a paining had been discovered that no one knew even existed."

"That's right" Bob said "You remember watching that piece on the news, don't you Ronnie?"

"Oh yeah" Ronnie answered, nodding, slightly disappointed. I imagine he liked the idea of a treasure being found in the mansion.

"Well, I have got to go" Bob said "You came here for lunch and I am taking up your time". he smiled apologetically.

"That is not a problem" I assured him "You have been very helpful. I had no idea that Mr. Doughty had made a discovery, but I assure you, I will try my best to find out what it was"

Lucy looked at Bill and they both rolled their eyes at each other. They obviously both thought it was a crazy idea. I didn't think it was though. We ordered our food, and my colleagues were talking about something, I had time to think about what I had learnt from the conversation with Bob. Could all of the strange goings on in the mansion be linked to Mr. Doughty's discovery? Very likely. I still didn't have any ideas what it could have been, but at least I knew where to start with the computer file. Bob's story about the messages between the guy who came to see Mr. Doughty and Mr. Doughty himself on the piece of paper were very helpful indeed. Maybe the computer file was linked to the discovery? Maybe, it wasn't far-fetched. Why else would it be protected with a password?

Bill and Lucy had been quiet for a few minutes and both were closely looking at me.

"What are you so happy about?" Lucy asked.

"Well, I just realised how helpful the conversation with Bob was. Some of the things he said will help to clear a few things up" I said, looking at them. "Do you think it's not possible to find out what Mr. Doughty's discovery was?" I asked. I tapped my index finger on my temple lightly. "We all have the necessary equipment to do it, it's not impossible."

Bill started laughing "So what, now we are all going to play detective?" he asked me.

"If you're not up to it that's fine, I will give it a go." Lucy said confidently.

"Find out what the discovery was? Hmm, I will definitely have a laugh watching you two compete to see who finds out first. But don't involve me. You are making a bigger deal out of this than necessary. I am sure there is no mystery, Mr. Simpson or the solicitor will know about the discovery, and I am sure it's nothing big, or they would have told us about it don't you think?" He looked at me and Lucy. "There, mystery solved".

I didn't think it was as simple as that. Mr. Doughty had obviously kept it a secret, judging from the way he communicated with the guy that had come to see him. He didn't want Bob or the doctor finding out about it, so I doubted he told anyone about it. He died suddenly, no one expected his death.

"Well, what about the people who are trying to get to it even now, after his death?" Lucy asked.

"What people?" I asked her, pretending not to understand what she had meant.

"Oh come on, you seriously don't believe its ghosts that visit us at the mansion?" she asked, looking at me as if I was crazy, "But how am I supposed to even think about this mystery, when we are working all day? If I had some time and peace and quiet, then maybe I could think about it."

"I am sorry, but we came here to get a job done, and that is the most important thing." I said.

"The most important thing will disappear right from our noses, we won't even know when" Lucy said angrily.

"So you think that things like this can be solved just by sitting and staring into space?" I asked.

"How would you know?" she shrugged her shoulders. "It is not like you have ever come across anything like this"

Her comment irritated me. I was annoyed that she had formed her opinion about me before she had even met me. I recalled their conversation I had heard when we were waiting for Mr. Simpson to see us and I felt my temper rise.

"So you think that you can solve this mystery, and you know how to do it, do you?" I asked.

"That's right" she said, standing her ground.

"And you're dead serious about it?" I asked again.

"Yes, I am very serious" she said.

"Well, let me tell you something then. To even begin to understand what this discovery was, how he found out what he did you need good historical knowledge and understanding as well as experience and expertise in the field." I said, looking at her and Bill "And that takes years of hard work, working in museums, doing precisely what we are doing at the mansion, you know." I paused "Tell me, what you understand from the symbols that Bob showed to us, the ones that Mr. Doughty and his friend used to communicate?"

"I don't know…yet, but I will find out" Lucy answered, not so sure of herself anymore "You can't say that you understood them, can you?"

"I don't know what they meant to them, but I know their meaning and origins" I answered.

"Really..?" she asked "Would you care to explain?" she obviously doubted that I had any idea about the symbols the two men had used.

"Well, let's take a look then" I said, taking the napkin on which Bob had drawn on out of my pocket.

"Here we have the first one. It looks like a diamond shape, but not quite, any ideas?" I asked, placing the napkin in the middle of the table so everyone could see the symbols.

"No" Lucy shook her head, Bill shrugged his shoulders.

"It's a well known Masonic symbol, used widely in Europe in the 18th century, the square and compasses. The second one is also Masonic, the inverted crown and dagger were used in most of Europe, again from the 18th century, used by the Masons which had revolted against the throne."

"You're right; I even remember studying about it at university..." Lucy said, not so sure of herself anymore. Bill laughed to himself, enjoying my victory over her.

"This brings me to my next point, the encrypted file on the pc, remember, it asked for a symbol. So if Mr. Doughty was using Masonic symbols to communicate with his visitor, then maybe the password is a Masonic symbol, what do you think?" I asked, looking at my two colleagues in triumph.

"You're right!" Bill exclaimed "We need to see if now we can open that file. So do you think Mr. Doughty was a Mason himself?" he asked.

I shook my head "There is no evidence to suggest that, he was a loner who had no friends. No, I don't think he was".

Lucy didn't say anything, and we walked the rest of the way in silence. I felt a bit guilty; maybe I was a bit hard on her. I wanted to get home and try to open the computer file. We reached the mansion and headed straight for the library. Bill switched the computer on.

"The clue is 'The key is the symbol of beginnings'. "He read "ok, so what now? We know the symbol is probably Masonic, and?" he asked looking at me and Lucy.

"We need to figure out what a Mason may have meant by that, what the symbol for 'beginning' would have been to them. Who were the Masons we need to ask ourselves, what was their way of thinking, where did they originate... Any ideas?" I asked, looking at them. Neither of them even seemed to have a clue. "Their name gives it away" I smiled.

"Their name?" Bill asked.

"Yes, as in stonemasons" I replied.

Lucy nodded, grasping the concept.

"Well, since they were builders, if you like, that used stone, what was the first thing they would lay?" I asked, still giving them a chance to figure it out for themselves. Bill looked like he was thinking about it; Lucy tapped her finger on her chin.

"The cornerstone? Isn't that right?" she said eagerly.

"That is exactly what I was thinking exactly. Let's try it" I said "Lucy, will you do the honours?" I asked, gesturing towards the pc. Bill stood up and let her put the password in. We all held our breath as the computer verified it. A window popped up on the screen- open file- it said, Lucy looked over at me and I nodded. Finally, we got the file open, hopefully it would be of some use to us; maybe even give us a clue as to what Mr. Doughty's discovery was. She clicked on the open file button. The file opened and all three of us drew closer to the screen, wanting to be the first one to see. There was nothing there. A blank page stared at us. We looked at one another. That didn't seem right at all.

"Why on earth would he create a password protected file and not put anything on it?" Lucy asked. None of us had an answer to that question. It didn't make any sense.

"Can you check when it was created?" I asked.

" I can help you with that" Bill said " Scoot" he said to Lucy " We can check when it was created, whether anything was printed off it and stuff like that, any changes that had been made" he said as he started typing on the keyboard. "Right, here we go, file created in September this year, it was 54 KB, so quite big. Unfortunately, it doesn't tell me what was in it, but here is something that may explain what had happened to it. File deleted 10th November." He looked at me and then at Lucy.

"That can't be right; it's the day after we arrived." Lucy said. "We didn't even know how to open the file, let alone delete the contents." She looked at me with a worried look on her face "What is going on here?" she asked.

I thought for a minute. It was obvious that someone had access to the mansion without our knowledge. The strange sounds that we kept hearing, books falling by themselves, glass breaking- it wasn't a ghost, it was someone that was looking for something in the mansion- Mr. Doughty's discovery. But how did they get in? There must be another way into the house, they managed to get in when the mansion was locked and sealed. Ronnie and Vanessa saw the lights way before we got here. There must be a secret way in, I thought, if only I knew where it was, I could maybe do something about it. But even without knowing where it was, there was something I could do to stop these 'visits'.

"It's obvious that someone is trying to get to Doughty's discovery before us." I said "I don't think there is any use in reporting it to the police, we have no proof of their visits, we don't know what they are looking for, and nothing has actually gone missing. We can't even prove that we were not the ones who deleted the file on the computer, it's not listed in the inventory that we were given."

"So what can we do?" Lucy asked, looking to Bill and me for answers.

"We need to find out what Doughty had discovered, it must be big if someone is still trying to get to it after his death. " I looked at them " I guess we will never find out what was in that file, but we can do one thing- all the doors have locks on them and we did have that big bunch of keys. We can lock all the doors and put an end to the problem of the visits that we get."

"That's a good idea" Lucy said "Where are the keys?" she asked.

"Didn't we leave the keys in the desk?" Bill asked. He started rummaging through the drawers. Lucy checked the ones on the other side.

"Nothing" she said "are you sure it was this desk, maybe it was the one it the study?" she asked, and headed for the door. Bill and I followed her. I had a horrible feeling and Lucy confirmed it. The keys were nowhere to be found. We split up and checked the kitchen and the other rooms we were using. No keys. But they were there when we had arrived. I decided that I needed some space to think about everything.

"Right, that's it. I am going for a drive, I need some space to think about all of this and clear my head." I said and put my coat on. "I would appreciate it if you guys stayed indoors whilst I am gone. I won't be too long." I went downstairs and went outside. The weather was unpleasant again, so I hurried to my car. I didn't just need to clear my head; I know it seemed a bit rude that I left Bill and Lucy to guard the house. I had a plan, but I didn't want to involve them in it.

# CHAPTER 4

It took me about an hour to reach Berwick. It is a small town, bigger than Cromdale and attracted a lot more tourists with its history, a magnificent 17$^{th}$ century church and a good selection of places to stay as well as restaurants and shops. It would serve me well for my purpose; I found the supermarket and parked my car. I went in and bought a packet of corn flour. Satisfied with my purchase, I had everything I needed for my plan. I looked at my watch and decided to grab a coffee. I loved latte, but the restaurant in Cromdale didn't have great coffee, so I wanted to use this opportunity and treat myself. I drove into the town centre and found a small cafe. I went inside and looked to see if there were any empty tables; but I couldn't see any. It was raining quite heavily and it seemed like everyone had picked this particular cafe to get out of the cold. As I don't like to impose on others I decided to give the coffee a miss after all and was heading for the door, when I saw someone waving at me from one of the tables. It was Walker. Andy Walker. We had known each other for years, we studied at university together. He was sitting at one of the tables in a far corner and I hadn't spotted him. He waved for me to come and joined him.

"It's good to see you, it's been a while, what have you been up to?" he asked as I sat down after placing my order. "What brings you to this part of the world then?" he continued.

It was a chance meet, but I immediately grew suspicious. I had not seen him for years, but I heard a lot of unpleasant rumours about him. We studied together, and he was really good, top of the class. Like me, he was passionate about history and like me he was adventurous. He was great at solving mysteries and we even made a few discoveries together and foiled the plot for forging known paintings. But this was as far as our similarities went. After university, we went our separate ways. I soon found out that he resigned from his placement; rumours circulated that he was involved in forgeries and scams. He travelled all over Europe, claiming it was to continue his studies, but the story did not ring true. Of course the rumours were never confirmed, but he wore expensive clothes, had a couple of expensive cars; it seemed unlikely that he could afford such a lifestyle on a salary of a history graduate.

"Are you still working for the National Heritage Society then? "He asked, smiling at me.

"Yes, I am. I have been sent here to organise a museum" I replied.

"And treasure hunting and 'cold cases'? Do you still get involved with that? I heard about your recent success in Bruges. Congratulations are in order. If it was me who found them, then I would not just give them up so gallantly, you should have asked for a raise at least" he chuckled quietly.

I looked closely at him, and remembered about a few other matters with which his name had been linked. I knew for a fact that that he was very smart, and he was involved in treasure hunting, as he called it. But I found it very hard to believe that he had never found anything; he had never donated any findings to a museum, did he sell it all to private collectors or on the black market? I had no proof, but I had my suspicions.

"So you must be the new curator for the museum that is supposed to open in Cromdale" he continued. "I know the estate, a big collection of antique furniture, a few paintings, but nothing special"

"Well, you seem well informed" I said.

"I think I must know all the private collectors in this area of Scotland" he said proudly "I have to, for my work you know. With my knowledge I assist in sales and purchases to collectors, a sort of antique dealer on the move. They pay me for my expertise and knowledge, it saves me from opening a shop and hunting around for the stock" he laughed quietly. "And it's not just private collectors, you know, people are getting tired of their contemporary furniture, the want classic pieces in their homes, they don't make them like that anymore, but they don't know what they are buying, so they need someone like me. That is how I met Mr. Doughty, he needed some cash quickly for repairs or something, and I found him a buyer for an 18th century desk and that is as far as that went" he took a sip of his coffee." I am not doing anything illegal, you know. I thought I would point that out, I know what you're like" He put his cup down and looked at me.

I took a sip of my coffee, finishing it. It was time for me to get home.

"It was great catching up after all this time" I said and lowered my voice to a whisper" Just a word of warning, my friend. Stay away from Blackhill estate, stay away from Cromdale. Do what you want, buy, sell, trade antiques but listen carefully, stay away from the museum".

"What are you talking about? Are you crazy?" Andy said, looking at me in disbelief.

"Stay away" I repeated, and with that I left the cafe.

I got into my car and drove back to Cromdale. This chance meeting with Walker was troubling me. I didn't have any reasons to doubt what he had said about his work, maybe he was here on business, but the strange goings on at the mansion and the fact that I bumped into him in Berwick seem a bit too much of a coincidence. Something was definitely going on... or was it? Maybe all the strange happenings were easily explainable with good reasoning? Nothing was missing; the books Mr. Doughty could have borrowed to someone and they simply did not return them. The keys we did not find, but maybe one of us put them away and just didn't remember. The strange noises? It is an old house and maybe we blew everything out of proportion? The lights that the kids saw in the windows could easily have been reflections or something. The only thing I couldn't explain was the deleted computer file, as well as the picture 'conversation' Mr. Doughty had with the guy that came to see him the day he died, and of course the supposed discovery.

None of it made any sense, nothing tied in together, and nothing was clear about this whole situation. This is the reason why I found it all so intriguing and I was sure that more unclear situations would crop up. The only thing I was sure of is that Mr. Doughty had made some kind of discovery at the mansion, and someone was trying to get to it. They were searching in such a way that no physical evidence was left behind. This is why my suspicions rose when I saw Walker; he was cleaver and could be very deceitful if he wanted to. Was it possible that he had already got to the discovery and it was gone? It seemed possible, but I didn't think that it had actually happened. What if I still had a chance to find it? Was there a way for me to foresee what steps they would take next in their search? If I knew what they (he? she?) were looking for than I could have a chance, but so far I didn't have a clue as to what it was. It's impossible to solve a puzzle if you don't have any hints or clues. So my only option was to wait and see. I reached this conclusion as I reached the estate. I parked the car and made my way towards the front door. I could see the kitchen lights were on so I made my way straight there.

Lucy was leaning against the kitchen table, reading. As I came into the kitchen the book slipped out of her hand and fell to the ground.

"Oh my gosh, you scared me" she said as she realised it was me. The kitchen was warm and cosy and the kettle had just boiled so I decided to make some tea to warm myself up a bit.

"Relax" I said to Lucy as I poured the water into my mug "You seem a little jumpy, next you'll be telling me you're hearing voices" I said as I sat down at the table.

"How did you know? Did you hear it as well?" she asked and sat down next to me. She looked scared.

"What?" I asked, surprised.

"When you went for your drive, Bill said he was going to the village to see if they were playing any good films tonight. I decided to go to the library and do some research on Masonic symbols and their history in general. I selected a few books and made myself comfortable in one of the big chairs in the library I even made myself some tea..." she stopped speaking and gazed into the window and into the night. "It got dark outside, I switched the light on. Everything was so quiet and the whole mansion seemed a bit strange, a bit eerie and then I heard it, a whisper. Something was whispering 'go on get out of here, whilst you still can'. It was coming out of thin air." She shivered at the memory. "I got so scared, I run to my room and slammed the door shut. A few minutes later, Bill came and brought Susannah with him, he is giving her a tour of the mansion. I think they are in the basement right now."

"Right..." I muttered, not happy about the fact that Bill was showing the mansion to a stranger with everything that was going on. " Right and the voices you supposedly heard? Did you maybe have a concussion when you were young?" I asked her.

She looked at me angrily and didn't say anything; only crossed her arms to let me know she was angry. Bill and Susannah came into the kitchen chatting and laughing. Bill was holding a bottle of wine in his hand. "Look what we found" he grinned and held it out for me and Lucy to see. "It was just sitting there, tucked away on one of the shelves. We can have a wine and cheese evening if we have any cheese in the fridge." He said.

I looked at him "I am not sure if we can, it's not really ours" I said

"Oh, come on, we are staying here now, we use the plates and stuff, it's not like Mr. Doughty will miss it" he laughed "We are allowed to enjoy ourselves you know".

"I don't see any harm in it" Susannah added "Won't you join us?" she smiled at me.

I shrugged. Maybe I was being a bit silly, Bill was right after all. "I think you're right" returning her smile.

"So... how about that ghost you promised me?" she asked as Lucy got the glasses out of the cupboard and poured each of us some wine.

"I promised you a ghost?" I asked surprised.

"Yes, you did" she answered.

"Oh, right, I think he isn't around today" I said.

"So you only have the one ghost here? I thought that in an old house like this there would be dozens" she said, with a playful smile on her face.

"We do, of course, but these ghosts are lazy, they only haunt on Saturdays." I replied, playing along.

"It's Saturday the day after tomorrow" she said.

"Well, maybe they will show themselves then" I answered jokingly.

"If Jimmy here won't manage to conjure one up for you then maybe I will" Bill added. It was a pleasant and relaxing evening, we were sitting around the kitchen table, chatting and joking with each other. Susannah picked up the book that Lucy had been reading.

"'Freemasons- a brief history.' Who were the Freemasons?" she asked." Are they the same people as the Masons?" she asked.

"Yes, it's just a shorter name for them." Lucy replied.

"My dad had a friend who always said that all wars and political disturbances around the world are because of their meddling." She said.

"That's a harsh opinion, and completely wrong." I replied.

"Well they are like a sect are they not? With their strange rituals and secrets and stuff." She tried to sound convincing.

"Lucy seems to think that they are responsible for all the strange things that go on in the mansion. And since she started blaming them, she has started to hear strange voices." Bill started laughing.

If looks could kill, Bill would be sprawled out on the floor, dead that very instant judging from the look Lucy shot him. But because that wasn't so he was still sitting at the table, laughing and drinking his wine.

"So do you think that as well Jimmy?" Susannah asked me.

"No, maybe Lucy does, since she started reading about them, but I don't." I answered.

"So who are they then? You're saying that my dad's friend is completely wrong, but a lot of people think that." Susannah replied and looked to me for an explanation.

"Well, I can tell you a bit about them if you like" I said and picked up my wine glass and took a sip.

"Freemasonry is an organisation that originated in the late sixteenth or early seventeenth century, but there is speculation about it. It exists in various forms all over the world. Freemasons correctly meet as a lodge, not in a lodge as most people see it. Often they are referred to as a secret society, but Freemasons themselves argue that it is more correct to say that it is an esoteric society, in that certain aspects are private. The most common phrasing being that Freemasonry has nowadays become less of a secret society and more of a society with secrets." I took another sip of the wine. "It's true to say that they conduct their meetings in a ritualised format, they make use of the architectural symbolism of the tools of the medieval operative stonemason. Freemasons as see themselves as speculative masons, meaning philosophical building rather than actual building, use this symbolism to teach moral and ethical lessons of the principals of 'Brotherly love, Relief and Truth'. There have been many conspiracy theories and hoaxes dating as far back as the eighteenth century and these have often become the basis for the criticism of the Freemasons. These were often political or religious in nature and that still resonates to this very day. It's a bit ironic in fact when you consider that there is no 'one' Masonic God. The masons believe in a 'supreme being' which therefore allows a man of any religion to join them. That's quite refreshing don't you agree?" I asked Susannah, but noticed that even though she had asked me about the Mason's she looked bored by the short speech I had made. She didn't even bother to answer my question, instead she changed the subject.

"So who is responsible for the strange things that happen in the mansion? It was Masonic signs that Mr. Doughty and the man that came to see him used, wasn't it? And the lights that were seen in the library when the mansion was sealed and the noises in the library that you guys keep hearing?" She asked.

"It's not the Masons that are responsible for those things" I smiled "I think it is just our imagination that's running away with us. We just joke around so we won't get bored here. It's just harmless fun."

I tried to sound sincere with my explanation "But don't worry, there is plenty of ghosts to go round, I am sure that we will sort one out for you" I said to Susannah.

"To all those who believe in ghosts and all of those who don't, I say cheers" Bill said and had a sip of his wine. We all did the same and then sat in silence for a few seconds. A loud knocking came from the front door.

"Who could that be?" Lucy asked. "Don't know, don't care" Bill answered and didn't even budge to get the door.

I got up and went to see who it was. It was Ronnie and I guessed that the girl he was with was his friend, Vanessa. I asked them to come in and we joined the others in the kitchen.

"Good evening" Ronnie said "This is Vanessa" he introduced his friend to everyone.

"Hi" Vanessa greeted everyone "We are coming back from rehearsals for the Christmas play" Vanessa explained. "I got the lead" she beamed.

"Stop showing off" Ronnie said.

"I am not, I am just explaining to everyone why we are out in the park at this time of the evening." She replied. "We saw the light on and Ronnie suggested that we come and see you to find out if you have heard anymore from the ghost." She carried on "We really want the ghosts to be very active, which will help bring in tourists to our village even during the winter and make our lives a bit more exciting" she added.

"Well, as a matter of fact, yes, Lucy here heard voices this afternoon." I answered.

"Voices?" Vanessa asked surprised and excited at the same time.

"Thanks a lot Jimmy" Lucy said to me angrily "are you trying to make me look silly or something?" she asked.

"What's the problem?" I asked. I didn't want to make her feel silly.

"I told you that in confidence, and you go and tell everyone" she said, giving me a stern look.

"You told Bill the same thing in confidence and he told Susannah in confidence" I tried to explain myself to her "And I told Ronnie and Vanessa in confidence as well"

"Was it a man's or a woman's voice you heard?" Ronnie asked "Don't worry, you can trust us" he added.

His question seemed to get her even angrier.

"That's enough" she said "What do you kids want? Spill" she said looking at them as if she didn't think she could trust them. Ronnie looked at Vanessa.

"We have an important matter, but we can only talk to Jimmy about it" Ronnie tried to sound mysterious as he said it. He didn't like being called a kid.

"Oh, no, not another mystery" Bill sighed.

I smiled at Ronnie and Vanessa and shoed them through to the hallway. "We can talk in here" I said.

We sat down on a small sofa that was positioned in one of the alcoves. "What's up?" I asked, wondering what this important matter could be. I looked at them in turn and tried my best to look serious.

"I was there when you and my dad were talking about the incident that happened the day Mr. Doughty died." Ronnie said "He was talking about the guy that came to see Mr. Doughty and the signs they drew to each other. We saw him that day because we were walking through the park on our way from school. Not him, his car to be more precise."

"A jaguar XF" Vanessa interrupted "I will get one of them for myself when I am famous"

Ronnie looked at her, then back at me and carried on "Anyway, he is back at the B&B, he checked in today"

"The same guy?" I asked.

"Yep, even my dad recognised him. He has the same car and we are sure it's him. Why do you think he came back? So long after Mr. Doughty's death?" he asked.

"Maybe he likes it here" I replied.

"Really?" I could hear the irony in Ronnie's voice "Do you really think so?"

"This whole thing is very suspicious" Vanessa added. "Should we keep an eye on him?"

"Keep an eye on him?" I asked and thought for a minute. I didn't want to put any ideas into these kids' heads, but I supposed that they just wanted to have some fun. "If you happen to see him in your spare time, and then keep an eye out. Let's not get carried away. You can't spy on him, just keep an eye out" I said.

"It is obvious that he is back for the same reason he was here before. He didn't manage to get what he wanted the last time he was here so he came back again." Ronnie said.

"What, to sort something out with Mr. Doughty? He knows he died, he was there, remember?" Vanessa said.

"No, but he might talk to you or Lucy or Bill" Ronnie pointed out.

I looked at him thoughtfully "That's not going to happen, but thanks for the heads up"

"If anything interesting happens we will let you know. We have to get going, it's getting late" Vanessa said.

I looked into the kitchen "Ronnie and Vanessa are going home, are you going with them? Is very dark and I thought it might be better if you walked with someone." I said to Susannah.

"You might be right there, but you haven't finished your wine." She pointed to the wine glasses. "Cheers then" she said and sipped the last of her wine. Bill and Lucy did the same, so I grabbed my glass and finished the wine.

"Blah" I said" It's so sour" I didn't like the taste of the wine at all.

"It is a good wine, you just don't know what you are talking about" Bill said.

"Maybe I am no expert, but I still didn't like it" I replied and followed Ronnie, Vanessa and Susannah out of the kitchen. I saw them off from the front door and then locked it shut. Now was a good opportunity to carry out the second part of my plan. I quietly went to my room and got the flour and the sieve which I sneaked out of the kitchen earlier. I then quietly went to the library and dusted a light layer of flour all over the floor where the books had fallen. If anyone walked over it in the dark we would see their tracks and where they went. I would just have to wait and see. I went back down to the kitchen and joined the others. Lucy was still not happy with me, Bill was yawning.

"Just one thing that I would like to say and then I am off to bed. If either of you hear the ghost upstairs, leave him be. Just ignore it please." I looked at them. They were probably thinking I was crazy. Lucy just shrugged her shoulders. "I don't care what he does, I am so tired tonight" and she let out a big yawn. "Good night." She said and went straight to her room. Bill followed; muttering something under his breath which I assumed was 'good night' and did the same. I felt really tired as well, I could hear the rain drumming gently against the window pane and I thought that maybe the gloomy evening weather was to blame for all three of us feeling so sleepy all of a sudden. I switched off the light in the kitchen, checked the front door and headed straight to bed. I fell asleep the second my head hit the pillow.

I was abruptly woken up by a loud banging at the front door. I had a splitting headache; in fact my whole body ached. I felt absolutely rotten. I looked towards the window and could see light seeping through the closed curtains. It was morning and someone was at the front door. I heard the banging again and I groaned as I got out of bed. I quickly threw on a pair of trousers and went to see who it was.

"Morning" a man said "Everything all right? I've been knocking for the past ten minutes and I had no answer. I was just about to go" he said looking at me strangely "I have a special delivery that needs signing for here" he said and handed me an envelope. It was the postman, but I hadn't realised that because I felt so bad. I looked at my watch; it was past ten in the morning. I scribbled something in the slot where my signature was supposed to go and thanked him, and then I closed the door and headed for the kitchen. I took a look at the letter; it was from the museum in Glasgow. It was a short message from the curator; it read 'There is a conference with regards to the new museum at Cromdale tomorrow morning at 9.30 am. You have reservations at the Sheraton hotel and tickets for the theatre for tonight.' I put the letter on the table and went to see what was going on with Lucy and Bill. I looked into both their rooms in turn and realised that they were still fast asleep. I shook Bill to wake him up and he just mumbled and groaned at me. I went to Lucy's room and tried to wake her up. She stirred and moaned.

"Ohhh, my head" she said as she tried to sit up. This was very odd. She looked very pale and was holding her head as she sat up in bed. I went to check on Bill, he was standing in the doorway pale and ill looking. "It must have been the wine" he moaned at me "That's why I feel so bad". I thought for a second. There were four of us last night so we had a glass each. We shouldn't feel so unwell after just one glass. Then something occurred to me. It seemed impossible, but the more I thought about it, the more likely it seemed. I run towards the kitchen "It was the wine; it must have been laced with sleeping pills!" I shouted and gestured to them to follow me. We left the bottle and the glasses on the table last night as no one felt like washing up. Anyway, there was still some of the wine left in the bottle. We run into the kitchen, but the only thing that was on the table was the letter which I had put there this morning. The bottle and glasses were all on the drainer next to the sink, washed.

"Are you sure you didn't finish the wine off by yourself?" Lucy asked, picking up the clean bottle.

"No, of course I didn't, I went to bed at the same time as you two. Someone must have poured the rest of the wine out a washed everything so there would be no evidence to prove anything, but I also set a trap" I said, looking at them triumphantly. "Come, follow me" I said and headed for the stairs. Bill and Lucy looked at each other, Bill shrugged and they both followed me. We went upstairs and into the library. I showed them the place where I set my trap. To my surprise there was nothing there, not even a speck of flour.

"So where is this trap then? What is it?" Bill asked me.

"I don't understand, I sifted flour all over the floor last night to track this 'ghost'." I explained, not understanding what had happened to the flour.

"Oh, good, so at least I know where the sieve went, I couldn't find it yesterday." Lucy said. Then she looked closely at me "Are you sure you are feeling ok?" she looked concerned.

"Yes, of course." I said, she must think I am crazy, I thought to myself. "Just forget I said anything."

"Right" Lucy said and looked at Bill who had wandered over to the window. All of a sudden he started laughing " I think I found your flour" he said as he bent down to pick something up from behind one of the armchairs. He straightened up and held in his hand a dustpan with a pile of corn flour on it. I felt confused. Lucy looked at my slippers; they were covered in corn flour. "So you set the trap, and then cleaned it up? What was the point?" she said, trying very hard not to laugh.

"Was this supposed to be a joke?" Bill asked "Well it isn't a very good one" he said and looked at me waiting for an explanation. "It's still funny though" he added after a few seconds.

"Do you sleepwalk maybe?" Lucy asked, concerned.

"I promise both of you that this wasn't a joke and I don't sleepwalk. The ghost played a dirty trick on me that's all" I said, hoping that they would believe me. But neither of them did.

# CHAPTER 5

I felt ill right until lunchtime. I had a terrible headache, I felt tired and sleepy. Bill and Lucy were the same. There was definitely something in the wine but again, I had no proof for it. We decided to do a relatively simple task of checking the inventory of what once used to be the grand drawing room at the mansion. The room was big, and obviously had not been used for that purpose for some years. Most of the furniture it would seem had been removed some time ago, there were only a couple of small sofas and a few chairs that dated back to the same period as the when the mansion had originally been built. The room had large windows on one side and probably the most striking feature was the way it was decorated. All the way around the whole room panels had been created by cleverly using columns carved in what appeared to be oak. The two that were at the end of the room that enclosed the fireplace seemed to be slightly larger. The other striking feature in the decoration of the room was the colour of the wallpaper that was covering the walls, it was dark green. The colour was so intense and deep it looked almost black even in the daylight. I was surprised at the way it was decorated; it did not seem cosy and pleasant. It was very formal, but it wasn't the formal drawing room of the house, that one was at the front of the mansion. However, I was glad that we had this room and that it hadn't been changed from when originally the mansion was built, it would be great as the main exhibition room for the new museum. It didn't take us too long to finish the work. We decided to take a bit of a break, so I quickly threw my coat on and went outside. I was hoping that a bit of fresh air would help clear my head and get rid of my headache. It was a bright morning and it was nice to see the sun shining for a change, although it was still pretty cold. I took a few deep breaths of the cool air and made my way down one of the paths. I started thinking about what exactly had happened last night. Was the wine laced with sleeping pills? I didn't have a good reason to think so, no proof. Maybe the wine was left in the old cellar for too long and that's what brought on our headaches? Bill did say he found it tucked away, so who knows how long it was there for. But if it was tampered with then there was only one reason why they would do it: to have the time to look for whatever it was that Mr. Doughty had discovered at the mansion. But he (she? /they?) didn't even leave a clue that they had been there, my trap had also failed. But I knew that it wasn't me who had 'cleaned' it up. Or was it? Maybe sleepwalking was another effect that the wine had on me. But I was sure that I had not been in the library at night. Unfortunately, I couldn't convince my colleagues to that. They had little trust in me from the start, it took me ages to convince them otherwise and now that was lost again. They had a good laugh at my expense when they saw the flour in the bin with the dustpan and brush. Once again they had stopped taking me seriously. Would I do the same if I was in their position? Probably, and the worst thing was that if anything odd or strange were to happen again, they would blame me for it, I was sure.

I reached a part of the garden I had not been in before. The garden was not well tended to, overgrown and shabby. In the distance I could see the grey- blue of the sea. I drew a deep breath in; I could smell the fresh sea air. I followed the path that lead away from the house and into the trees. I could see a small building on a small clearing next to the path and went to have a look at it. It was a shell grotto. The building was old and unpleasant. Once white, now the paint was peeling in several places, and the roof collapsed at one end of the building. The door however was solid and looked brand new. I tried to open it but it was locked. I thought it was a little odd, since there was nothing of value inside. I had a look through the small window, and all I could see was an old, broken bench, a few statues that were being stored here for the winter, even a broken one of cupid, poor fellow, he didn't have an arrow drawn on his bow.

"Sad, isn't it?" I heard Lucy's voice behind me. "I saw you from my window and thought a walk was a great idea." She looked at the statues again. "It's sad to see that, once they were considered beautiful, and now they have been dumped here, forgotten and useless."

"Maybe they never were beautiful" I said as I turned to face her.

"I don't think that, look at the one of cupid" she looked in again through the small window "It's sad that he will never shoot his arrow at someone's heart again, make someone fall in love..."

"You don't know that" I replied with a smile "Maybe he puts a fresh arrow on and draws his bow at night, I'd be careful if I were you, don't come here after dark; he might aim at you..." I said jokingly.

"So you do have a sense of humour after all" she said, laughing.

I returned her smile. The sun was shining and I thought this might be a good moment to patch things up, but it wasn't going to happen. There was Dave walking hurriedly towards us with a concerned look on his face.

"Hello" he said in his raspy, unpleasant voice "Is everything ok? I haven't had a chance to see if everything was ok, with the heating you know?" he said looking at me and Lucy.

"Yes, everything is fine" I replied wondering why he had the sudden interest in our wellbeing.

"Good, good, I was going to catch up with you this morning, but I overslept, and that never happens to me" he said.

"You weren't the only one, believe me" Lucy said.

"Well, as long as everything is ok at the mansion" he said, giving her an odd look "If anything at all needs doing, just tell me" he offered.

"That's great, we are ok for the time being" I said.

"So what's in here then?" I asked, pointing to the run down building.

Dave looked at me "Mr. Doughty used it for storage" he looked like he wanted to add 'as you can see' but didn't say anything.

"It has a brand new door and that is locked, do you know where the key is?" I asked.

"It should be in the house, all the keys should be" he looked at me.

I opened my mouth to say that the keys went missing, when Lucy held something out in front of her. It was the missing bunch of keys. "They were sitting on your desk, I don't know how you missed them" she said, handing the keys to me. I took the keys from her and tried each one in the lock but none of them fitted. Dave watched me and then nodded after I tried all of the keys and none of them had worked.

"As far as I know it was a long, flat key to this lock. It should be somewhere in the house if you haven't got it there. When the lock was installed, he locked it and that was the last I saw of it." He said. "I never saw him come in here, and why would he? It's only old and broken garden furniture in there" he shrugged his shoulders.

"Do you know why he fitted a new door in here? If there is nothing of value inside?" I asked.

" Oh yes, he found empty beer and wine bottles in here one day and asked me to get a door for here he said ' I don't want drunks hanging around the park Dave, ' so I did, he locked it and that was it" he explained.

"Right..." I said. I thought that there was a more significant reason for it, but I was wrong. Again.

"Anyway, I am off now, as long as everything is fine?" he asked.

"Thanks Dave, we are ok. If we need anything we will let you know. Thank you for asking though" I said. Lucy said 'bye' as well and he went towards his little house. Lucy watched him for a while and then turned around and faced me.

"Jimmy, I actually came out here to talk to you about something" she said, putting her hands in her pockets. The wind picked up again and it suddenly got colder.

"What did you want to talk to me about?" I asked, curious of what she wanted to say.

"Why are you trying so hard to convince me and Billy that something strange is going on in the mansion?" she asked.

"I am trying to convince you?" I asked surprised.

"Yes you are. Neither Billy nor I have noticed anything odd going on, it's just you. The night we arrived it was you who heard 'noises' in the library. You took that story about the lights shining in the windows when there was no one here seriously, then you set your trap which proved nothing, you couldn't find the keys and said they were missing when all along they were sitting on your desk. To top it all off you are the one who said the wine was laced with sleeping pills. That is a serious accusation, don't you think? Maybe we felt ill because the wine was in that cellar for god knows how long?"

"But Lucy..." I tried to interrupt her and explain, but she didn't allow me to do that and carried on.

"There is nothing weird going on in the mansion, as far as we are concerned it's a figment of your imagination. Nothing has gone missing. You are trying to make a big deal out of every tiny thing."

I wanted to explain my actions to her, but there was nothing I could say. She was right in a way. Nothing really had gone missing, three books from the library? The file on the pc? There were reasonable and simple explanations for these matters.

"It's hard to work when your superior sees a mystery to solve in every little thing that happens" she added.

"Right, I am sorry if I've created an unpleasant environment to work in. It won't happen again" I said.

She wasn't expecting that response. She thought I would be defending myself, maybe accusing her of the same thing but no. Instead I agreed and took all the blame, although I wasn't the only one to blame for this whole mess. She looked a bit embarrassed

"Well, that's good, thank you" she said, turned around and went back to the mansion. I decided to walk for a bit more, I didn't particularly want to get back to Lucy and Bill at the moment so I carried on down the path. I walked around for a bit and I ended up at the building with the broken statues. Something was drawing me towards it; it intrigued me although I couldn't say why. Maybe it was the fact that the key to the door wasn't with all the others. I thought for a minute. That was the other thing that was bothering me. Yesterday the keys were not on my desk, I could swear by it. I rummaged through everything and couldn't find them. But today Lucy just picked them up off the desk, as if they were sitting there all that time. Maybe she was right, maybe I read into everything too much.

I was standing, thinking about all these things when I heard voices. They were gradually getting louder and finally I saw Vanessa and Ronnie emerging from the trees on one of the paths. They were wearing their school uniform so I figured that they were on their way back from school. I could hear them laughing and talking, and eventually they spotted me and came over to say hello.

"Hi guys, how are you?" I asked smiling at each of them.

"Hi, we're fine" Answered Ronnie. He was holding a football under his arm.

"It's a good thing that we run into you like this" Vanessa added.

"Oh? And why is that?" I asked.

"Well, actually, it's two things. Firstly you can help us figure something out." She gestured towards Ronnie's school bag "Why don't you show him what you found" she said.

Ronnie reached into his bag and produced a beautiful gold Parker fountain pen.

"Wow, I said, where did you find that then?" I asked, surprised as clearly it was worth a lot of money. I picked up the pen to have a good look at it. It was beautiful.

"Well, I always take my football to school, even during the winter when it's not raining; I always kick it along the path when we walk through the park. " Ronnie started explaining "Today, Vanessa decided to have a kick around with me and kicked the ball into the bushes. I found the pen when I was looking for the ball."

"So why did you want to see me about it then?" I didn't know where she was going with this.

"That is the other thing, you see the two are connected to each other" she started to explain as Ronnie stood there patiently. "We know who the pen belongs to and we know that he lost it here last night."

"That's your theory" Ronnie interrupted. "That's why we wanted to see you about it, to get your opinion"

"If you know who the pen belongs to you need to give it back, it's very expensive and I am sure they are missing it" I said, looking at them "How exactly do you know that he lost it here last night? And how do you know who it belongs to?" I asked.

"Last night my parents and I were having the evening meal at the restaurant" Vanessa started explaining "Sitting at one of the tables I saw the guy who came to see Mr. Doughty the day he died, you know, the one with the car" She said "Somehow I find it hard to believe that he found Cromdale so charming that he returned for a visit in December." She said matter-of-factly.

"So does the pen belong to him then?" I asked, wondering again where this was going.

"No, it doesn't. The guy was waiting for his friend and they had dinner together, his name is Peter by the way, I don't know what his friend's name is though, but he had the pen. I was keeping an eye on them whilst I was there, and I saw Peter's friend drawing something on a piece of paper with this very pen that's how I know who it belongs to." Vanessa said.

"OK, but that still doesn't explain why you think he lost the pen last night, its coming up to noon, and he could have lost it this morning" I said.

Vanessa looked at me " The restaurant closes at 11pm" she said " So if he had the pen on him last night when I saw it at 8pm, and now it's here in the bushes then he must have lost it between then and now. If he was walking through the park today he would notice that he dropped it and he wouldn't be walking through the bushes, would he?" she asked with a triumphant glimmer in her eye.

"I am not sure, maybe you do have a point" I said uncertainly.

"I am right and you both know it. It's all down to logical thinking."

Vanessa continued "He didn't stay at the B&B; he just came to see Peter, who is staying there. Since they were having a meal and the restaurant closes at 11pm, he came here after."

I decided to put an end to the conversation.

"It was probably someone local and they took a short cut through the park and lost the pen on their way" I said, thinking that the simplest explanation is usually the right one.

"I would agree with you" Vanessa said "But we know nearly all the locals, and he doesn't live around here. Besides he didn't need to take a shortcut through the park, he drove here. His car was parked outside." She said.

"And how do you know that?" Ronnie asked.

"I have my ways" Vanessa replied. "Next time he comes I will return the pen to him, or you can do it" she said to Ronnie.

"And what if he doesn't come back?" Ronnie asked.

"Oh, I know he will, in fact I am sure he will" Vanessa said "If not, IO will give it back to this Peter guy and tell him where you found it" she chuckled quietly" I would love to see his face when I tell him" she added and turned her attention back to me "So how is the whole ghost situation then?"She asked.

"The ghost is on vacation at the moment" I replied, deciding not to tell them about the trap and the wine business.

"Really?" she asked "Because I think that the ghost should be getting more active by the day. This Peter has come back and he even brought a dodgy friend with him…"

"Why dodgy?" Ronnie asked

"Well, if he takes walks through a strange park in the middle of the night, that's dodgy, don't you think?" she asked." Anyway, let's get going, I can't be late today, my mum wants me to go shopping with her" and with that she said bye and started down the path towards home. Ronnie shrugged his shoulders, put the pen back into his bag and followed her. I was on my own once again. I looked at my watch, it was nearly one o'clock. It was time for me to get back and head for lunch. I made my way back to the mansion only to find Bill and Lucy already at the door.

"We were about to go looking for you, are you ready to go?" Bill asked.

"Yes, I am, let's go." I nodded and waited for Lucy to lock the front door. We walked in silence all the way to the restaurant. We entered the restaurant to find it nearly empty, only Susannah was sitting at one of the tables. She didn't look very well.

"Hi, what's wrong with you?" Lucy asked as she took her seat at the table.

"I don't feel very well, I think it was the wine we had last night" she said.

"Same as us then" I said.

"I have a terrible headache, I took the day off work, and I didn't even wake up on time this morning" she made a sad face.

"I wouldn't worry about it, I think we are just not used to well aged wines." Bill sympathised "James here seems to think it was laced with sleeping pills, but I don't think that's true."

"You're kidding, laced with sleeping pills? How?" Susannah gasped.

"Don't worry, it's just his suspicions, he is overreacting again" Lucy said. "It's this 'ghost' that is responsible for everything, that is what he thinks anyway"

"Did you get another visit from the ghost? Any new developments?" she asked.

" There is no ghost" Bill answered her " Jimmy is just making it all up, trying to convince everyone that there are odd things going on in the mansion".

Susannah looked closely at me and smiled. Even she didn't believe me, and why should she? So far there was no physical proof for anything, just my suspicions. To be honest I would probably think the same. I decided that it would be best to ignore everything and just concentrate on finishing what we came here to do.

"We have a meeting tomorrow about our museum. It's tomorrow morning and although the curator of the museum in Glasgow is providing us with accommodation and theatre tickets, if we leave at 6.30am in the morning then we will make it easily." I informed them. I completely forgot to tell them about the letter that I received in the morning by special delivery. "I don't want to leave the mansion empty overnight"

Bill and Lucy stared at me in silence for a minute. Then they both started speaking at once.

"You can't be serious" Lucy gasped.

"Oh, come on, we need a break you know! " Bill said loudly.

"It's not exactly going to grow little legs and run off when we're not there" Lucy added.

"Nothing is going to happen if we leave the mansion empty for one night!"

"The trouble is that things happen when we're there, so what will happen when it's empty?" I asked looking at them.

"You can't be serious?" Bill asked, shocked. "Please don't tell me that you take all this seriously, I thought that you and Lucy had a chat about it before, didn't you?" he asked worryingly.

"Well, Lucy here heard voices telling her to 'get out' if I recall correctly" I defended myself.

Susannah laughed quietly. I could only imagine how the conversation must have sounded to her. Lucy looked at me stunned. She raised one eyebrow and said

"Maybe I did, maybe I didn't. The truth is I have been told in the past that I can get influenced by other people quite easily, and that is what has happened here. You keep telling us of these visitors at the mansion even though we never see any proof of it; you can't say anything to Mr. Simpson for that same reason. Maybe it was your suggestive behaviour that made me think that I heard those voices." She looked at me sternly.

"Why shouldn't we go today, and enjoy the show?" Bill asked " Don't you think it would be better to arrive fresh and well rested tomorrow, rather than getting up at 6am to get there? What if we get stuck in traffic and we're late? What if the car breaks down and we miss the meeting?" He looked at Lucy and asked "What will you say to Mr. Simpson, that you couldn't leave the mansion by itself? And what is he going to think?" Both of them looked closely at me.

"I guess you two have a point, we will go tonight" I said and concentrated on eating my lunch. We finished the meal, said goodbye to Susannah and made our way home. Although we still had a lot of work planned for today, I decided that it would do all three of us well if we had a break. We would have to finish early anyway getting to Glasgow at a decent hour, we still had to get ready and it was quite late in the day already. I went to my room, packed an overnight bag and then went up to the library to have some peace and quiet. I needed time to think. Everything I had done so far didn't get me anywhere; on the contrary, my colleagues were very close to thinking that I had lost it. Deep down I knew I was right, that there was something going on, but there were just too many things too difficult to explain. I didn't have any physical proof either, I couldn't ring Mr. Simpson up and say that something was going on for certain for that very reason. Bill and Lucy either didn't see it or chose not to, I don't know which one it was.

I was so deep in thought that I didn't realise that the afternoon had slowly turned into evening. I heard a quiet knock on the door and Lucy poked her head into the room

"Still working I see?" she asked.

I looked up at her and smiled. I wasn't sure whether she was being sarcastic or not. I decided that it was up to me to patch things up between us; after all I didn't want her and Billy thinking I was losing it. I took this position on and it was up to me to be a good leader for the two of them, I didn't want them to feel uncomfortable in their first job after university. They were young and inexperienced and maybe I just wasn't settling into my new role very well- I had been solving mysteries for so long, maybe I was looking for one here even though there wasn't one?

"I wouldn't call it work" I smiled again "I was just thinking about a few things" I replied. She looked very pretty, she dressed up for going out and it was a rather pleasant sight.

"I am ready to go" I said and got my bag. Billy was already in the kitchen.

" I am so glad that we are getting out of this dusty place at least for one night" he said " I am getting bored and tired of this place"

"How can you get bored here?" I asked " There are so many interesting and rare books here, the whole feel of the place, Mr. Doughty had done well over the years with his collection" I said, a bit surprised.

"Serious lack of entertainment and excitement" he replied with a cheeky grin.

"And the ghosts?" I asked.

He and Lucy grew serious. She gave me that stern look of hers again.

"I thought we agreed not to talk about that anymore" she said.

"That's right, anyway, isn't it time we left now?" Bill asked "We're going to be late".

I nodded and took the keys that Lucy found this afternoon. I went round the whole of the mansion and checked all the rooms and then locked them. Lucy and Bill got their bags, and after locking and checking the front door we made our way to the car.

Lucy sighed as she sat down in the passenger seat.

"Maybe we should tell Dave to keep an eye on the place until we get back?" she asked "Would that put your mind at ease James?" she asked me.

"No, I don't think that is a good idea." I said "I don't really want anyone to know that we won't be here for the night"

"Jimmy, you would be such a great person to work with if you weren't so suspicious of everyone" she replied "Suit yourself".

I ignored her comment and we set off. It was already getting dark and to make matters worse it started to rain. There was no trace of the nice weather from this morning. We drove for a while and we finally got onto the M8. The traffic was still heavy so I drove slowly.

"Can't we go a little faster?" Bill asked "The limit is 60 miles per hour"

I shrugged my shoulders and ignored him. The weather wasn't great and I hated when people told me how to drive. We drove in silence for a while. No one seemed to have anything to say so I put the radio on. The journey took a while and we didn't talk. I supposed that we all had things to think about.

We finally made our way into Glasgow. I used the GPS to find the hotel as I didn't know the city. It looked very posh. I parked the car in the short stay car park and we went into the hotel. We left our bags in the car as we were going to drive to the theatre so we could take them with us when we came back and check in then. We picked up the theatre tickets at reception and we made our way straight to the theatre.

"Oh this is so nice after being in that mansion, I didn't realise how much I missed going out" Lucy said "We need to do this more often, I thought life in a village was relaxed and stress free, but I do miss London"

"Me too" Bill added "Although this isn't exactly my cup of tea, it is nice to get out".

We went back to the car and made our way back to the theatre. I parked the car on one of the available parking spaces just outside the theatre. The performance was about to start so we made our way in. One of the ushers showed us to our seats. They were up in the balcony section and I thought it was very nice of the curator of the museum to get us such good seats. The show started but I wasn't paying much attention to it, I had too much on my mind. I think it was some sort of love story as Lucy kept whispering to me every so often.

"Oh, they love each other so much. It's so sad they can't be together." She whispered.

I just nodded and didn't say anything in return. I still kept thinking about everything that happened in the past few weeks.

Act one was over and the actors went off the stage. We went to grab a quick drink before act two. The foyer was full of people, chatting and enjoying a quick drink as well. Bill looked slightly bored as he sipped his coke.

"What do you think of the play then?" Lucy asked him.

"To be honest I would have preferred concert tickets, like I said this isn't really my cup of tea" he replied.

"And you?" she turned to me. "Would you prefer a concert? Or maybe something else altogether?" she asked.

"No...No, this is fine" I answered.

"So you are enjoying the play?" she asked again.

"Yes..." I said. Something didn't feel right and I was trying to figure out what, but I just couldn't put my finger on it.

She misunderstood my distraction "So you are a romantic after all" she said smiling.

I didn't respond to that as it was time for us to get back to our seats as the second act was about to start.

"It was so nice of the curator to get us such great seats. We should say a big thank you, we got put up in the best hotel in town, right in the city centre and everything..." she said as the curtain went up on stage.

Just as it did, it finally hit me. Something was definitely off. I have been working for the National Heritage Society for years now and I have been to so many meetings and training courses. But I had never been put up in the best hotels, let alone had any sort of entertainment provided for me. The most I ever got was a room at Travelodge and a petrol allowance to get there. But here we had rooms booked in a posh hotel and theatre tickets for a play. If I was Mr. Simpson, then maybe yes, but not us, it just didn't seem right. I grabbed Bill by his arm and nudged Lucy.

"Get up, we've got to go right now" I said as I stood up and pulled Bill up from his seat.

They were so surprised; they both got up and followed me to the foyer.

"What is wrong?" Lucy asked, looking at Bill, not sure what is going on.

"This is all a scam, the theatre tickets, the hotel..." I said as I hurried to get my jacket.

They both looked at me in disbelief.

"What scam?" Bill asked as he caught up with me. One of the ushers was standing near the front door and was looking at us.

"All of this!" I raised my voice "We need to get back right away".

I hurried towards the cloak room to get our jackets.

"Are you not enjoying the play?" the attendant asked.

"It's not the play mate; I just need to leave ok?" I said in an annoyed voice.

He looked at me and stepped back.

"Are you ok? Is everything ok?" he asked looking towards Lucy and Bill.

"Yes, yes, its fine" Lucy assured him "Our friend just isn't feeling well, that is all".

At that moment someone else approached the cloakroom and the attendant went to see if he needed anything and left us alone. I rushed out the door and dragged Lucy and Bill with me. Lucy stopped in front of the theatre and pulled her hand out of my grasp.

"If you don't stop, I'm going to scream" she said.

"Hurry up, please" I said taking no notice of her. I nudged Bill again and went to the car. "We need to get back as soon as possible, do you not understand? This is all a scam just to get us out of the, mansion" I tried to explain as I hurriedly got into the car.

"I swear you really are losing it Jimmy" Lucy said as she put her seat belt on.

"I don't mind, Jimmy, I wasn't really enjoying the play anyway, but next time can you stop nudging me?" Bill said as we pulled away from the curb.

"Well, maybe at least some good will come out of this" Lucy said "We will be late for the meeting tomorrow and then you can explain why. I am sure that Mr. Simpson will take into consideration all of your actions and that will be the end of all of this." She crossed her arms.

I ignored her and concentrated on driving. I wanted to leave the city as soon as possible and get onto the motorway. The traffic wasn't as heavy as it was on the way to Glasgow so the journey back should take less time as well.

"Do you not understand that there is no meeting tomorrow?" I asked her.

"And what makes you so sure of that? What if there is a meeting?" she asked

"Then we will be a bit late" I said.

I had just got onto the motorway and I was concentrating on the road and didn't have time for arguments. Another car tried to overtake.

I moved over to the left lane to let him pass. Bill looked at the car as it went past us.

"An XF. They are really nice, those jags" he said and then started grinning "Look it's the guy that left the theatre right after we did, I guess he didn't like the play either. I think he fancied you" he said to Lucy and started laughing" And now he is following us, maybe he wants your number" he started laughing. I looked over at the car, it was just ahead of us and he indicated he was going to go into my lane.

"What are you talking about?" Lucy asked, slightly embarrassed.

"He kept staring at you in the theatre" Bill said, still laughing.

I suddenly remembered what Vanessa had told me. The guy who came to see Mr. Doughty on the day he died drove a jaguar XF. And he was back in town; she saw him and his car. This was too much of a coincidence, him being in the same place as us on the same evening. He was there to keep an eye on us and now he wanted to get back to Cromdale before us. Why? Maybe to warn someone that we were on our way back tonight. I suddenly felt angry at myself. Something was going on at the mansion and I still didn't know what. The stakes must be pretty high if someone is going to such lengths to get to whatever Doughty discovered. Well, I wasn't going to let anyone get away with it, maybe they were smart enough until now not to leave any evidence of their actions but now I had the chance to catch them red handed.

"Do you have your seatbelts on?" I asked Bill and Lucy.

"Yes, we do, don't worry" She said, and Bill nodded.

I put my foot down on the accelerator pedal. Even though my Mercedes was old, it still had a kick. The hand on the speedometer slowly went up. I got into the middle lane and sped up a bit more. The motorway was empty; there were no other cars about so I could go a bit faster.

"Good stuff, I knew that this old thing had in him" Bill said jokingly.

We caught up to the jaguar, I could see his rear lights in front of me I indicated that I was going to overtake him. He sped up, so I stayed in my lane and tried to keep the distance between us.

"Why is he rushing so much?" Lucy asked.

"Do you not understand that he was there to keep an eye on us, and now he wants to get back before we do?" I asked. I spotted a sign warning about road works and a speed limit of 50 miles per hour and average speed cameras. I took my foot of the pedal and the XF driver did the same. I slowed down, he did the same and we entered the average speed check bit.

"Great, this is going to carry on for the next 3 miles" I said. I wanted to get in front of him, but I couldn't do it here, he was driving at exactly 50 and I didn't want to end up with a ticket to pay.

"Even if you're right, why doesn't he just ring?" Bill asked.

"Wow, I can't believe you just asked me that" I said, looking at him in my rear view mirror. "You were the one who moaned about the phone reception in Cromdale."

"Oh, yeah, it's virtually non- existent, you have to know where to stand to make a phone call" he said, answering his own question.

We finally got to the end of the road works and the guy in the jag sped up almost instantly. I put my foot down as well and was catching him up. We were nearly at the junction with the A1 and I knew I wouldn't over take him before we got the so I kept the distance between us.

We left the motorway and the chase continued. We were now on a single carriage way and if I wanted to over take him I had to do it at the right moment. We had just less than 20 miles left to Cromdale, so it was now or never. But the driver in the jaguar knew this as well and he wasn't going to make it easy for me to overtake him. He sped up even more and because the road had a few bends I couldn't see far enough in order to see whether it was safe or not for me to jump out onto the opposite lane. By the time I managed to get in front of the jaguar we only had 6 miles left to Cromdale. I put my foot down on the accelerator pedal to put as much distance between me and the other car as possible. But it wasn't much; the junction on which I had to come off was just coming up. Although I couldn't see the lights of the car that was chasing us, I knew he wasn't far behind. I sped down the country road, but here I had to slow down a lot because I had to watch out for pedestrians as well as other cars, although I didn't expect to see anyone here at this time of the evening.

Just as I turned into the gates I could see a glimmer of headlights from the car that was chasing us. I drove as quickly as I could down the driveway but I had the head lights off so I wouldn't let whoever was in the mansion known that we were home. I really did want to catch them in the act and put an end to everything. But this was enough for the driver of the jaguar to catch up with us. Just as I got close enough to the house to walk, he drove up the driveway, revving his engine and blasting his horn. He stopped next to my car, jumped out and started yelling.

"You nearly drove me off the road!! What kind of a driver are you?!" he was shouting angrily at me.

But I jumped out and ignored him. I wanted to get inside as soon as I could although I knew it was probably too late.

"Bill, you argue with him, I haven't got time for this" I said without even looking whether Bill had heard me and I sprinted towards the front door. He wanted me to start arguing with him so whoever was inside would have enough time to get away and remove any signs that someone was inside during our absence. I opened the front door and bounded up the stairs. I got the keys to all the rooms out and opened each room in turn checking them over for anything odd. Everything seemed fine. I went in the library. I drew the air in with my nose. There was a strange smell in here. I couldn't put my finger on it. Also the chair next to the computer was pulled out as if someone had just been sitting there. I walked over to it and touched the seat. It felt warm. I looked around the library but everything seemed in order. Had someone been in here or was it my imagination? I shrugged my shoulders and decided to join the others. I went downstairs to find them closing the front door.

"Is everything ok?" Lucy asked.

"Everything seems fine, what about him?" I asked pointing towards the door.

"He just had a go at us, and said that you need to get your driving test done again." Bill said. "He went on for a bit then he got in his car and drove off"

"Right, I am going to park the car properly "I said.

When I got back inside I saw Billy and Lucy coming down the stairs.

"Everything seems in order, I don't think there was anyone in here" Bill said as he reached the bottom of the stairs.

"What if there is a meeting and we aren't there?" Lucy asked.

"No, there is no meeting. It was all a scam to get us out for the whole night. That guy's behaviour confirms it wouldn't you agree?" I looked at them. They both just returned my gaze without saying anything. "During our absence someone was in here looking for something. The guy in the jag was meant to keep an eye on us and warn whoever was here if we were coming home. Which is exactly what he did? How did we know we live here? He is staying in Cromdale, that is the exit before ours and yet he drove after us off the A1" They were listening to me, Bill was even nodding in agreement. I continued "I don't know what it is that they are looking for.

They were so clever so far that even you started to doubt me even though you were here and witnessed all the odd things and coincidences. But at least I have proof this time; I have the letter that arrived today. We have something to go on now and something to show to the authorities." I went to my room and opened the desk drawer. I opened the file that contained incoming mail.....only to find it empty. The letter I had put there this morning was gone.

# CHAPTER SIX

The next morning I decided to try and straighten this whole mess out. I drove into Cromdale and went into the post office. I wanted to get to the bottom of this whole mess. In the light of day all of last night's events seemed unreal. My suspicions slowly disappeared. After all I didn't find evidence of anyone being in the mansion. Anyone of us could have left the chair like that. It felt warm, but that could have been because I had been running in the cold, so my hands were also cold. The letter that I couldn't find? When it was delivered I was still half asleep. I know I read it in the kitchen, but maybe I didn't put it in the file after? Maybe I put it down somewhere and now I just couldn't remember. After all I wasn't feeling well after the wine...who knows.

As soon as I had reception on my phone I rang Mr. Simpson only to find out that he was away from the office for a few days. His mobile was off as well. I decided to try and get a hold of the curator of the Glaswegian museum and if there had been a meeting this morning I would just say that my car broke down on the way. It was a nerve-racking few minutes before he answered his phone.

"Hi James, how are you getting on?" boomed the curator of the Glaswegian museum down the phone "I am sorry I've not been in touch with you sooner, I am sure you are very busy and you know that I am here for support if you need me?" he asked.

"Yes, all is fine, we are getting there slowly, but surely" I answered, relieved that I was right and there was no meeting. "We are just fine. We should be finished within the next few weeks, and I think that Mr. Simpson will come and see us. Any plans for a meeting regarding the plans for the new museum in the near future?" I asked cautiously.

"No, James, not as far as I know. I wouldn't be involved in it anyway, I have nothing to do with new museums, I've got my own to worry about, you know?" he said, and that finally put me at ease. We talked for another few minutes and then said goodbye to one another.

There was no meeting; it was all a scam to get us out of the mansion for the whole night. Maybe I could find something out at the post office though. The letter had been sent by special delivery, so the post office must track it. They should be able to tell me who the sender was.

I made my way to the post office. There was a bit of a queue and I had to wait for a few minutes. I finally made it to the cashier.

"Good morning, I was wondering if you can help me" I said with a smile to the young lady on the other side of the desk.

"Good morning" she replied.

"I received a special delivery letter yesterday, to which I need to reply, but I've lost the envelope and I don't know what the return address is. Is there any way that you can check for me who the sender was?" I asked. It sounded like a good story in my head but now that I had said it, it sounded a bit lame.

"Umm, let me see, I wouldn't be able to check here, but what I can do is give you the tracking number, you can give Royal Mail a ring and if they can they will give you that information." She said.

"I don't know if they can because of data protection, but you can certainly give it a try."

It wasn't great, but it was a start.

"What do you need to track the number down?" I asked.

"Just your address, or the delivery address and when you received it" she said.

"Well, I am staying at Blackhill Estate, Cromdale, and the letter arrived yesterday" I said.

"And was it before 9 am or 1 pm?" she asked, typing the address into her computer.

"It arrived after ten, so it was the second one I think" I replied.

She typed the information I had given her into the system and after a few seconds she looked at me.

"I have nothing in the system for that address, are you sure you got the date right?" she asked.

"Of course I am" I said, getting a bit annoyed.

"Right, from what I can see here, the last special delivery for

Blackhill Estate, Cromdale was back in September." She looked at me questioningly.

"Oh, ok, well, I am sorry to have bothered you, maybe it's my mistake" I mumbled feeling rather awkward. "Thanks for checking, bye" I wanted to get out of there as soon as I could. The girl at the counter just gave me an odd look and called the next person in the queue over.

I went back to the car and went back to the house. It was clear to me that someone wanted us out of the mansion for the night. I wanted to share the news with m colleagues as soon as possible. It wasn't hard evidence, but at least it showed that after all I had been right all along.

I got back and found them in the kitchen finishing their breakfast.

"It was all a scam!" I shouted after greeting them "I spoke to the curator in Glasgow, there was no meeting, I checked at the post office and there was no letter that came through to us. Someone just thought of this whole thing just to get us out of here for the night so they could look for whatever it is they want." I rambled on.

"Well, to be honest, I am not too upset about it. I am stuck here all the time, there is nowhere to go out and it was nice to be away from here for a change." Lucy said as she started doing the dishes.

"All we do is work, we don't even have a TV" Bill added "The only problem I had with the whole scam is that it was theatre tickets and not concert tickets".

I looked at the two of them. They did have a point. We felt cut off from civilisation here; our only break from the mansion was going out to lunch to the village. I thought for a minute and made my decision.

"It is obvious there is another way into the mansion, like a secret passage. We are going to look for it before we do anything else today" I said.

"Ok, how do you want to do that?" Bill asked "I have never done anything like that before. I thought that secret passages existed in castles in the medieval times."

"There are several ways that we can go about it. For example, you can fill a room with smoke and see if it seeps out anywhere." I said. "The most common method is by knocking and tapping on walls to check for any hidden doors or passages. This is the method we can use here."

"The only thing that needs checking is the state of your mind" Lucy said under her breath, and the in her normal tone of voice she added "There aren't any secret passages here. But if you want to waste our time that's fine, you're the boss" she shrugged her shoulders.

We each took something that we could use and went to different rooms. Soon there were echoes of tapping and knocking coming from different rooms in the mansion. We carried on until it was time to go for lunch and we didn't discover anything. As usual, Susannah was waiting for us before she ordered so we could eat together. She looked very pretty today and my mood lifted a little bit.

"I think we should put an end to this ghost business." She smiled at me "And I know how to do it" she smiled again.

"Oh really?" I asked.

"The ghost is giving you a bad name so you need to get rid of it, simple" she said jokingly. "We need to summon it and tell it to go away. The sooner we do it, the better, how about tonight?" she asked "Do you guys have anything planned?" She looked at each of us in turn.

"Well, I guess we are free" Lucy said. "It's just a bit of harmless fun, right?" she looked at Susannah questioningly.

"Oh, this is very serious business" she answered, looking serious but I could see a smile playing on her lips. "We can use an Ouija board and see why the ghost keeps returning to the mansion. What do you think?"

I thought about it for a minute. It was just a bit of harmless fun. I had heard about this sort of thing before, but never actually took part. It could be an interesting experience.

"Sure why not? It will give us something to do tonight" I said and smiled.

Our food arrived at the table and we all tucked in. Susannah broke the silence after a few minutes.

"How was your trip to the theatre last night?" she asked.

I looked at Bill and Lucy, trying to let them know that I didn't want any details from last night discussed with someone outside of our team. Bill pretended not to understand.

"It was all great fun. They play was really interesting and the actors performed really well" he said.

I managed to kick his ankle under the table.

"What was the play about?" she asked.

"It was a love story" Lucy answered her.

"Did it have a happy ending?" she continued asking "I love happy endings" she smiled.

"Unfortunately, it wasn't a happy ending for us" Lucy explained "Jimmy here felt unwell during the second act and we had to return home."

"You're kidding" Susannah said, then she turned to me "Are you feeling better?" she asked.

"Yes I am" I replied, giving Lucy a stern look. I wasn't too happy about telling Susannah anything about last night it was too late. We had arranged the plans for tonight; Susannah was to join us at the mansion at 9pm. We finished lunch and we were just heading out the door when one of the waitresses approached us.

"You forgot this" she said quietly as she handed me a folded piece of paper. Lucy looked at me.

"Have you got a secret admirer?" she laughed and nudged Bill with her elbow. He started laughing as well. "Is it a date?" she asked.

I took no notice of her comments and stopped to have a look at the note. It was from Vanessa and it read 'This morning our friend with the jaguar packed and left. He said he is never coming back.'

"Well, what is it?" she asked, trying to look over my shoulder at the note.

I crumpled it up in my hand and stuffed the note in my pocket.

"It's nothing" I said. I didn't want to tell them that it was from Vanessa. I needed all the allies I could get and I didn't want her to know this. We walked all the way home in silence. As we got to the door, I decided to have a word with Dave.

"You guys get started, I will be back in a few minutes" I said. Neither of them asked where I was going and I wondered if they thought it had something to do with the note. Neither of them asked so I didn't bother explaining. They went in and I slowly walked over to Dave's little house. It looked quite run down and I couldn't help asking myself why he still stuck around. The house belonged to the estate, it wasn't his. I knocked on the door and waited. There was no answer. I knocked again and waited. I was just about to turn away and head home when the door opened abruptly.

"'Afternoon" he said attempting something that resembled a smile. "Come in and get out of the cold." He said and gestured towards the inside of the house. I smiled back and returned his greeting. I went inside and followed him to a room at the back which I supposed was the living room. It was dark and quite messy inside. He sat down in an armchair and pointed to the other one in the room.

"Won't you take a seat?" he asked and offered me tea. I declined and we sat in silence for a few seconds. He picked up a small knife and the piece of wood that were sitting on the table and started whittling.

"Do you want one?" he asked pointing to one of the objects he had finished.

I picked it up to take a closer look. It was a smoking pipe. It was quite simple and the only design on it was two snakes intertwined together.

"I don't smoke" I said, still holding the pipe.

"It's just as well then, it's not been impregnated properly" Dave said, putting down the one he was working on. "Take it, I don't smoke either, but you can have it, it can be a souvenir for when you leave." He said.

I wanted to ask him about the motif in the pipe, but decided to hold off with that question just yet.

"Dave, listen, as you know the museum will be opening before next summer. We will need a care taker for the place and I don't see why it shouldn't be you" I paused for a second "After all you have been the care taker here for years, am I right?" I asked.

Dave nodded and didn't say anything, waiting for me to continue.

" You did offer your help and I would like to take you up on that offer" I carried on " I won't be able to pay you for your help as I don't have the budget sorted out yet, but something is going on here and I think I need your help."

"Did anything happen?" he asked, looking at me intently.

"I don't think so. Not yet, anyway." I said "But I have good reason to believe that something dodgy is going on. I am sure that someone is entering the mansion at night or when we are not there despite all the doors and windows being locked. This has led me to the conclusion that there must be a secret or hidden way in." I looked at him to see his reaction "Frankly, you have been working here for many years; you must know something about it."

His expression didn't change one bit. I was beginning to think that I had made a mistake asking him about it and telling him my suspicions. He sat in silence for a while and finally cleared his throat.

"I am sorry, but I don't know where it is, I wish I could help" he said.

"But it does exist, right?" I asked eagerly.

"Yes it does" he confirmed. "Mr. Doughty knew where it was, but he never showed it to me. In the last few weeks, before he died, he suddenly appeared in the park even though I knew for sure that he had not used any of the doors. It happened a few times. But when I asked him about it, he just laughed, but didn't tell me his secret."

"And you really don't know where it is?" I asked.

"I am sorry, I don't" he stared off onto the distance. "I really wish I could help you but I don't know myself."

I looked at him and decided to give him the benefit of the doubt. I didn't have a reason not to believe him. At least I knew that there was a hidden way into the mansion and that was a good start. "Well if you could at least keep an eye out for anyone in the park especially after dark that would help" I said getting ready to leave.

"I can try" he said "But you know, a lot of people cut through the park on their way home, it's much faster than taking the road and walking round"

" I know, but just in case, if you see anyone acting suspiciously or anything like that, it would be a big help" I said

"Sure thing, I'll do what I can" he said and I left.

On my slow walk back to the house I couldn't help but ask myself whether I could trust Dave. How was it possible that after working here for so many years and taking care of the mansions he didn't know about any of its secrets? I was sure there was more than one, but I didn't have a sound reason for not believing him, maybe he had been telling the truth. The guy with the jaguar had left this morning. Did he leave with what he had come for? I doubted that. But did this mean that we wouldn't have any more visits? I wasn't sure. I think that the 'prize' was still out there to get for whoever was clever about it; I was still very much in the game.

It was only 4 pm but it was already slowly getting dark. The wind blew in clouds and that gave the afternoon an even gloomier feel. I hurried inside out of the cold. I left my coat in my room. I joined Lucy and Bill and we carried on working for the next few hours. We didn't really talk much, just when it was necessary. I guessed they were still upset with me. We had eventually finished the day's tasks and each of us went to our rooms. I sat down at the desk and took the pipe that Dave had carved from my coat pocket. I looked at it and wondered about the design. It resembled the design on one of the paintings in Mr. Doughty's collection entitled 'Within the inverted crown lie the snakes'. It was a Masonic painting and the symbol was Masonic as well. I wondered if Dave knew that and whether he had placed it there intentionally or if it was a coincidence. It was meaningful though. Doughty wrote it on the piece of paper when he wrote his last wish but it was considered gibberish given his state of mind, but maybe he did mean something after all, but what?

I sat there for a while staring at the pipe. It had gotten dark by now so I switched on the desk lamp. I had been here for such a short time and nothing seemed to be going right. We were on schedule with the preparation work for the new museum but I had not been a good example for my two young colleagues. Things were pretty bad between us; they even thought I was losing my mind. Even the events of our outing to Glasgow didn't help in convincing them that I was right.

The second thing that was bothering me was Doughty's discovery. Mr. Simpson had not mentioned anything about it to me and I've not had the chance to ask him about it. Surely he would have said something about it so perhaps he didn't know. But our nightly intruders did. It's what they have been searching for. Once again I asked myself whether their visits would stop since the guy with the jag had left. Probably, but maybe not, time would tell.

I heard a quiet knock on the door. Bill popped his head into the room.

"Lucy made some tea and sandwiches if you are hungry" he said and closed the door behind him. I looked at my watch. I didn't realise I had been sitting and thinking for such a long time, it was nearly eight. I got up and went into the kitchen. There was a big plate of sandwiches sitting on the kitchen table and a cup of tea was already made for me.

"Thank you" I said to Lucy as I sat down with them.

We ate and drank our teas but none of us started a conversation. Finally, when we finished our food and bill was clearing up the table as it was his turn to do it I suddenly said

"It is time to put an end to all this nonsense with the so called ghost".

I said it quite abruptly and it startled them both.

"Jimmy, rather than thinking about these ghosts you should put more effort into creating the new museum. Mr. Simpson is due to show up any day and we still haven't finished cataloguing everything, let alone having an idea of what the proposed museum is to be" Lucy said.

"Well, yes, maybe you're right. The work we're doing is on schedule, but you can't deny the fact that we had hotel reservations and theatre tickets" I explained "It wasn't a ghost that provided them, it was a person. We know that it wasn't anyone from our end as the letter was a fake, there was no meeting, remember?" I asked looking at her.

" Fine, but how do you explain the fact that we have so many valuable things in here, but nothing has gone missing, despite these 'visits'?" she challenged.

"What about the deleted file?" I responded.

"We discussed it so many times and none of us can explain it, so I think we should just leave it at that. We don't know what was in it and I suppose we will never find out. We haven't found anything relating to it" Bill joined into the conversation.

"Exactly" Lucy added "The computer wasn't even listed as one of the things for us to use, which is to say that the file wasn't his personal business?" she asked.

She was right so I decided to give it a rest.

"If the hotel reservations and theatre tickets are bothering you so much I am more than happy to take the train into Glasgow tomorrow to see if I can shed some light on the matter." She said

"Would it be ok if I took the day off and did that? Would it put your mind at ease Jimmy?" she asked.

"That would be great" I said. I wanted to get to the bottom of that matter myself but I wasn't too keen on taking a trip to Glasgow and leaving Lucy and Bill alone in the mansion in the light of things.

"What about you Bill, are you going to help?" I asked, but I knew straight away what his answer would be.

"I am not getting involved in your games. I want to finish what we came here to do and get home as soon as possible" he said.

His response didn't surprise me at all. I was glad that at least Lucy was willing to help even if her reasons for it weren't the same as mine. We carried on chatting and joking when we heard a loud knock on the window. It startled all of us.

"Not again" Lucy muttered under her breath.

I looked towards the window only to find Susannah waving to us. I got up and went to open the front door for her.

"Hey" she said smiling as she took off her coat "I knocked on the door but I guess you didn't hear me" she gave me another one of her charming smiles. I spotted a few snow- flakes starting to melt in her hair and looked outside. It started to snow and already here was a thin layer of snow on the ground.

"It's snowing" Susannah said excitedly.

"I can see that" I said and returned her smile. "We are just in the kitchen".

She was holding something under her arm and I wondered what it was. I guessed I would find out soon enough and made my way into the kitchen.

Susannah put the large piece of card she had brought with her on the table. It had a large circle drawn in the middle and the circle in turn was divided to accommodate all the letters of the alphabet. Around that were all of the zodiac signs.

"It's a homemade Ouija board, it's the best I could come up with on such short notice" Susannah explained.

"Oh, I think it will do for us" I said.

"My aunt has the proper stuff for this kind of thing, but I have attended a few of her séances, all we need now is a small plate, a candle and the right room to do it in." She added. "The basic principle is that we all gather together around the board, place the tips of our fingers on the plate and we can communicate with the ghost. The ghost will channel it's thoughts through us" she continued to explain.

Lucy listened to her sceptically and then walked towards one of the cupboards and opened it

"There are plenty of plates, I am sure we will find a candle kicking around somewhere as well" she said.

"Great "she said and took a small plate out of the cupboard. Lucy rummaged through the drawers to find a candle. She finally produced one and Susannah took that from her as well.

"Now all we need is the right room" she said.

"We have plenty of ghosts in the mansion, several in every room in fact" I said, playing along with the game.

"As long as you guys don't use my room for this" Lucy pointed out.

"How come?" I asked.

"You really don't expect me to actually believe that we will communicate with a ghost?" Lucy said sarcastically. "I'm going to sleep soon; I'm not staying up to play games."

"But you have to" Susannah said "There has to be at least four people for this otherwise it's not going to work"

"You were complaining about lack of entertainment" I pointed out "It's better than sitting and doing nothing, don't you think? It's just a bit of harmless fun" I looked at her.

All of a sudden Lucy let out a gasp and she jumped to her feet. Susannah let out a quiet scream and did the same. I looked at Bill not understanding what was going on. He pointed to something in the corner of the kitchen. I looked closely only to find a small mouse sitting, munching on what appeared to be a crumb.

"What's the matter?" I asked the girls, giving Bill a sign to play along.

"It's a mouse, right there" Lucy said pointing to the mouse.

"I can't see it, can you?" Bill asked.

"No, I can't say that I can" I said and pulled a face.

"Get it out of here!" Susannah was on the verge of screaming.

Suddenly the chair Lucy had climbed on started to topple over and she lost her balance. I just managed to catch her falling so she didn't end up on the floor. The mouse runs off startled by the sudden noise.

"You are monsters you two" she said accusingly to me and Bill "If I had known there are mice here, I would never had come" Lucy said, still looking around to see if the mouse had really gone.

"There must be lots of them here, you should call someone from pest control" Susannah added, sitting back down in her chair, curling her feet up on the seat.

"Well, I first need to win with the ghosts and get them out of here" I said jokingly "Then I can get rid of the mice"

Lucy sat down as well, but kept looking around.

"I really am scared of them" she said quietly.

I wanted to change the subject so she wouldn't think about it anymore. Susannah did it for me

"I don't think we will be starting the séance before ten, let's go and find a good room for it first" she stood up.

"Ok, that's a good idea" I agreed and we all followed her out of the kitchen. We went round some of the rooms downstairs, following Susannah as she did know more about this sort of thing than any of us. We finally got to my room and she stopped. She closed her eyes, took a couple of deep breaths and said without opening her eyes

"I think this room is the best" she opened her eyes and blinked a few times.

"Right" Bill said "Shall we get started then?" he asked.

I looked at my watch; it was only coming up to 9.30pm.

"Let's go and have one more cup of tea" I suggested "We can discuss what sort of ghost we will contact, what we want to ask him and stuff like that"

"That's a good idea" Susannah agreed and we all returned to the kitchen.

"What kind of a ghost shall we try to contact?" Lucy said after she poured herself some tea from the freshly made pot.

"I think it should be the local ghost, we can ask why he or she keeps coming back" Susannah suggested and we all nodded in agreement.

"That's good" Bill said.

We all agreed so we passed the remaining time chatting and joking. Lucy seemed to have forgotten about the mouse and relaxed a bit. Soon 10pm arrived and we were ready to start.

# CHAPTER SEVEN

We took the Ouija board, the candle and the little plate and went to my room. We sat down around the small round table that was there. Susannah placed the card on the table and the little plate in the middle of it. Lucy brought a candle holder from her room and we lit the candle. Bill turned the light off and closed the door.

It was very quiet. The light from the candle flickered every now and again. I couldn't help myself but a strange feeling came over me. I think the atmosphere got a hold of everyone, Lucy and Bill had very serious looks on their faces. I looked towards the window. Everything was pitching black, except for the thin layer of snow already forming on the ground. It was quite eerie.

"Ok everyone; place just the tips of your fingers on the plate." Susannah said quietly.

We did what she asked us to do. Then she closed her eyes very slowly and took three deep breaths.

"Oh spirits, spirits of the damned, can you hear me....can you hear my plea?" she said. Her voice sounded different, deeper. She sat in silence for a few minutes and we watched her, none of us daring to say anything. We didn't want to spoil the mood.

Susannah opened her eyes and looked at us.

"I think that maybe you need to close your eyes too" she whispered.

We looked at each other and again did as she asked. We knew that this was just a game, a bit of fun, but it's like I always say- If you're going to do something, do it properly. Since we all agreed to do this then we had to take it seriously, otherwise it would spoil the fun.

Lucy closed her eyes first, and then I did. Bill did it as well because Susannah gave her call one more time.

"Oh spirits, spirits of the damned, can you hear me? Can you hear me? Show yourself!" she raised her voice at the end.

"Oh great spirit, if you are hearing my call, answer me...answer me...answer me!" she chanted.

Suddenly the plate moved. I could feel it vibrating slightly under my fingertips. I opened my eyes and saw that the others did the same. The plate suddenly started moving, and the small arrow which Susannah had drawn on it earlier started to point to letters- I A M H E R E and then stopped.

"Wow, who is pushing the plate?" Bill whispered.

"Shhhh" Susannah looked at him "It's the supernatural energy emitting from our fingers"

"Yeah Bill, the message is from the ghost" Lucy whispered.

Susannah gave them a stern look and they both stopped whispering. She waited a few seconds before continuing.

"Oh spirit, tell me your name" she said in that strange voice into the darkness.

R O B E R T O the plate went in turn to each letter and returned to the centre of the card.

"Why are you here, in the mansion?" she asked him.

The plate went round all the letters, but didn't stop at any of them.

"I think you asked him the wrong question" Lucy said.

"Does the mansion have any secrets?" I called into the darkness.

The plate went round the card a few times, and then finally a message emerged.

M A N Y

"Where are they? What are they?" Bill called out this time.

Again the plate went round the card a few times, but didn't stop at any of the letters.

"Clever clogs, he knows them but won't say what they are" Lucy whispered.

"Rude and arrogant, that's what he is" I muttered under my breath.

Susannah heard what I said.

"You can't say that about him" she said angrily.

I looked at her, surprised. She was taking this a bit more seriously than I thought.

"You offended him" she said "do you want the ghost to punish you for offending him?" she asked.

I shrugged my shoulders.

"I don't believe in ghosts" I said, not understanding why she got angry over a little thing like that.

"Really? Fine, let's ask the ghost for, proof that he does exist" she said. "Let's blow out the candle and ask for a sign" she was all worked up.

I wasn't having a good evening, first Lucy over the mouse, now Susannah over this ghost. I didn't realise she would get so upset and wanted her to enjoy the evening with us.

"What do you propose?" I asked "Because I don't want to get a punch to the ribs as a so called sign from the ghost"

"We can ask for something else" she said, calming down a bit.

"How about the ghost conjures up a plate of nice sandwiches for us" Bill suggested.

"Maybe he can change Jimmy's hair from blonde to back?" Lucy suggested.

"Guys, I don't want to change my hair, hey, can we leave me out of this?" I opposed.

Bill opened his mouth to make another suggestion, but Susannah spoke before he had a chance to do so.

"How about if we let Roberto, our ghost, decide." Susannah suggested.

"Right, as long as it's not involving me directly, I don't care" I replied.

Bill shrugged his shoulders and yawned. I think he was getting bored of the whole thing. I must admit, so was I. Lucy didn't say anything. Susannah put her finger-tips on the plate. She looked at us and we did the same. She closed her eyes, and after a few seconds she called out-

"Oh spirit, Roberto, we can feel your presence with us!" she paused. "I command you to give us proof of your existence, give us a sign, give us a sign, and give us a sign!" and with that she blew out the candle.

No one even stirred. I opened my eyes and noticed that everyone else did as well. Bill yawned again. I looked towards the window; the only brighter thing around us, the room was pitch black.

Then, to my astonishment, I heard a noise and one of the huge shutters swung shut and a second later the other one did. I sat still for a minute. None of us could do it as the shutters were on the outside.

"Oh my gosh" Lucy whispered.

I jumped out of my chair and switched on the light. I went to the door and grabbed the handle. I wanted to catch whoever was outside and had shut the shutters. But this is as far as I got. The door was locked. I pulled on the handle a couple more times, hoping it was stuck. The door was locked, and we were locked in. Bill went to the window and tried to push the shutters open. They didn't even budge.

"Great, we're locked in" I said angrily. Lucy and Susannah sat in the chairs, shocked.

"But....but why?" Susannah asked.

"I wish I knew, But I don't" I replied.

The girls both jumped up from their chairs as they realised the situation that we were in. Someone had locked us in the room, we were trapped.

"We're trapped!" Lucy shouted as the realisation sunk in.

"Yes we are, and you said you don't believe in 'ghosts" I replied, taking a seat in one of the armchairs.

"I have my mobile on me" Bill said getting his phone out of his pocket " Maybe we can call someone for help" he took a closer look at the phone's screen " No reception" He muttered " Ok, that isn't going to work."

"Who is responsible for this?" Susannah said angrily "Is this some kind of a stupid joke?"

"Ummm, I don't think it's a joke, at least it's not a very funny one" I answered, crossing my arms.

"But how am I supposed to get home now?" She asked.

"I don't know, perhaps you can ask 'Roberto'" Lucy said.

"I didn't know this was going to happen, it was just supposed to be a bit of fun" she said. "I don't believe in ghosts"

"What?" Lucy almost shouted "But this was all your idea, the séance, the ghost giving proof of existence...."

"Jimmy offended the ghost..." Susannah tried defending herself

"Great, blame me for everything, as always" I said.

Lucy got up from her chair and went towards the window

"Hello?!" she shouted "Please let us out! This isn't funny" she started banging on the shutters.

"How dare you lock us in!!!? It's an outrage" her pleading turned into anger. "You'll be sorry when I get out of here!!!"

She carried on running from the door to the window, shouting. Bill went and sat down on my sofa. Lucy finally got tired of running and shouting, she turned her attention to me.

"Why are you sitting there with your arms crossed, do something" she was almost shouting again.

"I'm sorry, do you have any suggestions?" I asked "Because I really don't know what I can do in this situation. It's your chance to shine, so show me what you got"

"What?" she asked, not understanding what I had meant?

"This is partly your fault you know" I explained.

"My fault? How is any of this my fault?" she got all worked up. "This séance wasn't my idea and I certainly didn't get us locked in here"

"I didn't say that" I started to explain patiently "But every time I said that something was going on here, you would tell me I am losing it and seeing things and making a big deal out of nothing. Do you still not see what is going on here?" I asked

"We're locked in this room" she answered.

"By a ghost?" I asked with irony in my voice.

"Well...no" she replied.

"Well then who? And why?" I asked her again.

"I don't know, do I?" she answered, angrily.

"I'll tell you then. None of this wouldn't have happened if I hadn't let my guard down." I told her "I let my guard down because you constantly told me that I was imagining things. Unfortunately, I wasn't. Someone kept entering the mansion, looking for something. They didn't 'break in' in the general sense, yet I could feel someone's presence here. How else will you explain the fact that someone managed to lock us in here without us realising? I locked the front door when Susannah came, I can assure you. So how did they come in?" I looked at her triumphantly. She didn't say anything, neither did Billy.

"Can we all be very quiet for a minute, I want to see what these people are doing" I said and put my finger on my lips.

We all sat in silence, listening out for any sounds coming from behind the locked door. We heard footsteps upstairs. Silence again for a few seconds and more steps coming from upstairs. I accessed the mental map I had of the mansion in my head and my guess was that whoever it was, he (she?) was in the library. Next we heard a loud bang and something that sounded like the furniture was being moved. He loud bang was heard again, followed by knocking.

"What are they doing?" Lucy whispered.

I shrugged my shoulders. All we could do is guess. We were at the mercy of the people who locked us in. I was just hoping that they would be civil enough to let us out. I didn't want to think about that at the moment.

"They are looking for something" I said.

"Well, we can't just sit here and let them do what they want, we have to do something" she jumped up with those words and went to the window again.

"Heeeelp! Police! Anybody?!" she shouted.

I looked at her and sat down again. Screaming at the window at this time of night was pointless. I doubted anyone would be walking through the park at this time. Dave wouldn't hear her shouting, his house was too far away from the mansion, plus the shutters muted the sound. We had no reception so we couldn't use the phone to call for help either.

Bill got up and moved her away from the window. Then he closed it again as the room got cold whilst she attempted to call for help.

"Lucy, there is nothing we can do; we have to wait till the morning." He said as he sat her down on the sofa "If they don't let us out we will have to think of a way of getting out of here ourselves. Besides, Dave will see the shutters are closed, so he will come over to find out what is going on, you know how nosy he is" he chuckled quietly, trying to cheer her up.

She sat down next to Susannah, who had nodded off. I think she finally accepted the position that we were in and realised there was nothing we could do. We all found a comfy position and listened to the sounds coming to us from various corners of the mansion.

"I am sorry, James" suddenly Lucy said "I'll never doubt you again" she gave me a little smile.

"Thank you" I smiled back at her.

Each of us took a blanket and eventually even I dosed off.

Something woke me up. I wasn't sure if a couple of hours had passed or if it had been a few minutes since I had dosed off. I looked at my watch. It was a few minutes past five. I looked around the room, the other three were still sleeping, and Billy was even snoring quietly.

I listened. I couldn't hear a sound. I had no idea how long I had been asleep for, but the intruders seemed to be gone. I sat still listening for a while. I heard nothing. Silence. They were gone. I got up and checked the door. Locked. How on earth were we going to get out of here? I thought it might be a good idea to have some sort of a plan before I woke the others up, but no such luck. Lucy stirred and opened her eyes.

"What time is it? What's going on?" she asked sleepily.

"A few minutes past five" I said.

She looked around.

"What's our situation?" she asked, looking slightly more awake.

"Well, the door is still locked" I replied.

She looked around rather helplessly. Just then a gust of wind blew and one of the shutters opened slightly.

"Oh, look!" Lucy said "The shutters are open"

I went over to the window and pushed the shutters open. We were free. I climbed out of the window. In the freshly fallen snow I could see tracks leading from the front door to the window and...Back again. There were no other tracks in the snow. I jumped out and run to the front door quickly. The intruders may still be inside. I garbed the handle and tried the door. It opened. I rushed in and turned the key in the lock to my door, letting Lucy out. She peeped out, and I put my finger on my lips.

"They intruders might still be inside" I whispered in her ear "Get Billy up and check all the rooms, but be careful"

"What are you going to do?" she asked

"I've got a good opportunity to check where the secret entrance is into the mansion thanks to the snow," I replied "I'll go round the whole building and see if I can find it"

She nodded in agreement and went to wake up Bill. I quickly threw on my coat and my shoes and went outside. I looked around; there were no tracks visible except for the ones leading to the front door. I quickly made my way around the mansion to see if there were any tracks leading away from it, but I didn't see anything.

Perhaps they were still inside and finally we had a good chance of catching them. I quickly made my way back inside. Lucy was emerging from one of the many corridors on the ground floor; Billy was making his way down the stairs.

"Anything?" I asked.

Lucy shook her head and looked at Bill

"Nothing" he said "no sign that anyone has even been in here" he replied.

"Yes.... very clever indeed" I muttered under my breath.

I went to double check myself. Everything was just as we had left it, nothing was out of place, and nothing was missing. I went into the library, had one last look and was just about to join the others downstairs when something caught my eye. There was a tiny puddle of dirty water next to the clock. It looked like melted snow. Perhaps the way in was through the library somewhere? But where? And then I started to doubt myself again. It could have been me or Bill that had brought the snow in on our shoes. Most likely it was, so there was no point speculating over it. Everything was in order, as always, but I couldn't help but wonder, did they find what they were looking for? I was hoping that wasn't the case. I went back downstairs to find Susannah getting her shoes and coat on.

"How am I going to go to work today? I am so tired" she moaned as she grabbed her bag and went towards the front door. She looked upset and didn't even say goodbye to us properly, she just went home. Lucy shrugged her shoulders and didn't say anything.

"Well, never mind" Billy said," I think I might go to bed for a bit" he said.

I looked at my watch, it was past six. A bit too early to start work, there was nothing better to do.

"I can still make my train to Glasgow if I leave now, do you thing I should go?" Lucy asked

"Are you sure?" I asked surprised that she was still willing to go after the night we just had "Aren't you tired?"

"There is no point putting it off for another day, I am up already and I wouldn't fall back asleep anyway" she said "I can always sleep on the train"

"That would be good, if you're up for it" I said "Did you want me to drop you off to the station?" I asked.

"I'll walk, its fine" she smiled "It's not like I have any bags and by the time you warm up the car I'll be half way there anyway"

"Ok" I said. Lucy got a few things together and went. Bill was already fast asleep so I followed suit and went to bed for a couple of hours. I would decide on the best course of action when I woke up, hopefully a bit refreshed and thinking clearly.

# CHAPTER EIGHT

I ate breakfast alone. I sent Billy to the local police station to at least make them aware of the situation we had at the mansion. At least we had a witness for last night's events so we could give them a statement if they wanted one. I didn't go with him because I didn't want to leave the house empty again. I cleared up after myself and wondered around upstairs for a little while. I kept returning to the library, where I had found a bit of melted snow this morning. Was the secret way in through here? But if so, where was it? I knocked on the wall in a few random spots but that didn't lead to anything. I looked at my watch again. Billy was certainly taking his time at the police station. I was beginning to wonder where he had got to when I heard a loud knocking from the front door. I went to see who it was.

"Good morning" a police officer was standing at the door with Billy.

"Good morning" I replied somewhat surprised.

Billy brushed past me as he came in. I invited the police officer in and wondered what he wanted. I took him through to the kitchen and offered him a seat.

" Thank you" he said as he sat down " I've come down with your colleague just to clarify a few things about last night and see if I can be of any assistance" he smiled and took a small note pad out.

"Right "I said sitting down at the table as well. Bill was pottering around the kitchen making him some breakfast. He offered the police officer some coffee but he declined.

"I am PC Macleod" he introduced himself "Bill here gave me a quick account of what happened here last night. Was there a break in then?" he asked and looked at me.

"Well, not exactly" I replied wondering what Billy had actually said to him. I told PC Macleod quickly about what had happened last night and about the entire strange goings on we had experienced in the weeks before, as well as my suspicions as to who was behind it all. He listened, taking down the details.

"Based on what you have told me, there isn't a lot I can do. There was no official break in, there are no signs of intruders and nothing has gone missing. From my point of view, no crime had actually occurred. As to last night, you have a witness who can confirm that someone had locked you I your room, yes?" he asked.

"That's right" I replied, unsatisfied with his response.

"Can you show me the room?" he asked.

I nodded and went to my room. He took a quick look around the room, the corridor and went to take a look at the shutters. He returned after a while and asked to see the library. We went upstairs and he took a quick look around, pausing briefly next to the clock.

"Well, this is what we can do" he said after looking at the notes he had made "I can send a forensics team down here to check for fingerprints, but that is all I can do. At the most, the incident from last night can be classed as a prank. The snow has now melted, so we can't even see the tracks leading from the front door to the window and back again." He paused "This is rather a toughie"

"I think that they are after the discovery that Mr. Doughty had made. I have not been able to confirm it with anyone, the B&B owner told me about it. As far as I know it could just be a rumour, although with everything that has been going on I don't think that's the case." I told him.

"Well, I suggest we leave things the way they are for now and see what happens. I will keep an eye on things discreetly from my end. We don't want to scare them away if we're to catch them." He said as he stood up "They have been very clever up to now, but now that I am aware of the situation, I can help I hope. You should have come to us sooner; maybe we could have caught them by now."

I thanked him and saw him out. Maybe he did have a point, but like he said, with no evidence what was I supposed to say? That I thought someone was entering the mansion during our absences? I did have a good feeling having him on my side, maybe everything would turn out well after all. I watched him walk down the drive towards his car when Dave came out of his house and quickly went over to him. PC Macleod talked to him for a few minutes and then got into his car. Dave looked towards the mansion and went back to his house. I was a bit annoyed at him, following our conversation the day before. I had asked him to keep an eye out for anyone suspicious in the park at night and then we got locked in. The little bit of sympathy I had for him vanished. I was pretty sure that he was involved with the intruders somehow, but I couldn't prove.

I closed the door and found Billy clearing up in the kitchen.

"Well, let's get some work done" I said "I think it will be best if we go to lunch separately though, I really don't want to leave this place empty with everything that's going on, ok?" I asked.

"Fine" he said.

We got to work and finally it was lunch time.

"You can go first "Billy offered "I had my breakfast later than you".

"Great" I said and went to get ready. "I won't be too long"

I set off and walked briskly through the park. There were still bits of last night's snow lying in shaded parts of the park, unable to melt. It was pretty chilly and I wrapped my scarf tighter around me to keep warm.

The restaurant had attracted more people on a cold day but our usual table was reserved. I looked around as I started my meal but I couldn't see Susannah anywhere. I wondered if she did manage to get to work this morning. I was just finishing my food when Ronnie and Vanessa came into the restaurant. They saw me sitting so they came to my table and sat down.

"Susannah wasn't here for breakfast this morning" Vanessa said "I wonder why?"

"Oh, she probably didn't wake up in time" I replied and told them about our adventure from last night.

"Oh dear, that's terrible" Vanessa said.

"Why is it terrible? " Ronnie asked "Nothing bad actually happened, did it? Nothing has gone missing?" he asked looking at me questioningly.

"No everything seems fine" I answered reassuringly.

"Well, do you have any idea who it was? Any suspicions?" Vanessa asked.

I had my suspicions but I didn't think it was wise to tell them about it.

"Time will tell" I answered.

They looked at me and then at each other. Ronnie shrugged his shoulders as if to say that there was no point on insisting, I wouldn't tell them anything else.

"Did you get my note yesterday?" Vanessa asked "The one about the guy with the car?"

"Yes I did, why?" I replied smiling.

"Well, he left Cromdale but I don't think he went very far." She said, bringing her voice to a whisper "On our way home from the costume rehearsal for the Christmas play we saw him again. He was sitting in his car. It was parked on the side of the road, just as you get to the bridge with the headlights off. We thought it was a bit odd so we crept around so he wouldn't see us. We hid behind one of the trees and decided to wait and see what he was up to. We waited and waited but we got cold and we were about to go when someone went up to the car and he opened his window. Guess who it was?" she asked with a cheeky smile on her face.

"Ummmm, Dave?" I asked.

"No" Vanessa started laughing "It was Susannah"

"Oh" I said quite surprised. I wasn't expecting that at all.

"Take a guess at what happened next" Vanessa was clearly enjoying this guessing game.

"She got into the car and they went somewhere to have coffee" I took a stab at it.

"That's too simple don't you think?" she laughed again. Ronnie was smiling as well.

"They didn't go anywhere" she continued "Instead, that guy got out of the car and they were chatting for a few minutes. We couldn't hear what they were saying, they were very quiet. After a few minutes, he got back into the car. As he was about to drive off she said to him 'I'll be by the clock'. He drove off and she went in the direction of your mansion. Oh, and she was carrying something as well. Don't you think that was odd?" she asked and looked for my reaction.

I didn't think that was odd. She was on her way to meet with us and she was carrying the Ouija board. The fact that they decided to meet by the bridge and not in a cafe for example was a bit odd, but people arrange to meet in the oddest of places. I shrugged my shoulders. I really wasn't sure what to think about it all.

"Maybe he wanted to arrange to meet with her and he wasn't sure how to get hold of her?" Ronnie suggested. "So he waited in a place where he could spot her easily"

"I don't think so" Vanessa said "He knew where she is staying he could have passed on a note and not been sitting in his car at the side of the road" she obviously had made up her mind that their behaviour was dodgy. Maybe she was right.

"Are you going to come and see our Christmas production?" she asked, changing the subject. "It's tomorrow night. I've already asked my teacher and she said it would be really nice if you did come"

"Sure, why not. At least you will stop wandering through the park so late at night" I replied

"Late at night?" Ronnie asked "I wouldn't say six o'clock was late at night"

"You saw Susannah at six yesterday?" I asked surprised.

"Yes, why?" Vanessa asked.

"And she was carrying the Ouija board with her?" I asked again

"I don't know what she was carrying, but yeah" Vanessa said looking at Ronnie "How come you are so surprised?"

"Well in that case it took her three hours to walk through the park, because she didn't arrive at the mansion until nine o'clock" I said.

The kids looked at each other

"Maybe she forgot something and went back again as she got near to you, and then made her way there again?" Ronnie suggested.

"Maybe..." I said but I wasn't convinced.

"Speak of the devil" Ronnie said pointing to something outside.

I looked and saw Susannah walking quickly on the other side of the road. I finished my coffee and got up, leaving the money for the meal on the table.

"I'll go over and see how she is feeling after last night." I said and said goodbye to Ronnie and Vanessa. I left the restaurant and started walking quickly, trying to catch up to her. I had a few questions I wanted to ask her, and I was very curious as to what her answers would be. Susannah was walking very quickly and she had had a head start. By the time I reached the other side of the road, she was already making her way across the bridge. As she reached the other side she slowed down and then stopped. She looked around and I hid behind the telephone box. I don't know why, but I didn't think that she should see me. I was right to do so, as after a few seconds the jaguar had pulled up and stopped next to her. It was exactly like Vanessa had described it. The guy got out of the car, they chatted for a few seconds looking around as if checking to see if anyone could see them. It looked very suspicious. They finished talking and he got back in the car and drove away. Susannah gave one last glance around and went towards the park. I waited for her to get onto the path and after a few seconds I lost sight of her.

I left the safety of the phone box and quickly followed her. I figured that if I kept my pace up I should catch up with her near the house. I walked quickly down the winding path and emerged onto the lawn in front of the mansion expecting to see her, but she was nowhere in sight. 'She must be inside already' I thought to myself and hurried to the front door. I went inside to find Billy sitting in one of the arm chair in the drawing room. He jumped to his feet when he saw me.

"Wow, if I'd known you would take that long I would have gone first" he said.

"Where is Susannah?" I asked surprised not to see her with him.

"How should I know?" He asked as he put on his coat.

She obviously didn't come in, so where did she go? I didn't want to bother Billy with this mystery so I didn't say anything.

"I'll see you soon!" he yelled as he left.

I nodded, not even realising I was doing it. 'Where did she go?' I wondered. I went back outside. Maybe she was in the park and she only came for a walk, not to see us. I thought I might take a quick walk to see if I could find her, I really did want to speak to her. I made my way down one of the paths. I walked slowly enjoying the fresh air. There were still patches of snow lying around here and there. The sun wasn't strong at this time of year and hadn't managed to melt all of it. I walked around enjoying the sunshine and eventually found myself next to the old shell grotto. I looked at the door. With everything that had happened I forgot about the fact that we didn't the missing key. I looked inside through the window. Everything inside was the same as last time....except? I took a closer look. Next to a broken bench there was a wet footprint. It had small droplets of dirty water on it, as if from the left over snow. I rubbed my eyes and looked again. My eyes were not playing tricks on me, it really was there. Someone must have gone inside and left it there recently, it was still wet. But how? The door was locked, wasn't it? I grabbed the handle and tried it. The door opened without any problems. I opened it wider and slipped inside. I stooped down and took a closer look. There was another footprint behind the bench. I looked at the tracks. They stopped in the middle of the floor behind the bench. As if the person who made them had jumped up in the air and didn't fall back down again. I took a closer look. There was a faint rectangle on the floor. I tried to see if I could put my fingers in the gap to try and lift it but it was too narrow. I searched my pockets and got my pen out. If I could just wedge it into the gap, I could check if I could lift the panel to see what was beneath it. A thought struck me; maybe this was the way into the secret passage into the mansion? Dave did say he saw Doughty appear out of nowhere in the park, so maybe this really was it. I wedged the pen into the gap and after a few unsuccessful attempts I managed to lift the panel enough to grab it with the tips of my fingers. Something creaked, and the panel swung open, like a door. It had hidden hinges. I sat still for a while. Whoever came in here may still be down there, I had to be careful. I listened for a few minutes but all I heard were crows in the park and seagulls in the distance. I checked my pockets to see if I had my lighter on me. It was there. I didn't want to go to the car to get the torch and decided it would do. I slowly made my way down the steps and could feel the weight of the panel on my hands. I had to close it behind me; there was no way to keep it open. I let it close gently and tried to lift it again. It gave way easily so I went down the stairs carefully. I light my lighter to have a look around. At the bottom of the stairs I could see a corridor. The bricks looked very old and it was pretty cold, I wrapped my jacket tighter around me. I could see a faint wet track on the stone floor. I had to be quiet and very careful; I didn't want whoever was down here to know I was here as well. I thought about going back to get Bill, but I quickly discarded that idea. If when we came back the door was locked again, my chance of finding the intruders entry point was gone. If I got a locksmith, they would know that I had found the way in and our chances of catching them would be gone. I decided to check it out now, and run back if I had to, but maybe I would get far enough to work out how they got into the mansion. I listened out for a few seconds and decided it was safe to continue. I lit my lighter again to see the way. The corridor continued for several meters and then there was a turn. I extinguished the lighter and slowly started down the corridor, feeling my way along the wall. I got to the corner and lit the lighter again. Another straight bit and another corner. I tried to work out the direction in which I was going and figured it was towards the mansion. I carried on in darkness again until I got to the corner. I light my lighter again. I could see a straight bit in front of me and then the corridor had two more coming off the one I was in. I let the lighter go out again and felt my way along the wall until I got to the bit where I had a choice. I light the lighter. Both tunnels looked the same. I thought for a minute not sure which one I should take. They both went off in slightly different directions, so I chose the one on the right, the direction in which I thought the mansion should be.

I followed the corridor, mostly in darkness, from time to time I lit my lighter to see where I was going. This corridor was straighter than the first one, it didn't have as many corners and bends to it. It felt like I had been walking for ages but when I looked at my watch I realised I had only been down there for maybe twenty minutes. I stopped and checked the way again. I could hear a faint rumbling noise coming from the direction I was walking in. I had no idea what it was. I listened for a few seconds, but I couldn't work out what it was. I couldn't hear any footsteps or any other sounds. I cautiously made my way towards the next bend. The rumbling sound grew louder; I reached the bend, turned the corner and stopped. The rumbling sound was very loud but I was staring at a wall. A dead end. All this time wasted to reach a dead end. I sighed and made my way back. I thought about the noise coming from behind the wall I had reached. It was possible that it was the water in the river, the corridor was probably long enough to reach it. In the darkness and with so many turns along the way I lost my sense of direction. I had no choice but to go back and take the other corridor.

I eventually made my way back to the place where the other corridor was. I was pretty tired, walking in the dark as I didn't want to waste any more of the gas in the lighter. I lit it again just to check that I was going the right way. I listened out again, but couldn't hear anything. I made my way down the next one. It was a bit drier than the other one I had been in before. This was a good sign. I walked, partly just feeling my way along only checking every now and again that there were no obstacles in the way.

I carried on for a while and decided to check my position again. I lit the lighter and peered into the darkness before me. I couldn't see much further ahead and thought it might be quicker if I walked with the lighter on. I took a few steps forward and saw stairs in front of me. I hurried to where they begun and saw that the material from which the walls were built was different to the one in the corridor. It was stone, the same type as the mansion. I couldn't help but feel excited. I had made it to the mansion.

I went up the first few steps, lighting the lighter every now and again so I wouldn't trip or stumble in the dark. Gradually the staircase got more and more narrow and I suddenly realised that I was in the mansion, in the secret corridor. On one side of the corridor the walls weren't stone anymore, I looked closely and realised it's the oak panels from the main staircase I was looking at. I looked at my lighter and realised I would have to continue my trip up the stairs in darkness as the flame got smaller and smaller. I let it go out, hoping there would be a little bit of gas left in it if I needed it. I waited for a few seconds letting my eyes adjust to the darkness when I spotted a faint ray of light coming through the panels into the corridor. I went a bit closer to it. The whole was quite small but seemed big enough to see through. I stooped down as it was quite close to the floor and peered through it. I could see the bottom part of the stair case, the door to the kitchen, the small corridor off which our rooms came off, even the front door. It was a good place to see who was coming in and out of the mansion without being spotted yourself. That was the intention of it; it wasn't there out of coincidence. Our intruders could see exactly when we were going in and out and they knew exactly when it was safe to come in through the hidden door. I needed to carry on and find out exactly where it was. For once we could give them a nasty surprise. I carried on up the stairs slowly in darkness so I wouldn't miss any more of these 'peep holes'. There were more of them, each strategically placed to give the widest point of view. I carried on up the stairs and realised there could only be one place where the hidden door was, it had to be in the library. But where exactly? I knew I was seconds away from finding out. I hurried up the stairs as fast as I could, in my excitement forgetting that someone else was in here with me. Suddenly I felt a painful hit on my head and everything fell into darkness.

# CHAPTER NINE

I don't know how much time had passed when I opened my eyes again. For a few seconds I couldn't remember what had happened. I thought for a minute and everything came flooding back to me. I found the secret passage into the mansion when someone hit me on the head pretty hard and knocked me out. I tried to touch my head to see if there was a cut but I couldn't move my arms. I fumbled around for a second and then realised that my hands were tied behind my back. I felt something rough in my mouth and realised I had been gagged as well. I was sitting in complete darkness, I had no idea where I was and to top it all off I had a pounding head ache. I felt around with my hands and realised I was on the ground, propped up against a brick wall. Was I still in the corridor? Maybe, but how was I ever going to get out? How long had I been here for?

I had no idea whether it was night or day. Some time must have passed since my attacker had tied me up because I was shivering and my hands and legs felt numb. I tried to move them a little bit to get the blood flowing again, but my movements were restricted. I continued for a bit and that helped with the cold as well. At least I stopped shivering. Everything seemed quiet at first but when I listened out I could hear echoes of what sounded like footsteps and murmurs of conversations. This was a good indication that I was still in the mansion. I had no idea who hit me on the head though. It was my own fault that I got myself into this mess, I should have been more cautious when exploring the tunnel. How could I get myself out of here? There was nothing I could do, I was tied up and I didn't have anything sharp to cut myself loose with; I had no chance of wriggling out of the ropes, they were pretty tight. All I could do was sit and wait, but for what? I chuckled quietly to myself, but this was certainly no laughing matter. Was I really going to rely on my captor to just turn up and let me go? It was naive of me to think that, what else could I do? I didn't know who was behind all of this, although I did have a pretty good idea. If it was Andy Walker as I suspected, then maybe it would all turn out ok. I knew that he was always very clever, he never seemingly broke the law, and no one could ever prove any of his dodgy doings. Would he want me on his conscience? I doubted it. But then again there was nothing stopping him just leaving me here. Who would ever find me? No one. My colleagues would probably report me missing with the local police; they would do their investigation and find nothing. I would just become another statistic, another cold case. Would they ever find the secret passage? Probably not. Even I didn't know where it was, and if it wasn't for the fact that I spotted the wet footprint in the grotto it probably would never had occurred to me. And maybe some years down the line when the mansion needed renovating or the grotto was to be demolished the contractors would find the tunnel leading from the shell grotto to the mansion and within it a skeleton. The police would look up their file for missing persons and find my name on it. Then everyone would realise what happened.

I shook my head. Thinking like that wasn't going to get me anywhere, maybe into a state of panic; and that was the last thing I needed at the moment. As depressing as it seemed, my only hope was with my captor. Once he would get what he was searching for maybe he would let me go, and disappear with the loot. 'Wishful thinking' I thought to myself and I let my head slump. I needed something better than assumptions that my captor was a softy.

Suddenly I saw a ray of light shine into the corridor. It seemed to be one of the peep holes I spotted earlier. It was nearly opposite me and I wondered if I could see anything through it. I started slowly shuffling along the floor to get to it. It was just high enough for me to look through if I got to my knees. It took me a few minutes for me to get myself into position. Every time I moved my head throbbed with pain. I finally managed to get myself to the peep hole and looked through it. I realised that I was looking into the library once my eyes adjusted to the light. I tried to shout but the gag in my moth prevented me from doing so. I tried again but the sudden dizziness stopped me. If I tried again I was afraid I would pass out so I gave up, instead I concentrated on observing what was happening. Billy came into the library followed by someone. They sat down and when I looked closer at his guest I thought I was seeing things. Billy was accompanied by Andy Walker. If I wasn't tied up I probably would have rubbed my eyes to check that they weren't deceiving me. There he was, sitting in an armchair, dressed in what looked to be a designer suit. My suspicions were confirmed. He was behind all the odd things that happened in the mansion. How did I know? Simple. He would never have come to the mansion if he knew I was there, so he was responsible for my current situation. I shifted slightly so I could see what was going on and I was hoping that I would be able to hear their conversation as well. My assumptions proved to be correct; I could hear every word they spoke.

"It's a shame that the curator of the future museum isn't here" Andy said. "I was really hoping to meet him. I heard he is a really nice guy"

"Yes, he is" Billy replied, unconvincingly "Unfortunately he isn't here. He is a nice guy, a bit odd maybe. He should be back any minute, I think. He was here when I went out to lunch and his car is in the garage, so he couldn't have gone far" he rattled on "We can wait for him if you have time"

"Well, that's fine, but I need to send in my team of contractors in tomorrow. As I have told you, Mr. Doughty had contacted me some time ago to investigate the suspected subsidence, and my surveyor has confirmed it. I've had a look at the plans of the mansion and his report and it seems that the problem lies within the left wing, where the drawing room is. It's not a huge amount of work, but I am afraid it's necessary." Andy said.

I thought for a minute, taken aback. His surveyor? Subsidence? What was he talking about? It seemed he was passing himself off as an architect to Bill. I wondered how he had managed that.

"Well, I don't know anything about that; I don't know anything about that technical stuff." Billy replied "But I guess you're the expert in that field so you know better."

"It will take a couple of days at the most. You won't have access to the drawing room for those two days but it shouldn't be a problem, the museum isn't open yet, is it?" Andy smiled at him.

"Well, it's up to the curator, Mr. Jones, I am afraid. I cannot make that decision without him." Billy replied. "He is responsible for everything here; it's up to him to make the decision. He should be back any second now, I am sure he will agree with you."

"And what happens if he's not here?" Andy asked, smiling again.

"Why wouldn't he be back?" Billy asked, surprised "I am sure he only went for a short walk, he likes his walks in the park"

The door to the library opened and Lucy came in. She still had her coat on and was about to take it off when she spotted Andy.

"Hello" she said, looking at Billy as if to ask who the stranger was.

"Did you find anything out?" Billy asked, forgetting about his guest.

Lucy gave Billy a funny look and looked at Andy.

"I am sorry, where are my manners" Andy said as he stood up and helped Lucy with her coat. "My name is David Chapman; I am an architect from Edinburgh. I am here because Mr. Doughty contacted my office some time ago asking us to investigate possible subsidence of the mansion. I am afraid there are essential works that need to be carried out to the property in order to stop any permanent damage." He explained as he sat back down.

"Hi, I am Lucy." She said and sat down as well "I don't think that we know anything about that, we've not had anything regarding that in our paperwork as far as I know"

"Well, Mr. Doughty contacted me shortly before he passed away, I have just completed my analysis recently and felt that the matter couldn't really wait much longer, so here I am" Andy replied.

She looked at him and then turned her attention back to Billy.

"Where's James?" she asked.

"I dunno" he shrugged his shoulders. "He wasn't here when I came back from lunch, and I haven't seen him since"

"That's odd" she said "It's not like him to go somewhere without saying"

"Well, I am afraid that I need someone to make the decision today" Andy butted into the conversation.

"What decision?" Lucy asked.

Andy explained again about the works that supposedly needed to be carried out at the mansion. She listened to his story nodding a couple of times.

"Right, well, like I said before, we haven't been told anything about it. The decision maker is the curator of the future museum, but it seems he isn't here at the moment." She replied "I am in no position to make that decision, so we will have to wait for James to return."

"Ok, but how long do we wait?" Andy asked and looked at his watch.

I sat in the dark corridor, watching all of it play out in front of my eyes. I couldn't believe Andy's nerve; he knew perfectly well that I was sitting behind the wall. I supposed that his plan was very simple. He would agree to wait for me, but knowing that I wouldn't be back any time soon he could pressure my colleagues into letting his team of contractors into the mansion to carry out the 'work' as a matter of urgency. He would get away with whatever it was he was after and we would be none the wiser. Where did releasing me fit into his little plan? I had no idea. At least I knew where to look for the discovery; it had to be the drawing room since he was so interested in it. But I still didn't know what it was exactly but I was sure it had to be something spectacular for him to go to all these lengths to get his hands on it.

Billy suddenly got up from his seat and left Lucy and Andy alone. A few moments later he came back to the library, followed by Vanessa and Ronnie.

"Hello" Vanessa said shyly, noticing Andy.

"Hi" Ronnie said and also looked at Andy.

"Is James here?" Vanessa asked, and walked towards the big table and put an envelope on it.

"I am afraid Jimmy went for a walk and hasn't come back yet" Lucy answered "What is that?" she asked pointing to the envelope.

"They are invitations to our school's Christmas production. Jimmy said that you guys might want to come and see it" Ronnie explained.

"Christmas production?" Billy said "I think that we can give it a miss. I can't say that I am a big fan of school plays"

"Right" Lucy added "I remember from when I was at school; the only people that enjoy them are the performers"

"Well, Jimmy said that he would come" Vanessa said, seemingly a bit upset that they weren't going to go "And our head teacher would like to meet all of you"

"Maybe James will want to go, I don't know what he does in his spare time" Billy said " Quite frankly I wouldn't be surprised if he enjoyed school plays and attended them on a regular basis."

"But he will come, won't he?" Vanessa asked.

"I cannot answer for him, you'll either have to wait or come and see him when he returns." Lucy said.

"Well, when is he going to be back?" Ronnie asked. "Where did he go?"

Andy just sat there, listening to the conversation with a smirk on his face.

"He's probably on a date with Susannah" Billy said, trying to put an end to the questions from the kids.

"Is he meeting her by the clock?" Vanessa asked and not quite realising what she was doing, she looked straight at the grandfather clock in the room.

I watched as the smirk disappeared off Andy's face. Suddenly he didn't look so relaxed. I couldn't help myself and tried to smile with the gag on.

"What clock?" Billy asked "What are you talking about? He's just probably met up with her in the cafe"

"Well, that's where Susannah meets up with people from what I've heard" Vanessa started to explain "So if they're meeting up it's probably by the clock"

"Oh dear, it's unbelievable what these kids can come up with sometimes." Lucy started to laugh.

I smiled as much as my gag would allow me. Vanessa was brilliant; she just solved one of the many mysteries of the mansion. Of course Susannah met with people by the clock, the library clock that is. And by the looks of things I was sitting on the other side of it, but no one in the room had the slightest idea, except for Andy who knew perfectly well where I was.

"We're not kids" Ronnie said.

"Well, there is no need to get upset over that, everyone has parents, so that makes everyone a kid." Billy said "Anyway, thanks for the invitations, but I don't think we will be coming, sorry"

"Ok then, never mind" Vanessa said and started to walk towards the door. She looked a bit upset. She looked at Ronnie who was still standing next to the table. He didn't seem quite ready to go. He reached into his school bag and took something out.

"I believe this is yours" Ronnie said, putting the pen they had found in the park on the table "I found it in the bushes when I was looking for my football in the park the other day. You must have lost it the night before."

Andy looked stunned just for a second then he pushed the pen away with from him.

"You're mistaken, that's not mine" he said "I have not been in the park at night..." he added.

Ronnie looked at Vanessa.

"I am sure it's your pen. I saw you take it out of your pocket when you were having dinner with someone in the restaurant in Cromdale. I was there, and I noticed the pen because it's so beautiful." Vanessa explained and looked at him, waiting for his response.

Andy sat there for a couple of seconds, not sure how to respond. I laughed to myself, I couldn't believe it. Andy was always so clever and he had just been put on the spot by two children. I waited for his response. He suddenly picked up the pen and took a closer look. I think he figured out that there was no way out of the situation. He had lost all of his confidence.

" Right, you are right, it seems that this is my pen" he said as he got up in a hurry "I don't know how it ended up in the park, but thank you for returning it to me" he got his things together and got ready to go.

"I have to go, I am afraid I cannot wait any longer for Mr. Jones, I'll just try to catch him tomorrow. Thanks for the tea" He said "I'll see myself out" and with tat he left the room.

"It's time for us to go as well, it's getting late" Ronnie said and made his way towards the door.

"See you "Lucy said. Billy went with then I assumed he wanted to lock the door behind them. Lucy sat down in one of the armchairs and took some papers out of her hand bag.

I was frustrated at my situation. Here I was, stuck behind the wall, helpless. I tried to bang on the wall but because I was tied up it didn't quite work. I managed a quiet thump, and Lucy didn't hear it. Billy returned to the library so I gave up on trying getting their attention. As long as they stayed in here I could hear their conversation and maybe learn something new. Just the past hour had been so beneficial to me.

"So are you finally going to tell me what you have found out in Glasgow?" Billy asked eagerly.

"Wait, I'll tell you in a minute." she said "First you tell me what you think of that guy, the architect" she asked Billy. "Don't you think it's all a bit ...odd?" she asked

"Odd? What do you mean" Billy asked "You're starting to sound like Jimmy now" he added.

"Well this business with the pen, surely you won't say that's normal. First he said it's not his, then he said it was and then he run out of here like his pants had caught fire or something" Lucy pointed out.

"He had dinner with the guy that followed us to the theatre and nearly run us off the road. I don't know, it's all a bit too much. Did he have any I.D. on him or even a business card?" she asked.

"Well, I didn't ask him for I.D., he knocked on the door and when I opened he introduced himself." Billy said scratching his head. "It would have been weird if I had asked him for I.D. . . . He did give me a business card; I put it on the table." Billy got up to get the business card.

"That's funny, I put in on the table when we came in. It's not here" Billy said.

Lucy looked at him and thought intensively for a minute.

"Unless those kids took it, which I doubt they did, it must have been him" Lucy said "I am afraid we have been made fools of once again, and I think that he is involved with the 'Roberto' gang" she looked at Billy.

"Really?" he asked "I don't know, maybe you're right." He added after a short pause.

"Of course I am right. What did he do in here?" Lucy asked.

"Well, he said he needed to double check the measurements in the drawing room, so we went in there and I helped him out with them." Billy replied, looking worried. "He then checked over his paper work and said that the measurements that he had just taken confirmed the subsidence"

"Billy, I can't believe you just did that, you let a stranger into the mansion, and you even let him measure walls without checking his credentials first." Lucy said accusingly "You know that someone is looking for something in here. I am sure that this so called architect has something to do with the people who have caused us all the trouble."

"Well, at least can you not say anything to Jimmy about it?" Billy asked.

"Don't worry, I won't" Lucy assured him "His opinion of you is bad anyway, I don't want to make things worse" Lucy chuckled. They sat for a while not talking.

"Tell me honestly, what you think about all of this? " Bill asked "These weird things that keep happening, dodgy architects and the rest of it. Did your trip to Glasgow help answer any questions?"

"I didn't really get anywhere at the hotel" Lucy said, shaking her head "Someone booked the room, paid for it all in advance by cash and left the theatre tickets for us. That's it. Apparently it was a youngish man, that's all they could tell me. They can't tell me his name because that would be breaking data protection laws." She propped her head on her hands. "The receptionist told me that he paid by cash, but he was very well informed because he knew our names...makes you think, doesn't it?"She looked at Bill.

"Obviously it was someone who knew exactly what is going on in the mansion." He said thoughtfully "Maybe Jimmy was right after all?" he asked Lucy

"I definitely think he had a point about all of this." Lucy started nodding as she took a small notebook out of her bag. "I had a couple of hours to kill before my return train so I went for a walk around the town centre" she said.

"What, you mean shopping?" Billy interrupted her and started laughing.

"Well, yes, but that didn't take me too long, so I decided to go to the library and check out the books that are missing from the collection here" she gestured to the shelves around them. " I had enough time to read through both of them and I even made some notes...You'll never guess what I found out! " she said excitedly " Well, go on take a guess, it's about our mansion" she smiled at Billy waiting for him to start guessing.

"I don't know, I don't have a clue" he replied "Just tell me...please?" he asked leaning towards her in his seat.

I tried to do the same in the corridor behind the wall. I could feel excitement rising in me once again as I realised we were probably just about to solve one of the mansion's mysteries. I tried to shout through my gag for Lucy to hurry up and make her revelation, but couldn't manage it.

"Well, the mansion was supposed to be a meeting place for a Masonic Lodge." She told him.

Billy looked disappointed.

"What is so exciting about that?" he asked her. "There are still plenty of lodges about; do you mean to tell me that at all of them you have weird people searching for something? Or is it just our one?"

"I am sorry to say, but Jimmy is right about you" she said looking at Billy. "Just think about it, and use your imagination a little" she continued. "When was our mansion completed? What year?" she asked him.

"1799?" Billy answered, not entirely sure if he was right.

"Wow, you don't pay much attention to detail do you?" Lucy asked him. "Yes, 1799. Historically, does that date tell you anything?" she asked.

"Not really" He didn't seem too bothered and certainly didn't share her excitement. I on the other hand knew exactly what she was going to say next.

"That was the year that threatened Freemasons in this country from carrying on, don't you remember anything form school? The parliamentary proclamation of Unlawful Societies Act of 1799? It was only thanks to the Grand Master of the Masons at the time, and the letter he had written to the prime minister to exclude the Freemasons from that Act that it all didn't end for them. Do you really think that they would have stopped their meetings? I don't think so; it would all become a lot more secret.

They would need a better location to hold their meetings, a new one, and a secret one." She continued explaining.

"It could be a coincidence that the mansion was finished the same year as that happened." Billy said.

"But is it a coincidence that Lord Blackhill was a Mason of the third degree? The highest degree, other than Master Mason?" she asked and waited for his reply. Billy thought for a few seconds.

"All of this confirms it don't you think? That Mr. Doughty did discover something in the mansion connected to the Freemasons, it's not just a rumour. We need to find it before it slips away from us" Lucy said.

"Well, Doughty took the secret with him, we don't even have a clue as to where we should begin looking" Billy shrugged his shoulders.

I could feel the frustration growing inside me. I tried to shout 'But you do have a clue' to them, but I strained myself too much and I could feel myself slipping into unconsciousness again.

# CHAPTER TEN

I didn't know how long I had been out for. I woke up and opened my eyes. I figured out that it was night because everything was dark around me, there was no light seeping in from the library. I was shivering again and my arms and legs felt numb so I tried moving them as much as I could to get some heat in my body. I sat for a while listening out but I couldn't hear anything. Lucy and Bill were either in bed or maybe in the kitchen. I re-analysed my situation. After seeing Andy in the library tonight, posing as an architect, I knew that he was behind everything, so I had hope of getting out of this corridor. Andy was always very clever and his slate was clean as far as the police went, he never did anything that would land him in trouble. He probably already had a plan as to what he will do with me; he wasn't going to keep me here forever. But what would his next move be? He would have to get what he came here for to let me go. He unwittingly told me where to look for it but I doubted he would give me a chance to get to it before him. So I needed to get out of here as soon as possible. I tried wriggling my hands out of the ropes which they had used, but they tied them pretty hard. I gave up trying to get out for the time being and sat in the dark, listening. Nothing stirred and I couldn't hear anything that would indicate that my colleagues were still awake.

Suddenly I thought I heard an echo of footsteps somewhere. I held my breath as I listened out to make sure I hadn't imagined it. I heard it again. It sounded like someone was making their way through the tunnel. I continued listening out with a glimmer of hope at the back of my mind that someone had actually found the secret way into the tunnel and was coming to my rescue. The footsteps were becoming louder with every second and I could hear muffled voices in the distance. I tried to shout but the gag sat firmly in my mouth and once again no sound came out. I decided it would be better to sit and not waste my energy on pointless shouting. I sat still on the floor and waited to see who was coming. Eventually I saw light bouncing off the walls and realised that it was someone with a flashlight. As the people approached me I could see two, maybe three figures looming in the tunnel. As they came closer the guy at the front shone his torch straight into my face. I instinctively closed my eyes and realised that it was my captors, not my rescue party.

"Don't worry, just sit still" said the one that shone the light in my face. "You'll be free by dawn"

I thought I recognised the voice but I couldn't quite place it. He stepped over my legs and stood next to the wall opposite me. I heard a quiet rumble and a creak as he activated some kind of mechanism in the wall and a small part of the wall gave way and swung open and he went through it. I blinked a couple of times, trying to readjust my eyes to the dark again. The other two men stepped over my legs and followed him. The first guy came to the opening and pushed it shut again. I realised that it was the clock that was disguising the hidden door. I could see faint light peering into the tunnel through the peep hole and decided that it must be their torches. I could see them for a few more seconds until they left the library and went into the corridor. I sat once more in the dark and felt my anger rising. There they were, going about their business in the mansion, Lucy and Bill were asleep in their rooms and I was sitting here, on the other side of the clock, helpless. I tried listening to try to figure out what room they were in and what they were doing, but the walls of the old mansion were too thick to allow any sound to pass through. I hated feeling so helpless, but there really wasn't much I could do, so I sat and waited.

I don't know how much time had passed; it was hard to try to figure it out. I wondered if there was anything I could do about all of this once I got out. Again I had no proof of what went on here, I knew who to point the finger at, but it was like PC Macleod had said, without any concrete evidence there was nothing we could do. They were in the mansion right now, taking whatever it was they came for. They would probably loosen the ropes so I would eventually free myself. Even if I did go to the police with the claim that it was Andy who had imprisoned me, he would have a solid alibi and that would be the end of the story. Once again I would have no solid proof of what went on here.

I sat in the dark with my thoughts, trying to listen out for any sounds that came from inside of the mansion but I couldn't hear anything.

Whatever they were doing, they were pretty quiet. I supposed that they would have to if they didn't want to wake Billy and Lucy up and get caught red handed. I wasn't sure how much time had passed when I heard footsteps in the library once again. The clock swung open and two of the three men came in from the library. They were carrying big bags. One of them had a flashlight and they slowly made their way through the tunnel. A few minutes later their accomplice came in from the library and closed the secret way into the mansion.

"I've left the front door unlocked for you in case you don't figure out the way in which this mechanism works." He whispered to me, attempting to change his voice so I wouldn't guess who it was. He did sound like Andy and I was pretty sure that it was him.

"Game over, you lost, I am sorry to say." He added "We've got what we came for and it is time we went our separate ways. I'll loosen the ropes so you can free yourself. I'll take the gag out so you can call for help, but I would wait till the morning for that, I don't think anyone will hear you right now, these walls are pretty thick you know" he said and chuckled to himself.

I sat there as he started to loosen the ropes. I didn't say anything back to him, but I could feel my anger rising once again. He took the gag out of my mouth, lifted the third bag that he had brought with him and went down the corridor. I could see the flashlight growing fainter as he made his way down the tunnel and it eventually disappeared.

I swallowed a few times, trying to get rid of the horrible taste that the gag had left in my mouth. It didn't really help so I concentrated on freeing myself from the ropes. I took me some time to loosen them enough to be able to get my hands free. It was a real struggle and I was hoping that the knots on the ropes binding my legs weren't too complicated and that I would be able to untie them.

As I sat there untying my legs slowly I thought about the whole situation. They won, I lost. Andy finally figured out where the thing that Doughty had found was hidden and because his plan to get to it didn't work thanks to Ronnie and Vanessa, he decided to get it tonight. The worst thing about it is that he will most likely get away with it. By the time I come out of the tunnel and can try and do something about it, everything they took will be long gone and hidden away. This time he had outsmarted me and again I had no proof for any of it. I still didn't know what the discovery was and where it was. It wasn't in plain view, I knew that much but where had it been hidden? Somewhere in the back of my mind a small idea appeared, but it was so ridiculous, I dismissed it. I was nearly done untying the complicated knots that were binding my feet, and the thought kept coming back to me. The more I thought about it, the less it seemed unlikely. There was still hope to recover the discovery, but I had to be very smart about it. I finally stood up and bent my legs a few times to get the circulation going again and to get rid of the pins and needles.

I took a look at the hidden door that lead to the library. It wasn't complicated; the back of the clock just neatly covered the hidden doorway. It swung open like a door and the hinges were cleverly hidden and inlaid into the oak panelling. I cast my mind back to the night when we arrived. We rushed upstairs because we heard footsteps. The intruders weren't expecting us and they rushed into the corridor to hide in time. They didn't pull the clock far enough to close the doorway and left a small gap. Realising that Billy, Lucy or I would spot it and find the secret way in, one of them pulled on it to get it completely shut. He must have used too much force and that's why the glass cracked.

I realised that I had solved another one of the unexplainable things that had happened in the mansion and I almost laughed out loud when I realised how simple it was. I would hopefully solve all of them in time, including Mr. Doughty's discovery, I was sure of it.

I went into the library and pushed the clock in order to close the hidden doorway. I took a closer look at the finish and was surprised at the workmanship. The clock fitted the panels so snugly, that even when looking closely at it you couldn't tell what it was hiding. I felt around with my fingers along the whole clock and found a small handle at the bottom of the clock. I pulled on it slightly and the clock swung open. I closed it again and shook my head in astonishment again. It was amazing that Doughty had even found it. I looked around the library and saw the tickets to the Christmas play that Ronnie and Vanessa had dropped off. Looking at them I smiled to myself as an idea formed in my mind. I knew exactly what I needed to do in order to recover Doughty's discovery. I switched the light off and quietly went downstairs. I checked the time only to discover that it was just coming up to three in the morning. I could still get a couple of hours sleep, so after locking the front door, I jumped in my bed. I fell asleep as soon as my head hit the pillow.

... I could see Andy running in front of me. Every time he turned around I couldn't help but notice the enormous grin on his face. He was carrying something in his arms, but every time I tried to see what it was, he would get further away from me. I could hear him shouting 'you'll never get the secret; you'll never know what the mansion was hiding! I've got it now and there's nothing you can do about it!' I could hear him laughing. I- could feel myself getting tired and suddenly I felt someone shaking me. I could hear Lucy's voice, gradually getting louder and louder 'you're here, where were you! Jimmy? Jimmy!'...

Suddenly I woke up to find Lucy shaking me and shouting "Jimmy! You're here!" I sat up, at first unsure of where I was I realised that it was a dream and that I was in my bed in the mansion. I could see Billy standing behind Lucy with a concerned look on his face.

"Where were you? You gave us such a fright yesterday" Lucy asked. "We were so worried when you didn't turn up last night"

I rubbed my eyes and looked at my hands they were covered with dust and dirt from the corridor.

"Guys, let me get dressed and wash up" I said "I would love some coffee first and then I promise that I will tell you everything ok?"

"Sure" Lucy said, looking at Bill "I'll go and put the kettle on" she got up off my bed and they left the room. I got dressed quickly and joined them in the kitchen. We sat around the table and I told them everything that happened the day before. They were listening carefully, sometimes asking a question. I finally got to the end of my story and we went upstairs where I showed them the secret door into the corridor. They were both surprised and amazed just as I had been when I first saw it.

"So now what?" Billy asked, after he opened and closed the secret door a few times.

I thought for a minute whether I should tell them my suspicions but decided not to. It wasn't because I didn't trust them; I just felt that the less people knew about it the better.

"I think I should get down to the police station to have a word with PC Macleod." I said "But first we should have some breakfast, don't you think?" I asked them.

"Sure, but I'd call it brunch, not breakfast" Lucy said.

"It's a very good idea, I must say" Billy said smiling,

I looked at the clock and realised that it was after ten. It wasn't exactly an early start of the working day for us today, but with everything that's happened, I didn't think it would be a big problem. At least my colleagues were smiling again, maybe not everything was a failure.

"Right, I'll see you in the kitchen then" I said.

Billy and Lucy went downstairs and I picked up the invitations. These would come in very handy tonight, I knew exactly what I was going to do, all was not lost yet, I just had to play my cards right. As I was walking down the stairs I heard a loud knock at the door. 'Who in the world could that be?' I asked myself, genuinely surprised. I went to the front door and opened it. To my surprise I could see Mr. Simpson standing there.

" Hello, Jimmy," he said " I've not heard form you for a while and I thought that I would just pop in and check how you are getting on" he said, grinning at me.

I stood there unsure whether my eyes were deceiving me. I felt like rubbing them to make sure that he was actually there. I had not been able to get in touch with him for the past two weeks and the timing just couldn't be better for his visit.

"Come in, come in" I said and showed him in. He took off his coat and waited for me to show him in.

"Guys, we have a visitor" I said to Lucy and Bill as we both came into the kitchen.

"Good morning" Lucy said, with a surprised look on her face Billy just nodded as he was finishing his sandwich. "Would you like some tea or coffee?" she asked "We've just finished breakfast, but if you're hungry, I'm sure we can sort something out?" she looked at him.

"Tea would be great, thanks" he replied as he sat down at the table "I see you guys have a very relaxed and homely atmosphere here, it makes a nice change."

"Well, we are stuck here by ourselves, so we make the most of it" Billy said, finally finishing his sandwich "Is this an official visit then?" he asked.

" I wouldn't call it that" Mr. Simpson replied " I was just on a visit up in Inverness, so I thought I'd come down and see you on my way back since it's been very hard to get in touch with you here" he looked at me a bit sternly.

"Well, the network coverage is pretty bad here, virtually none." I explained "We need to go all the way into Cromdale to get it I have tried ringing you at the office, but of course you weren't there so I left a few messages on your mobile."

"Well, I am here now so I can take a look at your progress with everything, maybe we can go over what you have planned for the museum. I have a return train tomorrow to London so that gives us plenty of time." He said.

"So much has actually happened in the past few days, I am not sure where to start" I said scratching my head.

"Well, start at the beginning, and then you can take me round the mansion, how about that?" he said and smiled Billy and Lucy looked at me, neither of them knowing how to explain everything that's happened. It was up to me then, so like he suggested, I started telling him about everything that had happened since we arrived. There wasn't really anything he could do now; it was up to the police. He listened carefully to my story, Billy and Lucy left me to do all the talking. I could sense his good mood disappearing gradually as I got closer to the end. When I finished, he sat in silence for a minute or so.

" You need to get to the police station straight away" he said " I don't know how much good it will do, but we can't just leave matters as they are. I will go and see this caretaker...Dave is it? And see if maybe he spotted anything last night."

"Right" I agreed and got up to get ready to go.

"When you get back, we can sort the museum business out" he said. I could tell he wasn't very happy and thought that he probably had more to say about the whole thing, but maybe he didn't want to say it in front of Lucy or Bill.

I set off for the police station and left the three of them in the mansion. Luckily PC Macleod was on duty so it saved me a lot of explaining. I told him about the events from the night before and about my suspicions as well as my idea. We spent a long time going over all the details, but by the end of the visit I was sure that all would turn out well. I left the police station in a better mood and I was enjoying my walk through the park. It was another beautiful morning, the sun was shining and the air was crisp. As I walked onto the lawn in front of the mansion I saw Ronnie and Vanessa. I waved to them and they waved back.

"Hello" Ronnie shouted.

"Hi" I shouted back and walked towards them.

"How are you?" Vanessa asked when I finally reached them. "We came by yesterday but you weren't there. We brought the tickets for the Christmas play. It's tonight" she said proudly.

"I know, and thanks for that" I smiled.

"Will you come?" she asked.

"Of course we will we wouldn't miss it" I said.

"So where were you yesterday?" Ronnie asked "Billy said you were on a date?"

"Umm, not exactly" I answered.

"Are Billy and Lucy coming then?" Vanessa asked "They weren't so keen on it yesterday" she said, frowning.

"They were only joking, of course they are coming. My boss from London is here and he wants to come too" I reassured her.

"Why is your boss here?" Vanessa asked. Ronnie gave her a funny look.

"Stop being so nosy" he said.

"I'm not, I am just asking, you don't mind do you?" she asked me "You don't have to tell us if you don't want to" she crossed her arms.

"Oh, it's fine, it's not a big secret, he just came to see how we are getting on with everything" I said, trying not to laugh.

"Cool, did you tell him about the ghosts? Ronnie asked "It would be an added bonus if the museum was haunted. What did he say?"

"Well, I did tell him about everything, he wasn't too happy about it to be honest. But you should both know that I am going to put an end to this ghost business once and for all. The museum itself will be a good addition to your little town, believe me" I replied, smiling.

Vanessa thought for a minute

"I suppose you're right so you are definitely coming?" she asked again.

"Yes, we are" I reassured her.

"Vanessa, if you ask one more time he is going to change his mind" Ronnie said.

"Oh, be quiet" she answered jokingly. I couldn't help but laugh. It seemed everyone was in high spirits today. We got to the drive and we said goodbye, they made their way home and I went back to the mansion. I thought about what still needed to be done in order to have everything in place for tonight, and I hoped I wasn't wrong in my calculations and that my plan wouldn't backfire. Time would tell, I just had to wait and see.

I came into the kitchen after getting my coat off to find Mr Simpson, Lucy and Billy still sitting at the table, talking.

"I hope I'm not intruding" I said.

"No, not at all, I've just been getting some feedback about how you are doing at your new post" Mr. Simpson said. "Your colleagues are very happy with the way you have been running things here, well done"

I looked at Lucy and Billy and smiled I couldn't help it. If Mr. Simpson had come a week ago, they probably would have said that I was rubbish, but now they knew that it wasn't me imagining things, that something odd really was going on here.

"Good to hear it" I said "Feedback is always good" I smiled.

"In the time that you were away, I had a little tour of the mansion from your co-workers." Mr. Simpson said "The progress of work is very good, have you had any definite ideas about what you want here? In the museum I mean?" he asked.

" Well, yes , actually I have thought about it and I'm pretty sure what would be a good theme for the museum " I said " But I would like to tell you about it this evening if you don't mind"

Mr. Simpson looked surprised.

"Why this evening? Can't you tell me now?" He asked, looking at Billy as if he could answer that question for him. "Why should anything change by this evening?"

"Oh, nothing really, I would just prefer to do it tonight" I said with a playful smile on my lips. "I am planning on finally putting an end to this ghost business and lay them to rest"

"Not this again, I thought you said that the police were dealing with the matter now" he said.

"Well, yes, but we can't even say what's missing, can we?" I asked "I am determined to find that out" I said confidently.

"That's true, but it's out of our hands now" Mr. Simpson said in a tone that indicated that he didn't want to discuss it any more. "Our main concern is the museum now, not what's missing, or isn't"

"Sorry to interrupt, but there is one thing that you need to know" Billy said.

"What's that? Mr. Simpson asked "I am always interested in fresh input from our young co-workers" he said, gesturing to Billy to tell us his idea.

"Lunch" he simply said.

"Lunch?" Mr. Simpson asked.

"Its lunch time" he clarified "So we really should get going if we want to make it. The restaurant closes between three and five thirty you know"

"Right you are, let's get going then" I said, looking at my watch.

Mr. Simpson wasn't happy with that but all he could do is to grab his coat and to join us on the walk to Cromdale. I was sure that he had already made up his mind about what he wanted for the mansion and after lunch he would do his best to convince me that his ideas were better than mine. We started walking, Lucy and Billy were leading the way, and Mr. Simpson and I were following. I slowed down on purpose to put enough distance between us and the pair in front so they wouldn't hear our conversation.

"We have a rare opportunity to promote the new museum tonight" I said lowering my voice just a little.

"Oh, what's that?" Mr. Simpson asked, not sounding very interested.

" Well, I've met two kids from the local school here, who are very keen on the idea of having a museum here" I explained " They are doing their Christmas play tonight and they have invited us to come along and watch. The head teacher is keen to meet us as well, so it might be a good opportunity to maybe talk about it a bit. There will be parents there, we could maybe spark an interest in the community, I am sure they will have some questions for us, what do you think?" I asked "Besides, it would give us a chance to go out, there isn't much entertainment around here you know"

Mr. Simpson thought for a minute about my proposal.

"It's not a bad idea, you know" He said after a few minutes "It is a good opportunity, and maybe some of the locals can give us some points on what they would like to see here" he nodded.

"Well, the problem is that Lucy and Billy are not too keen, maybe you can persuade them to come?" I continued "It would look better if the whole team was there, supporting the idea."

"You're right, I'll see what I can do" he said.

We caught up with Billy and Lucy.

"I've told Mr. Simpson about the Christmas play at the local school." I said to them "He thinks it might be a good opportunity to go along tonight and promote the museum."

"Yeah, he had to go and tell him about it" I heard Billy whisper to Lucy.

"We don't really want to go, come on it's a Christmas play, we all know the Nativity story, we don't really need reminding" Lucy said.

Mr. Simpson looked at them.

"I think that we all need to embrace this opportunity. After all, museums are there to educate and broaden our horizons. I am sure that the local school will want to get involved with exhibitions as well as organise trips and such. The museum will be an important addition to this small community. We all need to be there to create a good impression. I am sure that many people want to know what has happened so far and what the plans for the future are. We should all be there in order to answer any questions and I am sure there will be plenty." He looked at the two of them, looking to see if either would disagree with him. Neither of them did but Lucy gave me one of her looks of disapproval. I knew they weren't keen on going, but neither of them was able to say no to what Mr. Simpson had just said. I smiled, happy with the outcome. Slowly everything was falling into place just as I wanted it.

"The mansion can't be left empty, I'll stay to keep an eye on things" Billy said, having one last attempt on getting out of going to the production.

"There is no need" I replied "On our way back from lunch I'll ask Dave to stay at the mansion for the duration of our visit to the school"

Billy wasn't too happy with that so he shrugged his shoulders. He couldn't think of another excuse so he just gave up.

We carried on walking, chatting about nothing in particular; Mr. Simpson told us about his visit to Inverness and what the curator was doing there. The conversation returned to our museum once again when we were all just finishing our lunches. Mr. Simpson told me what pieces he wanted to take from the mansion, and just as I suspected, some of them he wanted to be transferred to Inverness, some were to go to the British Museum in London.

"That's fine" I agreed to his proposal "But to replace them, we would like some of the artefacts from the British Museum that are specific to Freemasonry."

He looked at me surprised.

"Freemasonry? But why?" he asked.

"Lucy here found out that our mansion was built with the intention for it to become a place for the Lodge to hold its meetings, so I think it will be a good idea to capture that within the new museum." I explained.

"Well, maybe you're right, but I think you'll need more than that to borrow exhibits from other museums, we'll see" he replied.

I could see that he wasn't convinced, but I didn't insist. I hoped that tonight's events would help him see things from my point of view. I had just finished my last bite of steak when I spotted Susannah outside.

"I'll let you finish your lunch, I'll wait outside, I need a bit of fresh air" I said as I got up from the table.

Billy winked at me.

"I saw her as well, going for a quick chat?" he asked.

"Well, I've finished eating, so I'll pop out for a second. You finish your food before it gets cold" I replied and threw my coat on. Lucy just smiled and didn't say anything.

I went outside and tried to catch up to Susannah. I am sure she had already finished playing her part in the story, but there were some things that I really wanted to talk to her about. I could see that she was on her mobile and I took it as a good sign. I was too far to hear what she was saying, so I waited for her to finish. She put the phone back in her bag and went into the small cafe. I quickly followed her and saw that she sat down at one of the tables after ordering at the counter. I came into the cafe, greeted the girl behind the counter and approached Susannah's table.

"This seat isn't taken, is it?" I asked and pulled out a chair.

She looked a bit startled and surprised to see me.

"No it's not. Hello" she said but she didn't give me one of her usual charming smiles.

"Hello" I replied as I sat down "I really didn't think I would see you again" I said.

"Really?" she asked "I didn't say I was leaving?" she asked.

"Well, I presumed that you'd be leaving with the frequent visitors to the mansion with the loot" I said, quite sure of the role she had played.

"How dare you accuse me of anything..." she said, but I stopped her.

"Let's stop pretending, we both know that you played a part in all of this. No one can hear us here, I have no proof, can we be honest at least now?" I asked. "The minute I spotted Andy in the cafe, I knew it was no coincidence that he was here. I know that he always has a pretty girlfriend, and you are just that... very pretty. Your interest in the mansion was also a bit suspicious for someone who had just arrived here to cover sickness. It would be useful for Andy to have someone who would keep an eye on things within our team on a day to day basis. You are linked to all the events, the wine- correct me if I am wrong, you brought it with you, and it was already 'prepared' wasn't it? The séance... well I won't go into the details, but I am right, aren't I?" I looked at her. She didn't seem too bothered or surprised.

"If you are so clever, why did you let us do what we wanted? Why didn't you stop us?" she asked, realising that there was no use in pretending anymore.

"Because I didn't know what you were after" I replied "I wanted you to point me in the right direction"

"Well, now you know, don't you?" she asked. I nodded in agreement. "It's a bit late now; you just said that the loot is gone. I hope that that there isn't too much missing?" she asked. I could hear the sarcasm in her voice.

"You know that nothing is missing" I shrugged "Nothing that we knew about"

"Well, so this whole incident can stay between us. Officially nothing is missing; you don't need to tell anyone about all of this. You win some; you lose some, as they say. This time it was your turn to lose" she said and finally smiled, as if she wanted to make me feel better. Her coffee arrived at the table and I waited for the girl to get back behind the counter before I replied.

"We win some we lose some, you're right" I got up and smiled back at her.

"I am glad to see that you're not letting this get you down, that's good. You'll still have your victories I am sure" she said.

"Yes, so am I" and with that I left the cafe. I was sure that this whole thing would be added to my victories, not loses like she insisted.

# CHAPTER ELEVEN

After lunch the weather changed. The wind picked up again and blew in clouds that were lingering on the horizon. They had that look about them as if it was going to snow. The temperature dropped and it was very cold. It started to rain, but I was sure we would see snow again by the morning. I took Mr. Simpson around the mansion to show him what we had done. He was pleased with the progress of work but still had a lot of decisions to make and a lot of questions, so I left him with Lucy and Billy. I grabbed a chair and went to the drawing room. The thought that Andy was so interested in it wouldn't leave me alone. I sat in the middle of the vast room with my small notepad on my lap. I kept drawing the same design that Dave had carved on the pipe. I had a feeling it was the key to answering all of the questions that were bothering me, the answer to the mystery. The solution was in the back of my mind I could feel it there but it kept escaping me. I sat there, doodling and trying to figure it out and then it finally came to me. I couldn't help but smile to myself. I knew what the mansion's secret was, and what's more important, I knew exactly where it was. I felt a feeling of triumph wash over me. Once more I asked myself whether my plan would work, and I was sure that I would have the last word to say in the matter. For the first time in weeks I felt a sense of peace.

I had no idea how long I had been sitting in there with my thoughts, when suddenly the door opened and Lucy came in.

"Here you are" she said "I was wondering where you got to. Dave is here, to look after the mansion like you asked, but I really don't think we will be going?" she looked at me.

"Why not?" I asked as I got up. I looked at my watch and realised it was time for us to get ready to go.

"Well, the weather is terrible, it's so cold, maybe we can give it a miss?" she asked.

"That's out of the question" I said shaking my head "It's a really good opportunity for us to explain to everyone what we are doing here. We have to go. Anyway, I saw Vanessa and Ronnie today, so I am sure that they have said at the school that we are coming so they are expecting us. Let's go".

I switched off the lights and went to get changed. On the way to my room I peered into the kitchen to find Dave sitting at the table.

"Hello" he said when he spotted me. He had brought a newspaper with him and was reading it.

"Hi" I said. "Thanks for coming by. I see that you have something with you to pass the time" I pointed to the newspaper. "Will you be ok to stay in here? You can help yourself to tea and coffee and any food that we have in the fridge."

"Yes I'll be fine" he said in his raspy voice. "Thank you".

He was still his usual odd self and I wondered whether he was involved with Andy and if he was helping him in his attempts to get to the mansions secret. I wanted him to house sit so that I would find that out once and for all whether he was in on the whole thing.

"Good. I'll lock all of the rooms anyway so you don't have to worry about. Maybe I am being a bit too overcautious, but like I've mentioned before, we've had strangers in the park at night, so I don't want to tempt fate and risk a break in. Better to be safe than sorry, don't you think?" I asked him.

"I suppose you're right. I'll keep an eye on things here" he said and gave me a crooked smile.

"Right" I said and left the kitchen. I went to see if the others were ready and asked Billy to lock all the rooms whilst I got ready. When I went into the entrance hall, I found Billy, Lucy and Mr. Simpson all ready. I put my coat on and we left.

"I know you're up to something" Lucy said as we made our way to the car "I am sure of it"

I didn't reply anything to that. We got in the car and were on our way when suddenly Mr. Simpson had a change of heart.

"This isn't a good idea" he said "We will be imposing. I am sure the children all worked hard on their production and we will be stealing their thunder by talking about the museum. Let's go back"

I shook my head.

"We are almost there, it's too late to go back. " I said "We don't need to steal all the attention, we can maybe ask the head teacher to mention the fact that we are there. I am sure that parents will be more interested in their children's performance. I know that the head teacher is keen to meet us and that's the main reason why we are going. We can maybe arrange for a time in the near future to go and talk about the new museum at an assembly or something, but things like that are always arranged in person don't you think?" I asked and looked at him. He didn't look too convinced so I added "You'll be off to London tomorrow, I won't have time to go to the school, and we still have a lot of work to do if we want to finish all the preparations before Christmas."

He thought for a minute and nodded in agreement. We had reached the school by now and I looked for a parking spot. I managed to find one very close to the school entrance so I parked the car and we all got out. The wind was very cold so we hurried inside.

The school was bustling with excitement; there were parents and children making their way to the school's assembly hall. We were greeted by one of the teachers who showed us where to go. Mr. Simpson introduced himself and the teacher said he would tell the head that he was here. We went into the assembly hall and took our seats. The stage was decorated and there was the school choir sat in two rows of chairs next to the stage. The hall was nearly full and I looked at my watch. The performance was about to start.

The head teacher went onto the stage and greeted everyone.

"Good evening everybody" she said smiling.

"Good evening Mrs. Randall" all of the children and some of the parents replied in unison.

"I am pleased to welcome you all here for this year's Christmas production. All of the children , teachers and parents who helped to make all of this possible had worked very hard so a big thank you to all" she smiled again " I won't keep you in suspense any longer, please sit back and relax. We will have refreshments at the end as well as a surprise. Enjoy" she said and stepped off the stage to let the children start.

The performance started with the choir singing a few carols as well as Christmas songs. A lot of the audience joined in but I've never had a good singing voice so I just listened. Then the Nativity story started and I spotted Ronnie on stage with Vanessa. He played one of the shepherds and she had the leading role of Mary. I couldn't help but smile when I saw her on stage, taking her role very seriously. We were sitting and watching the children perform when out of the corner of my eye I saw the clock and realised what time it was. I grabbed Mr. Simpson's and Lucy's hands.

"We have to leave, right away" I whispered.

"What?" Lucy whispered back "Again?" I could hear the disbelief in her voice even though she was whispering.

"Is this some sort of habit that I didn't know about?" Mr. Simpson asked trying to pull his hand away.

"Yes, you can say that" I said so they wouldn't question me and we quickly went out of the assembly hall. The only person I didn't have to explain anything to be Billy. The second he heard me say that we were leaving; he got up and went out without any fuss. Once we were in the corridor they tried to stop me to explain what was going on, but I wouldn't allow them.

"We need to get back, now, hurry" I said and practically run out of the school building.

"He's gone mad" Lucy said to Mr. Simpson.

"I think you're right" he agreed "Jimmy, stop, what on earth are you doing?" he asked and tried to grab my arm to make me stop. By now we were outside and I opened the car door.

"Please get in. I don't have time to explain right now." I said as I jumped into my seat. "When have I ever let you down?" I asked Mr. Simpson as I started the engine.

"Well....never" he replied hesitantly.

"So can you please just trust me and not ask any questions, I need to concentrate on the road." I said and pulled away from the curb. I sped through the little town and pulled out onto the road that went around the mansion's park. I wanted to get back as soon as possible, before it was too late.

As we reached the gate to the estate I slowed down and stopped at the side of the road. I turned off the engine.

"Get out and be quiet. We need to walk the rest of the way." I said to the others. They did as I told them, realising that it would be pointless to argue with me. I saw Lucy tapping the side of her head as if to say I was crazy. I didn't care anymore what they thought of me, too much was at stake.

"Be quiet" is said to them quietly. I went first and they followed me. After a few steps someone stepped out of the shrubs growing next to the path. It was PC Macleod. Mr. Simpson opened his mouth to say something but the police officer gestured for him to stay quiet.

"Everything is going according to plan. My men are in position, so you don't have to worry about anyone getting away. What do you want to do now?" he said quietly.

"Well, like I said I want to catch them red handed, so let's take the secret way in. I want to surprise them." I said to him "Follow me, but be quiet" I said to the others. They nodded in agreement, afraid to even utter a word. They finally realised that something was going on, and I was sure they were keen to find out what. I led the way, followed by PC Macleod and then my colleagues. We made our way down the path in the dark, not using our flashlights so we wouldn't make ourselves seen. It took a while but we finally made it to the old shell grotto. The door was open and we slipped inside. I opened the trap door and one by one we went into the secret tunnel. I heard Lucy gasp in amazement and Billy shushed her. We slowly went down the corridor, and finally made it to the stair case. I turned around and put my finger against my lips to remind them to be extra quiet.

"We can turn off the flash light here, we're nearly inside. I know my way around well enough to get to where they are in the dark. We wouldn't want to scare them off." I whispered.

PC Macleod nodded and switched off the flashlight. We got to the hidden doorway and I opened it. We entered the library and went down the stairs. We could hear loud bangs coming from the ball room. I hurried along and burst into the room flicking on the light switch as I did.

Inside we saw Andy and Peter with flashlights and crowbars pulling off the floor boards. In the corner of the room nearest to them sat Susannah in a chair. Another man that I'd never seen before made a dash for the window which was slightly ajar. He didn't get very far, the mansion was surrounded by police men and he stopped in his tracks.

"Well, I never..." Billy said in amazement as he came in to the room. Lucy gasped again and Mr. Simpson looked a bit shocked.

"Stop what you are doing, you're under arrest for breaking and entering and attempted burglary" PC Macleod said. His voice echoed in the room.

All four of the intruders looked shocked, especially Susannah. Andy and Peter dropped their tools.

"I did warn you, didn't I?" I asked Andy. He looked at me angrily, but didn't lose his temper.

"I am sorry, on what basis are you suggesting the charges?" he turned to the police officer. "We did not break into the mansion, the caretaker downstairs let us in. We only wanted to have a look around the mansion. We didn't know that we weren't allowed. We didn't come in with any intentions to steal anything, How can you prove that?" he asked.

The PC looked annoyed and helpless at the same time. Andy did have a point.

"What about the floor boards?" he asked. "You've got tools with you; do you mean to tell me that you always carry them around with you?"

"Well, no. I happened to have them in the car" Andy replied quickly "Whilst we were taking a look around the mansion, I realised that there is a secret, hidden room under this one. I probably should have had waited for the curator to get back and tell him about it, but the idea of discovering it was very exciting. So I asked my friends to help me to try and get to it. I do realise it was the wrong thing to do. I am happy to pay for the damage." He explained. I realised that he was probably right. It would be hard to prove that he intended to steal something. The damage to the floor wasn't great, and probably the police would only be able to charge him and his friends with trespassing and the damaged caused, unless they could prove everything else. He wouldn't get the punishment he deserved, but I couldn't do anything about it.

"It's your own fault" I said to him "I warned you to stay away from here when I saw you in the cafe, remember? I know that you won't get the sentence that you deserve, but I want you to know that it's me you need to thank. All I had to do is to wait for you to get to the secret room and catch you when you are taking the treasure out of the mansion, or driving away with it. Your punishment would have been a lot more severe, believe me. The police would have proof and evidence of your break in and everything, but do you know why I didn't allow it to get to that? I didn't want you to damage the mechanism that opens the way into the secret room. You would have made a hole in the floor to get to it. I wanted to preserve the mechanism to show to our future visitors of the museum." I explained. We had discussed this with PC Macleod and he agreed reluctantly to do things my way. It made his job a lot more difficult, but I managed to persuade him to see things my way. I had saved Andy's back, and I wanted him to know it.

"So you know where the mechanism is and how it works, do you?" Andy asked sarcastically.

I nodded.

" Yes, I do, I am even willing to demonstrate it to you if the police here will let you stay on for a bit before they take you to the station" I said, looking at PC Macleod.

"I don't see why that would be a problem. This lot won't get away even if they try. I am interested to see what all the fuss is about to be honest. Let me just go and take care of the caretaker. Unfortunately he is an accomplice to all this, I'll go and tell him the news." He said and left the room to talk to Dave. Everyone grabbed a chair and sat in a small circle around me. I laughed to myself. Here we were, like in all of the crime novels that I had read, where the detective gets everyone involved together to explain everything.

"This is just unbelievable" Mr. Simpson muttered to himself as he made himself comfortable.

"You're a liar" Lucy turned to Andy "You told Billy that you are an architect." She said accusingly.

"Well, you got me there" Andy laughed "But you have to admit, there is a lot at stake here" he shrugged.

I could see that Billy was looking at Susannah, as if he couldn't believe that she was part of the whole scam.

"It was you who brought that wine with you, you never found it in the cellar like you said you did" he said to her. "It was laced with something, just like Jimmy said it was." He crossed his arms waiting for an explanation from her.

"Well, I drunk it as well you know" she said.

"So that makes it ok then?" I asked "You drank it so none of us would get suspicious. You went home to sleep, and you knew that we would be sleeping all night so Andy and his friend could do whatever they wanted in the mansion" I looked at Andy. He didn't say anything, just smiled.

"There is one thing that I don't understand" I said to him.

"What's that?" he asked, still smiling.

"You were in here nearly every night, even before we came, and yet you couldn't find the way to the secret room. You're a smart guy, I thought that you would have been able to figure it out" I said.

"I know where the secret room is" he replied, the smile disappearing from his lips.

"Yes, you know where it is, but you don't know how to get to it. You were looking for it, and when you realised that it was only a matter of time for me to find out about it you decided to take the easy option- break your way into it, right?" I asked.

"Doughty lived here for years and he didn't find it until a few months before he died." Andy said.

"Well, it only took me a few hours to figure out the way in, I did it this afternoon" I said. I wasn't being modest, in fact I was showing off a bit but I couldn't help it. I could finally show my colleagues that I was smart and clever and not someone who imagines things to make my life more exciting.

" Don't sound so proud of yourself, you are the curator of the museum, you can come and go as you please so it was easy for you to find it" Andy said.

"On the contrary" I opposed "Yes, I am the curator and I can do what I like in here, but you didn't exactly make it easy for me to find it. I didn't even know about the discovery let alone what it was relating to. You made sure that all of the books that would tell me something about the history of the mansion were taken out of the library. It was only last night when Lucy returned from Glasgow I had found out what the intention with which the mansion had been built. Then, along with the phrase he had used as his last words so to speak, it dawned on me as to what the discovery was. It was you who erased the file from the computer and I am sure that it had something about the discovery in it, did you at least make a copy of it?" I looked at him. "I had a lot of time to think about everything when I was stuck in the corridor, you know"

Andy didn't say anything, he just looked at me. I felt a shiver and realised that I he hated me for what I had done. He wouldn't get the punishment he deserved, but he wouldn't get away with the treasure.

PC Macleod returned to the ballroom.

"Dave has been taken to the police station for a statement" he said "Now, let's finish up in here, shall we?" he looked at me.

"Sure" I turned to Andy once again "You had made three fundamental mistakes. The first was that you thought that you would outsmart me."

"I told you, didn't I?" Susannah interrupted me. "I told you he was smarter than he looks" she hissed at Andy.

"Oh, be quiet" he replied angrily. "So what were the other two mistakes? I don't want to make them again" he asked.

"Are you planning on doing this sort of thing again then?" PC Macleod asked sternly.

"No, of course not" Andy replied.

"Your second mistake was that you came here, posing as an architect and telling Billy and Lucy that you will be sending a team of builders to work on the drawing room. Thanks to that I realised that the room in question was the drawing room, but you had not managed to find the existing way into the secret room, so you were planning on getting in by making basically a hole in the wall or floor. But then it turned out that Lucy wouldn't let you do anything without my permission. So you came up with another solution. You decided to let me go, but first you did the little performance with your friends to make me believe that you got what you wanted from the mansion and it was over. That way, I'd stop looking for the discovery, and sooner or later you would have the opportunity to get to the treasure. I have to admit, it did work at first, but one thought kept coming back to me- first you wanted to excavate a hole, but now you came in and just took the treasure away? It didn't make sense. I realised that the treasure was still here, by the way, what was in those bags you took?" I paused.

"Fire wood for the fireplaces from the cellar" Andy replied after a few seconds.

" Right, very clever" I said " I decided to speed things up a bit, after all the tables had turned and I was calling the shots now, although you didn't know that. I spotted the invitations to the Christmas play on the table and that gave me the idea to "allow" you the opportunity to get to the treasure. I also wanted to find out once and for all whether Dave was I on all this so I asked him to stay at the mansion whilst we went to the school. I guess I was right about him from the start. So here we are now, my plan worked perfectly, thanks to the police officer here who had helped me with all of this. And that was your third mistake Andy" I said to him smiling triumphantly. "Now let me demonstrate to you what all of the fuss was about".

But before I could start another police officer came in and told us that there are a couple of children waiting downstairs, wanting to speak to me and they refuse to leave until they do. I nodded and asked him to bring them upstairs. It could only be Ronnie and Vanessa and I wanted them to see this as well because they had done their little bit in helping me to solve the mystery. A few minutes later the pair joined us.

"So that's how it is? " Vanessa asked accusingly "Was the production so bad that you had to leave early?" she asked, looking very upset. I smiled at her

"Of course not, I thought that you two were wonderful, but unfortunately my work required me to leave and return to the mansion. I am sure that you can understand that?" I asked her.

She looked around and noticed everyone else in the room. She smiled shyly.

"Sorry, I didn't know" she said quietly.

"It's ok; I am glad that you are here. Finally, I've chased the ghosts away for good and cleared up this whole mystery. I have to admit, you two have been a really big help. You're the ones who spotted the lights in the mansion when there was no one here; you were the ones who linked Andy to Peter here when you found the pen, so I am very grateful to you both." I smiled at them again. Ronnie didn't say anything, Vanessa just nodded. Both of them had big grins on their faces, they were very pleased with what I had just said.

"Now, as long as we don't have any more interruptions, I will reveal the secret to you" I said and gestured to everyone to come closer.

# CHAPTER TWELVE

Everyone gathered around me. The atmosphere was tense, everyone was excited. I lowered my voice just a little and pulled out big screwdriver which I had picked up earlier.

"Can you all imagine that I am holding in my hand a dagger used in Masonic rituals? We are, after all in an old mansion that was built with the intent for Masons to meet here in secret if it ever became necessary. And the symbols are the key, literally, to opening the secret room. You've all seem the inverted crown and the dagger piercing it, yes?" I asked them. "Even Doughty had drawn it on his deathbed, isn't that right?"

"Yes, and so what? Do you think I've not seen it? It's even on some of the panelling..." Andy said.

"Even Dave carves them into his ashtrays and such. Even in this room you will find those symbols, here, on the columns that form the panels." I said pointing to the columns around the room.

They all nodded once they took a closer look.

"All the other columns have slightly different carvings on them, the symbol in question is only on this one here" I pointed to the column next to me.

"You're right, but do you really think that I hadn't noticed that?" Andy asked" So what that it's different?"

"Andy, you need to have a good eye as well as a good imagination to solve things like this one. I kept asking myself why on earth the room that was intended as the main party room had such a depressing look about it. I mean it's dark and somewhat unwelcoming, I couldn't understand why someone would do that intentionally. It was when Lucy had found out when the mansion was built it clicked, and I realised the real purpose of the room- it wasn't intended as a drawing room, it was a meeting room for all the members of the lodge. But we all know how society looks at mason's, with their rituals and initiation ceremonies... not everyone wants to admit to society that they are a lodge master, so they need to keep it a secret. So they all gathered here, entering via the secret passage and held their meetings in.... well not in this room, in plain sight, in the hidden one beneath this one. So what better way to start the meeting than using the old Masonic symbol of the dagger piercing the inverted crown? Can you imagine the master using that as a sign that everyone has gathered and they are ready to start?" I asked them.

"So have you tested your theory?" Andy asked.

"Well, I am about to; I didn't really have the time to do it yet." I aid "Will you help me?" I asked him.

He nodded, forgetting about the situation he was in. Once again I felt excitement wash over me and I was pretty sure he felt the same thing. After weeks of searching, finally the mansion's secret would be revealed.

"You measured the walls well; there is definitely another room under this one. However there is no way into it through the cellar. I am guessing that you were in the room weren't you?" I asked Andy.

"He took me inside" Andy nodded "Doughty, I mean. He blindfolded me so I wouldn't see how to get inside by myself, but he showed it to me. He was proud of it and wanted to share it with everyone, but then if he did, it wouldn't be secret anymore. He was very odd you know. He said he would show me everything once I had found him a buyer for the stuff. He only told me about it, no one else knew."

"That's not entirely true" Mr. Simpson interrupted him "A few weeks before his death he wrote to me telling me about the treasure he had found in the mansion. I think he maybe wanted to find out if he would get some sort of reward if he donated it to a museum. Before I had a chance to write back to him he died, so I came down here, honouring his last wish to make a museum. However I didn't find any of the things he had listed in his findings. That's when I came up with the idea of sending you here Jimmy." He explained.

"So that's why you sent me here, to get to the bottom of this, not to organise the museum" I said, finally understanding his decision.

"No offence, but you really didn't think that when I said to you that you are the best person for the job, I meant for you to sit in an office did you?" he asked ironically.

"Well, no...But why didn't you tell me about the letter Mr. Doughty had sent to you? It would have been really helpful" I asked.

"To be honest I wasn't sure what to make of it. None of the stuff which he had described was here, I didn't know for sure whether he was being serious about it; I didn't want to make a fool of myself." Mr. Simpson replied. "This is the real reason for my visit. I came here to tell you about it all and to show you the letter. If I had known that all these things happened, I would have told you sooner." he shrugged.

I supposed I couldn't blame him for not telling me about the letter, Andy at least had seen the treasure so he knew it was there. By the time Doughty contacted Mr. Simpson, it was too late for him to show or explain anything to anyone. I should've had more faith in myself as well, there was no point blaming anyone for anything, we got there in the end.

"Can we please just get on with it? I want to see the secret room" Billy said impatiently.

"Yes, let's do that, after all, it's what everyone wants to see" I said and grabbed the screwdriver once more. "Where did I get to?"

"To the part where the dagger pierces the inverted crown" Lucy said.

"Well, that's it then, all we have to do now is to find the crown and pierce it" I said.

"Hang on..." Andy said as he got up and went over to the column next to the fire place. "This column has crowns carved on it. The two at the top are too high, besides, they are the right way up, and so it must be the bottom ones." He leaned in and took a closer look at the panel "There seems to be a metal opening in this one here, Jimmy, pass me the screwdriver please" he said. I passed the screwdriver to him. He took it without looking at me and inserted it into the metal slit.

"Now I think this can turn...?" he turned the tool and we all heard a noise coming from behind the panel.

"Now I think all it needs is a push" I said as I applied pressure to one side of the panel. Andy got up and helped me. Again we heard the noise of the mechanism hidden in the wall. As we pushed one side, the other came out of the wall revealing a staircase concealed by the panel. I grabbed a torch and was the first to go into the newly found stair case. Mr. Simpson went after me, closely followed by Billy and Lucy, Ronnie and Vanessa. PC Macleod was kind enough to allow Andy to come down with us and to have a look. He left the others with a couple of police officers. We slowly made our way down the narrow staircase. I reached the bottom of the stairs and entered a surprisingly large room which was located directly underneath the drawing room. I directed the light from my torch around the whole room.

It had been most certainly intended as a meeting room for the lodge. I could see what remained of the fabrics that once draped the walls of the room. You could still see some of the Masonic symbols on a few of them- the compass and the square, the all-seeing eye and other symbols. Along two of the walls there were wooden chairs lined up for the brothers to sit on during their meetings. Beneath the third wall was a long table with four chairs. On it were items used in the rituals, as well as more symbolic objects, mostly in gold and silver. Two smaller tables were in the corners of the room and on them were more objects which had been used for initiations a long time ago. I walked up to the table. On it was a thick book, covered in leather. I opened it very delicately. It appeared to be a list of members of the lodge and their degrees. The Master Mason was Lord Blackhill himself, which didn't surprise me. It had other information in it, I was sure, but it seemed so fragile I was afraid to look any further. I turned around to see my friends staring in awe, as if they still didn't believe me that all of this was here.

"This is unbelievable" Mr. Simpson said after a few minutes. "How is it possible that this is all still here after so many years? It looks as if it had never actually been used?" he asked.

"Well, Mr. Doughty had a good explanation for it and I think he was right about it." Andy answered his question. "When Lord Blackhill was building the mansion, we know that Freemasonry almost came to a halt, or nearly went underground. He built the mansion with the intent for the lodge to have a place for their meetings if the Unlawful Societies Act of 1799 had passed and had included Freemasons on it. He was simple going to carry on in secret so the lodge had needed a secret place to hold their meetings in. As it turned out, Freemasons were excluded from the act as long as Each Private Lodge's secretary placed a list of members once a year with the local 'Clerk of the Piece'. By the time he had finished, he no longer needed the room, and so it was never used".

I nodded as I listened to his explanation. It made sense.

"But why didn't anyone else know about it? For example his son?" Lucy asked.

"Well, he never became a Freemason, like his father, so the secret was never passed onto him. We will never know I suppose if Lord Blackhill actually told the Lodge about this place, but they wouldn't disclose the information to anyone outside of the lodge. So if it wasn't used, then I guess it was eventually forgotten about." I explained.

"That's right" It was Andy's turn to agree with me "Mr. Doughty told me that when he had bought the mansion, no one could really tell him anything about it. As we know he was an antiques enthusiast and he had an interest in history. On one of his trips around the country he came across a text which related to the mansion. From that he managed to decipher the fact that there was a secret passage out of the mansion through the library. He started to research the subject to find out why a mansion would need a secret way in our out and eventually found out about the real story behind the mansion. He wrote a book about it, and don't worry, I just sent it to the solicitor, he should have it soon. I didn't want you to get your hands on it too soon, but I didn't want to destroy it either, it's an important piece of research that the old man did." He smiled at me slyly.

I shot him a look but decided not to comment. At least the manuscript was safe, that was all that mattered.

"I think I was the only person that he brought down here with him." Andy continued. "Doughty was quite odd you know. He was desperate for historians to take him seriously and he knew that this discovery would guarantee him that. But at the same time he wanted to keep it to himself- once he shared the news with someone, it wouldn't be a secret anymore. I think he wasn't sure what to do with this."

"But he made up his mind at the last minute, wouldn't you say?" I asked Andy "His last wish and request was to make a museum in the mansion and to share the discovery with others, and so we will." I looked at Mr. Simpson.

"That's right. We will honour his last wish and let people know what he accomplished" He nodded.

We all took one final look around the room and then each of slowly climbed the narrow staircase.

"Well guys" I turned to the kids "Although you can't say that the mansion is haunted, d you thing the new museum will attract tourists?" I asked them.

"Definitely" Vanessa said with confidence. "It has something that no other museum in Scotland does, lots of secrets and an interesting story to go with them" she looked very pleased.

Everyone laughed.

"I am sure that visitors to the museum won't get tired of hearing it," Lucy said.

It was time for them to go home so we said goodbye. PC Macleod took Andy and his friends with him back to the police station. I can't say that I felt sorry for them, I was glad that they didn't get away with stealing the mansion's secret and its treasure. I knew that they would get off lightly, but I wanted to preserve everything in the mansion, I didn't want them to ruin it. The rest was up to the police, it was out of our hands.

When everyone had left we went down to the kitchen for a cup of tea. We sat and talked about the evening's events, reliving the whole thing again. Mr. Simpson looked very pleased with the end result and I couldn't say that I wasn't. Although I had my doubts about the whole thing along the way, everything worked out for the best.

"Well, all is well that ends well" Mr. Simpson finally said. "I have some bad news I am afraid though". He looked at my colleagues and then at me.

"What is it?" Lucy asked with a concerned look after a couple of minutes. Billy had a puzzled look on his face. I had no idea what he was talking about either.

"I think you are not suited for this post at all Jimmy" he finally said "Tomorrow you are to return to London with me. I have an important matter which I need you to look into for me. For the time being, Lucy can take over as curator. I will see how she gets on in the role, and if necessary I'll appoint someone else. Do you think that you want to take on that responsibility Lucy?" he asked her.

"Erm, yes, definitely" she said surprised. "But Jimmy is a good curator and a good team leader" she added.

"Well, I don't agree with you on that" he replied. "Besides, I want to give someone young a good opportunity, so do you want to take the post? Or should I look for someone else?" he asked.

"I do want the post, thank you" she looked very pleased. Billy however didn't look too happy, but didn't say anything to that. I don't think he would have taken the opportunity if Mr. Simpson had offered it to him. I couldn't be happier with his decision. I am not the type of person that can stay in one place for too long and the promise of a new case made it even better for me.

"You'll come to visit us when you come back from Bruges, won't you?" Lucy said after a few minutes when everything finally sank in.

"Of course I will" I replied and I smiled. I realised that despite our differences we had become friends. We all sat in the kitchen for a while longer, still talking about everything that happened. I thought I would miss my colleagues and the mansion. I had become attached to the old house. I would definitely come to visit. When we all eventually went to bed I lay in bed, listening to the sounds of the old house, to the wind outside and I knew that finally nothing was going to wake me up in the middle of the night. That was a comforting thought and I fell asleep with a smile on my face.

Printed in December 2021
by Rotomail Italia S.p.A., Vignate (MI) - Italy

Royal Tea

The Chronicles of Kerrigan, Volume 4

W.J. May

Published by Dark Shadow Publishing, 2015.

Also by W.J. May

**Hidden Secrets Saga**
Seventh Mark - Part 1
Seventh Mark - Part 2
Marked By Destiny

**The Chronicles of Kerrigan**
Rae of Hope
Dark Nebula
House of Cards
Royal Tea

**The Hidden Secrets Saga**
Seventh Mark (part 1 & 2)

**The Senseless Series**
Radium Halos
Radium Halos - Part 2

**Standalone**
Shadow of Doubt (Part 1 & 2)
Five Shades of Fantasy

Glow - A Young Adult Fantasy Sampler
Shadow of Doubt - Part 1
Shadow of Doubt - Part 2
Four and a Half Shades of Fantasy
Full Moon
Dream Fighter
What Creeps in the Night
Forest of the Forbidden
HuNted

The Chronicles of Kerrigan

# Royal Tea
Book IV
By
Copyright 2015 by W.J. May

This e-book is licensed for your personal enjoyment only. This e-book may not be re-sold or given away to other people. If you would like to share this book with another person, please purchase an additional copy for each recipient. If you're reading this book and did not purchase it, or it was not purchased for your use only, then please return to Smashwords.com and purchase your own copy. Thank you for respecting the hard work of the author.

All rights reserved. No part of this publication may be reproduced, stored in or introduced into a retrieval system, or transmitted, in any form, or by any means (electronic, mechanical, photocopying, recording, or otherwise) without the prior written permission of both the copyright owner and the above publisher of this book.

This is a work of fiction. Names, characters, places, brands, media, and incidents are either the product of the author's imagination or are used fictitiously. Any resemblance to actual person, living or dead, events, or locales is entirely coincidental. The author acknowledges the trademarked status and trademark owners of various products referenced in this work of fiction, which have been used without permission. The publication/use of these trademarks is not authorized, associated with, or sponsored by the trademark owners.

All rights reserved.
Copyright 2014 by W.J. May
Cover design by: Book Cover by Design

Edited by: Chelsa Jillard

No part of this book may be used or reproduced in any manner whatsoever without written permission, except in the case of brief quotations embodied in articles and reviews.

http://www.wanitamay.yolasite.com

Facebook:
https://www.facebook.com/pages/Author-WJ-May-FAN-PAGE/141170442608149

**Cover design by:** Kellie Dennis - Book Cover by Design

*The Chronicles of Kerrigan*
Book I - *Rae of Hope* is FREE!
Book Trailer: http://www.youtube.com/watch?v=gILAwXxx8MU
Book II - *Dark Nebula* is Now Available
Book Trailer: http://www.youtube.com/watch?v=Ca24STi_bFM
Book III - *House of Cards* is Now Available
Book IV - *Royal Tea* - Now Available
Book V - *Under Fire*, coming June/July 2015
Book VI - *End in Sight,* Coming Fall/Winter 2015

## ROYAL TEA

The Queen of England has requested the help of the Privy Council. Someone is trying to kill her son's fiancé. HRH, the Prince plans to marry a commoner, and his bride has a secret no one knows but the Privy Council. She has a tatù. When the Privy Council turns to Rae for help, she can't possibly say no; not even when they make Devon her partner for this assignment. They are to pose as a couple and work undercover, as bodyguards, to protect the soon to be Princess of Wales.

Rae would rather be anywhere but with Devon, especially since she believes her mother to be alive, despite the Privy Council's assurances to the contrary. The question is, how can Rae find proof of life for her mother, come to terms with her feelings for Devon, and manage to save the Princess, all while dressed for tea?

When the enigma, the secrets and the skeletons in the closet begin to be exposed, can Rae handle the truth?

*What we try to hide about ourselves in life, is often revealed in death - our nobility, our fears, but most of all, our secrets.*

# Chapter 1

"My mother's alive," Rae whispered. "My mother's alive," she repeated louder, trying to grasp the unbelievable. In the movies, this would be where the main character would say that they had always felt the truth; that they had believed it, deep down inside, all their lives. Rae had never had that feeling. She had never sensed her mother's presence, except when she thought of her in the quiet moments. That didn't mean it couldn't be true. She stared at Carter, Jennifer, and Devon's faces only to see disbelief, pity and sympathy. *No shock? Why isn't anyone saying anything?*

"Impossible." Carter shook his head. "You can't use your mother's tatù. It must have been something else. Someone else's tatù you mimicked."

*Seriously? Are you still on that?* Not the fact that her mom could still be alive? "What if they have her? What if they're torturing her? For twelve years!"

"Who's they?" Jennifer, her Botcher, asked.

"You don't have your mother's tatù," Carter repeated. "You only have your father's."

An exasperated breath shot out of Rae's mouth. They weren't going to get anywhere until Carter had proof. She lifted her right hand and rubbed her fingers lightly together; a small blue light rose from her palm and turned to a yellow flame at the tips. She held it out so Carter could see it and then turned to show Jennifer and Devon. "It's fire. Not electricity, not a ball of ice... Fire." She clenched her hand into a fist, and the flame disappeared.

Carter stood, visibly shaken. "It can't be! Think hard. Have you touched someone with something similar? Did you pick up a new tatù and not realize?"

"That's impossible," she said, using his favorite word of the day directed back at him. "I would *know* if I picked up a new tatù. They don't just slip in unannounced."

"Maybe you got it from Kraigan. Did you touch him?" Carter walked around his large desk toward her.

"It's not from Kraigan." She pointed at her ex-boyfriend. "Dev, you saw it. I've used it before tonight."

The sympathy on Devon's face disappeared, replaced by dawning realization as he came over beside Rae. "I've seen it. She's had it for a while, but we didn't realize what it was."

"It can't be." Carter refused to accept it. "When were you with her? I thought I specifically asked -"

He trailed off, perhaps realizing what he had inadvertently revealed. Rae chose to tuck her questions about the unspoken part of his statement for later. Making Carter face the truth was more important at the moment. Her mind spun, trying to think of something that he couldn't argue with. *I've got it!*

Rae swung around and jerked up her shirt, exposing her tatù. It was larger than any of the other inks she had ever seen. It spread across her lower back, a sensual, delicate fairy with hues of pink, purple and green on her dress and the wings behind her. In the dimness of Carter's office, she stretched her arm behind her back and created a small flame so they could all see her tatù in detail.

"It sparkles." Jennifer tilted her head and squinted. "I've never seen that before."

Rae glanced at her from the corner of her eye. She had never shown Jennifer her tatù but had assumed she had seen photos from her file. Carter had taken about a zillion pictures that day in the infirmary. He wasn't saying a word now, or pulling out his camera. He seemed frozen to the spot. She focused her attention on Jennifer as she lowered her hand. "Look at the bottom of the tatù."

Below the fairy-girl, lay an ornate design with Celtic or Gaelic detail.

Jennifer's breath caught.

"You see them, don't you?" Rae asked. "They're miniature suns, part of my mom's tatù."

A warm finger traced the circles with the wiggly lines. *Devon*. Rae's heart sped from the realization that it was his touch.

He jerked away from her as if he had been burned. "Ow!" He blew on his finger.

She turned to see what had happened. "Oh, sorry!" She had burned him. She swore the flame snuffed when she spun around, but maybe, just maybe; it had grown when her heart had started racing.

She looked at Carter and waited until she held his gaze. She needed to convince him. She recreated the flame once more. "I just burned Devon." She brought the flame toward her face.

Jennifer caught Rae's wrist. "Don't."

Rae glanced at her, trying to read the hidden expression on her face. Did she know something? About her mom? "It's not going to hurt." She reached for Jennifer's hand with her free one. Jennifer would not let go. Rae let the flame disappear and only then did Jennifer drop her grip on her wrist.

The minute Jennifer let go; Rae rekindled the flame and stepped back, out of her Botcher's reach. She ran the blaze over the skin of her left forearm.

No smell of burning flesh, no pain, the flame just continued to flicker. Nothing happened.

"Impossible," Carter whispered, his eyes following Rae's hand.

Jennifer released an impatient sigh. "It's seems like her mother's ability." She sat on the corner of Carter's massive desk and set her long boots on the other end.

Rae shot Devon a look. He seemed just as surprised as she felt. That was a pretty bold move even for Jennifer; her leather covered derriere on one end with her legs stretched out across the head of the Privy Council's desk. She so hoped she would have that crazy courage when she was Jennifer's age.

Ironically, Carter didn't seem to notice. He began pacing. "Cromfield predicted it. There are notes in his journals and references. He mentioned the ability to carry two tatùs, but it was a theory. No one has ever carried two. Your father couldn't. His parent's tatùs combined and became one. Like everyone else's."

Rae could not see what the big deal was. Her tatù allowed her to carry and mimic hundreds, maybe thousands of tatù abilities. Her mothers' was just one more she carried.

Carter leaned over Jennifer and reached for something on the other side of his desk.

Rae did not miss the look that crossed Jennifer's face. She blinked. *She's in love with him.* Rae glanced at Devon to see if he had noticed. She nearly rolled her eyes, he was as oblivious as Carter. The thought crossed her mind. "How do you know my dad couldn't use both of his tatùs?"

Carter tapped the book he was flipping through. "Cromfield had a theory... he believed there had to be a matching of bloodlines or abilities." He scrolled through more pages. "I read it a few days ago. He believed, even tested, mixing tatùs had a negative effect. Every pair he bred created a combined tatù. Never two abilities."

Rae shrugged. She wanted to talk about finding her mother, not this. "Who cares? I already can use other people's tatùs, what's one more ability?"

Carter slammed the book closed. "Don't you see?" He glared at her, the old Carter coming through, the one Rae remembered from her first year at Guilder. The one she didn't like.

She stiffened and then straightened. "Nobody sees!" Her hands went automatically to her hips. "My mother is alive and all you can talk about is a damn theory! You can't get past some idea that's already happening. I have more than one ability. It's not new for me."

Carter crossed his arms over his chest, both of them forgetting about the presence of others in the room. "You are so your father's daughter! Your mother would never have acted like this."

Rae fired back. "I am NOT my father. I'm not evil or scary. The sins of the father are not the sins of this daughter! I might not be able to undo the past, but I am NOT being punished for who my father was!"

"Selfish child! This isn't just about you! Kraigan is going to have the same ability! He might already know it. He can use his father's and his mother's ability. Did you ever think of that? He might not need to steal other people's tatù. That psychopath is out on the loose!"

"And whose fault is that?" Rae hissed between clenched jaws.

"You tell me."

"I didn't let him out of prison. Only an idiot couldn't have figured he would go straight for me."

"Watch it, Rae." Devon had moved behind her and gently touched her shoulder.

Rae saw Jennifer standing beside Carter now as well. She jerked her shoulder away from Devon's touch. "Kraigan always wanted me dead. He needed the journal so he couldn't kill me until he had it."

"You had the journal?" Carter looked ready to explode.

"Yeah." The cat was out of the bag, and she didn't care. "He gave it to me just before you captured him. I've had it ever since. Not that it matters. I never got to read it and then I burned it." She inhaled a slow, long breath between her flaring nostrils. "Had I known there was a chance I could have my mother's ability, I might have been a bit more careful." She shot Jennifer an angry look. "Or knowing her ability in more detail could have helped as well."

"We did not know," Jennifer responded, each word perfectly enunciated. She had her emotions barely in check.

"Really? I find that hard to believe. The high and mighty Privy Council appears to know everything." She couldn't keep the sarcasm out of her voice. "Don't you think it might have been a good idea to tell me that my mother was still alive? Maybe when I got here? Or after I received my tatù? Or after Lanford tried to kill me?"

Carter tossed the book onto his desk. "Your mother is dead! I'm sorry, Rae. No one is sorrier than I am. If I-If we could have saved her, we would have!" His eyes begged her to understand, but he revealed more than he realized.

*He loved my mom!* Rae stepped back in surprise, bumping into Devon, who caught her before she stumbled and fell. It was all too much to take.

Carter's voice softened. "Your mother died in the fire."

Jennifer took a step closer to Rae. "Only your mother could have created that fire."

She still refused to believe it. "If she killed my father with her tatù, she would have survived the fire."

"No." Carter shook his head. "There were two bodies."

Rae blinked back the tears of frustration trying to force their way out. It had been one hell of a long day. Her next thought was crazy, but she knew it had to be true. "It wasn't my mom. It was Kraigan's mother. She died in the fire."

"Kraigan's?" The pity in Carter's eyes as he stared at her made her want to lash out at him. He didn't believe her. None of them did.

"Kraigan said his mother took off on him. She didn't. She must have died in the fire. Maybe my mom killed both of them."

"And then what, Rae?" Carter's voice dropped to a calm, quiet one. "What's your theory on what happened next?"

Theory? He was turning her words against her. She had mocked him on his theory of two abilities. "Maybe they kidnaped her. Maybe you guys did, and you're hiding her somewhere safe."

"Like under a witness protection program?" Carter asked, rubbing his neck.

Rae clapped her hands. "Exactly!"

Carter shook his head. "Don't you think if we had done that, we would have put you with her?"

She didn't have all the details figured out obviously. "Maybe you needed me around so you could figure out what my tatù was when I turned sixteen."

"And we couldn't have done that under witness protection?"

She threw her hands up in the air. "I don't know!"

Jennifer took both of Rae's hands in hers.

The action threw Rae of guard; Jennifer didn't comfort. She was hard as nails. Tougher than anyone.

"Your mother is gone. I honestly wish I could tell you she's alive somewhere, but I would be lying. I would have done anything to trade places with her. Anything."

*So you could have Carter all to yourself and make him love you, not her?* Rae shut her eyes tight, forcing that terrible thought out of her mind. *How could I even think that?* She let out a long sigh. "Okay."

"Okay?" Jennifer straightened and dropped Rae's hands. "You good then?"

"Yeah." She faked a yawn. "Sorry. It's been one heck of a long day."

"It has." Carter nodded. "Why don't we meet, here again, at thirteen hundred hours? We'll go over your assignment before you leave."

"We're leaving tomorrow?" Rae had barely had time to process what had happened, and she had agreed to jump immediately into another mission?

"When the Queen of England requests, you do not make her wait."

"We'll be ready, sir." Devon moved close beside Rae. "I'll take her back to her dorm. Make sure she's all right."

"Good." Carter nodded and walked across the room, opening the door for them. "Tomorrow. Thirteen hundred hours."

Rae let Devon lead the way out of the office. She stared at his strong back as she followed him. She thought of her tatù and swore she could feel the Gaelic suns burning against her skin. Her mother was alive. Just no one else believed it.

All she needed to do was find proof of life... and save the future Queen of England in the meantime. *Cake...right?*

# Chapter 2

Just outside of the Privy Council building on the concrete steps, Devon tried clearing his throat quietly. He did it again as they walked side by side across the parking lot.

Rae stared straight ahead to where his car was parked, all the while trying to watch him from her peripheral vision. His awkwardness wasn't something she was accustomed to.

He pulled out his car keys and pressed the button to unlock the doors.

When he cleared his throat a third time, Rae couldn't take it anymore. She was short on patience after the emotionally and physically draining day. "Just say it!"

His head shot up. "Pardon?"

"You've never been nervous around me." She rolled her eyes as she jerked the passenger door open. "Scratch that. You were. One time. When you dumped me." She closed her eyes, not wanting to see how that affected him, regretting the tone of her voice and the words she had said. "Sorry. That was a low blow and totally uncalled for." She tried to soften her voice, "Is there something you want tell me?"

Devon sat down in the car, while she leaned back against the seat and closed her eyes. He started the engine but didn't put the car into reverse to pull out. "Rae? Are you okay?" His voice trembled with emotion.

"Really?" Rae couldn't stop herself from blasting him. "Now you want to talk about feelings?" ***Now** he's all concerned how I felt about his breaking up with me?* She opened her mouth, ready to drown him in a tirade of words she had never used in her life, only to hesitate. Her brain was on overcharge, she was so full of a myriad of emotions, and she was shaking with it. The feeling was almost overwhelming, but there was a still, small, quiet voice in her mind telling her that she needed to look at Devon's face.

She took a deep breath, let it out slowly and turned to meet his concerned gaze. That's when she saw it, the truth. Devon wasn't talking about their break up. He simply meant today and everything that had happened inside Carter's office.

She turned away, closing her eyes and trying to supress her embarrassment for her outburst while simultaneously trying to still her shaking body, which she didn't seem to actually have control of at the moment. She barked a laugh, then coughed, trying to cover it. "I'm exhausted." Her laughter turned instantly into tears. She tried to smile and force them away, but inside the small confines of his sports car, it was just the two of them. No accusing eyes, no sense of responsibility, and no wall of civility that needed to be upheld at all costs; just her and Devon - the only boy who had managed to steal her heart, who then had rudely handed it back to her. *Jerk face...I don't want to be here. I don't want to feel this. I don't want him to see me like this. He doesn't deserve to see me like this. Who am I kidding? He doesn't care.*

The thought brought a fresh supply of salt water to her eyes. She buried her face in her hands. "I'll be f-fine. Can you jus' take me 'ome?" Her words came out muffled, but she refused to move, to let him see her face.

Stony silence was the answer, at least for several minutes. It felt like a lifetime later that Devon finally gave it some gas. Gravel crunched under the wheels as Devon pulled the car out of the small parking area of the house and down the lane to the main road. He said nothing.

When Rae felt the car turn left instead of right toward the dorms, she lifted her head. "Where..."

"You need to eat." Devon answered firmly. "I bet you've barely had anything all day."

*I'm a snotty, tear-stained, emotional mess. The last thing I want is to spend more time in his company looking like this.* "I'm not hungry." She tried to wipe the tears away without him noticing.

Devon concentrated on the road. "Then I'm hungry. I'll be quick. Just let me hit a drive through and grab a burger or something."

A golden pair of arches lit up the sky on their right. He pulled in and drove up to the intercom where they were greeted by a very unexcited male voice. "What can I get you?"

Devon raised an eyebrow and glanced at Rae. He tapped on the door handle as he checked out the menu. "How about a cheeseburger and fries? Make it a number four combo with a coke."

"Sure," came the monotone reply. "Anything else?"

Devon pointed at Rae.

Rae shook her head, only to have the scent of deep fried potatoes waft up her nose. *Oooh....fries...* Her stomach rumbled in protest to the action her head was doing. "Oh, fine." She leaned over Devon toward the intercom. "Can you add a number six, please? With sweet and sour sauce? And the lemonade." Her hand reached for Devon's arm to steady herself. She inhaled, hoping for the cool fresh air outside to mingle with the scent of French fries again, but instead, Devon's musky cologne filled her nostrils. He smelled good. Too good. She quietly drew in another breath, trying to get the scent to linger longer. She glanced up to see Devon watching her with an amused look on his face. Anger and embarrassment instantly had her already blotchy face glowing red. She quickly pulled away and dropped back against her seat wishing she could just disappear entirely.

Devon said nothing as he drove the car forward to the pickup window. He collected their order and paid for it.

Rae held the warm bags on her lap and stared out the window into the darkened night. She wanted to be away from him as soon as possible almost as much as she wished she could turn back time to when they had still been together. More than both those things, she wanted to gain back some control, because she was feeling decidedly out of it. *Why can't I just be cold? He seems to be. Why can't I be whatever the hell I want to be? I'm tired of emotions for now. I feel like I'm about to explode I'm so full of emotions. I need...I need to burn off some of this somehow.* "Are you feeling crazy? Like a bit of a rebel?"

Devon's foot lifted off the gas pedal as his words stumbled out. "Wh-What do you mean?"

Rae giggled as she felt a bit of the power balance between them shift her way. She'd caught him off guard. Right then, that helped somehow. She pulled a fry out of the bag and popped it in her mouth. As she chewed it, savoring the salty flavor, she commanded, "Pull the car over."

Devon turned into an empty shop parking lot and idled the engine. He turned in his seat to face her fully. *Look at Mr. Serious Face...I wonder what he thinks I have in mind?*

She tossed him his hamburger bag. "Let's eat in the car." She leaned back, set her feet on the dashboard and dug into her combo for another fry.

He caught the paper bag with one hand, still holding it in the air, staring rather pointedly at her feet. "What?"

"This car still smells brand new. You've had it a year now?" She stuck her straw into her drink. "I bet you've never eaten in here." A breath escaped from Devon's lips. Rae thought it sounded disappointed, but she couldn't be sure. "Be a rebel and wipe a greasy finger on the leather seat. I dare you."

Devon shook his head. He turned the car off and opened his window a bit. "I eat in here."

"Really?" Rae laughed as he stared at her feet on the dashboard. "You're going to clean this spotless tomorrow aren't you?"

"No, I won't." He shrugged and grinned, opening his bag and pulling his burger out. He hesitated before taking a bite. "The

PCs have a concierge type service that cleans and takes care of their agents' cars. I won't have to clean it myself."

It had been a long, hard day, and she could feel her body start to relax as her tummy grew content. The shaking had almost stopped completely. She was only mildly vibrating now, and most of that she could truly mark up to pure exhaustion. She would be fighting drowsiness on the ride home, but for the moment, she wished she could hang here with Devon all night. It felt like before, when she had first come to Guilder, and he had tutored her on what tatùs were, had introduced her to the world she now inhabited. She kind of didn't want it to end. "You can go outside. I'm good right here."

They ate in comfortable silence as the front window began to fog up. A man walking his dog went by, and Rae wondered if he assumed the windows were fogging for a different reason.

Devon must have had the same thought cross his mind. He started the engine and switched the defrost on high. "Is the journal really gone?"

She tossed her left over wrappers into the paper bag and balled it up, purposefully tossing it into the backseat while staring straight into his eyes. *Is that an eye twitch I see on his face? Serves him right for ruining the moment.* "I'm 'fraid so."

"You had it this entire time?"

And the good feeling that had been there a minute ago disappeared liked the fog on the windows. "Are you trying to accuse me of something?"

"I'm just wondering why you might have had the journal and not bothered to give it to the Privy Council."

He was such a dufus sometimes! "It's my journal."

"It's not yours. It was Simon Kerrigan's."

*What nerve!* "No, it was my uncle Argyle's and he entrusted it to me!" Her voice rose as she finished the sentence. She made a mental effort to lower her volume and control her tone, but her words still came out clipped and short. "It doesn't matter who had it, or what happened. It's gone now. Burned to nothing. Gone." And all the information in it, the information she had never had the chance to review.

"Did you make a copy of it?"

Good question. He was always the organized one, thinking and planning, two steps ahead of everyone. "No. I wish I had now, though." She hated how he put so much importance on the rantings of a dead man, her father. *No, I hate that he's right.* It annoyed her. *He's always right.* She sighed. "There was nothing in it that mattered. It was a high school club that never lasted and then some ramblings of a teenager with crazy plans. My dad was nuts."

Devon put his hands on the wheel but didn't put the car into drive. "Some people think he went coo-coo because of the double tatù." He kept his eyes straight ahead, refusing to meet her gaze.

His tone, his posture... it was obvious what he was implying and it made her even angrier. She leaned forward and using a tatù, forced his head to turn to look at her. "Is that what you think is going to happen to me? You think I'm going to go crazy because I'm double marked?"

His eyes softened a moment before turning unreadable. "I've never thought you were anything but normal, for our kind." He blinked before breaking the hold of her tatù and shifting away to face her properly. "I'm not the enemy, Rae. I never have been, nor will I ever be."

"Sometimes I wonder, Devon. You were so keen on getting close to me when I came here, and now it's like my touch burns you. What did I ever do to make you so scared of me?" She couldn't believe she'd said those words to him. She had barely let herself think them but as she said them aloud, she knew they were true. He was scared of her.

"I'm not scared of you."

"Then what is it? Why do you run like a dog with your tail tucked between your legs whenever I'm around? Why do you watch me from the shadows?"

"I don't!"

"Really?" Frustrated anger boiled inside of her. She tried to keep it down but after all the crap she'd had thrown at her in the last 24 hours, she needed to vent. Devon was an unfortunate, but convenient target.

"I almost hurled a fireball at you because I thought you were Kraigan!"

Devon rubbed his face with his hand. "RRGGH! You have no idea how frustrating you are!"

She blinked, surprised at his words and the agitation in his voice. It just didn't sound like him, like the controlled boy he'd become around her.

"You have no idea what it's like to be around you!" He threw his hands in the air. "You have all this amazing talent. You're smart, incredibly beautiful, and you rock a freakin' tatù that blows everyone's mind. The Privy Council sees you as an indestructible tool, but they are terrified you'll turn on them. Only Jennifer and Carter don't see it that way. They are constantly arguing with everyone, trying to convince them you are on our side... that you are not your father! Julian fights too. He's always defending you. He's furious at me because I don't say anything."

"Why not?" She knew she should focus on those who supported her, but at the moment, she only wanted to know why he didn't want to be her knight in shining armor.

"You don't need me to defend you. Every day you prove how much of an asset you are to the PCs."

She was always questioning herself and what the Privy Council thought of her. They were right to worry about her allegiance. She didn't know herself which side of the fence she wanted to be on. It made her so mad. She didn't want Julian to have to fight with people he worked for. She appreciated Carter and Jennifer's commitment, but the Privy Council had hired her, she hadn't asked if she could work for them. She clenched her fists tightly at her sides, her anger centering on Devon. The only person who seemed to be willing to tell her the truth. Well, at least some of it. "You always pick the safe route, don't you? Afraid to rock the ship?"

Devon pounded the steering wheel. "I'm not scared of you! Or your tatù!"

The anger boiled over. "Then what the hell is your problem?" she screamed. "Why are you avoiding me?"

"I'm scared of what I'll do when I'm around you!" His chest and upper body heaved up and down as he stared at her, and she knew she was seeing him lose control. Not completely, but enough, enough to see inside his shell.

# Chapter 3

Rae did not know how to respond to his words, to the intensity in Devon's eyes, the way he fought to control himself or the air inside the car that had grown thick with unspoken thoughts. Emotions ran through her at a pace so rapid, even she couldn't figure them out. As her body tensed, her tatù shot warnings off inside her like a nerve ending firing messages to the surrounding tissue.

Devon recovered quicker than she did. He closed his eyes and inhaled a long breath, slowly exhaling it before opening his eyes again. His face became a mask, hiding the emotions that had been so clearly displayed a moment ago. "I apologize. I was completely out of line. I shouldn't have said that."

*But you did.*

"They were heat of moment words." Devon shifted the car into drive and slowly pulled out of the parking lot. "I didn't mean them. That came out completely wrong."

She straightened her jacket and flicked an imaginary speck off her thigh to cover the sensation of having the ground open up beneath her. She felt like they had been on the verge of some actual truth, raw, unfiltered. But he had shut down so quickly. *How can he do that? How can he be like that? How can I feel safe with him one moment, then totally exposed and defenseless the next? How....How can I be like that? How can I have the same protection? I deserve it.* "Okay." So the conversation was over, before it even had a chance to start. Well she could do that too.

"What I mean is, we are about to be working together on a mission. That needs to be our primary focus. Whatever Carter has planned, there is a reason he wants the two of us working as partners. If the Queen of England requests the Privy Council's help, we don't say no." He grinned at her, leaving her wondering if something was truly wrong with him. *After that outburst he turns all controlled and dimpled again?* She loved his dimples, but at the moment they left her cold.

There he sat across from her, dimpled and back on track. "Carter would only hire the best for this mission. That says something about your skills and mine."

"I never doubted my ability, or yours." She pressed her lips tight and stared out the front window at the passing forest as it gave way to the buildings and surrounding walls of Guilder Boarding School.

"I just meant..." Devon's voice trailed off as he pulled into the front gates of Guilder. The mood inside the car shifted back to complete professionalism as if Guilder and the Privy Council had some kind of hold on their personal feelings. It felt oddly combative to Rae, to maintain the cool, controlled façade. She wondered if Devon felt the same way underneath it all.

When Devon parked his car, Rae jumped out before he had a chance to cut the engine. "See you tomorrow in Carter's office." She couldn't get away fast enough.

Devon got out, standing between his car and the open door. "Do you need a lift?"

She shook her head and turned to go. She paused and glanced back, her mother had taught her to be polite... her father had taught her to be tactical. "I'm just going back to Aumbry House. Thanks for the food, and for the clarification on where you and I stand." She had meant to try and make the words sound grateful. Instead, she sounded sarcastic. She turned, cursed herself for missing the mark, and ran to her dorm room, using Jennifer's tatù, knowing Devon wouldn't be able to keep up with it.

Once safely inside Aumbry she raced up the stairs, thankful for the lateness of the evening. No students were around to stop her; they were all probably sleeping. Once inside her dorm room, she slid down against the door in a boneless puddle and let the tears fall.

Everyone seemed to have lost faith today. She lost the journal, Kraigan had escaped, Devon was out of reach and her mother might be alive, but no one seemed to believe it other than her. There was no denying it. Today had kicked her butt, hard core.

She took a deep breath, trying to collect herself, while trying not to think about how the phrase sounded as if she had shattered into a million pieces, or about how that truly matched how she felt. She told herself tomorrow would be a fresh start. She would concentrate on her job, ignore Devon as much as possible, and on her own time, work to prove that her mother was still alive.

Right now, she needed to shower and go to bed.

She stood and walked over to her desk, tossing her phone on it. A small blue light flashed indicating a text message. As she shucked off her jeans, she checked who it was from.

Luke.

**Heard there was a situation in Stoke. Word on the street is Kraigan's escaped. Wanted to make sure you were ok.**

She wrinkled her nose at the smoky smell coming from her jeans and reached in to turn them inside out. A pinging noise sounded as something fell out of her pocket. She glanced down and around the floor but saw nothing. Her phone buzzed again.

**Luke again. Are you alright? XKs know for definite that Kraigan's escaped. They think he left the country. Please reply.**

Rae didn't want Luke to worry. She picked up her phone and sent him a reply that she was fine and appreciated his concern. She hesitated after she hit the send button. How much did he know about Kraigan? She believed his concern was genuine. She just wished she knew how much he knew.

After tossing her fire smoked clothes into the garbage in the bathroom, she jumped in the shower. The hot water splashed against her face and she chose to focus on Luke instead of Devon. Luke was a decent guy. He knew about tatùs, about her past and did not pass judgment. He liked her, had not lied to her as far as she knew, and she was crazy not to give him the attention he deserved. *Compared to Devon...*that made her wonder. She hadn't yet actually compared them. He wasn't tatùed like Devon. She groaned. *Devon*. Nothing would ever happen between Devon and her. The sooner she accepted that, the better. Yet her heart played back their history in her mind anyway.

Had it been two years already since she had woken up with the fairy tatù? It seemed a life time ago that she had been a normal person, and yet the time seemed to have flown. The ink that covered her lower back was different from a tattoo, it gifted her with her supernatural power. Devon had a tatù, a fennec fox, which gave him heightened senses, super speed, and agility. Rae had her father's—and her mom's—tatù. The newly discovered fire ability came from her mother, the ability to mimic other tatùs came from her father, the one person in the world she had no issue with being dead. Her power was unique, even in their already exclusive and insular world. She could copy anyone's tatù. No one had been able to do that except her father, and Kraigan, her half-brother. He didn't have the super ability she did of being able to recall any tatù she had ever used. He had to steal an ability, and when he touched someone else with a tatù, he stole their ability till he touched another. Or can he? She had only just discovered her second ability. Given their history and genetics, she couldn't afford to discount the possibility that Kraigan also had a second ability that he'd kept hidden. Of course, at the same time, she knew nothing about his mother or her father's parents so any speculation would be premature. Something else was far more important.

Kraigan wanted her dead. *Nice guy.* He had run, and she would have to be ready for his return.

The Privy Council wanted Rae because of her singular ability. So did the Xavier Knights, another black ops division for British Intelligence. Supposedly Kraigan worked for them, as did Luke, and he knew about Kraigan but didn't seem to be a fan. Rae turned the water hotter against her back. If Kraigan was a loose cannon she would never trust, how could she put any faith in the Xavier Knights or Luke? He might not be tatùed, but he apparently worked for the enemy.

Or maybe the Xavier Knights weren't bad. Maybe Kraigan had duped them into thinking he was the good guy, and she was the baddie. It didn't seem too impossible to make people think she was her father's daughter; many of her actions in the last few years could conceivably be misinterpreted. Even her Uncle Argyle, the man who had helped raise her since her parent's deaths when she was six, seemed to have his doubts.

Now that was another running theme in her life. People watching her, waiting for her to turn into a monster. From some of what Devon had said, they still were. What would it take to prove herself? Did she even want to prove herself? Could she possibly be fighting for the wrong side? Her mind spun with questions.

*Enough!* Rae jerked the shower handle to off and whipped a towel around her. She stomped back to her room and still half wet, fought to put her pj's on. She flicked her finger to switch the lights off and jerked the covers back and then over her. She threw her head onto the pillow and shut her eyes tight.

Half an hour later Rae lay in her bed, hands behind her head, eyes staring at the ceiling, trying to get her brain to relax so she could fall asleep. At least the inner anger and frustration had dissolved. Now, the course of the entire day kept running over and over in her head. It played from beginning to end, hovering painfully over the moments in the car with Devon, before slipping forward to when she'd removed her burned jeans and heard a sound.

*Her mother's key!*

She shot into a sitting position and glanced at her desk. She'd left it in the pocket of her jeans. She burst out of her room to the bathroom to check in the bin. A strong smoke smell greeted her when she flung open the door and raced to the garbage can. Thankfully it hadn't been emptied; her jeans were still there. Just no key.

She checked the entire bin and sighed. *Not there.*

She traced her steps. Maybe she had left it in Julian's car, or Carter's office, or Devon's car when they had stopped. She had come into her dorm and jumped in the shower-

Wait! When she sent Luke a text, she'd stripped down. Something had fallen. *It had to be the key!*

She raced back to the room, flipped on the light using Molly's tatù and dropped to the floor. Checking on the bed with no success, she crawled over to the desk and tilted her head to check the area. She finally found it near the radiator, half hidden by dust and shadows. She grabbed it and stared at it.

The brass key had a number on the side, seventeen. Rae knew nothing about the key. Hand, not machine, had engraved the number. It was precious to her in a way her father's journal could never have been. The journal had been something hated as much as she had wanted to crack its secrets. This key, by comparison, was priceless to her. It could be, literally, the key to finding her mother alive somewhere in the world. She had to protect it, much better than she had the journal. At least no one knew it existed. That was something at least. She needed an excellent spot to hide it. She turned around, eyes scanning the room and everything in it, searching for inspiration. It didn't take long.

She went over to the little china cabinet of porcelain figurines and felt along the back. A little nail stuck out, and she leaned over to hang the key off the protruding metal. No one would look there, and if they did, they wouldn't realize it was anything special. With time, it could help her solve the puzzle of her mother's so called death. She had no idea how it connected together, but she had no doubts she'd find out eventually.

She turned off the lights and went back to bed, snuggling deep into the sheets, and even though her brain refused to stop thinking, her body finally fell asleep from pure exhaustion.

She began dreaming, a reminiscence from her first year at Guilder somehow metamorphosed itself into a nightmare. The memory itself was a nightmare, just with the added twist that only dreams can provide.

A very large man with an overgrown comb-over stood over her in a dark, round room where the shadows on the wall seemed as malicious as the hateful man looming above her. Rae lay stretched out on the floor, her arms and feet in shackles.

*Lanford.*

She pulled and twisted, trying to break free of the prison holding her. She was helpless. Lanford glared at her, his face rotting away from death and pure evil. He said nothing, but a recording echoed in the cold, stone room. Rae knew it was her father's voice. She shut her eyes and tried to ignore the words, but her hands were tied so she couldn't plug her ears or turn off the sound.

*A lifespan is spent, seeking success and happiness. People chase after dreams, careers, ambitions, faith, partners, and money; all in the hope of finding the success and contentment they so long for. The only place we need to search is within ourselves. Our inner powers will move us forward-we must show the world our tatùs. Our capabilities and potential are far greater than anything man has ever done, or will do. We are above mankind-above the law which rules over them...*

"Turn it off," she begged, her head twisting side to side. "I won't join you."

A horrible laugh escaped Lanford's terrible mouth, his lips shaking, rotten teeth falling out.

One hit Rae in the face. She thrashed and kicked. "No!" she screamed as he leaned down, closer and closer to her.

"Rae! Rae! Wake up!"

Rae's hand broke free, and she shot a bolt of electricity at the evil leaning over her. The body hit the wall with an oomph. She sat up, her body covered in sweat, ready to throw another bolt of electricity.

The body scrambling to get up was much smaller than Lanford's... and more feminine.

"Rae! It's me, Molly!"

Rae flicked her finger at the switch by her door, and the lights blinked instantly on.

"Molly?"

Molly stood slowly, rubbing the back of her head. "I'm lucky you used electricity. You'd have nearly killed anyone else with the bolt you just sent through me."

Rae blinked against the bright light, trying to clear the remnants of her dream away. "I was dreaming."

"I know. You were screaming. I could hear you from my room."

"How'd you get in?" Rae couldn't shake the caution warnings her body still felt from the nightmare.

"You left your door unlocked." She yawned. "You okay?"

Rae laid back down. "Yeah. Stupid dream."

"Do you want me to stay?"

Rae's eyes had closed; she smiled against her pillow. Molly was awesome. No friend could be truer, or more loyal. "I think I'm okay." She could feel herself drifting back to sleep. The bad dream seeming silly now as she thought about her friend.

"Good." Molly said something else but Rae couldn't make out the words nor did she have the energy to ask Molls to repeat them. She did hear Molly say as she turned out the light, "Relax. Dreams don't mean anything."

# Chapter 4

Rae slept through her alarm and woke late. She pulled her hair into a ponytail, threw on black stretch pants and a tight fitting black shirt. She grabbed a zippered cotton jacket as she raced out the door, stopping in the bathroom to brush her teeth and throw on mascara. As she sped down Aumbry's staircase, she switched to Jennifer's leopard tatù, and raced from Guilder to the mains gates of the Privy Council's secret location. A normal person running hard would have taken at least half an hour to get there. She made it in just under ten minutes with the leopard ink.

She skidded to a halt just outside the main gates and dropped her hands to her knees, expecting to be out of breath and gasping for air. She worried her heart would explode from the exertion she just put on it.

*Nothing.*

Not even winded.

She grinned and made a mental note to remember that for future reference. No wonder Jennifer always appeared calm and collected. Her tatù had serious pros.

She punched her code into the gate, impatiently slipping through as soon as it began to open. Rae knew that cameras hidden everywhere were watching her every move. As she passed the narrow road that lead to the training facility, she glanced down it. The leaves on the trees had just been budding and now were full. Had spring happened that fast? It was like she had blinked and now nature had come to life. Little seedlings fell to the ground. With the breeze pushing through the tree tops, they fell like floating feathers. It was picturesque to watch, and Rae suspected by later this afternoon rain would fall and change their flight to straight downward spirals. She paused a moment to watch, wanting to capture the beauty of the moment. Nature was more powerful and magical than anything a tatù could ever do.

A black car pulled in through the gates and passed her. The darkened windows hid the faces inside. She picked up her pace and followed it toward the large, old Tudor house that worked as the offices for the Privy Council. *Or office.* Rae had no clue if anyone else worked out of it. She only ever saw Carter there; it could even be where he lived for all she knew.

She took her sweet time making her way up the concrete stairs to the main door, curious to find out who would exit the car. Unfortunately, she reached the top of the steps without any signal that the occupant of the vehicle was in the mood to oblige her curiosity. Not wanting to make it obvious that she was stalling, she pulled open the door and stepped inside.

Several, slightly raised voices floated out of Carter's open office door. She recognized Devon's, Carter's, and Jennifer's, but there was another male she did not know.

Instead of stepping into the middle of what didn't seem to be a pleasant conversation, she leaned against the doorframe, deciding to wait until someone noticed her and invited her in. She need not have bothered.

Devon looked up the moment she appeared, as if some inner sense had clued him in to her arrival. Carter, Jennifer and the boy she hadn't recognized continued to talk. He looked a few years older than Devon, with mousy brown hair and glasses. He spoke quietly and only seemed to add to the conversation when needed.

"Curtis, do you feel this will work?" Carter asked the boy.

Curtis nodded. "I believe it will. I've created documentation and records to show their connection. I've falsified some reports and also incorporated video with the two of them together. It will appear completely legit. If the Queen's guard or anyone looks into their history, it will show a connection." He pushed his glasses up his long, narrow nose. "No one's going to prove otherwise."

Jennifer flipped through the iPad Curtis set on the table. "These look real," she murmured.

"Rae!" Carter called out and beckoned her into the room. "Let's get you caught up to speed." He handed her a thick file and moved beside Jennifer, so the only vacant spot was beside Devon. *Just where I do and don't want to be...fabulous.*

"Sorry I'm late." Out of habit, she ran her fingers over her hair checking for escaping frizzies.

Jennifer slid the tablet in front of her. "Curtis has set all this up." She nodded at the boy to her right. "He's going to be your gopher."

"Gopher?"

"She means go for this, gopher that." Curtis chuckled. "Thanks, Jen." He held his hand out to Rae. "Nice to meet you, Rae Kerrigan." He smiled. *Hm...a handshake...freely offered...either he forgot my ability or...*

Rae had figured by now everyone knew that she copied tatùs by touch. There were people at Guilder who moved to the other side of the hallways when she walked down them to avoid accidentally touching her. In her world, to have someone offer a handshake was a big deal now. Rae leaned across Devon to return the hand shake. She avoided eye contact with Devon and shook Curtis' long cool fingers. His tatù immediately zinged through her.

She blinked and watched him with interest as she dropped her head to the side. "Your ability is similar to Carter's."

He nodded. "Slightly. Carter is able to see memories, like watching a video. His ability allows him to see things, with or without them knowing. I absorb memories through skin-to-skin contact as well, but differently." He stroked his chin and watched her. "You have my ability now?"

"Yes. Sorry." Crap, he didn't know! She waited for him to react, inwardly cringing.

"No problem." He waved his hand. "I'm a tech-guy, science nerd." He pushed his glasses up his nose again. "Can you touch your partner beside you and tell me what you see?"

"Devon's not my partner." Her heart fluttered at the assumption. Had he seen something in her past to make him think that?

Curtis flicked his wrist. "He will be for this mission."

"Oh yes, sorry." She reached for Devon and hesitated a moment before touching him. "May I?"

He shrugged. "Sure."

She tentatively brushed her fingers against his bicep. She quickly pulled her arm back. Nothing happened.

"You have to hold it longer," Curtis said. "The memories are only absorbed by skin-to-skin contact. You must remain touching the person in order to see the entire memory."

"That's the same as Carter's."

He shook his head. "It's different." He motioned again. "Try it again."

She reached for Devon's arm again.

"No, it has to be directly on the skin," Curtis said.

Rae gave Devon an apologetic glance. She slipped her hand into his and focussed on the strings of Curtis' tatù. She stared at their two fingers entwined perfectly together. She didn't know what to expect or what she was supposed to do.

Curtis cleared his throat. "Devon, think about something you did as a child."

A blurry image began to form in Rae's head. It slowly cleared. A bright sun reflected off the cars parked along the road and a boy appeared pushing a bike. Rae recognized him as the younger version of Devon. He walked his bicycle around the corner to an empty tennis court. He rested his bike against the chain-link fence as he clipped his helmet on. Rae moved closer to watch him. She could almost feel herself brush up the chain-link fence and mentally moved around the fence so she could see him more clearly.

Young Devon looked at her as she moved, and she almost wondered if he could see her. He grabbed his bike and moved it to the middle of the open court. He got on it and gave himself a push and began pedaling and trying to steer. The front wheel wobbled as he struggled to gain control. He managed to turn the bike around on the far end and picked up speed. Going too fast as he rode toward the fence, he tried to break with his feet on the ground but didn't have enough control. His hands jerked free as he reached out to protect himself.

Rae grabbed the bike to steady the handle bars and stop him from falling.

"Thanks!" the young Devon said in a squeaky voice. "I was about to crash."

Rae pulled her hand out of Devon's and gasped. The fresh summer air, green grass, and hot pavement disappeared. She was immediately back in the present, standing at the table surrounded by Carter, Jennifer, Curtis and a shock-faced Devon.

Devon rubbed the hand she had been holding, unable to tear his eyes away from her.

"My ability is unique," Curtis nodded at the two of them in understanding. "President Carter can search through memories." He chuckled. "I have the uncanny ability to step into them."

Devon cleared his throat; his eyebrows pressed together. "I remember that day. I was seven, determined to ride with no training wheels. I wanted to show my father I could do it on my own. I remember a teenager helping me when I went too fast and nearly lost control. She steadied the bike and then... disappeared. I never knew to this day that it was Rae."

Rae looked back and forth between Devon and Curtis. "I was never there."

Curtis pointed at Devon. "But he remembers it. He believes it to be true now. Somehow he now thinks that it has always been so. He's just thinks he's making the connection now that it was you."

"But it wasn't me back then. I'm younger than Devon. It couldn't have possibly been me."

"I know," Devon said. "You just shared it with me now, yet it seems like...like you were there that day. Someone was there." He hesitated. "And they looked just like you." He scratched his head. "Now that's one crazy tatù."

Curtis leaned against the table. "It does have its benefits." He watched Rae for a moment. "You cannot change the course of history with this ability, nor change a person's path. If you try to go back to save another, it won't work." He glanced at Carter before returning his gaze to Rae. "But if, say, you are friends with the soon to be Princess of Wales and someone questions how the two of you know each other, it just might come in handy." He crossed his arms over his chest.

"You want me to use this tatù, so the soon to be princess thinks we are friends?"

"No." Carter pointed to the thick file on the table in front of her. "You and Devon need to know everything inside there like the back of your hand. Memorize it all and be familiar with all of it. The two of you are going to work together to protect the soon to be princess. She knows you both have tatùs."

"She does?" Devon and Rae asked the question at the same time.

Jennifer scoffed. "You were right, Carter. They are going to be perfect together." She walked around the table. "The Queen has hired us, but she has no idea about our tatùs. The son's fiancé, on the other hand, does. She is one of us."

"What?" Devon shook his head. "You've got to be joking!"

"I'm not." Jennifer gave him an annoyed look usually reserved for Rae. "She's one of us and someone wants her dead. There have been several efforts to sabotage the Prince's relationship."

Carter continued, "Last week there was an attempt on her life. A clear message was left that no member of the royal family would ever bare the mark of a tatù. We need to find those responsible and protect her."

"That's where you two come in."

"What do you want us to do?" Rae detested the fact that the soon to be princess was being judged because of a tatù. It was probably some royal old fart who couldn't stand women or anyone with talent.

"Protect the soon to be princess," Carter said. "While posing as a couple. Rae will pretend to be a close friend of Sarah. She knows the background of your jobs."

Rae blinked and blinked several times again. *A couple?* She must have heard Carter wrong. "I'm sorry. A couple of what?"

Devon nudged her under the table with his foot so no one else would see.

Face completely serious, Carter continued. "Fake romance. Pretend the two of you are together. It's the only way we can get Devon and you into the castle and included in the Royal Tea fundraiser gala in two weeks."

Rae looked at Devon to see if he had known about this. He had the same questioning expression on his face.

Carter rubbed his hands together. "Don't look so frightened, you two. When Rae arrived, Devon you showed her the ropes. The two of you were best of friends that year and seemed close all through last year as well. I don't understand why you both look terrified by the thought."

"I know." Curtis took his glasses off and began cleaning them with his shirt. "The Privy Council and Guilder spend an unsurmountable amount of time on teaching us how wrong two people with tatùs is. Now it sounds like we're encouraging it."

"Yeah," Devon finally found his voice and spoke. "I'm not sure this is such a good idea."

"You can't pretend to think Rae's hot?" Jennifer gave him a disbelieving look. "Use your brain, mister-rule-book-boy. It's a mission. If you can't do it, we'll find someone else who can." She pulled out her phone. "What about Julian? Or Riley?"

Devon put his hand over Jennifer's. "I can do this."

"Good." She stuffed her phone back in her pocket. "Everything's arranged. Devon, you are going to be going as yourself. We want people to know you attended Guilder. It might entice the stalker if they know more tatù people are around." She turned to Rae. "You cannot go as Rae Kerrigan. Your background, character, lifestyle is all sorted inside your file. Your name is Karen Carter. You attended Oxford with Sarah. You've been out of the country and have just recently returned. We suggested America because of the accent you now have." She shot Rae a look, expecting her to disagree. When Rae didn't, she continued. "We've set you up in a flat, all your clothing and the belongings you will need are already inside. You needed new clothes... Higher ranking than a black ops." She pulled out a pair of keys and handed one to each of them. "The flat across you will have two other black ops working behind the scenes to make sure you two don't mess everything up."

"Jennifer!" Carter warned. "They are there to help you out. Any background info you need, gadgets, I.D." He waved his hand and looked at Devon. "You know, the usual stuff."

Rae couldn't get around the fact that the Privy Council wanted them to pretend to be a couple! Were they crazy? "I don't think I..."

"Who's in apartment two?" Devon asked, cutting her off.

"I am," Curtis said.

Devon clapped him on the back. "Glad to be working with you again." He said to Rae, "You'll love Curtis' gadgets. He makes MacGyver look amateur."

Curtis laughed. "Wait till you see some of the neat tech stuff I've made."

"You said two techs?" Rae asked Carter, trying to ignore Devon and Curtis. They seemed like best friends. "Is Jennifer coming as well?"

Carter shook his head. "I'm afraid not. She's going to be trying to chase down any leads on Kraigan."

"I'm coming."

Rae turned at the sound of a quiet voice near the door.

A tiny, dark-haired girl peeked into the room. She clutched a cane in one hand and took a step into the room, using the cane for support. "Sorry I'm late. I got called into a mission as we pulled in. Is everybody filled in?"

Rae stared in amazement. "Maria?"

*You got it girl; it's me. You ready to kick some bad-guy ass?*

## Chapter 5

*Tough Maria?* When had that happened? Rae had always known her as quiet, slightly unsure and shy. Where did the cane come from?

Devon reacted faster than Rae. He rushed to Maria and held his arm out for support.

"I'm fine." She ignored his offered hand and made her way beside Rae. Maria smiled and gave Rae a big hug. "I've missed you." She turned back to Devon and shot him a shy smile. "Sorry, I'm just determined to get better and I need to do stuff on my own or I never will."

"What happened?" Rae relaxed. This was more the Maria she knew.

Carter cleared his throat. "Maria's been working with us since the summer. She was on a black ops mission where an accident happened."

"What were you doing?" Rae couldn't picture Maria doing the same stuff she had been doing.

"It's classified." Carter crossed his arms over his chest, his face giving away nothing.

Maria smiled, her brown eyes sparkling as she looked at Rae. "It's so good to see you. It feels like forever."

Rae hugged her friend again. "It does feel like a long time. Are you okay?"

Maria waved her hand. "Yeah. I hurt my back. Tried to play the hero when it's not really my style. I'm more of a behind the scenes kind of person." She gave Curtis a smile. "We working together again?"

"You got it, little one." Curtis winked at her. "No more super hero stunts for you then?"

Rae was dying to know what had happened but knew she couldn't ask. She glanced at Devon, but he looked as baffled as she felt, so she knew he had no idea either.

"Maria's tatù is a great way to communicate. She's able to send Intel in as needed without having to worry about wires or being traced."

Devon nodded enthusiastically. "Great idea. I could have used her a number of times already." He put his arm around Maria in a brotherly way. "I'm glad you're here."

"Wouldn't have it any other way." She leaned into Devon.

Jennifer walked around the table and stood by Rae. She flipped the light on the table that lit it up from underneath, revealing a blueprint of Buckingham Palace. "Maria's got a handy ability. The only problem is that whoever she's working with, can't send Intel back. We had some miscommunication, and she went dashing in to try and warn her partner." Her eyes darted over the blueprint. "That's why we felt she would be perfect for this mission. She can do her mind speaking thing to Rae, and Kerrigan can answer back." She pointed to a large room on the left side of the castle. "This is where the Royal Tea Masquerade Ball is going to be held. According to our theories, this is where Sarah is going to be most vulnerable. If someone wants her dead, it could happen at any moment, but this would be the perfect opportunity to do it."

Carter tapped on several locations. "There will be several entrances and exits that are guarded, but still permeable. It's tea with a soon to be princess, so everyone wants to attend. Tickets are sold at auction, and there are radio stations raffling off tickets. Anyone can attend so it's next to impossible to control who will be there."

Jennifer flipped Rae's file open and skimmed through several pages. "Here is a list of who is already attending. However, there are still another hundred to two hundred prize tickets to be won. This thing is massive."

From the long list in front of her, Rae could tell. "So you want us to guard S-Sarah?"

"Without being detected. She has body guards. You two need to go in undercover. No tatù abilities out in the open," Carter said.

"Or just don't get caught using them," Jennifer added.

"Do you know if it is someone working alone? Do you have any idea of who it could be?" Devon asked as he stared at the list on the table.

"We have almost nothing," Carter said.

Rae stared at the thick file. Sure looked like a lot to her.

"It is a viable, legit threat."

"What is Sarah's tatù?" Rae looked around the table.

Nobody responded. She checked the front of the file and found the page on the prince's fiancé. "Tatù unknown?"

Jennifer frowned. "It's not exactly a question you openly ask the soon to be Princess of Wales in front of the Queen of England!"

"So you mean, you don't know what she can do?"

"Not at the moment." By the expression on Jennifer's face, she didn't like having to admit to it.

"Have you checked with her father? Is he inked?" Rae checked the paper in her hand.

Jennifer let out an exasperated breath.

Carter touched her shoulder. "These are all good questions, Rae. All things we've looked into. Her father is not tatùed. Her mother passed away four years ago from cancer. There is no record of her mother's tatù marking. She could not have attended Guilder since it was still an all-boys school. She was a stay at home mother. She entertained and was well received in London. Her husband built a millionaire business from the ground up, which brought himself, his wife and daughter into the elite circle. Sarah met Prince Philip at Oxford."

"If they met at Oxford, won't the Prince find it weird that I attended Oxford, and we never met?" Rae asked.

"Sarah is older than you. She's twenty-two. You attended Oxford one year, then went abroad. You're nearly nineteen now, so we've thrown two more years on your ID." Jennifer closed the file and handed it over to Rae. "Study it, know everything. You'll find answers around the questions."

*I already know it.* Maria told Rae through her telepathy ability. *If you forget something, I can help. I have all your information so you can just ask me.*

*I think I'm going to have to.* Rae smiled, loving that no one else in the room could hear them. *How far can you reach now with communicating?*

*Further, than you'd believe. What about you?*

*I'm not really sure. I haven't used it in a long time.*

*Then we'll have to strengthen yours.*

*Thank you.*

*For what?*

*For doing this mission with me. It helps having someone normal in this group.*

Maria giggled, then realizing she had done it out loud she straightened. *Let's go get us some bad guys.* "When do we leave?"

"Now." Curtis grabbed a backpack off a chair near the door and slipped it over his shoulder. "You driving with me or with your friend?"

"She should drive with you," Carter spoke before Maria could respond. "Devon and Rae need to go over the file and get to know each other."

Devon cleared his throat. "I think we'll be fine, sir."

Jennifer handed Rae a backpack as well. "Curtis has a bag of computer gadgets. This one's more yours and my style." Her eyes met Rae's and held them. "You are beyond talented, Rae. Get through this."

*And we'll focus on finding my mother?* Rae asked her using Maria's telepathy.

Jennifer gave her a brisk nod. "Devon?"

"Yes?"

"Rae's talented, but she has a habit of thinking with her heart instead of her head. Be the smart one here."

*Hold up a sec... What?*

"Yes, mum." Devon nodded.

*Smug little, brown-nosing...* Rae was so going to kill him before this mission **was** finished.

As Maria headed out with Curtis, Rae made sure to be a step ahead of Devon. She could hear Jennifer questioning Carter how she and Devon were going to pull the couple thing off.

Devon obviously heard it as well because he came up beside her and said quietly, "There's nothing wrong with thinking with your heart."

She didn't know if he was trying to hint at something between the two of them, or just trying to give her a boost of confidence for the mission. She didn't need the later. She was a Kerrigan, confidence came with the name. "You should try it sometime then, Dev. Being the responsible, logical one isn't always what it's cracked up to be."

He fumbled for his keys as they stepped outside. Maria and Curtis were already pulling out of the parking lot. "It seems to be working fine for me."

She sighed, wishing that for ten minutes they could just talk without rules, barriers or anything hanging over their heads. Hanging over *his* head. "You should go out on a limb."

"Pardon?"

She opened his passenger car door and got in, setting the backpack on the ground between her feet. "Go out on a limb, Devon. That's where the fruit is."

## Chapter 6

Rae and Devon sat in awkward silence as he drove them out of the city. They only spoke when necessary. She asked him to stop at Guilder on their way past so she could pick up a few things. She wrote Molly a note and grabbed her make up bag and a few other necessities.

As Devon headed onto the motorway, Rae pulled her phone out of her leather coat. She dialed Luke's number.

"Watchya doing, Rae?" His low voice echoed through the phone making Rae smile.

"Calling you." She laughed and pretended not to notice the scowl on Devon's face.

"Everything alright? Your text last night seemed kind of cryptic."

"Sorry about that. It was a long day and late night." She wanted to ask him what he knew about Kraigan. Just didn't know how to approach the subject without sounding suspicious.

"I hope the PCs are paying you well."

She smiled. "I'm guessing much better than you."

Devon shot her a look. She remembered his ink gave him the ability to hear both sides of the phone conversation.

She cleared her throat. "Speaking of work. I'm heading out now."

"Again? Sheesh! They don't give you a break." Luke sighed. "Sorry. My bad. I'm just jealous how dedicated you are to your work. I won't keep you. Why don't you text me or call me when you have a chance?"

"I've got a bit of time now." *Now! Ask him now about Kraigan!*

"Sweet!"

"I wanted to ask you something..."

"Ask away."

He was so easygoing. It made her feel like she was using him. She straightened. That wasn't what she was doing. "What do you know about Kraigan?"

"More now than I did two weeks ago."

"Really?"

"I suddenly have a keen interest in kicking his butt."

Devon snorted, and Rae shot him a dirty look. She tried to ignore him. "You'll have to get in line."

"I know he's your half-brother. That just got added to his file."

"You have his file?"

"I don't have it, but the Xavier Knights have a file on him."

She now had a million more questions she wanted to ask. The top one would be to ask him to get her a copy of that file. *Out of the question, Kerrigan!* Did they have a file on her as well? Or maybe a better question to consider was; how big is the file?

"Are you alone?" He laughed quietly. "Of course you are, you wouldn't call me in front of a group of PC masterminds! Is your phone monitored?"

She turned so she couldn't see Devon's face and tried pressing her ear closer to the phone so Devon couldn't hear it. "No. What's up?"

"Let's keep this between you and me, k? I could get my arse into some serious suffering if anyone knows."

She didn't want him to get in trouble. She wasn't sure how she felt about him on the friendship to boyfriend scale, but she liked him. Luke was a good guy. She glanced at Devon from the corner of her eye. *He's a good guy too.* Just too scared to think with his heart. "Your secret is safe with me." What if he told her something about the Xavier Knights that Devon shouldn't know? She opened her mouth to suggest he tell her later.

"I'm going send you what we have on Kraigan. There isn't much you probably don't already know. Most came in after he left Guilder. But there is stuff about him before he turned sixteen. I can't risk emailing it to you or anything like that." His voice became a whisper. "I'll make copies. If, by chance, you want to meet me tomorrow while I'm taking Sandy to the dog park I'll have stuff for you."

"I can't. I wish I could." She glanced at Devon whose face had become completely unreadable. She knew she couldn't tell Luke much. "I have to work."

"No problem. I'll give it to you when you get back." He paused. "If you are hunting for him, I hate to say that you're wasting your time. He's left the country. He's not after you."

*For the moment.* She appreciated he wanted to watch out for her. "Good to know."

"Hold on a sec." He pulled the phone away from his mouth. He chuckled. "Molly just sent me a text. She's wondering if you're with me."

"Tell her to check the note I slipped under her door." Molls was going to be mad she had left without looking for her. "Can you do me a favor?" She wondered if talking to Luke was making Devon jealous. She had expected him to make a comment under his breath and was surprised he hadn't.

"Anything, Rae."

"This is going to sound weird. Would you mind giving Molly a shout?"

"Just call her? That's not weird."

"And maybe invite her out? Not like a date or anything." She started wondering where she was going with this. It had sounded good in her head a moment ago. "Just grab a burger or take her to walk Sandy or something?"

"Well, I was going to ask you out tonight, but I can try hitting on your roommate instead," he teased. "Maybe make you jealous? Pit two best friends against each other? Be the guy that comes between them. I have all these awesome ideas."

"Good-luck with that." She laughed.

"You don't think it could work?"

"Not with Molly n' me. Molls is..." What was the right word to use? "A bit of a handful."

"Really? She seems nice."

"She is. Hang out with her tonight. You'll see what I mean."

"Can I drill her on questions about you?"

She smiled. "Oh, you can try."

"She a hard shell to crack?"

"Not exactly."

"Now I'm going to have to hang with her just to find out what you find so amusing. You owe me if I do this."

"Owe you what?"

"Dinner. Movie. Some kind of proper date."

The car suddenly accelerated as Devon whipped by another car on the motorway. She had nearly forgotten for a moment he was there and could hear everything. She held onto her seatbelt. Because of him she was single. That fault belonged entirely to him. "You got yourself a deal, Luke."

He chuckled. "Why do I have the feeling I'm going to regret this?"

"You won't. Molly is awesome," Rae said. Devon swerved around another car and pulled sharply back into the middle lane. "I gotta go, Luke. Can I call you back later?"

"Definitely. See ya!"

She appreciated how he didn't question her about work or put any pressure on her what so ever. And he was taking Molly out tonight. If he could survive an evening with her, he was totally worth considering.

"Who the hell is Luke?" Devon snapped.

Rae blinked and reached for the dashboard as Devon accelerated and whipped by another car. "Seriously? You're going with road rage?"

"What?" He glanced down at his speedometer and lifted his foot off the gas pedal. "Who's Luke?"

"A friend." She got her answer on the jealousy question.

He scoffed. "That's it?"

She didn't owe him any explanation and yet she couldn't stop her mouth from talking. "He is just a friend, right now. He's a good guy. You'd like him if you met him."

Devon shook his head. "I *highly* doubt that."

She frowned at him. "You're the one who dumped me, remember?"

"What's his tatù?"

"He doesn't have one." She crossed her arms. "Is that okay with you?"

"Just peachy..." He shot her an annoyed look. "You sure he doesn't have one?"

"Yes. One hundred percent sure."

"Then how does he know about Kraigan?"

*Uh-oh. Here it comes.* "He works for the Xavier Knights."

"What?" Devon snapped his head to the side and stared at her in disbelief.

She pointed in front of them. "Can you please face the road?"

He scowled but turned back to concentrate on the busy traffic. "He works for the Xavier Knights? Are you working undercover to get inside?"

"No."

"Is this a personal mission?"

"No." She didn't dare say more on that one. Devon tended to have the ability to read through her. She had thought about it, but with Luke offering to send her information on Kraigan, she might not need to.

"Are you dating this guy?"

"That's none of your business."

His fingers tightened around the steering wheel. "You are."

"I am not getting into this with you right now, Devon. Can we just concentrate on the job?"

"This mission?" He scoffed. "We're supposed to be dating and you're already cheating on me!"

She rolled her eyes. They needed to change the subject fast - before they blew the mission. "Did you know my father started the Xavier Knights?"

Devon concentrated on the road and did not reply.

The silence grew uncomfortable, making Rae begin to worry they weren't not going to be able to work together.

"I didn't know that," he said quietly. "I wondered, but never asked. Did what's-his-face tell you that?"

"Luke. His name is Luke and yes, he did." She sighed.

"Did you do a background check on him?"

"No. I don't have to."

"You trust way too many people too easily."

"I trust no one these days." *Not even myself.*

"Sorry." Devon pressed his lips together. "I will try and keep this professional."

*Professional?* She giggled sarcastically. She didn't mean to, but it escaped.

Devon shot her a confused look; one eyebrow raised with creases appearing on his forehead.

"The Privy Council wants us to keep this professional? Our mission is to fake date! It's horribly unethical according the unspoken rule of tatùs. What are they thinking? What is Carter trying to do to us? It's like they want us together." She rolled her eyes. "If they only knew the half of it."

He shot her a wry grin. "Kind of ironic, eh?"

A tatù tingled against her skin and coursed up her spine. She misunderstood why it prickled as it happened so fast. *A warning.* It took barely a second to register. She pressed her hands against the dashboard, her body tightening all over. "Devon! Look out!"

A truck zinged past them and then cut back into their lane in front of the car ahead of them. The vehicle in front had to slam on their breaks. Its rear swung left to right as the driver fought to stay in control. He had to pull his car into the passing lane to try to avoid nailing the truck in front. The bumper clipped the bad driver's back end. Because of the difference in height, their bumpers entangled on the sides; the two vehicles stuck together like a magnet.

Rae watched in horror, unable to move as the scene unfolded in front of them. The truck tried accelerating and pulling away from the car.

This wasn't good. Devon had nowhere to go. He couldn't move left because a car was there, and he couldn't pull into the right lane and risk hitting the other stuck car. They were unbelievably close to the accident about to unfold.

The terrible driver in front of them jerked the steering wheel and swerved to the right. He hit a small car in the slow lane. Instead of breaking from the impact, the truck accelerated. It literally drove up the slow lane car and tilted, hovering on two wheels a second before hitting a bump and flying into the air. It began spinning.

Devon accelerated abruptly and pulled in the direction of the overturning truck. He hit the auto window, and Rae's window began to roll down.

Rae screamed.

"Push it away, Rae," Devon yelled.

She had no idea what he meant, but her tatù body did. She leaned out the window and using Haley's wind ability she pushed as hard as she could with her hands to mimic a strong wind against the car. She watched in awe as the overturning truck flew over them, and Devon sped under the small space.

Rae forced the spinning truck to move towards the grassy ditch on the side of the road. She arched and twisted as she kept her hands following the vehicle. As it flipped upward, its wheels on the bottom she tried to control it with one hand to stop spinning. Sweat ran down the side of her face as she concentrated. She managed to control the truck as it dropped heavily down.

She fell back against her seat exhausted. *I must be dreaming.*

"You okay?" Devon asked, his eyes darting to her, in front of them and to his review mirror.

Rae closed her eyes. "Did that just really happen?"

"It did."

She leaned over the seat to the halted traffic piling up behind them. "Should we stop?"

Devon shook his head. "No. Too risky. If anyone saw you hanging out the window with your hands steering the truck like magic, we're screwed." He pointed at her chest. "Put your seatbelt back on."

"I never." She looked down. *How did that come off?* "How long did that just take? A minute?" It felt like ten, maybe more.

"About five seconds. Not even."

*If this is the start of the mission, what else is going to happen?* She thought as she clicked her belt together. "Do you think that was an accident or meant for us?" Like she had told Devon before, she didn't trust anyone.

## Chapter 7

"Are you sure this is where we are staying?" Rae ducked her head to get a better view out of Devon's car window. "It looks insanely posh."

Against the setting sun, the building's red brick seemed to burn with fire. Devon drove down the gated drive and around to the front of the house. Beautiful orange-red bricks with stunning windows and pointed roof parts jutting out by the raised windows near the top.

"The place is called Heath Hall." Devon reached for a garage door remote inside his glove compartment and hit the button. "Some architectural billionaire bought the place, renovated it and now rents it out to football players, movie stars..."

"And the Privy Council," Rae finished and shook her head amazed. "The entire place isn't ours, is it?"

Devon pulled his car into one of the four parking garage spots located to the west side of the Heath Hall. He cut the engine. "There are four flats. We have the apartment on the right with the view of the forest and fields. Maria and Curtis will be staying in the wing across from us. The Privy Council rented out the top floors as well, but no one is staying in them."

"More secrecy?"

"Something like that, I'm sure." Devon opened his door and stretched his arms and back when he stood. "You coming?"

Rae stuffed her phone and purse into her backpack in front of the file for the mission. She took a deep breath as she opened her door. "How come you know the history of the building? Have you stayed here before?" She'd read through the file on the drive, and there hadn't been any information about their location.

Devon shook his head. "Last night while we were, uh, waiting for you to drive back from Stoke, Carter mentioned the place. He never says anything without a reason behind it so when I got back to my room last night I looked it up. We're going to be in high society here. We need to be prepared for anything."

Once Rae followed Devon out of the small garage, she noted that he didn't walk ahead or behind her, but kept perfect pace beside her. "So we have to try and stop a killer and blend in perfectly with royalty, like we've always been classy? This might be out of my league." Rae could barely keep up with Molly's fashion sense. Realistically she didn't stand a chance here. *All* this and pretend to be in love with the one boy she was trying to forget existed? *I am so screwed.*

Devon reached for her hand and squeezed it. "You've got this, Rae. I wouldn't have agreed to the mission if I didn't think you—we could handle it." He quickly let go of her hand and stuffed his into the pocket of his jeans.

She didn't know how to respond. They walked around the small water fountain at the front and into the arched wooden doors of the front entrance. Her eyes roamed the building like a child in a candy store.

Devon chuckled. "Shouldn't the posh be complaining, not gawking?"

"I can't get over the size of this place. Compared to our dorm rooms, which are pretty nice considering, this place is massive." She giggled, letting excitement flood her veins instead of the constant caution always flowing through them. "What do you think the inside looks like? Modern? Antique? Like a castle?"

Devon pulled his hand out of his pocket along with a set of keys. "I'm thinking old-fashioned. Old antiques cluttered in a million tiny rooms with rugs hanging on the walls as paintings. We'll barely have room to move around. I bet we'll have to move furniture to the upstairs apartments." He unlocked the front and handed Rae the keys. "The brass one opens the front door, the silver one is for our place."

Her heart melted slightly when he referred to the apartment as "our place." She knew he didn't mean it in the way she thought it, but it didn't stop her body from reacting. "Wh-What about you? Shouldn't we both have a set?"

"There's another one inside. Carter said he put one on the kitchen counter." He held the door for her.

The hallway had been painted a soft yellow color that seemed to absorb the sun shining in from the windows. A vintage, tall bench with hooks and an umbrella holder on each side, stood on the one side, near their door. Rae glanced back at Devon who winked at her. "*Told you,*" he mouthed.

Rae hiked her slipping backpack back up her shoulder. "Let's go see what treasures await us." She fingered the silver key before using it to unlock the door. She pushed the door open and stepped inside, jaw dropping as she took it all in.

Devon had been wrong. Well, partially wrong. The ceiling was a painted mural of clouds with gold crown molding and enamel painted detail along the edges. There were oval painted portrait pictures in each corner of the ceiling. Rembrandt himself must have painted them or taught someone how to. It was breathtaking.

The walls had been painted a beige color with white edges framing each part of the walls. The bright setting sun filtered in through the windows giving it a warm glow. The main room was very large, with three couches, reading chairs by the windows and two fireplaces. The furniture and lights were all modern, with simple, warm colors and gold pillows matching the detail on the ceilings.

Devon whistled behind her.

This room alone could entertain the queen or a prince and soon to be princess. It looked like a picture out of one of the books that showed royal weddings and Buckingham Palace.

She slipped off her runners and leaned around Devon to set them in the hallway. They did not belong in a place like this.

"Feeling underdressed?" Devon laughed quietly. He moved around her and tossed his bag onto the brown leather couch facing a bookcase. "I'm starving. Let's go see what the kitchen looks like."

Rae followed, her feet padding softly against the granite floor and expensive carpets. The enormous kitchen had counters running around with stainless steel appliances in between. An island in the middle had a stove top with a venting system above it. Bar stool chairs sat at one end, with an extremely large wine rack behind it.

Devon went straight for the fridge, barely bothering to glance around. "Good. It's stocked." He disappeared behind the door, appearing a moment later with everything needed to make a gourmet sandwich. He slammed the door closed with his foot. "Find some plates, will you?"

Rae did as he asked, mainly because she wanted to see what was inside each closed cabinet. The fourth cupboard she opened had the dinner settings. She slid two plates across the island toward Devon, who was busy cutting up cucumbers. Rae continued going through the drawers, finding another dinner setting much fancier than the first, along with wine glasses and crystal.

"Everything's expensive. We break one of the goblets, and it'll probably cost us a week's pay to replace."

Devon popped a crisp into his mouth. Rae hadn't even noticed him go to the food pantry shelves to grab the chips. "Privy Council is responsible for all breakages, not us."

Rae's eyebrows pressed together. "That something learned from personal experience?"

Devon grinned, his dimple teasing her with its cuteness. "Possibly." He handed her a plate with a sandwich stacked high with meat and vegetables on it. He turned and started back towards the living room.

"Uh-oh, mister." Rae shook her head. "You are NOT eating in there. Sit your butt down here and eat." She pulled a wood and snake patterned leather bar stool out for him, and then planted herself **on one** beside it.

Devon, thankfully, didn't argue. He sat down and finished his sandwich before Rae was halfway through hers. He got up and made another one and sat down beside her again.

Rae wanted to see the rest of their place. A thought crossed her mind. "How many bedrooms does this place have?"

Devon shrugged and stole a chip from her plate. "No idea." His hand paused mid-air, chip hanging between his fingers. "At least two, I think."

Seriously? Were the Privy Council actually trying to get them together? Maybe Carter was testing them to see if they were hiding something from the company. Rae jumped off her chair and strode to the other side of the living room. A long hallway with the same high vaulted ceilings as the living room offered three doors. The first was a bathroom, not simple by any means.

The second door opened to a large office with a desk and fireplace. The door on the far side obviously opened to a closet. From the size of the bathroom, she figured the closet was most likely a walk in one. The last door was a bedroom with a massive canopy bed and ornate gold furniture that matched the living room ceiling. Two opened doors show massive walk-in closets, each with a few pieces of clothes that hung in them. Hadn't Carter or Jennifer said they had their clothing organized?

Devon walked into the room a few minutes later. He glanced around quickly and then checked the men's closet.

"There's barely anything," Rae commented absently from her frozen spot beside a tall full-length mirror. One bedroom? She couldn't get past that one thought.

"Maybe it's coming in tomorrow. There's enough for a couple of days." Devon didn't appear worried.

"There's only one bedroom."

Devon shrugged. "It's fine. Th..."

"We are so NOT fine! I'm not sharing this bed!" Her voice rose. Last night he had brushed her off. She had no intention of going through that same feeling of rejection ever again.

"It's fine!" He used his hands in a patting motion as if to calm her down. "The office has a bed. It's hidden so no one would notice. It's in the office closet. It's fine." He gave her a half smile. "Even has a small ensuite bathroom. Tiny in comparison to the rest of this place, but it's good for me." He glanced around the room. "This is all a bit too much. How do rich people actually like this stuff?"

A relieved Rae plopped onto her bed, enjoying its perfect firmness

"Not too extravagant?" He leaned against the doorframe of his closet.

"I wouldn't complain if I had to live here forever." *With you, or without?*

Devon pulled out his phone and checked it. Rae waited as he typed and scrolled through emails or whatever else he was reading. He slipped the phone into his back pocket and moved to sit in one of the expensive leather reading chairs across from the window. He slung his feet over the tall side arms and leaned back. "Carter messaged. Clothes are upstairs; a Council designer is going to fit us tomorrow."

"Good." She was beginning to think this mission wasn't going to be as bad as she had initially thought. Then she remembered her manners. "Thanks."

Devon sat quietly for a few minutes before releasing a long sigh. "We should probably set some ground rules while we're undercover being... mates"

"What?" She sat up on the bed, leaning back on her elbows.

"You know... mates." He chewed on his lower lip and wouldn't look her in the eye.

Why did he look so uncomfortable? "You mean acting like boyfriend and girlfriend?"

"Yeah." He met her gaze but quickly looked away again.

"What kind of ground rules?" They didn't have to worry about sharing the same room, what else would be a problem?

Devon swung his legs around and set his feet on the floor. He shifted the chair, so he was facing her. He rested his elbows on his knees. "We have to be convincing. No one's going to buy that we are together if we don't act like we are."

"We'll be fine." She tried to envision any situation where it might be awkward. "It's not like the Privy Council is going to want us... you know making-out in public."

Devon nodded, his face still serious. "You don't know what we are going to have to do. I agree, we probably won't need to worry about full on, make-out sessions, but there will be times for public displays of affection."

"PDA's?"

"Yeah. Holding hands." His head tilted slightly. "You okay with that?"

Rae sat up, cross-legged on the bed. "Yes. Are you?" She couldn't help but tease him a bit; he seemed way too serious for this conversation. She had worried about it earlier but to see that Devon was struggling with the same dilemma; it calmed her.

"No! I'm totally fine."

"What about kissing?" Her insides trembled at the thought. "It might be required. I can keep it professional. Can you?"

Devon blinked once and then again. "Sure. No problem."

*Liar.* "The Royal Tea thing is a masquerade ball. Can you dance?" She wasn't about to admit she knew nothing about ballroom dancing.

"Uh..." He scratched the back of his neck. "I might need to take some dance lessons. I'll let Carter know. He can get someone here to teach me."

She shrugged, trying to appear nonchalant. "We might as well take the lessons together. It'll make it more realistic-professional then."

Devon stood. "I'll get that sorted now then." He pulled the phone out of his pocket and read something on it. "Looks like we are going to have some company."

"What?" Rae slid off the bed. "You're kidding!"

"I'm afraid not. Carter just received the message and contacted us."

"Who is it? Maria and Curtis?"

"Afraid not. They're already unloading their equipment into the flat across from us."

"Is it the stylist person?" Rae glanced at the closet. There wasn't much selection, and she had no idea if any of it fit. It was stupid to leave without taking a suitcase of clothes. Why she had never even considered, it was beyond senseless. At least the dress person was on their way.

"It's not the stylist."

*Seriously?*

"It's the Prince of Wales' fiancé."

"You're jokin'?! She's coming here? How soon? Crap! I need to shower!" She wasn't sure if her heart or her mouth were moving faster. Her body had switched to Riley's cheetah tatù, and she quickly swapped it for Jennifer's leopard tatù to get rid of the frenzy-panic caffeine feeling. The bathroom had better be supplied with towels, shower gel and anything else! *Wait! Slow down, Kerrigan. Someone stocked the kitchen; the bathroom should be as well.*

"Me, too." Devon checked his watch. "I'll meet you, uh, in the living room, shortly. Race ya!" He disappeared out of the door using his tatù to move fast.

"Could life be anymore disorganized?" Rae mumbled. She didn't have time to consider the answer at the moment. She rushed into the bathroom and flipped the fancy shower faucet on inside a large glass and marble shower. She threw her hair in a bun, not bothering to wash it, knowing there wouldn't be time to blow dry if she wanted to beat Devon. While slathering her body with foam, she checked out the large bathroom through the glass. The bathroom color-scheme was black and white with the same glass and marble accents as the main building structures. A large claw-foot tub looked inviting, and she planned on using that one night. At the end of a long, two sink make-up counter, a three piece full-length mirror section allowed full view for dress or hair styling. This bathroom equaled pure paradise.

Rae dried off quickly and wrapped a large fluffy towel around her chest, tucking it in under her arm pit. She swung her head around. No clothes. She had no bloody clothes!

She dashed out of the bathroom, straight for the walk-in closet. Out of the corner of her eye, she noticed a blur of motion come from the bedroom door. Her mind registered what it was a moment too late just as she crashed into Devon, both of them tumbling to the floor. Rae rolled and crashed into the wall. Devon stumbled and fell backward into the closet with Rae's clothes.

His towel wasn't as lucky. It landed in front of Rae. Actually, clutched in her hand. She let go of it and glanced down, double checking it wasn't hers.

"Rae?" Only Devon's head popped around the doorframe, his cheeks a hint of a shade of rosy. "Is my t-can you hand me my towel?"

She stood, keeping her arms tight around her. She leaned slightly as she handed him his towel, trying to get a slight glimpse of more skin. She grinned when he grasped for it, and she held it slightly out of reach.

"Rae Kerrigan!"

"You forfeit?" She wiggled his towel.

An exasperated breath escaped his lips. "Fine! You win!" He wiggled his fingers at her. "Towel?"

"The mighty Devon brought down by a loin cloth?" She giggled and tossed the towel into the closet.

Devon marched out; the towel held extra tight by his fist. His muscular chest taut with drops of water on his skin.

Rae watched him head into his closet and come out a minute later in black dress pants and a red polo shirt. He looked handsome. "That was quick."

He grinned. "We do have speed on our side." He raised one eyebrow. "Except for maybe you. Why are you still like that?" He gestured at her body.

*Whoops!* She slipped into her closet closing the door behind her. Three dresses rested on hangers. No pants, no clothing perfect for fighting and doing under cover intelligence stuff. She felt the material of the black dress. The shoulders were leather and ran down the front in a V. It was just above knee length. The garnet red dress beside was long and way too fancy for walking around the flat in. *More for a fancy dinner or something.* The last dress hanging had navy blue and white stripes, empire waist and no sleeves.

Rae found new undergarments in the drawers. She slipped them on and tried the black dress. The full mirror on the back of the door showed Rae someone she didn't recognize. The dress clung to her, and the low V-cut exposing more flesh than Rae had ever shown. She tried running on the spot, just to see if the dress rode up or anything fell out. Amazingly nothing did, and the dress clung perfectly below her derriere. The dress was made to move fast in, and the material stretched and offered the right amount of freedom for movement. She hung it back up not prepared to wear it today.

She then tried the long striped dress. It felt fancy to Rae but was by far the most casual of the three. In the mirror, she looked mature and graceful. She pulled her hair out of her bun and let one part fall over her shoulder. She imagined her mother in this dress, in this same situation and wondered how composed she would have been. Probably perfect under pressure. Rae appeared calm on the outside from the mirror's reflection, but everything inside her seemed to be running in circles and crashing together like her and Devon just had.

Could she keep it up in front of the future Princess of Wales, the next Queen of England?

The doorbell chimed, warning her that she didn't have time to contemplate.

# Chapter 8

Rae rushed back to the bathroom to check if, by chance, a drawer had any make-up in it. Thankfully she found one full of stuff. She referred to it as stuff because she only owned mascara, eyeliner, lip gloss and the occasional bit of eye shadow. Hers fit into a pencil case with room to spare. The drawer she found had more *stuff* than a cosmetic store!

She fluffed her hair with her hands and threw on some mascara and lip gloss, thankful for the speed that came with one of the tatùs she could mimic. She didn't even concentrate on which tatù she was using. It was becoming easier and easier just to let her body sense the one she needed and switch to it.

As she hurried down the hall, she heard Devon clear his throat and open the door. Rae was in the living room, her elbow resting against the white marble fireplace before Devon had opened the door all the way. She ran her fingers through her hair, hoping her run away curls weren't flying.

Inside the doorframe stood a very large, muscular man in a dark suit. "Devon Wardell?"

"Yes, sir." Devon held out his hand.

The man ignored it and lifted his arm, so he spoke into his wrist. "Hallway clear. Will confirm the flat is clear, then you can bring her in."

He spoke quietly, but Rae easily picked it up with Devon's tatù. As he stepped inside, his gaze darted everywhere. "Can I see some identification?"

"Sure." Devon patted the back of his pants before swinging around toward the couch. He glanced at Rae and hesitated a moment before leaning over and reaching into his backpack.

The royal security man charged inside the room and twisted both of Devon's arms, so they were behind his back. As Rae took a step forward to stop him, she realized Devon was letting the guard pin him. "What do you think you're doing, son?"

"Reaching for my I.D." Devon grimaced but didn't cry out. The man obviously had him in a tight hold.

"Where is it?" Holding Devon with one hand, he dumped the contents of the backpack on the couch. Devon's black leather wallet among the falling debris.

"I'd point to where it is, but you've got both my hands, sir."

Rae calmly watched, impressed with the guard's degree of protection for the soon to be princess. She wondered if she should be acting as the panic stricken girlfriend.

"Let him go, Alfie." A soft voice cut the tension in the air. "He's clear. The flat is clear, as is the entire building." A beautifully stunning blonde girl, about the same age and height as Rae stepped into the room.

"Alfie" grudgingly let Devon go. "Mum, if you let me do my job, then you can safely do yours."

The girl strode into the room with an air of confidence in her walk Rae knew she would never possess. "Sarah." The words slipped out of Rae's mouth before she realized she had said them out loud.

The soon to be princess calmly turned her attention to Rae as another man in a suite stepped inside the apartment and closed the door. He stood beside it, his feet shoulder width apart, and his hands crossed perfectly over each other as he stood guard.

"K-Karen?" Sarah smiled warmly at her and walked over to Rae like they were long lost friends. "Karen! You look gorgeous, petal."

*You idiot! You two are school friends. She's seen the file too. Well, part of it at least.* "Princess Sarah," she said as she tried to curtsey. "It's a pleasure."

The soon to be princess waved her hand. "Please Karen. Drop the formalities. I was Sarah growing up and your friend Sarah long before the future Princess got added to my name. Besides, I'm not a princess yet."

"Don't forget 'of Wales.' Should I say that as well?" Rae hoped her joke covered her rookie mistake.

A perfect tinkle of a laugh escaped the soon-to-be princess's smile. "You call me by that official name and I'll have Alfie strip search you."

"Mum!" Alfie straightened, his arms crossed over his chest as he walked over to check the kitchen. "How many exits does this place have?" he asked Devon.

"Two. This one and then kitchen has a set of sliding doors leading into the conservatory." Devon bent over to pick up the items belonging inside his backpack. "I will show you around once I clean up this mess."

Alfie ignored Devon as he disappeared into the kitchen. Devon rolled his eyes at Rae as he shrugged and followed him.

"Clear." The word echoed through the ear piece the bodyguard at the door was wearing.

Alfie and Devon appeared back into the living room a moment later. "I need to check the rest of the place.

Sarah shook her head. "No, you do not! You and Lenny can wait outside. Go get some fresh air. I'll be perfectly fine in here."

Alfie was already crossing the room toward the hall.

"Don't you ignore me-"

The guard by the flat entrance opened the door. "We never do, mum."

"I am under direct orders from the queen-"

"For Pete's sake!" Sarah stomped her foot. "Devon works for the Privy Council! They outrank you two any day! I'm in more than safe hands here."

Alfie refused to give up. "How can you be sure... ?"

"I know Karen! And I know Devon!" Sarah lowered her voice. "Outside, please, Alfie." The please did not sound like a request. Soon-to-be princess-power all the way.

"Yes, Mum." He bowed and with an unreadable face, followed Lenny out the door.

Sarah sighed. "I apologize. They seem wound a bit too tight these days."

"It's okay. They're just focussed on protecting the future queen." Devon's face looked like he agreed with them completely. He walked over and held his hand out. "Not sure if I'm supposed to do this or if your men would frown upon it. But I'd like to introduce myself. I'm Devon. This is R-Karen." He nodded toward Rae. "The rest of our team will be staying in Heath Hall also."

"Sarah." She shook his hand. "Just, Sarah. Unless we are in public, and it calls for something else, but I prefer Sarah." She strode to the couch facing the window and sat down, perfectly poised; her legs crossed at the ankles, and her hands folded neatly on her lap.

*No slouch in those shoulders.* Rae wished she could remind herself to sit like that all the time. She realized she had been kicking her big toe against the floor and quickly stopped. Bad habits were impossible.

If Sarah felt uncomfortable or nervous, she didn't show it. At all. She glanced a moment at the door. "We have about two minutes before Alfie returns. He won't leave my side if Philip isn't with me."

Devon came over to Rae and gently nudged her toward the couch. She blinked and quickly moved to sit across from the soon to be princess, realizing too late that she had used Devon's tatù to travel. Her hand went to her mouth as she felt her eyebrows rise.

Sarah smiled. "No sense in wasting time, right?" She tilted her head slightly. "So what type of tatù do you have? Speed? Is it an animal?" She sighed. "I hardly know anyone with a tatù. I wish we were not in such a rush right now."

Devon stepped forward, pulling his sleeve up to show his tattoo. "Mine gives me speed, agility, strong hearing, better night vision, plus more. Karen's is sort of similar." He shot Rae a look.

"Yeah." She cleared her throat. "Yes, it is." What was with her today? *Smarten up, Rae!* "What is your ability?" She knew better than to ask Sarah to show it to them. What proper soon-to-be princess would lift her shirt to commoners? Rae also didn't dare reach out to touch her either.

Quiet commotion outside that only Devon and Rae could hear, unless Sarah had a similar ability, sent them a warning that Sarah's bodyguards would be coming around the front of the house, ringing the front buzzer to be let in in seconds. Or they might just let themselves in without needing to press the outside button. She glanced quickly at Devon.

Sarah was oblivious to the sound or their silent communication. She giggled. "It's nothing fancy like yours. It gives me Omnilinguism."

"Pardon?" *At least I didn't say, What.*

Sarah's voice dropped. "It's the ability to understand any form of language."

"Spoken?" Devon moved toward the door.

She nodded. "And written."

"Very handy." He put his hand on the door knob.

"Especially for a soon-to-be princess. In a room full of foreign delegates." Sarah smiled. "Philip thinks I'm brilliant. I hate keeping the truth from him."

"Does it help protect him?" Rae asked. It wasn't hard to tell Sarah loved Philip. She smiled at his name and the sadness in her eyes as she spoke about hiding her tatù was obvious to Rae.

"It has, several times," Sarah replied.

"Then you're doing the right thing," Devon said. "It's not always the easiest choice, but in the end, it's the right thing to do." He glanced at Rae.

*He's warning me the guards are about to come back into the room.* Rae turned back to Sarah. "I'm an old college friend of yours."

"Yes. I've memorized the information that was sent to me. You and I both studied language and graduated together." She frowned slightly. "Philip took classes with me, too. He's going to wonder why he never met you."

Rae pressed her lips together and then snapped her fingers. Curtis' tatù! "It'll be sorted. Not to worry." She smiled. "It must be nice to travel the world and never have to worry about the language barrier."

"I love it. I..." Sarah stopped when Devon opened the door for Alfie and Lenny. She then continued as nothing surprising had happened. "Philip enjoys traveling as well. It is a shame we will not be leaving the country until after the Masquerade Ball, but until this," she gestured with her hand, "mess is cleaned up, we must be on high alert."

Lenny returned to his position by the door, and Alfie traveled around the room in a way that one barely noticed he was moving. Rae watched out of the corner of her eye. She wished she could learn to mimic that ability! "We—I agree. I can't believe someone would be after you!" Rae tried to play the part of a concerned friend.

"I'm so glad you came to visit." Sarah leaned forward. "I wouldn't have asked you to come and help me organize the Royal Tea Masquerade if your boyfriend didn't work for the Privy Council. I hear they are one of the best black op divisions in England."

Sarah was playing her part better than Rae. Alfie stopped scouting the room and turned his full attention to Devon. "You work for the Privy Council?" There was a teeny ounce of respect in his voice.

"I do."

"You working now?"

Devon crossed his arms over his chest. "I'll do anything to protect Karen. She wants to help Sarah, then I'm part of the package."

Alfie grunted. "Good." He moved strategically by the window but stopped searching the room.

"See Alfie?" Sarah beamed at him. "I told you there was nothing to worry about!"

He made no comment back to the soon-to-be princess, instead trying to appear invisible like part of the surroundings.

Devon moved not far from him, posing in a similar fashion.

Sarah clapped her hands. "We only have two weeks till the Masquerade! I have a massive list for the two of us to get through. Why don't you and Devon come by tomorrow? You can meet Philip. There's a small luncheon, come to it and then we can get to work for the afternoon. At the palace, we will have more time to catch up and go over *everything*."

"We would love to." Rae hoped their wardrobe would be in on time. She didn't plan on wearing the green grown or the tight black thing to a luncheon. *Crap!*

Sarah checked her watch and stood. "Wonderful. Why don't I have a driver come by and pick you two up around eleven?" Sarah checked her watch and stood. "I apologize for having to jet, but there are a group of children waiting to hear a story read by me. It's a mini tea party. I've been doing one a week for the past seven weeks, leading up to the Masquerade. Royal Tea with royalty." She giggled. "Everyone gets to be a soon-to-be princess. Big and small kids."

"It sounds like fun."

"It is. I'm really enjoying it." When Alfie cleared his throat, Sarah waved her hand. "I know, we are going." She began walking to the door where Alfie stood holding it open, and Lenny had probably already left to have the car ready. Sarah spun around and hurried back to Rae. She hugged her tight. "Thanks for coming here. It means the world." She straightened and smiled at Devon. "See you tomorrow, Devon."

As Rae watched Sarah leave, a new tremor zinged up her spine and exploded inside her brain. When the door closed, and she and Devon were alone, she whispered, "That's unbelievable!" She couldn't wait to try it out. "Are there any foreign books on those shelves?"

Devon checked the door to make sure it was locked. "New mission and instead of working on the case, you want to study a tatù?"

Rae's head shot up in surprise. She was tired. It had been a hell of a day yesterday, then off on a new mission today, a near-fatal car wreck, meeting the Prince of Wales' fiancé and now Devon had to make a snide remark? "You're a...a jerk!"

It was his turn to look surprised. "Excuse me? What did I do now?"

She huffed. "And a dummy! Why would you make a comment like that?"

"Like what?" He looked behind him to make sure she was talking to him. "I didn't say anything."

"I heard you loud and clear, Devon Wardell." Her hands curled into fists as she set them on her hips. This was not the place to shoot electricity or bolts of fire at Devon.

"I have no idea what you're talking about."

She opened her mouth to bark back at him and hesitated a moment. Had she heard the words or just made them up? "You're just jealous!" *There. Take that!*

Devon scowled at her. "I don't know what your problem is, but I am NOT jealous of you!"

"I think you are. I think you wish you had my ability." She couldn't believe she was saying the words to him and yet she couldn't stop herself. "You get annoyed with me all the time. Or you tell me to go faster or harder. You were always pushing me at Guilder."

"That's because of your talent!" He threw his hands up in the air. "Women!" he muttered as he headed toward the kitchen.

"I heard that."

He spun around. "You hear everything! But that doesn't make it right. You hear me pushing you and call it jealousy. Well, it's not. Just because you hear it, doesn't make it true." He ran a hand through his dark, thick hair. "You've got a tatù I'm sure a lot of people are jealous about. I'm not one of them." He stomped into the kitchen and came back out a moment later, his face red with anger. "You're still a child. You're trying to act like the big, all-knowing adult, but you don't know everything, Rae. You don't."

"I have never said I did!" She knew she was screaming, but his I'm-older-than-you-with-more-life-experience-voice ticked her off. "You, just like everyone else, just have to judge me! I always have to defend myself! Defend being a girl. Defend being a Kerrigan. Defend being good at my job. Defend-"

"Then stop doing it." A single eyebrow rose on Devon's face. "Why do you care what other people think? I don't mean your friends, but everyone else. Like the Privy Council. Do you think Jennifer gives a toss what anyone thinks about her?"

Rae shook her head, baffled why he sounded like he was now on her side.

"She doesn't. And everyone respects her."

"Or is crap-scared of her."

Devon's mouth twitched in one corner. "Crap-scared?"

She was still mad at him. He wouldn't be able to pull his sexy man-charm on her tonight. "Whatever. Don't make comments under your breath about me. So what if I get excited about a new tatù? I'm going to have to know how to use it tomorrow when we meet Philip."

Devon ground his teeth together. "I never said anything!"

Maybe he had said it in his head, and she had somehow heard his thoughts. Either way, it was still wrong. "Fine! Be the technical, by the book, guy you always are." She stepped toward him and poked him in the chest with her finger. "I'm the best person for this mission. That's why the Privy Council hired me. I'm not saying I'm better than you. I'm saying I can get the job done. You will never get the opportunity to work with someone like me again. Don't screw it up." *Like you did our relationship.* Funny how words could be a double edged sword sometimes. "We're partners here. If this is going to be even remotely believable you need to start respecting me or our *fake* relationship," she used her fingers as quotation marks around the word fake, "isn't going to fool anyone."

"I won't have a problem faking the relationship," Devon shot back, his bright blue eyes moving back and forth as he looked into hers.

Did he mean something by that? "Good!" She didn't know what else to say. She moved around him into the kitchen and poured herself a glass of water. She grabbed an apple from the fridge as well. As she slipped by him still standing in the same spot as before, she said, "I'm going to my room to study the file. I'll see you in the morning." She hurried using his tatù ability so he wouldn't have a chance to reply.

She heard him as he noisily banged pots and pans around in the kitchen and slammed cabinet doors. She tried to ignore it by switching her tatù to one without sensitive hearing. Going through the antique dresser, she found a drawer full of nightgowns. A lot of silk. And lace. Rae pulled one out and stared at her surprised reflection in the mirror. It was a negligee. Black silk with fancy black lace. What was the Privy Council thinking? A sound near the door made her jam the tiny thing into the back of the drawer and quickly shut it. She glanced at the door and realized the sound was coming from her backpack. The noise repeated again. Her phone.

She walked over to her bag and pulled out the iPhone. There were a few missed texts from Molly, and the last one was from Devon. From a minute ago.

She switched back to his tatù and listened to see if he was standing by her door. She could still hear him in the kitchen, just not slamming things down anymore or muttering to himself.

His text read: *Wardrobe person coming at eight tomorrow. Meet upstairs at eight am.*

She replied: *Got it.*

She set the phone down on the dresser and pulled open the drawer beside the sexy pj drawer. Empty. She tried the other one. Thankfully there were a pair of turquoise blue long silk pajama bottoms and a tank top style top. The material wasn't her style, but the design was.

She slipped into them and hung the striped dress back on its clothes hanger before retrieving her laptop from her backpack and her phone from the dresser. She settled on top of the comfy bed and nestled the pillows perfectly behind her.

The blue light on her phone flashed, indicating another message. She slid her thumb over the phone's face to turn it on. Devon had messaged again. "*Truce?*"

She typed back: *Okay.*

A moment later her phone vibrated again. *I'm making an omelet. Do you want one?*

*No thanks.*

*It'd be like breakfast in bed.*

She laughed. *Maybe tomorrow.*

*I'm using all the eggs now. I'm starving. And Bacon, I'm going to use all the bacon. I just found sausage too.*

*Explains the hungry, grouchy bear from before.*

*I thought you said Truce?*

*Sorry. My bad.* Rae laughed and tapped the keyboard again. *We're in the same flat. Why are we texting?*

*Too far to walk?*

*If I speak in the room here, could you hear me?*

*Maybe. I heard you laugh a moment ago. What about you?*

*Not sure. Say something.* Rae perked her ears and focused on any sound.

"Why don't you ever see hippopotamus hiding in trees?"

Rae blinked. "What?"

A second later her phone buzzed. *Because they're really good at it.*

"You're sad!" she called out, laughing.

"Got you laughing." Devon's voice sounded like he was smiling. "Sure you don't want an omelet?"

"Maybe a small one?" Her tummy rumbled in agreeance.

"I'll bring it to you... If you want."

"Sure." She reached for her laptop and opened it up. She knew she should be reading the file but opened her browser to google instead. She typed in: woman survives strange fire.

Several photos and articles showed up on her screen. As she scrolled through them, she mentally checked most of them off as useless. Devon knocked on her door five minutes later. "Come on in," she called.

Devon came in carrying a tray with two plates on it. He hesitated as his eyes grazed over her. He set the tray down on the bed and hopped onto the vacant spot beside her and handed her a plate before reaching for his own.

She took a bite of the hot omelet. Sausage, onion, egg and cheese teased her taste buds. She moaned. "This is really good."

"Thanks." He leaned over and glanced at her computer screen. "What are you looking at?"

She shrugged and took another amazing bite. "I just wanted to see if there might be something on my mom. I'm not exactly sure what I'm looking for."

Devon sat quietly eating for a moment. "I wouldn't know where to start either. Where do you think she is? Do you have a theory about what happened after the fire?" He typed: PEOPLE WHO DON'T BURN.

Rae stared at the screen results. "Thanks," she said. "For believing me." She couldn't look him in the eye.

Devon elbowed her gently. "I hope you find her."

"Me too." She tried joking, "Just not on the cover of some tabloid magazine." She closed the laptop and yawned. "And maybe when I'm more awake to focus."

Warm fingers collected the empty plate in her hand. Devon shifted, and his weight disappeared off the bed. Rae leaned back against her pillow and let her eyes close for just a moment. Soft lips pressed against her forehead. "'Night, Rae."

When she opened her eyes, Devon had already disappeared out of the room and closed the door.

## Chapter 9

Rae rolled over and tucked deeper into the soft covers. Her bed at the dorm didn't hold a candle to this luxurious piece of art. Even the pillows held dream-like feathery softness. She could lie in the bed forever.

Except for the irritating buzzing of her phone. Someone wanted to get a hold of her - persistently.

She reached for her phone sitting on the night stand beside her and swiped it on, keeping one eye closed for better focus against the bright sun shining behind her. She should have closed the shutters to the large windows in her room before she fell asleep. Too late now.

*Privy Council sent us a message to say the clothing-person is coming.*

*Rae, wake up! Did you get the message from the PCs? Jennifer just called me to say you aren't answering.*

*I'm giving you three minutes and then coming in.*

*Two minutes.*

*One Minute.*

"I'm up!" Rae sat up and rubbed her eyes. "Give me a minute." She made her way to the bathroom and skimmed over the messages from the Privy Council and Jennifer. She yawned and washed her face with cold water. The past few days had left her exhausted and she didn't have her healing tatù to fix her tired body. She sent Jennifer a text to see if there was any chance Charles could be up London way so she could get it back. His healing tatù only worked on himself, but if she mimicked it, she had the ability as well. She had lost it fighting Kraigan the other night. She didn't dare ask Carter. He might think she was weak. Then again, Jennifer might think that as well.

She ran through her tatùs and went for Riley's cheetah, thinking the hyped up caffeine feeling might get her body going.

"Rae?" Devon wrapped his knuckles softly on the bedroom door. "You decent?"

She had changed into a black pair of jogging pants and black fitted top she had found in one of the dresser drawers. She pulled the door open. "I'm ready." She pulled her curly hair into a messy bun. "We're just going upstairs, right?"

Devon nodded and walked beside her down the hall to the living room. Expensive cologne wafted to Rae's nostrils. It wasn't his typical smell, but it carried something deliciously tempting. She liked it and moved a little closer to smell it again, cracking her knuckles to try and distract herself.

"Why are you so jumpy?" Devon's eyebrows went up. "Hard to sleep in a strange bed?"

She shook her head a little too hard. The room vibrated with the movement. "Shoot! Forgot my phone! Be right back." She raced back to her room and returned a second later with her phone. "Got it!"

Devon watched her from the door to their flat. "Are you using Riley's tatù?"

The proud look on his face teased Rae. She quickly switched her tatù to Jennifer's leopard ink. Similar ability, without the over-caffeinated rush. Her body relaxed, and she inhaled, enjoying the loss of the jitters. "You're too smart for your own good sometimes."

He grinned and held the door open for her. "You would know."

She stopped suddenly in front of the antique staircase at the end of the hall. Devon managed to catch himself just before crashing into her. She laughed and raced up the stairs, leaving Devon to try to catch her.

They sobered at the top of the stairs and slowed their pace. "Which flat?" Rae pointed to both doors slightly across from each other.

Devon nodded to the one that wasn't above them. "In there. The one above us is supposed to have any equipment we might need."

"Equipment? Like gadgets and tazors and double-oh-seven stuff?"

"And guns, tranquilizer darts, superman capes..."

"Good. I got gum on my cape the other night. Do they have a Wonder Woman one? I refuse to wear Superman's."

"Your humor is bad, Rae. That's one thing I thought would get better."

She opened her mouth to throw a comment back at him and realized he was teasing her. "Yours has gotten worse."

The door they stood in front of them swung open. "RAE! DEVON!"

Rae jumped back. Devon reached his arm around her so she wouldn't fall. It was a mechanical reaction, but it still felt nice against her lower back. Rae barely had time to register the reaction. She was too busy staring at the person standing in front of them. "Molly?"

Molly beamed and posed with one hand in the air, the other on her hip. "In the flesh! The Privy Council needed a fashion coordinator and who better to hire than yours truly? I've been shopping and organizing like mad the past two days. I wanted to tell you the other night but then you were so tired and then you had that crazy dream."

"What crazy dream?" Devon asked.

Molly continued like she hadn't heard him. "I left way before you did yesterday. Jennifer filled me in on the mission a few days before you two even knew. I had to sneak into Devon's room and check his sizes. I already knew them, but I wanted to make sure." She moved into the room and left the door open so they could follow her. "So I put a few things in both your rooms downstairs for you yesterday. Do you like the black dress?" She turned to Devon. "Did you see her in it yet? She's going to be so sexy, no one is going to even notice you in a room. They'll all be staring at luscious-Lana here." She eyed Rae. "You tried it on first didn't you? I knew you would. I bet you put it on and quickly took it off. You are so wearing that dress! Not to the luncheon thing today but tonight for dinner."

"Does her mouth ever stop?" Devon leaned over and whispered to Rae.

The room had racks with clothes on them, models and fitted mannequins with fancy dresses and tuxedos. All the classy furniture had been shoved against the walls.

"Crazy, I know 'eh?" Molly did a full circle and jumped up and down in delight. "I'm going to be here the whole time you guys are here! I get to dress you every day for every occasion." She clapped her hands. "It's like playing Barbie but with real live people!"

Devon cleared his throat. "Does Carter know you are here?"

"Headmaster Carter?" Molly waved her wrist dismissively. "Of course. He had to sign off on me skipping classes." She cupped her fingers close to her mouth. "You do know he's the president of the Privy Council, right?"

Rae laughed.

Devon nodded. "I heard that."

"Good. I wasn't sure what you knew. I know Rae knows, but wasn't sure how much you knew. You never know, some people get told everything, others... Well they don't know too much. The less they know, the better."

"I can't argue with you on that, Molls." Devon walked over to a rack of clothing meant for him. "So what are we supposed to do? Pick some things out and take them down to our flat?"

Molly grabbed Rae's hand and squeezed it before pulling her toward a tall round rack of dresses. A small electric shock zapped against their skin. "Sure. You can do that if you want. You need regular day clothes that are classy." She frowned at Devon. "You won't find any torn jeans or cargo pants where you are going, Dev." She let go of Rae's hand. "Rae, go through these and pick out a few you think you would wear to the luncheon. I have to help your man here." She tsked and moved over to Devon. "Let's turn you into a man, Mr. Wardell. A handsome one."

Rae winked at Devon when Molly wasn't looking. She quickly pretended to check out the clothes in front of her when Molly gave her a stern look. It reminder Rae of Madame Elpis.

She pulled out several dresses and went behind a screen Molly had set up to try things out. She found a dark navy blue sleeveless dress with a matching short cardigan. The fitted top gave Rae free movement of her arms and felt like a second skin. It came down in a classy V-cut in the front without showing too much skin. The skirt part of the dress hung just at knee length and was loose with a sewn in belt. Rae liked the dress. It looked the part but also gave her the ability to run if she needed to or to move about in whatever way might be required of her. The cardigan fit perfectly as well.

"Let me see," Molly asked.

Rae stepped around the screen and stared at the floor. She refused to look up, even when a low whistle escaped Devon's lips. It wasn't meant to be heard by them, but Rae picked it up while Molly didn't even notice.

"It's perfect!" Molly moved around her fixing the hem at the back and pulling Rae's hair out of the bun. "What do you think, Devon?"

Rae held her breath as she looked up at him. He wore a dark gray suit with a blue shirt that matched his eyes perfectly. Classically handsome. She couldn't stop staring.

Molly laughed. "Seriously, you two. You guys need to get out more. It's like you've never seen each other. You both look perfect." She checked her watch. "All thanks to me, of course.

Now get going. The limo is going to be here in about ten minutes." She ran to a couch full of name brand gift bags and pulled out a pair of black heeled shoes with a matching clutch bag for Rae. "You need some eyeliner, mascara, and eye shadow. And lipstick!" She ran to the table and dumped the contents of a bag out. "Here! Quick, sit down." She pulled a stool over and set Rae down. "Close your eyes."

Five magic minutes later, Molly stepped back and handed Rae a mirror. "Perfect."

"Limo's pulling up" Devon said and moved to the window to double check his hearing.

"Get going!" Molly ran to the door. "Have fun!" She grabbed her phone and snapped some pictures of the two of them. "For the scrapbook."

Devon and Rae raced down the stairs and stopped just outside the front doors where a chauffeur was getting out of the limo.

"Shoot. Molls has my hair in a pony."

"You look gorgeous. You don't need it." Devon opened and door and put a bright smile on his face as he spoke to the chauffeur. "Hello! Beautiful day, isn't it?"

The chauffeur helped them in the limo as Devon made small talk with him. He put his arm around the back of the seat where Rae sat. He played the couple part perfectly as they drove. He would wink or squeeze her shoulder or ask an easy question at her to just engage her enough in the conversation. It gave Rae time to collect her courage and focus on where they were going.

"You okay?" Devon asked quietly when the limo parked in the parking lot of a beautiful, old building.

"I assumed the luncheon was at Buckingham Palace." She let him take her hand to help her out of the limousine. This place looked big enough to be a palace.

"It's the same location where the masquerade is going to be held."

More limo's pulled in to drop other people off. "I thought it was just going to be you and me with the prince and Sarah."

"Surprise!" A low laugh escaped Devon. "I'm still trying to get over Molly being here. She's going to blow our cover if they let her out of the room."

"She'll be fine."

*Rae?*

Rae nearly stumbled at the sound of Maria's voice inside her head. *Yes?*

*Just wanted to make sure you could hear me. Curtis and I parked around the corner. We followed you guys. Let me know if you need anything.*

*Okay.*

*You look gorgeous, by the way.*

*Thanks.*

Inside the building, Devon gave their names before they stepped through metal detectors and were ushered into a large hall. Name cards were set up on the longest table Rae had ever seen. It had to seat at least a hundred, maybe more. A pair of throne-like chairs sat in the middle with origami crowns made out of gold paper sitting on the plates in front of them.

A man dressed in a white tuxedo stepped onto the small stage behind where the prince and soon-to-be princess would be sitting. He rang a bright, shiny, brass bell. "Please find your seats." He stepped off the stage and rigidly walked over to a closed door. He stood straight and tall beside it.

"Queen's guard," Devon murmured close to her ear. He began looking at the names on the table, trying to find theirs.

Rae followed him, her arm loosely slipped into his. She smiled at people as they passed trying to remember their faces, and see if anyone acted odd. The only person out of place was her.

Devon straightened when they came around the end of the long table. Rae could tell he was using his tatù to read the names down the row. She smiled. Sometimes being normal was too slow.

"Found us." Devon grabbed her hand and walked down to the middle of the table, slowing as they passed the origami crowns. Rae realized they were sitting beside the prince and Sarah, on the prince's side.

Devon pulled her chair out and sat down beside her.

She smiled. *Really?* She said to Devon, using Maria's tatù to talk to him inside his head. He couldn't respond back to her but he could hear her. *I have to sit beside the Prince of Wales?*

Devon grinned and reached for her knee under the table, giving it a squeeze. "You'll be fine."

When everyone was seated, the Queen's guard introduced the prince and his fiancé. Everyone stood and clapped, and then sat down again once the royal couple was seated. The prince barely glanced at Rae.

Sarah rose to her feet and moved to the podium "Welcome everyone. We are so glad you could come." She smiled. "Philip and I hope you enjoy the meal. We are grateful for all of your help with the Royal Tea Masquerade, whether it be financially, volunteer..."

As she continued to talk, Prince Philip turned and looked Rae straight in the eye. His face grew hard and irate. "I have no idea who you are. Sarah says you were in her classes. I don't know why she is lying, but you have five seconds to tell me what the hell is going on before I signal my guards to come and drag you out of here."

Rae swallowed hard, her mouth as dry as a tumbleweed blowing in the desert.

# Chapter 10

How was she supposed to respond? Rae ran a million ideas through her head. Nothing seemed like the right answer or the perfect lie. She heard Devon suck in his breath beside her and knew she was taking too long to answer. She stared wide-eyed at the prince, the future king of England, while his fiancé continued to address everyone sitting at the table.

Philip grabbed her wrist and leaned forward. "Answer me!" he hissed in a low voice so only Rae could her.

She seized the opportunity. She let her tatù decide the best course of action. Leaning close to him and smiling sweetly, she said, "We did take a couple of classes together. You might not remember me, but it was hard to not miss you." She thought of a language class the prince might have taken. "I think it was Spanish. Do you remember that day it was pouring rain?" She hesitated, hoping Philip had taken a course or two in Spanish.

Philip continued to hold her wrist. *What had Curtis said about his ability? Skin to skin contact?* Rae mimicked the tatù and waited for the prince to pull a memory from his head. She figured a rainy day wasn't too farfetched for England.

A memory began to surface. Philip and Sarah racing into class, his hair dripping from the rain and her umbrella soaked. She shook it out before stepping in the door. They were laughing as they raced to sit down. Rae watched them settle into a row and positioned herself behind them. When Sarah bent down to grab her notebook, Rae tapped Philip on the shoulder and asked if she could borrow a pen.

Philip released her wrist. They were immediately back in the present.

Rae tucked a chunk of hair behind her ear. "I'm not sure if you remember... I borrowed a pen from you." She giggled, hoping it sounded girlish. "You probably don't remember. It wasn't as a significant moment for you as it was for me." She smiled confidently, knowing he would remember the moment.

"Funny you should say that. I do remember you borrowing a pen. It was the first thing that came to mind when you mentioned the rainy day." He shook his head. "I hated Spanish. Could never figure out the verb conjugations."

Rae's smiled broadened. "Language is like math to some people. You either get it or it never clicks."

"I'll stick with mathematics then. Language, I just never got it. Still don't." Philip's eyes flitted over to his fiancé. "That's why I'm lucky to have such a gifted, talented fiancé." He straightened in his seat. "My apologies for sounding harsh a moment ago. I feel the need to be over protective of Sarah these days."

"I don't blame you." Devon put his arm around Rae.

"And you are?" Prince Philip glanced at Devon, back to Rae and then at Devon again.

"I'm Rae's boyfriend."

"Who's Rae?"

*Oh shit.* She froze and felt Devon stiffen beside her.

"Karen. She's my ray of sunshine. It's a nickname I gave her." Devon leaned over Rae and held his hand out. "I'm Devon. Devon Wardell. I work for the Privy Council. The only way I would let Karen come here was if I stayed right at her side."

Philip obviously liked it that Devon worked for the PCs. It irked Rae she couldn't admit to working with them as well. "The Privy Council?" He nodded. "I'm impressed. And you're not here undercover?"

Devon shook his head. "My Rae's more important than work."

*Stop calling me Rae.* She warned him using Maria's tatù.

Devon grinned and shrugged. "I had a few weeks holidays owed, so I figured this would be an interesting break."

"Interesting indeed." Philip shifted and glanced toward his fiancé. "I'm not sure what you all know..."

Devon's face grew serious. "I've been informed. I'm here to be of assistance if needed."

"I may take you up on that." Philip smiled at Rae. "You sure landed yourself a jackpot. You've got a keeper."

Rae smiled brightly. "Your fiancé is about to finish her speech." She wondered if the Queen had told him she had sought out the Privy Council's help. Had Sarah suggested it to the Queen? When Rae had some time with Sarah on her own, she needed to ask.

As if on cue, everyone around them began clapping. The three of them joined in as well. The Prince leaned behind Rae when the noise started to die down. "Devon, make sure I get your number before you leave today."

Devon nodded. He turned his attention back to Rae as Sarah returned to her seat. He acted the perfect undercover guy. Rae couldn't help but be impressed with his James Bond kind of appeal. She needed to learn how he did it so she could copy it herself. He was good at his job. Lanford may have followed her father, but he had seen a good reason to set Devon up as her mentor. Had she not let her personal desire interfere with their relationship, she could have learned so much more from Devon. She planned on making up for that on this mission.

"Where is Sarah going?" Devon murmured quietly as the first plates of salad were brought out to the table.

Rae glanced up to see the soon-to-be princess head toward the hall. "I don't know."

Devon nudged her. "Ask Philip." He passed her the bowl of rolls just handed to him. "I need you to be all eyes and ears from now on."

She turned to hand Philip the rolls and realized he had his own. "Sorry. You have some already." She set the bowl down.

Philip glanced up.

She couldn't just ask him a direct question. She smiled and wiped her mouth with her napkin. "Excuse me."

Devon stood and pulled out her chair. "Everything all right?"

"Just nipping to the loo. Be back in a moment."

He quickly sat down again.

Rae headed out the main room to the hallway lobby where the restrooms were. Alfie stood by a door which Rae assumed led to the woman's bathroom.

He held his hand up when she approached. "You'll have to wait a moment."

"Okay." At least her hunch had been right on where Sarah had gone. Rae glanced around the beautiful brightly lit hall. The crystal chandeliers matched the enormous large ones inside the banquet-ball room. *Hey Maria. All's well here. How are you guys doing?* Might as well test to see how far their 'head-talking' could reach. Rae had once reached Carter through thick stone walls. How far could she reach now?

Rae pretended not to notice Alfie's raised eyebrows as she tried to whistle while waiting from the restroom door to open. *Maria? Can you hear me?* Where they too far apart? *Testing one, two... Testing one, two. Maria? Just seeing if you can hear me?* She cleared her throat. It had to work. Wasn't that one of the reasons the Privy Council wanted Maria working on this case? *Maria! It's me, Rae. Everything is fine. I'm just trying to see if we can communicate through the walls. This is where the masquerade is going to be and if it doesn't work, we need to come up with something else.*

Alfie knocked politely on the bathroom door. "Mum?"

Rae stopped trying to talk to Maria and walked over to the lady's bathroom. "Everything okay?"

Alfie frowned. Rae wasn't sure if it was because of the situation or because she was asking.

Rae's back tingled. She sensed another tatù nearby but had no idea if it was Sarah's or someone else. "Let me go check on her." She reached for the door and tried to pull it open.

Alfie held it tightly shut with his foot. "You are not permitted inside!"

She pulled and rattled the handle trying to get in. "If she's sick..."

Alfie grabbed her wrist and twisted it behind her back. "You are not permitted in there!" he repeated.

It took every ounce of control not to resist him with a tatù. He was doing his job, protecting the soon to be princess, even while in the loo. "Ow!" she whispered, the tight grip hurt. "I'm just trying to help. If she's ill, she'll prefer me coming in, not you."

Alfie loosened his hold then slowly let her go.

A loud crash inside the bathroom sent them both into action.

Rae shook her wrist and grabbed the door with her other hand. She switched her tatù to electricity, ready to zap an intruder should they be in there. She rushed inside, Alfie right on her heels.

A window near the far wall banged against its frame. The old brass and glass made an eerie horror movie kind of sound. Rae surveyed the rest of the room. Where was Sarah? The powder room section sat vacant. She ran into the toilet section and ducked down to check for feet under the three stalls. Empty.

Alfie spoke into his wrist. "Code Ice." He pulled out his gun and began checking the powder room under the long skirt tables.

Rae ran for the window and shoved it open. The old window hung by two hinges at the top and easily opened and slammed shut again. On tippy toes, she pushed her head through and switched to Devon's tatù for the better vision. She couldn't see anybody in the quiet parking area below, let alone some dragging or carrying Sarah in her red dress. There was black rope on the ground and a white van parked not too far away. Nobody was in it. About to mention it to Alfie, she bit her tongue when she saw

Curtis carrying two cups and slip into the back of the van. Dummy had gone for coffee while someone tried to get Sarah! She was going to skin him alive later.

"Sarah?" Alfie called. "Are you here?"

Rae dipped her head back inside.

A small noise came from inside one of the stalls. A metal click sounded, and the middle stall door opened slowly.

"Alfie? I'm okay." Sarah opened the door further and stepped down from off the toilet and onto the floor.

Rae rushed to her side the same time Alfie did.

"What happened?" he demanded and then into his wrist barked. "Stand down. Cancel ice."

Sarah looked shaken, and Rae grabbed a cup from the fancy sink and poured her some water. She handed it to Sarah.

Sarah gave her a smile as she took it. "I'm fine. Please, please don't alarm everyone. Do not get Philip! He will only worry. Everything is fine. Tell them, Alfie. Now."

Alfie didn't look like he believed her, but he did as commanded. "Stand down. False alarm. Back to your stations." He frowned before checking to make sure the bathroom main door was locked. "What the hell just happened?"

Sarah glanced at Rae before replying. "I freshened my makeup in the powder room and then stopped into the loo. I heard the window open which seemed strange because we are basically on the second floor. I panicked and crawled up to hide on the seat." She giggled, probably from shock. "Guess that was the smart thing to do. Someone climbed in through the window. They paused a moment before pushing open the stall beside me." She laughed again. "Then you two made a bunch of ruckus at the door and must have scared them off. I think they jetted back out through the window."

Alfie raced to the window.

"I saw something on the ground before," Rae said. "A black rope or a cable or something."

Alfie's head disappeared, along with the infamous wrist. He sent people to patrol and check the grounds before dropping the window back down. "There's nothing on the ground. You must have imagined it."

"I'm pretty sure I saw a rope."

"Maybe it was a branch." He pressed his lips in a tight line. "My men are checking now. If there's anything, they will find it."

"I need to get back to the luncheon. People are going to wonder where I am." Sarah moved to the sink to wash her hands.

Rae noticed they were calm, unlike her shaking ones clenched at her sides.

"We need to get you out of here, Sarah." Alfie raised his arm.

Sarah put her wet hand over his wrist. "No, you do not. I am staying. Nothing happened. I'm completely fine. No scoundrel is going to scare me from my duty."

Rae blinked. This was no faint of heart princess! She liked her more already. She offered her arm to Sarah. "Come on. I'll walk back with you. We can say we were gossiping in the bathroom."

Alfie cleared his throat.

"Fine." Rae rolled her eyes. "We were catching up."

Sarah slipped her arm through Rae's. "Alfie's mad at me, not you. However, catching up is much better."

"I'm just doing my job, Mum." Alfie followed them out but did not stop them.

"We keep this a secret." Sarah looked at Rae and then Alfie. "At least till after the luncheon?" Alfie frowned but gave her a curt nod.

As they returned to the large banquet hall, Maria's gentle voice sounded inside Rae's head. *Everything okay?*

*Where were you?* Rae didn't know whether to sigh with relief or scream in irritation.

*What do you mean?*

*I was trying to get a hold of you a few minutes ago.* Rae forced a smile on her face as she and Sarah made their way back to their seats, everyone oblivious to what had just happened in the bathroom. *Someone tried to attack the prince's fiancé! Then I see Curtis carrying coffee! What the hell?*

*What? I've been here the whole time.*

*Your van has full view of the restrooms. Someone climbed up and snuck into the bathroom.*

*Impossible! I would have seen them.*

*Something happened. Sarah wouldn't make this up. I was there.*

Maria didn't say anything for a moment. Rae took her seat beside Devon and let Sarah cover what happened.

*I'm sorry, Rae. Curtis and I screwed up. He went to grab coffee, and I grabbed us a sandwich. We were gone five minutes tops! One of us should have stayed here. I just didn't... You and Devon are inside... We figured... I guess we shouldn't have gone. Is everything was okay? Is the future princess okay?*

Rae felt bad for Maria. She could hear the guilt in her friend's voice. *The future princess is fine. Everything's okay. Her secret service men are scouting the grounds now.*

*It'll never happen again.*

*I know Maria. I'm sorry, too.*

Devon had switched places with Rae and was sitting beside the prince now. He leaned close to Rae and whispered so softly only she could hear. "Everything alright?"

"It is. Bit of a mix up. I'll explain later."

## Chapter 11

After lunch had finished, Devon and Rae made the rounds, saying hello and greeting the other people attending the lunch. Devon shook each person's hand as he introduced himself, giving Rae the opportunity to the same. No one else in the room carried a tatù.

The prince and future princess moved about the room talking. Rae watched them and marvelled at their ability to communicate and interact with whomever they met. Rae had never paid much attention to politics or royalty, especially growing up in America. She knew who the Queen was in England, and the royal family, but that was it. Now, she was beginning to realize they were so much more than just a cultural/traditional icon. Prince Philip and Sarah represented a new age of royalty. One with social media interaction, and the ability to reach out to a new generation, to make a difference.

From the conversations Rae picked up with her strong tatù hearing ability, they were both passionate about making a difference, and changing things for the better; the environment, poverty, endangered animals, education and more. Rae couldn't keep up with how much each of them knew on every subject. Rae and Devon had talents with their tatùs, but these two were using their social status to teach others. Rae could imagine little children following them and loving them. They were a fairy-tale couple.

"Rae?" Devon's lightly calloused fingers intertwined with hers. "Want to go for a walk?"

"Pardon?" She blinked trying to focus on his words instead of the tingling warmth his fingers created against her skin.

He smiled at her, his dimple appearing for a moment. "You're helping Sarah this afternoon and the Prince has asked me to join him. I just thought a walk would give us a moment alone."

Her heart sped. "S-Sure."

"I'll just let Philip know." Devon squeezed her hand before letting go and walking over to the prince.

He carried himself confidently. Rae could see he had changed since her first year at Guilder. He was still the same old Devon in some ways, but a more mature, grown-up version. It wasn't hard to see why the Privy Council wanted him. He was the better version of his father.

Was she the better version of her mother?

She highly doubted it.

Devon returned. "Ready?"

"Sure. Where are we going?"

Devon shrugged. "Just around the block." He held the door open for her as they stepped outside the antique building. He waved at the chauffeur to let him know they were walking. His fingers pressed against the inside of Rae's elbow as he steered her to the right and onto the sidewalk.

*Where are you going?* Maria's voice interrupted Rae's thoughts. She stumbled, not expecting to hear Maria.

Devon's hand curled gently around her upper arm to help her. "You okay?"

"Yeah." Rae rolled her eyes and tapped her forehead. "Maria just spoke in my head, surprised me."

"What does she want?"

"She asked where we were going."

"Tell her and Curtis that we're going over what happened earlier without spying eyes."

Rae felt her cheeks grow warm. She had misunderstood his suggestion for a walk completely. She straightened and cleared her throat. She needed to wake up and focus on her job. Whatever la-la dreams and hopes she was having needed to leave her thoughts completely. *Maria, just going over what happened earlier with Devon. No interruption. Did you guys find anything or find any information about the intruder?*

From the long pause, Rae assumed they had nothing.

*Not yet. Still working on it. Queen's guard haven't found anything either. They stopped and questioned us as well. When we told them who we worked for, they asked us to collaborate and help them out. We found nothing. You sure someone was really there? Could you have imagined it?*

Rae inhaled a harsh breath through her nose and forced it out again. *Sarah heard someone. She wouldn't lie. Whoever it was had a tatù. Maybe a shifting ability. Keep looking.*

"Sorry," she said to Devon. "Just seeing if they have any information."

"About what?" Devon asked. The sun peaked its bright head out of a pair of grey clouds and seemed to light the cement in front of them with a trail of the sunshine.

"There was an incident earlier." Rae had the feeling Devon wasn't going to be too impressed with what she was about to tell him. "When I left to nip to the loo, Sarah was using the bathroom, so I waited outside."

"Were there Queen's guards at the door?"

She nodded. "Alfie. At least I could see him. There were more, but they weren't exposed. After a bit, I went to go and check on her. I just had this hunch, you know... Alfie and I heard something and raced inside. I thought at first that someone had kidnapped Sarah-"

Devon grabbed her by the waist so stop her from walking. He swung her around, so she stood facing him. To any onlooker, it would have seemed he had spun her and pulled her close for a lover's embrace. "Slow down. Backup. Someone attacked Sarah?"

Rae found her breath that had gone missing when Devon wrapped his arms around her. "Yes. No. Wait!" She pressed her back against his arms. When he didn't let her go, she sent a small shock of electricity from her tatù against him.

He dropped his arms quickly. "Hey!"

She ignored him. "Nobody was in the bathroom when we walked in. An old window was banging either from the wind or someone escaping. There was no one about, down below or above. I thought I saw a cable or rope or something but it was gone when I checked again, and Maria confirmed there was nothing collected from the Queen's guards or them."

"Where was Sarah?"

"Hiding in a bath stall. She stood on a toilet and crouched down. Apparently when Alfie and I jostled the door to get in we scared the intruder."

"Did you see anyone?"

She shook her head. "I felt a tatù, but it could have been Sarah's. Whoever planned it, didn't execute it very well. Or wasn't planning on getting caught inside the toilets."

Devon began to pace, rubbing his hand along the small stubble of his chin line. "They could be amateurs with no clue what they are doing. Or experts knowing she would be in the bathroom alone and tried to seize the opportunity. They wouldn't plan on kidnapping Sarah. They'd kill her on the spot."

"Ouch! That's harsh." Rae couldn't believe he had said the words so matter a fact.

"But true." He stopped pacing. "What did Maria and Curtis see? They had eyes on the building."

Rae swallowed. "Um... That's where we hit a bit of a snag."

"What do you mean?" A single eyebrow rose on Devon's rugged face.

"Apparently Curtis went to grab them some coffee. I saw him carrying the cups to the van when I stuck my head out the window. And..." She began picking invisible lint off her small cardigan. "Maria said she nipped out to grab them some lunch."

Devon's jawline twitched as he clenched his jaw tight.

"Rookie mistake?" Rae offered.

Devon huffed. "Curtis isn't a rookie! He's one of the guys that helped crack the brainwashing device your father created! He knows better!"

"Maybe he thought Maria knew to stay on the lookout. She realized her mistake and apologized. I probably would have done the same thing."

"No. You wouldn't have." His jawline muscles twitched. "No way at all."

Rae watched him a few moments. "So what do we do now?"

"We let Carter know."

"Will Maria and Curtis get in trouble?"

"Rae, this isn't Guilder. There is a whole lot more at stake than worrying about being a tattle tale. Real life, real people. We may be pretending to be together in high-class society as our job, but for the rest of those people in there, this is their life. "

"I'm not..." She didn't finish her sentence. What was the use in arguing a point that she agreed with? She crossed her arms over her chest and stepped back to look at him. "When did you get so grown up, Devon Wardell?"

His head tilted slightly as he stared at her in surprise. "What do you mean?"

"You always had the mentor thing in you, since I've known you, but now you're all responsible. Wait! You've always been that as well." She pretended to stare hard at him and twirled with a strand of her hair. "It's something else about you." She snapped her fingers. "You're an adult now! That's it."

He didn't see the humor in her teasing. "This is a serious job, Rae. If you don't take it seriously, people die."

"People die when you take it seriously, too." She knew that better than anyone. "This job took my mother away. It killed her. Even if I believe she might still be alive, I lost her when I was six. I mourned her. *That* mother is dead. Nobody can give her back to me."

"She choose to work for the Privy Council. She went undercover to stop your father. She's a hero."

"She killed my father. That doesn't make her a martyr. She left me an orphan with no idea of what would happen when I turned sixteen."

"It's not her fault."

Rae blinked back the unshed tears. It hurt to swallow, but she did it anyways. She was not going to cry over this. "It is. She knew the risk of marrying my father, had an idea about inks crossing and still she choose to go through with it. She chose to work for the Privy Council. She sent me out to play in the treehouse as she casually planned on killing her husband!"

Devon reached out for her. "She sacrificed everything for you."

Rae stepped back so he couldn't touch her. "She didn't do it for me. She did it for the Privy Council. That was her only focus. I see that now. Job and country. Just like you."

"It's not ..."

"Don't defend it," Rae cut him off. "It's true. That's why you broke up with me. You can't have both. You're just like my mom."

"It's more complicated than that."

"No, it's quite simple. We've spent one afternoon with the Prince and soon-to-be Princess of Wales, and you can tell they love each other and are passionate about the things that matter to them. They'll make a difference in the world together."

"We make huge differences every day."

"Don't get me wrong, I work for the Privy Council to protect and serve, like you. However, I just see it through a different pair of eyes. I want to make a difference, but I also want to have a life. Have friends, a husband, kids. I'm not going to be the Privy Council's bionic machine. They will never own me." She had no idea where all this serious talk had come from. A minute ago she had been teasing Devon on how grown up he had become, and now she was telling him she wanted kids!

Something crossed Devon's face, but Rae couldn't figure out it was. "This is the job I dreamed about since I was a kid. I couldn't imagine anything else."

"I'm not asking you to." Rae wasn't sure what he meant. *Does he think...?* She wanted to get back to the beginning of this conversation and let everything else go. She blew her bangs away from her face. "For the record, when you broke up with me I didn't understand, but now that I'm here, where you were not too long ago, I understand the bigger picture. I respect what you're trying to do."

Devon looked like he wanted to say something but didn't. He closed his eyes a moment and finally spoke, "We should probably head back, or Philip and Sarah are going to wonder what happened to us."

They walked, side by side, back to the hall. As they neared the building, Rae asked, "You and me... We okay?"

Devon ruffled the top of Rae's head and then wrapped his arm across Rae's shoulders pulling her against him. He hugged her tight and after a few moments kissed her forehead before slowly letting her go. "We are."

Rae heard Devon's phone vibrate against his pocket.

He pulled it out. "Devon." He nodded and mouthed 'Carter' to Rae. As they spoke, Rae could figure out that Carter already knew everything that had happened. It sounded like the Privy Council didn't believe Devon and Rae needed back up.

Devon slipped his phone back into his pocket. "We should head back now. It seems like whoever is after Sarah might not wait for the Masquerade Ball."

# Chapter 12

Rae and Devon headed back inside the hall.

"No admittance, kids." A front guard doorman would not let them re-enter. "The hall is closed."

"We were just here with the luncheon."

"Place is closed now."

"Prince Philip and Sarah are waiting for us."

The large man let out a barking laugh. "And I'm Father Christmas's Uncle."

Devon gave the plain gray suited man the once-over. "Where's Alfie?"

The man barely glanced at Devon before turning his attention back to the view outside the front door.

Devon grabbed the man by the collar, getting his full attention.

Three men appeared suddenly behind Devon and Rae; guns pointed. Devon didn't even bat an eye. "Now that I have your full attention, where is Alfie?"

Rae's chest heaved.

Alfie came around the corner, his face tight with anger. Rae swore she saw him fight back a grin when he saw Devon holding one of his guys against the wall. "What's going on here?"

Devon let go of the man and smiled. "Alfie! I was just asking for you."

Alfie made a single motion with his hand, and the men put their guns away. "What can I do for you?"

"Philip and Sarah are waiting. There seems to be a misunderstanding down here."

"It's fine," Alfie spoke to his men. "Mr. Wardell here works for the Privy Council."

Some of the men looks impressed, others looked annoyed.

"He's here with Karen, his girlfriend, but I spoke with him earlier and he is completely on board with helping make sure nothing happens to the soon-to-be Princess of Wales. After the incident, earlier, I want him around."

"Wasn't the girl involved with the occurrence?" The gentleman, who Devon had almost accosted earlier, pointed at Rae.

"She was with me, trying to help. Sarah is comfortable around her, so she stays." Alfie shot Rae an apologetic look. "She's clear. She checks outs. I contacted the Privy Council."

"Excuse me?" Rae asked. What had Carter or whoever told him?

Alfie smiled. "Your boyfriend's company knows everything about everyone. You date one of their top; they have tabs on you."

"Oh, okay." She realized she should probably appear mad at Devon to play the part of the annoyed girlfriend. She crossed her arms and pretended to be mad at Devon. "You could have told me that! I thought you said you worked security."

A couple of the men chuckled.

She turned to head into the main banquet hall but not before she caught Devon shrugging to the men and mouthing, "*Women*!" She pretended she didn't see and pressed her lips tight together to suppress a smile.

"Karen! Devon!" Sarah came over when she saw them. She walked gracefully and flipped her long blonde hair over her shoulder. "I wasn't sure if something came up and you wouldn't be able to make it back."

Rae knew she was referring to the intruder in the bathroom. "We went for a walk. There was nothing out there but fresh air." She needed to work on her subliminal messaging; she sucked.

At least Sarah understood. She linked her arm through Rae's. "Let me show you the hall and what we are going to do for the masquerade. Do you have a costume yet? Don't tell me! It's supposed to be a secret who wears what. That way we are all equal for one night." She gave a perfectly pitched laugh. "That's the idea behind the masks. If it sticks is a completely other question." She began directing Rae to a part of the large hall away from Philip and Devon. A large stack of boxes were piled in the corner.

"Everything is going to be red. The Queen wanted purple to represent the royals, but since I am in charge this year I wanted to change it up. Red for England. It represents the people, not royalty. This ball is supposed to be about tea with the Royals." She opened one of the boxes and pulled out a napkin. "See?" She held up the fancy damask napkin with Royal Tea embroidered on the side in a garnet red thread. "It's going to be about a royal tea for everyone. A party that doesn't have a face for levels of society. We will all be equal."

Rae watched the Sarah opened another box to show garnet red wine glasses. She felt her tatù sift through its abilities. She ignored the feeling as it seemed to do it all the time now, as if trying to find the most effective one to keep on guard should she need it. "Everyone will be equal? You know that leaves you vulnerable, right?"

Sarah nodded. "I'm not going to hide. That's not who I am." She angrily slapped the lid back on the wine glasses. They clinked against each other in protest. "It leaves them susceptible, as well."

Rae hated to be practical, but Sarah had to realize how serious the danger was. "In what way? If they have a tatù like Devon, they've already got a leg-up over your guards. You have a unique ability, Sarah, but there are others with much more powerful inks."

"That's why Devon and you are here." She tilted her head and glanced back toward Philip and Devon. "What is your tatù?

Philip told me before that he remembers you in a class we took." Her voice dropped to a whisper. "I told him yes, but we never took a class together. What can you do?"

Rae began tapping her foot against the marble floor. She stopped when she stubbed her toe. "Ow!" She grinned. "Sorry, I'm okay." She reached down and rubbed her foot.

Sarah did not smile.

"I can make memories."

"You implant memories in people?"

"Sort of."

"Not sure how that makes you a worthy Privy Council member."

"Devon works for the Privy Council."

"So do you. What else can you do?"

Rae wondered why Sarah wasn't just accepting her one ability. "Just that."

"You're lying." Sarah stared hard at Rae. "I've spoken to you in ten different languages in the past two minutes and you've answered everything."

Rae blinked. *What*? "I have?"

"Oui. You could only do that if you had my tatù." Sarah put her hands on her hips. "But you just said you can implant memories. Devon said your tatù was similar to his the day I met you. So what is it? What can you do?"

"I... I..." Rae's eyes skirted across the room to Devon, or where Devon had been. The spot was not vacant. Philip and Devon had disappeared somewhere. She returned her gaze to Sarah and jumped back in surprise.

Sarah held a small pistol pointed directly at her. "Move one inch toward me and I'll shoot."

Rae held her hands up. How in the world had she become the bad guy? She opened her mouth but didn't say anything when Sarah raised the gun.

"Think carefully over what you are about to say, it could be your last."

"I'm on your side, Sarah."

"Really?"

"I'm not going to hurt you." Rae switched to Jennifer's tatù and in the time it took Sarah to blink, Rae raced over disarmed her and held it by the pistol end. She kept it at her side, nervous. This was the first time she had ever held a gun. "My tatù lets me copy other tatùs. I can mimic them."

Sarah stepped back, her hands held out defensively in front of her. She opened her mouth to scream.

Rae reacted quickly again. She covered Sarah's mouth so she couldn't. "Please don't call Alfie. He doesn't know I have a tatù. The fewer people that know, the better." She moved her hand, mortified she had just smothered the soon-to-be princess of Wales' mouth. She handed the small pistol back to Sarah. "You don't need this on me."

Sarah took it, her eyes big as she stared at Rae. "I've only heard about one person who could copy tatùs."

"Simon Kerrigan?"

Sarah nodded.

"I'm his daughter." The cat was out of the bag. Rae waited for the accusations to begin. She figured it would be less than ten seconds before Sarah raised the pistol and screamed for Alfie.

Sarah surprised her. "He had a daughter? Does the Privy Council know?"

Rae nodded.

"Did you attend Guilder?"

"I did. I started the year they opened it up to co-ed."

"Did they do that because of you?"

She shrugged. "Probably."

"Cool."

Wait... cool?

"I mean, it must feel good to be responsible for progressive changes without even trying to do them."

"I never thought of it that way. I kind of got lost in the fact that my father is known as a psycho. Made for a bit of a tough first year." She didn't bother explaining to Sarah that she hadn't known about tatùs until the day she arrived at Guilder. Or another about her father. Or that her mother died protecting her and stopping her father. Or that she might still be alive. Rae wanted to tell Sarah, but she didn't.

Sarah slipped the pistol into a pocket on the inside of her suit jacket. The material concealed it perfectly. She dropped her leg quickly when they heard male laughter, and then Devon and Philip appeared in the hall.

"You two all right?" Philip called out as they walked toward them.

"Fine," Sarah said. "I won't say anything."

"Neither will I." Rae forced a friendly smile on her face, trying to copy Sarah's.

Devon raised an eyebrow. He could obviously hear them but didn't say anything.

Rae would make up something later or tell Devon after they caught the guy trying to get Sarah.

"Are we allowed to see what's in the boxes?" Philip asked, slipping his arm around Sarah and kissing her cheek.

"Nope. It's still a surprise." Sarah winked at Rae. "Philip has no idea about all this." She gestured at the boxes. "I even picked out what he's wearing."

Philip groaned. "I'm not wearing pink. Or feathers. Please don't make my outfit into some peacock or something like that."

She stood on her tip toes and hugged him. "Never! It's very princely."

"Have you already picked out your dress and mask?" Sarah asked Rae.

"I have someone designing it for me... and Devon's too." Rae grinned. She pictured Molly creating this over the top outfit. She almost feared what it would be. Maybe it was better to not know until the day of the ball.

Philip chuckled. "She got you too, 'eh?"

Devon gave a low laugh. "Every time."

"They always do, mate." Philip clapped him on the back. "How about a drink?" Philip signaled to one of the staff standing near the wall. "Is there a bottle of wine we might be able to sample?" The staff nodded vigorously and nearly ran into the kitchen. "Or do you prefer beer?"

"Wine is fine." Devon stuff his hands into his pockets. "So Philip, what's been going on with Sarah?" He sat down on a high chair by a round bar-like table. "What's the situation?"

Philip sighed and sat down beside him. "We have no idea." He glanced at Sarah. "Come sit down, sweetie."

Rae followed Sarah and sat down between her and Devon. The staff came back with two bottles, one red, the other white. He returned a moment later with four lead crystal glasses. After he had poured everyone a glass, he scampered back to the kitchen.

"There's always a threatening letter or some worry to deal with. However, this is different. It started just after we announced our engagement. She would find a letter in her room or somewhere she was attending. At first we thought it was one of the staff and questioned everyone. Then things progressed, and a dead rat wearing a crown with a note was left in her bathroom about a month ago. The wedding is this summer, and someone or some group doesn't want her to be to be in line for the crown! It's a frightening thought."

"It's been going on while you were dating?" Devon asked.

"It pretty much started after the engagement," Sarah said.

Devon leaned forward resting his elbows on the table. "Why didn't you contact the Privy Council?"

"We have our guards and secret service." Philip seemed unimpressed by Devon's question. "You guys couldn't have done anything faster. But it's escalated to something dangerous now. It has to stop."

"I can't imagine someone not liking Sarah." Rae couldn't get around why anyone would want to hurt her. Devon's knee banging into hers reminded her of the real reason. Tatù. It didn't make sense. Sarah's tatù was a helpful one. She wouldn't use it to harm anyone. Something didn't make sense.

"We may have our guards, but I am glad you are here, Devon." Philip raised his glass of wine in cheers.

Sarah nudged Rae and winked at her from the corner of her eye. "I'm glad Karen's here too." She raised her glass.

They clinked goblets and Rae tried not to grimace from the volatile chemical reaction of the taste of wine inside her mouth. It sucked out all the water leaving it dry and tasting like wood. *Yuck*! So much for classy.

"What are your plans for the week leading up to the ball?" Philip asked, oblivious to the inner turmoil Rae's mouth was going through.

Devon saved her from having to speak. He must have noticed her struggling. "If they girls are hanging out together, I can keep an eye on Sarah if you'd like."

"I'd appreciate that. I have cleared most of my appointments and meetings this week. After what happened at the luncheon, I'm not taking any chances."

"How did...?" Sarah set her glass down and stared at her husband.

"Alfie filled me in." Philip reached for his fiancé's hand and held it. "If Karen hadn't barged her way into the bathroom, who knows what would have happened."

"What are the chances someone would try to sneak into the second-floor bathroom window the moment I was in there? It's not like there are cameras in the bathroom, and Alfie did his job, he did a full sweep of the room before I even walked in."

"I know, I know. But you can't be on your own until this bastard's caught. No one is taking her from me. My fiancé. No one is taking my fiancé, who is my life." He lifted her hand and kissed her fingers. "No one."

Rae stared around the room, anywhere but at the prince and soon-to-be princess. She realized Devon was doing the same thing.

Devon cleared his throat. "We should leave the two of you be. I think the chances of a repeat incident are not likely today."

"I agree. Alfie has upped the guard, and we will be leaving shortly to head back to the palace." Philip stood. Devon quickly followed, and Rae did too. "Why don't the two of you come around tomorrow? The two girls can keep each other entertained. Have you ever played polo?"

"I have."

"Are you any good?"

Devon lifted one shoulder in a half-shrug. "I can hold my own."

"Good!" Philip clapped him on the back. "I could use another man on my team! I'll have a service pick the two of you up around half ten tomorrow morning?"

"We would love to join you."

"Then it's settled. Let's hope the weather agrees to cooperate."

*And no one plans a surprise attack.*

## Chapter 13

They drove back to Heath Hall in silence. Once inside the flat, Rae kicked off her shoes and flopped onto one of the fancy couches. She blew a long breath out, let it blow her bangs away from her forehead, only to flop back down when she stopped. "What a day!"

Devon pulled his wallet out of his back pocket and tossed it on the stand by the door. "Such is the life of a super-agent." He walked around her into the kitchen and appeared a moment later with two bottles. "Water?"

"Sure." She raised her hand and caught the bottle without bothering to look up. She rested the bottom of it against her abs. The front door opened. Rae sat up. "Where are you going?"

Devon paused. "I need to check with Curtis to see if they found anything."

"Do you want me to come?"

He shook his head. "Don't worry. You rest. I'll fill you in if there is anything."

"You sure?"

"Positive. Why don't you check what we can make for dinner if you feel like it? Or we can order take-away. I'm easy."

When Devon closed the door, Rae fell back against the couch and closed her eyes. The events of the day ran through her head. She could not figure out why someone would want to go after Sarah. Her background checked out according to the Privy Council; her tatù wouldn't reveal the secret of the tatùs or have the power to dominate the world, control people, or be detrimental. She was sweet, and when together with her future husband, everyone loved them. A regular girl who overnight would become a princess. It was storybook perfect.

"So why does someone want her dead?" Rae asked herself out loud. She got up and went to her room to grab her laptop. A note lay on the dresser from Molly saying that she had filled up the drawers with some casual clothes and other needed items. Rae found a pair of jogging pants and casual long sleeve top. She changed into the comfy clothes and grabbed her laptop.

Back in the living room she settled back onto the couch and rested her legs along the length of the couch, setting her laptop on top of her thighs. She opened it and waited for the computer to load.

The monitor displayed a search engine on people surviving fires. She forgot that last night she had been trying to find information on her mother. She stared at the screen and wished it would be as easy as a Google search to find her.

*What does Jennifer know?* Rae wished to talk to her, just the two of them on their own. However, now was not the time. Jennifer had a mission of her own who knows where, and Rae had her own operation. She grabbed her phone and dialed Luke's number.

"Hello?"

"Hey, stranger." Rae smiled and glanced at the door hoping Devon wouldn't walk in.

"You still workin'?"

"Yup."

"Sucks."

"It's not so bad." Rae glanced around at her surroundings.

"I'm working, too."

"What are you doing?" She slapped her forehead. "Forget I asked. How are you doing?" They seemed to have an unwritten rule that they wouldn't discuss work.

Luke chuckled. "It's good to hear your voice."

"Yours, as well." She grinned and checked the door again. *Silly paranoia.*

"I have a feeling this isn't just a social call. What can I do for you?"

He knew her too well. "My first year at Guilder I read an article from some tatù kind of paper. Have you ever heard of it?"

"Yeah. Give me a sec." Clicks came through the phone line. Luke was probably typing into a computer. "It's old school. It stopped like ten years ago, maybe longer. It was big in the sixties, seventies. Actually the last article written was about the fire... Gosh, how'd you survive that?"

"You've never read it before?"

"No. I heard about the fire, but never read the article about it. I mean, it doesn't really have anything to do with me. No ink, remember?" He was quiet a moment. "Holy sh-sorry. How'd you not turn into some rebel, screwed up kid?"

Her aunt and uncle had kept her grounded. "Who says I didn't?"

"A little rebel never hurt anyone."

"Good to hear." She ran her finger over the mouse part of her laptop to turn the screen back on. "So the reason I'm calling..." She hesitated now, not sure she had a right to ask Luke to help her and unsure it might lead to trouble.

"It's okay, Rae. If there's something I can help you with, I'll try my best."

She didn't have anyone else. "The Privy Council believes my mother died in the fire. I don't."

"Do you have reason to think otherwise?" He lowered his voice. "You think they are lying to you?"

"No. Not at all. They really believe she died in the fire. There were two bodies recovered."

"Did they do any DNA testing?"

"I don't know. Probably. Maybe. I remember someone once told me they knew for definite my father perished in the fire." Lanford had told her that.

"Why do you think you the other body wasn't your mothers? Is it a hunch? Or maybe you're hoping so?"

He said the words as kindly as possible. "Kraigan's mother disappeared the same time as the fire. He believes she took off on him. I don't. I don't ever remember meeting her, but my gut is telling me she's the one who died in the fire with my dad." How could she explain it?

"But if your mother started the fire..."

"I think my mom's tatù made her fire-resistant. At least to the fire she created."

"Oh. Now that's interesting." He made some clicks that echoed through the phone.

"Why is it interesting?"

"There's this guy, Cromfield. He was around way back, like Tudor times. He had all these theories about tatùs. A museum in town has one of his books on display. We should go sometime to see it. Anyway, this guy theorized a whole bunch of stuff. He was like a scientist and tried all these experiments as well." A mouse clicked as he spoke. "I'm trying to find a paper I read on it a while back. I can't seem to locate it."

Rae didn't know what to say. She wasn't about to let Luke know she had broken into the museum to steal a sheet of paper from Cromfield's book. "I heard of the guy."

"You have? Of course, you would have. I'm sure Guilder has an entire class dedicated to the guy. He's got some theory on tatù evolution. I'm going to dig it up for you. Have you heard about it?"

"Not about tatù evolution." *Just that he drew a picture of me way before I was born.*

"I'll find it."

"Can you look for something else for me, too?"

"I can try."

"Can you see if the Xavier Knights have anything on my mother?" She took a swig of water from the bottle Devon had tossed her earlier. "I don't want you to get into any trouble." What if the Xavier Knights had her? It seemed kind of farfetched, but she didn't want to put Luke in any danger. "It doesn't have to be classified. Though if you do find any classified files about her, you have to let me know."

Luke gave a low laugh. "You are a rebel, with just enough crazy to make me like you. I'll see what I can find out. Can you email me your mom's full name, date of birth, all that kind of stuff? Send me a picture of her too if you have one. I'll see what I can find for you."

"Thanks, Luke. I really appreciate it." Rae's gaze shifted to the door to the flat. She could hear Devon coming in the main door. "I should get going now. You know, work to do and stuff."

"No problem! Give me a few days, and I'll see what I can find out."

"Thanks again. I didn't know if I should ask, I don't want you to get into any trouble."

"I won't. It's fine."

"I really appreciate it."

"You already said that," he teased. "Oh, Rae?"

"Yeah?"

"I phoned Molly the other day, but she hasn't gotten back to me. Have you spoken to her?"

*Oh shoot.* "I have. She's fine."

"Next time you see or talk to her, tell her to give me a shout."

Rae grinned. "Are you crushing on Molls?"

"Uh, no." He laughed and Rae could tell by the noise coming through the phone that he was shaking his head. "I'm still trying to impress you with my wit and charm."

"You are charming." Was she seriously flirting with him?

"Good to hear. Guess I just need to convince you now that I'm good for you."

He was good for her. A nice guy, he liked her, he didn't have a tatù but knew all about them and didn't judge her. He was perfect. "Hey, I gotta go. I'll call you later." She hung up the phone as Devon stepped through the door. She realized she had hung up on Luke before replying to his last comment. *That was rude.* Her head could be persuaded to like Luke; it was her bloody heart that kept beating to Devon's rhythm and making her do stupid things, like hang up on Luke. She vowed to not let that happen again.

She slipped her phone in her pocket, shut the laptop and then jumped up to check what food was in the kitchen. "How did it go?" she asked as she searched through the cupboards.

Devon came on and sat on one of the bar stool chairs. "Fine. I guess. They weren't able to find out anything about the intruder. There is nothing to prove someone was there. It's strange."

Rae closed a cupboard and crossed her arms over her chest as she leaned against the counter top. "I didn't make it up."

Devon's eyebrows shot up. "I never said you did."

"It feels like Maria and Curtis are accusing me that I did." She pursed her lips together. "Or hinting at it at least."

"They aren't! Plus Sarah and Alfie were there. All three stories corroborate."

"You checked?"

"No! They just do." Devon's head tilted slightly as he stared at her. "What's up with you? Why are you so defensive?"

Because you're getting in the way of me liking a boy. *Mature, Rae. Very mature.* "Curtis shouldn't have left his post for coffee. Neither should have Maria. Had they been watching..."

"What could they have done? They are Intel people. Their job is to get information out to us or warn us of incoming problems. That kind of stuff. They aren't trained to defend and protect. Do you feel responsible for not catching whoever was in the bathroom?" Devon tapped the granite top with his finger as he spoke. "You prevented something terrible from happening. That's what you need to focus on, not about letting them get away." He stared at her for a long time. "Is this because of Kraigan? Because he got away?"

"No!"

Devon pushed the barstool away and came around to where she stood. "He's not coming near you. I'm not going to let that happen again! Ever!" The fierceness in his voice reached his eyes making them bright. "I'll kill him myself!" He stood, legs shoulder width apart, hands on his hips, and his chest heaving.

"You shouldn't keep that hatred for Kraigan so bottled up inside of you. It's not healthy."

"What?" Devon stared hard at her and then his lips slowly curled upwards as he tried to fight a smile. "Are you taking the mickey on me?"

"I..." Rae's stomach growled loudly interrupting her. She looked down at it in surprise. "I guess I need to eat."

"I think you do, and quickly." Devon's body relaxed. "You feel like curry? There's a takeaway place around the corner. I can go grab us something. Or you can come if you want."

"Sure."

She followed him out to the car, and they drove in silence. The sun had begun it's descent, and the early night sky was changing from gray to black fast. It looked like it might storm tonight. The air held the scent of spring, but it was being tossed around in the wind trying to get rid of the last remnants of winter.

Devon pulled into the restaurant and parked the car near the takeaway door.

Rae held her hand on the door but did not open it. "Do you mind if wait in here?"

"Sure, why?"

She pointed at his clothes. "You're dressed to the tens and I've changed into jogging pants and comfy clothes. Seems a bit odd."

"You look fine." Devon shrugged. "What do you want?"

"Chicken Curry with rice. Or tikka masala. I'm good with anything."

"I'll get you some poppa dons to eat on the ride back. Don't want that tummy of yours growling at me." He nipped out of the car before Rae could throw a gust of wind or electrical spark at him.

While she waited, she thought about her conversation with Luke. Cromfield seemed to have had his hands in everything. He had worked for King Henry the Eighth, had written books, done scientific-y things, inventions, predicted the future and who knew what else. The guy seemed to have had free reign back then.

*What was the theory Carter had been so keen on?* The double tatù ability? Rae couldn't see the big deal about it. It should have proved to the Privy Council back then and now, that mixing tatùs didn't mean demon children. Hadn't Cromfield coupled two tatù people together and waited the sixteen years to see what happened to the child? The results showed two tatùs becoming one. Like a blending. Sure it lessened the amount of people with abilities but it didn't create stupid-devil spawn or whatever the PCs were so scared of. Rae tucked a loose chunk of hair behind her ear.

Jacked up people liked to keep journals. Cromfield, her father... Probably a bunch more crazies. Her dad's journal was gone thanks to Kraigan. Not that it was super important. It did have information about the brainwashing technique he had created but Devon, and the PCs had dismantled that thing a couple years ago. What else was in the journal? The fact her grandparents were both inked? She had been surprised when Carter mentioned it back in his office, but she had read it in the journal and must have forgotten.

Her stomach moaned, but this time not because of food. A weird thought crossed her mind. Her grandparents both had tatùs. Her dad ended up with a combined tatù and then married her mom. *Crap!* The sinking feeling in the pit of her stomach grew heavier. Why did she have the feeling that Cromfield had only tested immediate results, like two tatùs and then waited sixteen years? What if he had continued his research and combined two more tatù people together; as a second generation of tatùs... Like Rae. Her grandparents had both been inked; her parents had both been inked, she was unchartered history. That's why she had her mother's ability. It had just taken longer to show up because the dominant ink came first.

Kraigan would have it as well if he didn't realize it already. She needed to find out what his mother could do.

Cromfield would have loved to be around now to see Rae.

She stared at the front door of the restaurant as Devon stepped out. It had begun raining, and Rae hadn't even noticed. *Devon*! Imagine what kind of super-baby they could have? She shook her head and flushed the thought from her mind. That was never going to happen! She would never let her child go through what she had gone through.

# Chapter 14

The alarm on her phone grated her ears. Rae would have preferred another hour of sleep, but Molly had been insistent on the phone last night that Rae needed to come early to be outfitted perfectly for the polo match.

Rae yawned and stretched her arms. She shouldn't be tired. She had gone to bed early, right after eating actually. The thought of last night sent her rushing. If she hurried, she could beat Devon. She rolled out of bed and made her way to the shower.

She slipped into a long skirt and black tank top. "This is ridiculous. I'm telling Molly I need more clothes down here." She grabbed her purse and phone and headed down the hall to the front door.

"You want coffee?"

She jumped at the sound of Devon's voice. He stood leaning against the kitchen doorframe, a mug in his hand. He let out a low laugh. "Didn't mean to frighten you. I assumed you heard me."

She shook her head. "I'm just going to head up to see Molly."

Devon came toward her. "I'll come too. You sure you don't want coffee?"

"I'll get one later." She opened the door and made her way to the staircase.

"Rae?"

She paused, already half up the stairs. "Yeah?"

"Is something wrong?"

"No." she replied too quickly.

"Then why are you avoiding me?"

She scoffed. "I'm not avoiding you."

"Really? You wouldn't look at me the ride home from picking up dinner. Then you scarfed your food down so fast I thought you were going to eat mine as well."

"I was starving." She noticed the teasing in his eyes but looked up at the walls to avoid them.

"You literally ran for the bedroom as soon as you finished. You couldn't get away from me fast enough."

"I don't know what you mean." She sucked at lying. "I just needed to rest."

"I know you, Rae," Devon spoke quietly and with loaded implications.

When he didn't say anything else, she hesitantly met his gaze. He stared at her with big puppy dog eyes and she almost told him about her theory on Cromfield and tatù crossed children. She hesitated because he looked like he wanted to say more, but he seemed to be holding back as well. He didn't push her. It took every ounce of willpower to break the silence between and move forward, away from all the unsaid things they seemed to want to say to each other but couldn't. Somehow she knew that by not finishing this conversation, they would be closing the door to any future they might have had. She didn't know about Devon, but she had to let go of her feelings for him. There was no other choice.

Rae tried to speak but had to clear her throat to get the words out. "W-We should probably go see Molly. We don't want to be late."

"Yeah..." Devon forced a smile and made his face unreadable. "Let's see what she has in store for us today." He passed her on the stairwell taking the stairs three at a time.

Molly's door flew open as Rae reached the top step. "Finally! I was wondering if you guys overslept." Her eyes flitted back and forth between the two of them. "Are you two sharing a bed?" She grinned wickedly. "'Bout time Rae found her way between the sheets!"

"Molly!" Rae pushed a burst of wind at her friend, ready to kill her. Her face burned with embarrassment.

Molly flew across the room and landed on the sofa. "Give it up, Rae," she laughed. "If it makes you feel any better, I heard Devon's in the same boat as you."

This time Devon grabbed two pillows off the settee chair by him and drilled them expertly at Molly's head.

She threw her hands up in surrender. "I'm done." She then grabbed one of the pillows and held it up to protect her head and waited. When no more pillows came, Molly peered over the top of the lace cushion. "Sorry, guys. I didn't realize you were both so sensitive." She quickly ducked behind the cushion as Devon tossed a balled up sweater at her.

"Grow up, Molly." Devon walked over to the side of the room where his clothes were laid out and snatched up the pair of jeans and red shirt. "Do your job. Stay out of my personal business, or you'll be finding work outside of the Privy Council." He grabbed a bag filled with polo equipment and tossed it over his shoulder. "This everything I need?"

Molly nodded, her eyes as big as the "oh" shape of her mouth.

Devon spun around and headed for the door. "I'll be downstairs," he said to Rae and walked out the door.

"Sorry," Molly said softly. "What the heck just happened?"

Rae felt bad for her friend but also understood Devon's reaction. "Maybe you should sometimes keep comments like the ones you just said inside your head."

"I guess so. I never thought of him as sensitive. What's going on with you guys?"

"Nothing," Rae answered quickly, probably too quickly. She changed the subject. "What have you picked out for me to wear today?"

Molly grinned and slipped off the couch. "Let me show you. At least fashion is something I can't screw up." She opened the tall wooden dresser by the change screen and pulled out a white dress bag. Inside hung a short soft white dress with cranberry colours swirled throughout. It had just over the shoulder-length sleeves. It was classy and also sporty at the same time. "It's short so you aren't tied up in a long skirt, which will limit your movement. I know you prefer longer, but it won't go with the jacket." She pulled a hanger out of the clothes rack by her. On it hung a light beige stylish jacket with three-quarter rolled up sleeves and large buttons.

Rae took the clothes Molly handed to her and slipped behind the change screen. She stepped out a moment later to see how the dress looked in the mirror. She loved the jacket over the dress.

"Here's a matching purse and heeled sandals. The shoes are perfect. No pokey heel, just a raised filled in heel so you can walk on the grass without getting stuck." She dashed over to a table with millions of things laid out on it. "Here's a scarf to tie loosely." She hung it around Rae's neck and stepped back to view her handiwork.

Rae sat on the edge of a chair to slip on the shoes.

"You can run in those if you have to. Or karate chop people. Those suckers will stay on your feet if you went to war."

Rae laughed. "I might keep these to wear after this mission is finished."

"You can. Otherwise, the Privy Council donates it all to charity shops."

"Seriously?" Rae wanted to keep it all.

"That's what they told me to do when we finish here." Molly sat down across from Rae. "Can you tell Devon I'm sorry? I should have kept my mouth shut. That was kind of stupid of me."

Rae patted her friend's knee. "I'll tell him. It'll be fine."

"I hope so." Molly straightened. "Let's get your make-up done and your hair. You're leaving in about fifteen minutes."

"Fifteen? Shoot!"

"I can't do it. You'll have to wear your hair in a pony today. I won't have time to make it super glam. Next time come up here an extra hour earlier. For the masquerade, I'm going to need you the entire afternoon. Pretty takes time, you know."

Rae sat on bleachers beside Sarah in a covered tent. Prince Philip and a guy with a matching top had grabbed Devon the moment they arrived. Since Rae had never watched a match before, Sarah excitedly explained the game as it went on.

From what Rae could gather, Devon was a decent player. Very good in fact, according to Sarah.

When a horn sounded, Sarah stood and grabbed two champagne glasses off the table near the tent entrance. "You coming?" she asked Rae.

Rae stood and followed Sarah. "Where are we going?"

Sarah handed Rae one of the champagne flutes. "Divot stomping!"

"Pardon?" Rae held her glass as the players from the field stood by the roped fence holding bottles of champagne.

Prince Philip waved a small shiny metal thing in the air. "Great start to the match," he called with a grin on his face. "Though I don't like losing so much. Let's make the second half ours, mates!"

Rae squinted trying to figure out what he held. Her body switched its tatù to one with enhanced vision. "Is he holding a miniature sabre?"

Sarah giggled beside her. "We call it sabrage. It's the art of opening a bottle of champagne by using a small traditional sword called a sabre."

Philip shouted, "Sabre a Champagne!" He popped the top of the bottle off with the sabre and the bubbly liquid spilled over.

He quickly tipped the bottle to the ladies crowded around him and Devon.

The captain of England's polo team stood by Sarah and Rae. He popped his bottle and poured Sarah the first glass.

"Cheers." She smiled and waited for Rae. "Off to the field we go!"

They were the first to walk onto the field. Rae watched Sarah stomp down on a torn up piece of turn.

"Divot stomping," Sarah repeated laughing as she cheered her glass against Rae's. "Stomp away!" She greeted another lady beside them and chatted about the game.

Rae found a turned up chunk of grass and flipped it over with her foot before kicking it back into its spot. She owed Molly a thank you for the smart thinking shoes. Some of the ladies on the field wore welly boots and a few were struggling to walk on the grass in skinny heels. It made Rae smile.

"How's it going?" Devon came up beside her and offered her a refill of champagne.

Rae shook her head. "Still haven't finished the first one."

"It's better than the wine from yesterday, I promise." He chuckled. "Guessing from the face you pulled when you tried the red... Did it suck every ounce of sweetness out of your mouth?"

She raised her eyebrows and gave him an *oh-you-didn't* look. "Did everyone see me?"

Devon shook his head. "No. I think you're safe. Philip and Sarah were too busy ogling each other to notice." He leaned over and rubbed her shoulder with his. "You're secret's safe with me." He stretched his arms. "What do you think of the match so far?"

"Interesting. It's—"

A girl not far from Rae and Devon let out a shriek.

"She probably stepped in horse-oh shit!" Devon took a step forward and froze.

Rae followed his gaze. "You have got to be kidding me!" People were scattering from a spot just a few yards away from

Devon and Rae. The shrieking woman stood pointing at another woman who held a bloody sabre. A polo player stood clutching his shoulder. His blue shirt seeped red, and the blood ran between his fingers. He was trying to talk the miniature sword-wielding lady down. Rae's tatù switched to Devon's ability, and she took a few steps closer.

Devon held his arm across her chest to stop her. "Don't, Rae. Not in public."

"Put the knife down, Lily. There are people watching us," The injured polo player said.

The shrieking woman tried to move around them; she was caught between them and the back of a shed that housed the horses. Lily jabbed the knife in her direction. "Don't even try moving, you... You whore! Sleeping with my boyfriend!"

"I'm not your boyfriend anymore! We broke up months ago."

"That's not what you said last night."

The injured polo player had the decency to look embarrassed. "Can you please lower your voice? Put the knife down and let's talk."

"Talk about what? You sleeping with her?" Lily looked around at everyone watching. Her nostrils flared, and her heart rate quickened. She spun back to the polo player, her arm swinging wide.

There was no way Rae was going to let her stab her ex-lover-boyfriend - whatever he was. Tatù or not, she had a responsibility to protect people. She raced forward, keeping her speed slow enough to appear normally human and kicked her leg out. Her foot connected with Lily's wrist and the knife went flying on the roof of the horse shed.

Devon was right behind her and grabbed Lily. The other girl ran over to the polo player and hugged him, crying and asking if he was alright.

"Rae!" Devon hissed, loud enough so only she would hear. "What the hell were you thinking?"

Everyone around stood quiet and stared at them, Rae in particular. She shrugged and grinned sheepishly. "Guess I got lucky." She rolled her eyes to Devon and lightly tapped his arm. "I told you those self-defense classes would come in handy one day."

Someone in the crowd began clapping.

"That's some leg you got there," a security man said as he and another guard came by to escort Lily off the field. A medic jogged behind them, ready to help the polo player.

"Oh boy, was my adrenaline pumping! They say a woman can lift a car. Boy, were they right!" She lifted a shaky hand, playing the crowd. "Guess I could use another glass of that champagne." She had tossed her previous glass on the ground when she had decided to stop crazy-girl.

Devon slipped his arm through hers. It was meant to be playful but by the tight grip of his fingers, Rae knew he was ticked. "I can help you there, sweetie. Let's get you another glass." They walked through the crowd, and someone handed her a glass and someone else filled it.

"Where's Sarah and Philip?" she whispered behind her glass before she took a sip. The champagne was bubbly and sweet. Devon had called it when he said she would like it. She took another sip and then another.

"Alfie and some other under covers took them away. They should be back shortly, once the field's cleared."

"They okay?"

"Fine." Devon's eyes darted everywhere across the field. "You almost blew our cover."

She lowered the champagne flute. "No, I didn't."

"Nearly."

"I did not." Rae crossed her arms over her chest and snuck another sip of champagne. It seemed to be taking the edge off. She knew she had been extremely careful. "I made sure I didn't move fast and just kicked the knife away. Completely normal."

"It was close." Devon's shoulders dropped a small degree. "Did you see how the sabre knife landed?"

Rae arched her neck to see the top of the horse shed. The handle's glass jewels sparkled and shimmered in the sun. It stood straight up, a good inch or two embedded in between two slate shingles.

"Completely normal, 'eh?" Devon chuckled.

"That's just beginner's luck. I couldn't get it to land like that again if I tried."

"I'm surprised you didn't break the girl's wrist."

"There you two are!" Philip slapped Devon on the back. "I heard you saved the day, Karen." He nodded at Rae. "Shame about being in line for the throne, you miss all the action."

"It was nothing." Rae couldn't look him in the eye. "Devon's the hero. He's the one that taught me self-defense." She grinned, happy to pull him into the conversation. "I'm surprised he didn't react faster than me." She pretended to punch Devon in the arm. "He's the one that works for the big super-company."

Philip let out a loud laugh. "She's got one on you there, mate. Maybe you need to get her filling out an application." A man in a suit came by and spoke quietly to the prince. "If you two will excuse me, I'm going to check on our player with the hurt shoulder. We might be playing one man down." His eyebrows shot up as he gave Rae a once over. "You don't play, by chance?"

"No!" Devon answered before Rae had a chance.

Philip laughed again. "I think I was wrong before when I told Karen she had a keeper, it appears it's the other way around." He winked at Rae before jogging off to the ambulance parked near the large tent. The man in the suit had to race to keep up with him.

Devon put his arm around Rae and pulled her tight. "Does everything you touch turn to gold?" He kissed the top of her head. "I don't know how anyone ever thought you were like your father. You wear your heart on your sleeve. I'm not sure that man even had one." He kicked a divot into place and picked up her discarded champagne flute from earlier. "Shall we go find Sarah?"

The compliment made her day. "That's the nicest thing you have ever said to me." She finished the bubbly liquid in her glass. "I'll head over to Sarah. Let's not make the little kick thing any bigger."

"The adrenalin edge wearing off?" Devon teased. "Now getting a little paranoid, are we?"

She pushed him back toward the field. "Go warm up for the second half, silly, or do whatever you have to do. Pet your horse, feed it some sugar cubes or something."

"Sugar cubes?" His dimple appeared reminding Rae of her first year at Guilder.

"Go!" She forced her eyes and body to turn its attention to the large tent to find Sarah. The masquerade would be here before they knew it. Hopefully, they would catch this tatù-hunter before then and move on to another assignment, with different partners.

Or she could focus on finding her mother. Anything to distract her from... *Enough!* Her inner voice shouted.

# Chapter 15

The next few days passed without incident. No one went after Sarah, and Rae put all her concentration into the task at hand. She squeezed in some training, called and left a message with Luke and hung out with Molly upstairs during the little free time she had. She and Devon managed to squeeze in two ballroom dancing lessons. They were formal and awkward, but at least they got through them. Devon knew how to dance, Rae didn't have a clue.

The day leading up to the Royal Tea Masquerade Ball was spent at the spa in the early morning with Sarah, and then Rae rushed back to the house after lunch to meet with Molly. Her hair and make-up had been done at the spa. She felt silly in jeans and t-shirt with all the fancy on top.

Devon was getting into his car when the chauffeur dropped Rae off. "Everything go okay?" He too had been on friendly terms and seemed to be keeping Rae at arm's length. It made things easier for Rae.

"Great. Have you been up to see Molly already?"

Devon stared at her and then slipped his sunglasses on. "Yup. I'm all set to go. She's waiting for you." He grinned. "I wouldn't keep her waiting too long."

"I'm on my way up now." She paused in the doorway. "Where are you going?"

"Quick trip to Boots." He rubbed his face. "I need razors."

"Okay. See yah soon." She hurried up the stairs to Molly's place. Rae knocked on the door. "Molls, you in there?"

"Come in." Molly's voice rang out loud and clear.

Rae opened the door and stepped into the room. "I'm dying to see what I'm wearing tonight. Hook me up girl!" She moved to the middle of the room, trying to find the dress.

"Cover your eyes," Molly commanded. "AND close them."

Rae placed her hand over her eyes knowing that arguing with Molly would be futile. She peered through the small gaps between her fingers.

"No peeking!"

"I'm not!"

"Liar!"

"Okay. Now I'm ready."

"I know you, Rae Kerrigan!" Molly moved out of Rae's line of vision.

Rae didn't move her head to follow, or Molly would know right away she could see. She lurched backwards when a fingernail jabbed at her fingers. "I know you can see me."

Rae dropped her hand. "I'm not good with surprises."

"Ha! I knew you were watching!" Molly tapped Rae's wrist and shocked her.

"Hey!" Rae shook her wrist.

"That didn't hurt. I barely added any zing." Molly went behind the change screen she had set up in the room. "I should have known better." She appeared again with a massive puffy, black dress bag. "I found this dress yesterday. I had another design picked out in emerald green, but when I saw this, I knew it would be perfect on you. I found it online and then had to drive Devon's car to downtown London to pick it up. At a bridal boutique of all places! Who'd have thought?" She hung the hanger on the top of the change screen and began to unzip it. The stand creaked and shifted, as if shuddering because of the bag.

Rae craned her neck to see around Molly, who had positioned herself perfectly so Rae couldn't really get a look. Rae anxiously watched Molly wrestle with the bag for a minute.

Molly grunted and huffed in frustration. "A little help here?"

Rae jumped to lend a hand. She gasped as she lifted the long bottom of the dress out of the bag, and Molly held the hanger. "This thing weighs a ton!"

"Not when it's on. It just feels heavy now because all the material is bunched together." The stunning dark garnet red colour enhanced the silver and black detail. It was long, strapless and princess worthy.

"It's beautiful," Rae whispered touching the silver thread on the top of the dress.

"Do you know the magazine Allure? They made the dress." Molly fixed some of the bunched material. "It's a Quinceanera Dress. Strapless sweetheart ball gown." She gestured to the top. "Embroidered bodice with silver. It almost looks like platinum. The overskirt has pickups and a fabric flower on the side. You can store lipstick or even a weapon or whatever you need by the flower." She flipped the flower over to show the hidden pocket before turning the entire dress over. "There's a lace up back and the overskirt continues around here. It's long, but I found you these killer four inch heels that you are going to love."

"I can't wear that high of a heel!"

"They are extremely comfortable." Molly was dead serious.

"How am I going to dance in them? Or what if I'm chasing someone? I'll break my neck."

"No, you won't. You'll be fine." Molly pouted before smirking. "Be glad I didn't buy the six inch heels."

Rae's mouth fell open.

"There's a mask here somewhere as well." She reached inside the dress bag. "Aha! Here it is." A shiny black feather mask with silver detail and a shining stone reflected in the room sending a million sparkles dancing against the walls and ceilings.

"Is that a diamond?" The thing was huge.

"I wish! And don't say I didn't try for one. It's a Swarovski crystal. Next best thing in a pinch for time."

Rae gently reached for the mask and ran her fingers lightly over the black feathers. The embroidered detail was done in the same pattern as the dress. "It's beautiful."

"And matches Devon's outfit and mask."

"He's wearing a mask, too?"

"Of course. Isn't that the idea behind the Royal Tea ball? Not knowing who anyone is?"

Rae shrugged. She couldn't imagine Devon wearing feathers and lace on his face. She giggled; the picture in her head was not the boy she knew.

Molly stared at her. "You smoking something?"

"HA HA. You are so funny," Rae said sarcastically. "What kind of mask is Devon wearing?"

"Like a Zorro kind of cover. There's a mike inset so he can communicate with Curtis and Maria." Molly gestured for Rae to go behind the screen and start getting ready.

"Cool." Her hair and makeup were done; all, she needed, was her fancy dress. "Aren't I going to be ready too early?" She couldn't imagine sitting around in the dress for three hours waiting to go.

"I'm going to need to make sure it doesn't need any taking in or adjustments. Try it on and then I'll have the seamstress take in or let out whatever needs to be done. We can hang out while we wait."

Rae obeyed and sure enough, Molly had called it. They needed the seamstress. The little adorable lady was at the flat in less than twenty minutes with her sewing machine and everything else she needed. She fixed the dress so that it fitted Rae perfectly.

"You look like a princess," she told Rae as she finished up a few hours later.

"It is very pretty." Rae looked down, not recognizing the body connected to her head. "You did an excellent job."

There was a knock at the door, and Devon called from the other side, "Everyone decent?"

Molly scampered over and opened the door. "How's the tuxedo?"

Rae turned to see what he looked like as the seamstress handed her the mask she would be wearing.

Devon stepped in, his eyes going to straight to Rae. His eyes grew big as they travelled down and then up Rae.

Rae did the same. Devon wore a black tuxedo that fitted him perfectly. It accented his muscular shoulders and fit hips. Rae had never seen him look so handsome. She grinned. "You clean up nicely."

He gave her an appreciative smile. "So do you." He cleared his throat. "Molly you outdid yourself. Thank you."

Molly nodded, her face solemn. "I take my job very seriously. I won't mix personal with professional again."

"Really?" An eyebrow rose on Devon's face. "Stay you, Molls. Don't change for anyone, even me." He pulled a black string out of his pocket. "I need a bit of help with this."

Molly took it and grabbed Devon's hand, pulling him toward the couch. She climbed up on it and turned Devon, so he faced her. She spun him around showed Rae her handiwork. "Dickybow done to perfection!"

"A bowtie?" Rae tried to look at it, not Devon's striking face.

"How's it look?" Devon asked.

"Great. Perfect." Rae sat down to get her shoes on. The billows of the dress made it next to impossible while sitting in a chair. It would have been easier to do sitting on the floor.

Devon dropped down in front of her before she could slip off the chair. "Let me help." He slipped the first shoe on and adjusted the strap. "Okay?"

She nodded the warmth of his hand distracting her.

Molly held her phone up and snapped a picture. "You look like Cinderella and Prince Charming."

Devon put Rae's other shoe on and set the strap. He stood quickly. "Good to go?" He held his hand out for Rae.

She reached for it and let him pull her up. She picked up her fancy mask and slipped it on. "Let's go save a princess."

# Chapter 16

Outside Devon and Rae bumped into Curtis working in the back of his van.

"Everything okay?" Devon asked.

Curtis jumped. "You scared me, lad." He clutched his heart. "Aren't you two a pretty picture?" He grinned at Rae. "You look lovely."

She curtseyed. "Thank you."

"You have a job to do, but promise me you'll have some fun while you are there as well."

"I'll try." Rae nodded toward Devon. "I'm not sure about mister serious, though."

Devon pulled his mask out of his pocket and put it on. "There is a saying, a very old saying; when the pupil is ready the master will appear."

Rae stared at him. "Pardon?"

Curtis chuckled. "Don Diego de la Vega?"

"Yes."

"Who?" Rae looked back and forth between the two boys.

Devon grinned. "Zorro, Rae, Zorro."

He started walking toward his car.

Rae picked up the skirt of her dress and followed him. "Are you calling me the pupil?" She heard Curtis laugh behind her. "I heard you, Curtis!" She turned around and smiled at him, trying to speak with a nasal voice, "I'll get you, my pretty."

"Wicked Witch of the West?" He hopped back into the truck, poking his head out. "You'll never get the part, dear Rae. You are much too sweet."

She paused by the car door Devon held open for her. "Where's Maria?"

"Inside getting a few things organized. She'll be sad she missed seeing you dressed up." Curtis waved his hand. "We'll see you there. We'll be parked out of sight but within distance. Be careful."

"You, too." Rae said the words out of habit.

Devon closed her door and walked around to the other side. He looked like James Bond with his impeccably fitted suit and fast car. Rae felt like a bubble of lace and material as she sat in the low seat. She pulled her mask off and flipped open the sun visor to check her hair in the little mirror. It was fine, perfect actually. The spa had done a phenomenal job. Sarah had told her this morning they were amazing. She couldn't disagree.

They drove to the ball in silence, both seeming lost in their own worlds. As Devon pulled into the large parking area and waited in line for the valet parking, Rae tried to quietly clear her throat. "What do you think is going to happen tonight?"

Devon tapped his thumb against the steering wheel. "I don't know. There's a chance nothing will happen." He pulled the car up as the vehicles in front of them rolled forward. "I think what is going on is going to climax tonight. The attempt on Sarah during the luncheon was almost like they were scoping the building. I spoke with Philip earlier and he has the Queen's Guards on high alert. If anything happens, we'll all be there to stop it."

"Who could do this? Sarah is such a nice person."

"Sometimes it's not about the person." Devon put the car into park. "Mistrust everyone tonight. We'll catch whoever is doing this."

Rae's door opened. A valet dressed in black pants and a white jacket held his hand out to help her. Rae let her tatù chose what was the safest ability to use and settled on one with strong hearing. She watched other people getting out of their cars. "My mask!" Her tatù switching automatically, she grabbed the car door with lightning speed before it slammed shut and pulled it open. She leaned in and picked up the mask. She slipped it on and ignored the surprised look of the valet driver.

Devon came up beside her, his Zorro mask perfectly in place. "You ready?"

"Yuppers." She forced her shoulders back and tucked her arm inside Devon's mimicking the couples around them.

TV cameras and paparazzi were in full force leading up to the building. Rae automatically ducked her head down, forgetting that the mask gave anonymity until they neared the building. She switched to Maria's tatù and sent her a message. *We're entering the building now. Will keep you guys informed if anything is up.*

Maria's quiet voice came through Rae's thoughts. *Curtis said you looked unbelievable. I can't believe I missed it! I'm going to have to figure out a way to catch a glimpse of you dressed up. Too bad we can't send each other mental images!*

*That would be super cool. Molly took a picture. Get her to email it to you. I have to go, but I'll stay in touch.* Rae wanted to keep the inner chat line open for their job, not chitchat. She didn't think the Privy Council would approve.

"Wowza," Devon murmured once they passed through security and stepped into the main hall. The place had been transformed and the people standing around talking, drinking and dancing added to the atmosphere. The costumes ranged from simple to pretentious.

"I hear ya," Rae whispered to him. "How are we going to find Sarah? Or the Prince?"

Devon slipped his hand into hers and pointed with them. "See the peacock?"

"Oh no! She didn't dress Philip up as a peacock did she?" Rae's gaze ran down their arms to the emerald green and blue fancy tail that had to be at least four feet wide. The peacock turned around and Rae let out a breath when she saw it was a woman.

"Behind the peacock."

Rae had to wait for the lady to move before she saw Sarah. She didn't recognize her immediately but the man standing two feet behind gave her away. *Alfie.*

Sarah wore an emerald green dress with feathers on her shoulders. Her hair set in a bun, hidden by a cap that also had an exotic feather. She was a princess through and through. Philip stood at her side, wearing a mask similar to Devon's but in the same colour as Sarah's dress. Everyone else in the room wore their costumes, but the two of them, they belonged in them.

Orchestra music floated from the stage where a massive ensemble of instruments.

"Shame we have to work," Rae told Devon. "This is the kind of night little girls dreams are made of."

Devon nodded, his eyes scanning the room. "Yes. It's lovely."

She wanted to poke him in the gut. He wasn't even listening. Then again, he was doing his job, like she should be.

The center of the room had been set up for dancing. Rae watched couples twirl and dip in perfect time with the music. It was beautiful.

"Do you want to dance?" Devon asked.

Rae nodded, realizing a moment too late that he wasn't really asking her, he wanted a better position to see everyone there and the dance floor was the perfect spot to move in circles and notice everything.

"Watch everyone." Devon led Rae to the dance floor.

"I will." She looked down at her feet hidden under her dress. They had taken two dance classes leading up to tonight but it didn't stop the swirls inside her stomach. *What if I screw up and draw attention to us?*

"Let me lead, okay?" Devon looked down at her as he slipped his hand around her back. "It's my job. The guy is supposed to lead."

Rae nodded, her voice lost somewhere as he twirled her around. She thought back to the dances at Guilder and how so much had changed since those days. *Focus, Rae. Save the Queen. I mean, save the Princess... The almost princess.*

Devon twirled her around and led her through the dance steps perfectly. Their bodies fell in natural rhythm with each other. Rae's gaze settled on Devon's strong, handsome face. She felt like a princess herself, floating around a dance floor with her prince charming. *If only he would look at me the way he used to.* That seemed to have happened too long ago. She knew she should be focussing on their surroundings, not him. Devon guided her to the left and Rae mis-stepped. She tripped, her heel landing on Devon's toe. His face scrunched up in pain but he lifted her in the air to correct her position and continued on dancing as if nothing had happened.

She looked away, anywhere but his face. She could feel her cheeks burn but did not want to acknowledge why she had gotten lost in the music. Just then, her brain flashed a warning, a brief glimpse into the crowd. She thought she saw someone across the dance floor she knew, but couldn't be sure.

A familiar feeling tingled on her back where Devon's hand rested. Rae almost misunderstood it. A movement by one of the archways along the ballroom walls caught her attention. The halls around the main ballroom were like a maze around the building. Rae had studied the blue print to the building last night. She was fully aware that the layout of the building was a bad guy's dream. She and Devon had resolved to pay extra attention to people coming and going from the edges of the room.

She stopped moving her feet to focus on the archway again and switched to Devon's tatù for better eyesight.

Devon tried to get her to turn. "Everything okay?"

Rae squinted. "You have got to be joking!"

"What?" Devon lifted her and spun around to catch a glimpse of what Rae was looking at. "I don't see anything."

"Anyone." Rae stepped out of Devon's arms. "It's Maria. I bet she snuck in to see my dress." Rae moved again so she could see the arch where she had just seen Maria. "She sent me a mental message before that she wanted to see my dress." Rae stiffened. "There she is again. She just smiled and waved at me."

Devon huffed. "Get her back outside. She's going to blow our cover."

Rae chewed the inside of her cheek. "I'm sorry."

"It's not your fault." Devon frowned. "I don't think she's meant for this kind of work."

Rae felt bad for her friend, but she knew Devon was right. "I think Curtis might have put her up to it. I have a feeling something's off. I'm going to find out."

# Chapter 17

"Maria! What are you doing in here?" Rae lifted her dress and hurried over to her friend. She glanced around to make sure no one else would see Maria. "You can't be inside the building."

Maria shrugged. "I just want to see the hall."

"You aren't dressed." Rae's eyebrows pressed together. "You know you can't blow our cover."

"How am I going to?" Maria stood on her tippy toes and tried to see over Rae's shoulder. "Your dress is massive."

*Thanks. Nice compliment.* "How did you get in?" A sick feeling settled in the bottom of her stomach. If Maria could sneak in unnoticed that meant anyone could, especially someone with a shifter tatù or... worse.

"Curtis helped me."

"He did?" Rae spun around to check for Sarah. She needed to warn Devon. "Go back to the van."

"In a minute."

"No. This is serious. Something's going on. If Curtis isn't there, let me know. Go now-" Rae turned around. Maria was gone. Rae glanced down the hall but didn't see her. She switched her tatù to Maria's to speak with her friend. *Be on the lookout and be careful on your way back. Something's off. I just can't figure it out.*

Maria didn't reply, but Rae wasn't worried. Maria was probably racing back to the van. Rae hurried back to the hall and scanned the crowd for Sarah, Philip or Devon. The live band and orchestra were playing a ballroom dancing song. It must have been a popular song because it looked like everyone was dancing. The swirls of dresses and moving masks made it next to impossible to spot anyone. The lights had dimmed and dry ice floated off the stage to give the room a more historic affect.

Rae switched to Devon's tatù to get better vision. It didn't help as much as she liked. The smoke blurred her vision. She pushed through the dancers trying to find Devon and switched to another tatù. She tried to manage the panic building inside of her. She wished it was Riley's tatù inside of her making her feel out of control.

*Devon*! She saw him dancing with someone wearing a dark amethyst ball gown. She grabbed him by the shoulder and spun him around. "We have to go."

It wasn't Devon. The man wore a similar tuxedo like Devon's and had the same dark hair but the minute her hand grabbed him she knew it wasn't him.

"Sorry. I thought you were someone else." Rae pushed her way through the dancers to escape the dance floor.

Prince Philip stood beside a tall window talking to Alfie. The scene was wrong. Alfie always stood by Sarah, he never left her side.

Rae hurried over ignoring the fact she shouldn't be using her tatù to be noticed. "Where's Sarah?"

Line creased Philip's forehead. He stared at her wide-eyed and then at Alfie. "I thought you said she was with Devon and Karen."

Alfie blinked before raising his arm. Rae deflected and stopped him, holding his arm with the strength of one of her tatù abilities.

"What the hell do you think you are doing?" He scowled at her.

"Stopping you."

"From speaking to the Queen's guard?" He jerked his arm free. "I have a job to do."

"So do I."

He leaned down, his face inches from hers. "And what's that? Take down the future Queen of England?"

Prince Philip stepped between the two of them, his hand pushing Rae back. "What the hell is going on? Where is Sarah?"

Rae could feel the panic in his voice and the shaking in his hand against her as he tried to control himself. "I am not here to hurt Sarah. I'm here to protect her!"

Philip's head swung in her direction. "What?"

She sighed. *Cover's blown. Doesn't matter now.* "I work for the Privy Council."

"What?" Philip blinked. "You said you took classes with Sarah. I remember you from school."

Oh crap. "I just started with the Privy Council not too long ago." She waved her hand. "We don't have time to discuss this now. We need to find Sarah." She shifted her weight to see a very angry-looking Alfie. "Sorry for not including you in the loop. It was just easier. Now where did you say Sarah was?"

Alfie pressed his lips together, his jaw line twitching. Finally he spoke, "Devon was going to get her... with you. He said you and Sarah were going to the lady's room. I turned around and they were gone."

"Then Devon is with Sarah. She's safe with him." Rae turned to start looking for them.

Philip held her arm. "I don't trust you. Everything you've said is a lie." He motioned to Alfie. "Take her to a room and lock her in. Don't let her out until I know Sarah's safe."

Rae's mouth fell open. She felt her jaw drop. "I'm trying to help!" She didn't know what to do. Using a tatù would attract dangerous attention and people were beginning to stop and stare at them.

Alfie grabbed her arm and twisted it behind her back. "Let's go."

She did not resist. She let him lead her out of the hall toward a stairwell. *Devon! Serious mess up going on over here. I need your help. Fast!* She sent Devon a mental message and switched over to let Maria know as well. *Maria! Get Carter on the phone and clear this mess up. They think I'm the one after Sarah. Hurry!*

"If you hurt Sarah..." Alfie muttered and tightened his grip on Rae's arm.

The empty hall gave Rae the opportunity she was waiting for. She sent an electric shock at Alfie to break free. She spun and brought her foot under his legs and knocked him down. In a split second she moved and pulled Alfie's gun out of his holster.

He lay stunned on the ground a moment before raising his hands in surrender. He scowled at her. "What are you?"

"A well trained soldier." She had no intention of telling her about her ability.

"A lousy one who doesn't know how to hold a gun." Alfie kicked out at her. "Or take the safety off."

The gun flew out of Rae's hand and clattered down the hall on the marble floor. She reacted instantly and grabbed her dress so she could press her heel against Alfie's neck. If he moved he would never move again. "I'm not that lousy." She shifted her foot to show she knew exactly what she was doing. "I'm not here to hurt you or Sarah. Like I said before, I'm here to protect her. Now can I trust you to help me find her? I'd prefer to do this with help."

Alfie glared at her before finally relenting and nodding his head ever so slightly. He couldn't talk as Rae's heel was pressed hard against his esophagus.

She lessened the pressure and slowly set her foot on the floor. "I'm faster and stronger than you. Don't try anything or I'll have to lock you up in a room until I know Sarah's safe."

Alfie stood and dusted off his suit jacket.

Rae checked down the hall. *Where are you, Devon?* "Where do you think they went?"

Alfie spoke into the cuff of his shirt. "Amber alert. Anyone spotted the FQ?"

"What's FQ?" Rae asked as they waited for a response. Thanks to Devon's tatù and the quiet hallway, she could hear the crackle of Alfie's earpiece.

"Future Queen." Alfie waved his hand as replies started to come in from other Queen's Guards to say they had not seen the FQ. "Room check. Everywhere. Now." He walked over and scooped up his gun, unlocking the safety and standing ready by the nearest door. He pressed his fingers to his lips and motioned for Rae to get behind him.

She obeyed, feeling silly since she had the better skills to protect him. The music from the hall vibrated against Rae's chest. Laughter and muffled chatter came from the large ballroom also.

Alfie's hand turned the doorknob expertly in one slow, fluid and soundless motion. He pushed and barged through the door faster than Rae thought the older man could move. He cleared the room in a few seconds. Rae scanned the room with a tatù maybe a heartbeat faster. "You're good," she whispered as they made their way to the next room.

He cleared the next room just as fast. "You care to do this one?" He motioned to the door in front of them. His ear piece crackled as information came through from other guards clearing rooms above them.

Rae nodded as Alfie moved back toward the cleared rooms and spoke quietly into his cuff microphone. Rae wiped her palms against her dress and leaned her weight into the door as she tried to mimic Alfie's movements from earlier. When this was all over she would love to ask him teach her some of his techniques. It would never happen, but it would be cool.

She also needed to learn how to hold a gun. The lightning and ball of fire were handy, but a gun... It just represented a different kind of power. She opened the door slightly and burst in, thankful Molly had made sure the length of the dress wouldn't catch on her heels. Using Devon's tatù, she cleared the room and stepped back into the large hall locking the door behind her like she had seen Alfie do.

He watched her with eyebrows raised.

"No one's in there." She took a step toward the next set of doors. The hall was huge. They needed to move quicker.

Alfie followed her this time. "Do you have night vision glasses?"

"Pardon?" She glanced at him quickly before setting herself against the next door and waiting for Alfie to get behind her.

"You cleared the last room in the dark. How do you know there wasn't anyone hiding or if there had been a struggle in the room?"

"I-It's night vision contacts. They're new. The PC's are all about crazy devices and inventions." She grinned liking the story more as she told it. "I've also got this zapper-thing implanted in my pointer finger." She kept her voice low as she showed him a small spark by snapping her fingers.

"Oye! That's how you broke my hold before." He nodded more to himself than to her. "No wonder you don't carry a gun." He flattened himself against the wall. "You clear this room, I'm going to check the one adjacent." He pointed and scooted over.

They came out of the rooms at the same time and locked the doors. They continued until they reached the end where it split into two hallways.

Alfie shook his head. "Do you trust your partner?"

"With my life." Rae knew Devon had nothing to do with this. "I think whoever is after Sarah is either going to have his hands full with Devon or has somehow managed to incapacitate him." What if it was someone with a similar ability to hers? What if there was a team and they had taken down Maria, Curtis and Devon? Her heart sped. She noticed a long stick leaning against an antique chair down the one hall. *Probably an umbrella.*

"Okay. We need to split up. My men are nearly finished with sweeping the upstairs. They'll be down soon. I have four men outside. No one gets in or out of the building anymore. There are cameras set up on all walls outside. A team is on their way to start checking the video." Alfie stood to her left and pointed down the hall nearest to him. "I'll clear here. Call out if you hear or see anything suspicious."

Rae nodded. She could move faster without Alfie, a lot faster. "Let's find them ASAP."

Alfie turned and jogged silently down the hall to the office doors on his side.

*Maria! Are you there?* She didn't like the lack of response. *Curtis! What's going on outside? You can't answer me but can you make some alarm or something go off? Turn the electrical power off in the building if you need too.* Rae slowed her pace as she passed the ornate chair. She skidded to a stop and back tracked when she recognized the stick. *Maria's cane.*

Rae silently stomped her foot. Crap! Crap! Crap! They had Maria as well? Had they knocked her out? That's probably why she couldn't reply. *Maria, I'm here.* Rae planned on sending Maria a similar thought every few minutes in case she might hear. Rae left the cane where it lay against the chair and forced her way into the first room. Nobody had been in there. The desk sat empty and nothing was amiss. No sound of a heartbeat or breathing.

She closed the door and rushed over to the next one on the other side a few paces down. The room was probably empty as well. Using her tatù she couldn't hear or detect anything. The bastards had probably grabbed Maria just after Rae had bumped into her and dragged her down this way. They wouldn't hide out so close to the main hall. If they were here, they would be further down.

Or in some secret door. *Like the Oratory.* The building was Tudor era, it probably had secret rooms in it like most of Guilder. Rae began checking for drafts or odd spaces between the small office buildings. She hurried through each room, panic building as it began to feel like she was going to hit a dead end.

She faced the last door and noticed it slightly ajar. The hair on the back of her neck rose and she heard movement inside. Did she use the element of surprise or was stealth the better option?

Pressing her lips together, she swapped Devon's tatù for Jennifer's and burst silently through the door ready to flip Molly's electricity tatù on like a switch.

The door opened to another short hallway that had a staircase at the end. She ran down the hall, watching for any hidden entrances, finding nothing. The staircase was an old swirling, wooden one, probably a fire escape route from decades ago. Rae took them two at a time and hugged the stone wall as she neared the top.

She flattened herself against the wall at the top landing and counted to three before quickly peeking her head around the corner and jerking back to the wall again. Her brain processed what she saw. Three doors facing each other and - *wait a minute* - Alfie's guard. The guy who had been at Devon and Rae's flat the day Sarah had come by.

Rae leaned against the wall and banged her head lightly against it. Another dead end. The guard was clearing this hidden wing before heading down. What was his name again?

She came around with her hands in front of her so he wouldn't think she was attacking him. He froze when he saw her and reached for his hip.

She frantically shook her head. "Larry, it's me," she whispered. "Is it clear here? Alfie's checking the other end of the hall."

He hesitated a moment before letting his hand drop to his side. "Clear. Can't find anything. You?"

She shook her head. "Absofreakin'nothin'! It's like they vanished." She stopped halfway down the hall when he reached her.

"You carrying a gun?" Larry asked, standing arm's length away from her.

"No." She debated telling him the same thing she had told Alfie.

"Stick your hands out. Prove it." He didn't trust her, the same way Alfie hadn't earlier.

They didn't have time for this. She thrust her hands out in front of her palms out. Alfie's voice echoed through the earplug Larry wore. "We need to get downst-"

Larry slapped a set of cuffs on Rae's wrists. The same ones she had once seen on Kraigan. Privy Council issued.

"Come on! Larry, I'm on your-"

"It's Lenny!"

A small dribble of spit flew out of his mouth and hit her bare shoulder. She shuddered but thrust her hands at him. "Take these off. Contact Alfie, he'll let you know I'm working with you guys."

"You expect me to believe that?"

She huffed. "Look! I work for the Privy Council, just like Devon does. We're here under cover trying to protect Sarah. I can't do my job if I'm tied up here arguing with you. Get a hold of Alfie, he'll verify it."

Lenny lifted his left arm and spoke into the mike hidden in his cuff. "The wandering package is contained."

Huh? More code? Rae tried pulling a hand free of the bionic cuffs. "You found Sarah? Is Devon with her? My friend, she's not dressed for the ball, might be there also. Where are they?"

A muffled thump echoed from a door behind Lenny. He glanced back and then returned his gaze to her. A sly grin grew on his face, making him look mean. "Sarah's in there. She's a little fighter. You and her, my dear, will never see the light of day again." He jabbed a needle into Rae's arm and pushed the clear liquid inside the capsule before Rae could jerk her arm away.

Halos of light flooded her vision and sound seemed to have become subdued. She blinked, trying to focus, and felt her eyes roll as she fought the feeling of fatigue filling her body. Her legs seemed heavy and weak. Her knees gave out and she dropped to the floor, falling face first, unable to put her hands out in front of her to break the fall. She managed to get her cuffed arms bent in time to protect her nose from hitting the cold marble floor.

*Uh-oh.*

Then everything went black.

# Chapter 18

Why did she feel so tired? Rae tried rolling over but realized she was sitting, wedged between two walls. A corner maybe? She told her eyes to open, but they were too happy to stay closed and ignored her.

Moments flooded back in hazy blotches. Masks, dancing, Sarah missing; as each memory touched her brain, panic inched its way into her belly. She let her head fall forward and figured another few minutes of sleep would make it better. She focussed on inhaling and exhaling long slow breaths. She felt her jaw slacken and hoped she wouldn't start drooling, especially in the masquerade dress.

Masquerade! Rae switched to Riley's cheetah tatù ability. She needed the caffeine rush feeling. Larry-Lenny, whatever the dummy's name was, had drugged her. That needed to get out of her system. How long had she been asleep?

The tatù coursed through her body, eating up the knockout drug Lenny had shot into her. She coughed and forced her eyes open.

Cuffs were still on her wrists, and her legs were tied together by some plastic looking tie. Her dress had somehow managed to remain miraculously wrinkle free. Molly had done her homework on this one.

Molly!

Rae blinked to clear the few remaining cobwebs out of her head and focussed. *Molls! It's Rae. Don't panic but you need to get a hold of Carter. Something's gone wrong. One of the Queen's Guards has kidnaped Sarah. He's also taken Maria and tied me up.*

*I don't know where Devon is. We need back up. We're at the ball. I'll send you coordinates as soon as I can.*

She hoped the message would reach Molly. She didn't know how far her ability could go. She glanced around the dimly lit room and tried to figure out where she was. The cold ground and trapped feeling brought back memories of the night Lanford had locked her in the tower at Guilder. Just to be sure, she glanced up to make sure there was no monitor or brainwashing device above her. Nothing but bad lighting.

Rae tucked her feet under her and tried to stand up. It was awkward, and the hard plastic cut into her ankles. She sat back down and kicked her dress out of the way. Her hands were tied with some device the Privy Council had invented. It didn't stop her tatù, but the weird material wouldn't break as hard as she tried with every strength tatù she had.

"Crap!" She dropped her head back against the wall. She needed to get out of here - wherever here was. Starring at her legs, an idea hit her. She slid both legs toward her bending her knees. With her pointer finger, she used her mother's fire ability and spread her ankles as far apart as she could. She held the small flame on the plastic and applied pressure. It broke, and she quickly scrambled up and headed for the door.

*Devon! I found Sarah. Lenny's involved. I think he's got Maria as well. He used some needle on me that knocked me out, but I'm awake now locked in some room. I'm okay. Don't worry about me. I'll get out. Trust Alfie, find him and warn him about Lenny. I'll find Sarah.* She tried the door, not surprised that it was locked. *We're down the hall where Alfie and I split up. At the end is an old abandoned fire escape stairwell. There're three rooms at the top. I think we're still there. Each in a room.*

The cuffs needed to go. She tried burning them with fire knowing her mom's ability wouldn't burn her skin. The damn things were fire resistant! If she made the flame any bigger, she would set her dress on fire. She brought her tied hands to her face and rubbed her temples.

"Think, Rae, think!" She began to pace. "If I was back at school in the Oratory doing some class assignment, what would the other kids do to break free? What skills could they use?" She snapped her fingers. "Nic!" She switched to the MacGyver tatù and tried running through possibilities.

"Ice!" she whispered and froze when keys jingled outside her door. She stepped back frantically looking for some weapon while at the same time focussing on her wrists. The sweat on her palms wouldn't create enough ice. She needed more, fast!

Rae bent down and grabbed the plastic tie she had burned and squeezed her left hand around it and then pulled sharply with her right. She felt the plastic cut into her skin across several fingers and bit her lip at the sudden pain. She should have made Carter bring Charles in before they left for this trip. A healing tatù would be handy today.

The brass lock above the doorknob clicked and turned.

As fast as she could she smeared her blood onto the cuff, trying to freeze it at the same time.

The door swung open, and Lenny stood in the frame. He glanced first at the corner where he had dropped her and then over to where she stood. He scoffed when he saw her standing, blood dripping and her hands still shackled. "Trying a little escape?"

Rae moved slightly so her long dress would hide the plastic wrap that lay on the floor. He wouldn't know she had broken free of the ankle wrap. "You drugged me." She needed to distract him long enough to freeze the blood smeared on her wrists. She pretended to hobble back away from him, hoping she looked scared.

Lenny shrugged. "I couldn't use chloroform. It would take too long to drug you, and you might fight back and stop me before it set in." He apparently enjoyed her struggling to break free. "So I used the synthetic opioid etorphine to induce unconsciousness. It worked better than I thought it would. On you and Sarah."

Rae could feel the cold metal start to freeze against her skin. She might risk frostbite but if it allowed her to break the cuffs, she didn't have a choice.

Lenny stepped in and closed the door, locking it behind him. "She needed another dose after you showed up. Probably should have put a bit more into the syringes. No worries."

Rae needed a bit more time. Her hands were starting to shake from the cold. She turned slightly so Lenny wouldn't notice. "Why would you want to hurt her?"

"It's simple. Sarah cannot become Queen."

"You're the Queen's Guard. Your job is to protect her."

Lenny's face turned red. "No, my job is to protect the throne. She is not allowed on the throne."

"Why the hell not? Who are you to judge who is able to sit on the throne?"

"I'm the Queen's Guard!" he yelled and then lowered his voice. "She's one of you!" The disgust in his voice rang clear. "No tatù will ever sit on the throne."

Rae blinked in surprise. He knew? "Are you-?"

"Hell no!" he cut her off before she could finish. "Who do you think started the Queen's Guard? The King's Guard?"

Rae's body was shaking everywhere. It looked to Lenny like fear, but it was the cold on her wrists that was chilling her. Goosebumps rose on her arms as her wrists began to burn from the freezing. Frostbite had to be setting in.

Lenny didn't appear to notice, he was too caught up in delivering his history lesson. "King Henry believed in you guys. He trusted you to give him a male heir. When he knew you couldn't complete the task, he grew weary of his Privy Council. He used you for the purpose of controlling the crown and England, but he hated every one of you. England will never have one of you sit on the throne! He created the King's Guard to protect the throne from that very threat!"

"What?" Rae spun around. "I refuse to believe that." She switched to Jennifer's tatù and with a burst of strength pushed her hands away from each other to break the cuff on her wrist. It cracked under the pressure. She spoke again, trying to hide the noise. "Sarah wouldn't hurt anyone! She has a unique ability to understand languages. She's protecting the future king, her husband." With a final jerk, her arms broke free. She caught the cuff before it clattered to the ground. She set it on the desk in front of her. Rubbing her wrists to try and warm them, she was careful not to use her mother's ability. The fire would only cause more pain against the frostbite. She spun slowly around. " Does every one of the Queen's Guard swear to this oath of stupidity?"

Lenny barked out a ferocious laugh. "There are only a few selected to maintain this precious task." He jabbed a finger at her. "You will not stop us." He reached for the gun at his hip.

Rae moved swiftly. She raced to where he stood and kicked his hand away from his holster. She spun him around and pinned his arms behind him, pressing his face against the wooden door. "You don't know me very well." With one hand on his wrists, she searched his pockets and found a syringe in his vest. She bit the lid off. "Who do you work for? You couldn't plan this all by yourself." She jabbed the stick into his neck feeling around until she felt a pulse and knew she had found his carotid artery. "Where's Sarah?" She held her finger over the top of the needle threatening to push the etorphine liquid inside him. "I'm not going to ask you again."

"Then don't." Lenny arched up forcing Rae's finger to push down on the top of the needle. She injected the etorphine before she could react and pull the needle out. Lenny slumped back against her and crumpled to the floor when she let go of him.

"Crap!" She muttered and dragged his body to the spot he had dumped her in earlier. She pulled his gun out of the holster and slid it away from him. She checked his other pockets and found an old set of skeleton keys and the plastic he had used to tie her ankles up. She did the same to his ankles and wrists. She checked every pocket again to make sure she hadn't missed anything.

She pulled his ear piece out and wiped it off before tucking it into her ear. Then checked his cuffs. Alfie always spoke into a microphone. There was no wire or phone or mike, just Lenny's cuff links. Maybe he had taken it off so Alfie and the other Queen's Guards couldn't find him.

Rae grabbed the gun and everything else she thought he might use and tossed it into the garbage bin by the door. She then unlocked it and set the can outside of the room. Before leaving, she glanced back at the unconscious man, and quickly ran back to him, grabbing his cuff links. Maybe they had a mike embedded inside of them. She tossed everything in the garbage. She wasn't taking any chances.

Outside the room, she fumbled through the keys to lock the door and finally let out the breath she had been holding when a resounding click echoed inside the brass fixture. She checked the area to make sure it was clear and dug through the garbage for the cuff links along with the last needle vial - just in case. She stuffed the needle into the hidden pocket under the flower on her dress. Then she lifted the cuff links to her mouth. "Alfie?" she whispered to them. "Can you hear me?" She tapped the earpiece in her ear to see if it might click on or make some noise. Nothing.

She shook the cuff links and banged them together. "Alfie? It's Rae. Have you found Devon?" She waited a moment then huffed and rolled her eyes. "Crap!" She tossed the cuff links back into the garbage and ripped the earpiece out, throwing it in the bin as well.

She had no idea how much time she had or if Lenny had other Guards working with him. They could have taken Alfie down and were keeping this hallway clear. Rae headed for the door where the thump had come from earlier before Lenny had knocked her out. She tried the door. Locked.

Flipping through the keys, she tried the third one and forced it to turn. The door unlocked. Rae swung it open and jumped inside the room, ready to attack.

Sarah sat tied to a chair with a rag over her mouth. She was alone in the room. She stared at Rae with big, weary eyes.

Rae raced over and untied the rag. "Are you okay?"

Sarah shook her head free of the cloth. "Lenny," she gasped. "He's... He's the one."

"I know. He's incapacitated at the moment." Rae created fire and burned through the plastic tie around Sarah's wrist. She dropped down and freed her legs as well. "You lose your mask, too?"

Sarah stared at her before bursting out laughing and wrapping her arms around Rae. "Thank you."

"We need to get you out of here." Rae helped Sarah wobble toward the door. "Did you just wake up?"

Sarah's eyes rolled, and she swallowed hard, trying to focus. "I- I think so. I... I don't know. Lenny knocked me out twice." She stumbled. "I don't feel well." She sucked quick breaths and leaned over to rest her hands on her knees.

Rae managed to help Sarah out into the hall.

"I think I'm going to be sick." Sarah turned a few shades yellowish green.

Rae dashed over and grabbed the garbage bin she had set in the hall previously. She placed it in front of Sarah just in time.

Sarah wiped her mouth with the back of her hand. "Not very lady like." She shot Rae a shaky grin.

"Not very princess-like," Rae teased then turned serious. "We need to get you out of here." She put her arm around Sarah's waist. "I'll carry you if I have to."

"There's... a... girl..." Sarah nearly fell. Rae caught her just in time. Sarah's head rolled back as she lost consciousness.

*Maria.* Rae picked Sarah up in her arms and glanced back at the third door. She hesitated. Sarah needed medical help, what did Maria need?

"Oye!"

She spun around to the sound of the voice that called from the hallway. Alfie stood at the top of the stairwell his hair a mess but relief clearly written on his face. Until he saw Sarah in Rae's arms.

He rushed toward her. "What happened?"

Rae let him take Sarah. "Lenny injected her with etorphine. Twice. I don't know if she's having a reaction or if the drugs are still in her system." She nodded behind her. "Lenny's tied up in the room directly behind me."

Alfie's eyebrows rose. "Lenny?"

"He doesn't want Sarah to become Queen." She didn't know how much detail to reveal. "He sounds a bit mad." She twirled her finger by her temple to stress the point. "Get Sarah down to safety. I'll wait here."

Alfie opened his mouth to argue.

Rae held her hand up. "He's tied up. Have you seen Devon?"

Sarah coughed suddenly and struggled against Alfie. He held her tight and spoke in a kind voice Rae didn't know he even possessed. "Shhh... Sweetie. It's ol' Alfie. Let's get you some water and clear that fog out of you head." He walked briskly toward the stairs. He looked at Rae before heading down. "Devon was helping me. There were a few Guards." He grunted. "He's making sure he got them all."

Rae rubbed her left wrist. It burned and was beginning to turn itchy. "Go. I'm okay here. Protect Sarah."

## Chapter 19

Alfie disappeared down the stairs. Rae immediately rushed to the third door. She slid to a stop just before it and had to run back to the room Sarah had been locked in to get the keys. She moved quickly to the locked door and tried the first key. It slid in and opened with no noise. *Odd*. Like the handle had been oiled or used recently or not locked.

Hand on the knob, she turned it slowly and leaned her weight into the door and pushed it open. She crouched slightly, ready to pounce on anyone that might be hurting Maria.

Maria sat at a desk behind a computer. She glanced up and looked back down at the laptop before shutting it. She stood and shoved her hands into her pockets. "I was wondering when you were going to come." She walked toward Rae and grinned. "Heck of an evening, isn't it?"

Rae blinked. "You okay?"

"Fine."

"Did Lenny drug you?"

"No." She hesitated. "Did he drug you?"

"Yes."

"Did it work?"

Weird question. "Yeah. Entrophine. It knocked me out."

"For how long?" Maria started walking toward Rae again.

"Pardon?"

"How long were you out?"

"I don't know. Is it important?"

Maria waved her hand. "Not really. I was just curious. I figured you could heal yourself so it wouldn't work."

Rae rubbed her wrist against her dress trying to ignore the pain from the frostbite. "Kraigan messed with my tatù. I lost the healing ability. I didn't have time to see Charles before we headed out here." She stared at Maria. "You're so calm."

Confusion crossed Maria's face. "I am?" She rested her hand on her chest. "Inside I'm not. I'm shaking like a leaf. I'm just so relieved you're okay."

"Why did you come inside?" Rae couldn't help feeling angry that her friend had risked her life just to see a fancy dress. They walked side by side toward the stairs.

"It was a stupid mistake I guess."

"Devon was kind of ticked. I don't think I can cover for you on this." Rae tilted her head. "How's your leg?"

"My leg?"

What was wrong with Maria today? "Your cane is downstairs."

Maria touched her thigh and limped a little. "Must be the adrenaline. It hurts now." She stuffed her hands into her pockets. "Do we just go downstairs? Will it be safe?"

Rae pressed her lips together. It might not be. Alfie had gone down but who knew who else could be the double agent. "What did Curtis say when you told him you were coming in?"

"Curtis?" Maria stared at Rae with a confused look on your face.

Maybe she had been drugged and didn't remember.

"Oh, Curtis! He told me it was okay."

A bad feeling hung in the pit of Rae's stomach. "What else did he say?"

"What do you mean?"

"I think Curtis might be working with Lenny. Don't you find it strange he left you alone in the van the other day and then let you sneak out tonight? That's not PC protocol. Something's not adding up." At the top of the stairs, she touched Maria's shoulder. "Hold on a sec. I'm going to go and grab Lenny's gun. I don't want him escaping the room and getting anything." She turned around to head back.

"Watch out! Rae!"

She cringed and ducked, then stood frozen on the spot at the sound of Devon's voice.

Someone crashed into her back and sent them both tumbling to the floor - someone who seemed powerful. Rae's head connected with the marble floor. She felt an instant goose egg forming from the tightness of the skin on her forehead. Blinking away the double vision, she tried to roll onto her back. Whoever was on top of her had her pinned tight. "Get. Off. Of. ME!" Her tatù burned. She switched to Jennifer's leopard ability and grabbed the leg of the person on top of her.

The ankle was thin and smooth. Not the thick, hairy man leg she was expecting. She concentrated her power to the center of her body and flipped over, hoping to throw the attacker off of her.

Her hair hung in her face and whipped across, and she turned, her hands stretched out to send a bolt of electricity the moment her tatù changed. She shook her hair out of her face and hesitated a millisecond when she saw who was sitting on her.

*Maria.*

With the angriest, most despicable look on her face. It didn't even look like Maria.

"What are you...?" Rae's voice trailed off, unable to zap her friend.

"Hit her now!" Devon shouted.

Maria pressed a black handheld machine into Rae's neck.

*A tazor.* Rae knew the moment everything below her neck went numb. Her arms flopped helplessly at her sides. If the tazor was anything like the ones Devon had trained her with, she'd be useless for the next thirty seconds, maybe longer. She fought against the paralyzed feeling only her head thrashing side to side.

Maria grinned wickedly at Rae. "You stupid, stupid, girl." She pulled a syringe out of her pocket and dropped the tazor on Rae's chest. "This one will be permanent." She clutched the needle with both hands and went to plunge it into Rae's heart.

Rae lay useless. She shut her eyes tight and waited for the burning pain.

It never came.

But the sound of bodies crashing against the wall and glass shattering on the marble floor away from her resounded in her ears. She opened her eyes to see what had happened.

Devon must have barrelled into Maria in his effort to get her off of Rae. Because of the tazor effects, Rae hadn't felt the pressure lift. The needle lay useless and broken on the floor away from all of them.

Maria fought Devon with a lioness-like strength. They fought and rolled toward the stairwell. Rae was terrified they would clatter down. What was Maria doing?

A tingling sensation began to return to Rae's toes. Her left foot twitched, and the feeling ran up her leg. It would take a moment for it to recover fully. She closed her eyes and focussed, waiting for the moment the sensation would reach her arms. A headache throbbed against her temple. She tried to push it away, but it persisted, trying to get her to sink into blackness.

Her right pinky finger twitched. Rae inhaled a sharp breath and focussed everything into her tatù. She felt Devon's ability and sprang to action. In one fluid motion, she grabbed the tazor off her chest and hit the 'on' button as she scrambled up and leaped toward the tangled bodies of Devon and Maria.

As she came down to the floor, she positioned, herself perfectly to avoid Devon and sunk the tazor into Maria's neck. "Traitor!" she hissed and pushed the device hard into Maria's skin. She did it again and again as Devon held Maria's limp body.

"Enough!" he cried.

Maria wasn't done. She head-butted Devon and went to do it again, a crazed look in her eyes.

Devon dropped Maria on the ground and grabbed the tazor from Rae. He flipped the device open and with his fingernail switched a button. Then he snapped it shut and hit Maria on the neck, legs and arms. She glared at him with hatred in her eyes, unable to move.

"What did you just do?" Rae sank to the floor, using the wall for support. She was dizzy, and her head killed. It took every ounce of concentration to not pass out.

"The tazor is PC issued. There's a switch inside that will set it to continued paralysis. At least until she is tazored again. Then it restores the neurology and physical function returns." He glared at Maria. "I'm not taking any chances." He lifted his sleeve and spoke into his cuff.

A loud pounding echoed behind her.

Rae blinked trying to clear the double vision and blurriness. She couldn't hear what Devon said as a ringing in her ears grew deafening. "D-De-phon," she mumbled. "I donnen..." *feel so well...* She couldn't finish the sentence out loud. She felt herself begin to fall sideways, unable to stop herself. It was probably because of the drugs and then the tazoring. *Or did I bump my head?* She couldn't remember.

Strong arms slid under her and picked her up. She felt her body jostle up and down in a steady rhythm. Her head fell against a strapping, warm chest. The bumping stopped.

She felt like she was falling, but those strong arms held her tight. A finger brushed her forehead, and she winced at the sharp pain that ran across her head. The fingers gently moved to her cheek.

"Rae?" She had never heard so much emotion held in a single word. In her name.

Her eyelids fluttered as she tried to focus.

"Rae?" The voice cracked as he said her name again. "Stay with me."

*Devon.* She smiled, feeling safe.

"Stay with me." He swallowed. "I thought you were near indestructible. I was such an idiot!"

He sounded so worried. Her head killed, but he would protect her. It was his job.

"Rae, don't go dying on me. You are my heart. My whole heart."

*Am I hearing things?* A softness pressed gently against her lips. It was tender, but there was an urgency in the touch she had never felt before. Fresh air floated over her mouth before the incredible touch brushed against her lips again. She had to be dreaming. That was the only way to explain it. *Like the moment you realize that fate has outdone itself.*

Had Devon just kissed her?

# Chapter 20

A bright light flashed in front of Rae's left eye, and then her other one. She scowled and tried to cover her face with her hands. Someone grabbed her hands and pulled them down.

"It's fine, Karen. Just relax."

Rae knew the voice but couldn't place it. Annoyed, she opened her eyes only to quickly shut them tight again from the blaring light that hurt her head.

"Miss, you need to sit still. You have a concussion."

*Concussion? Who said that?* She felt nauseous. She focussed on breathing deep and steady, trying to get the pain to subside. The person tied some kind of rubber band to her upper arm. When a pin pricked the inside of her elbow she flicked her fingers and shocked the person trying to hurt her. The bright light disappeared from her face, and she opened her eyes to assess the situation around her. Ready to run or pounce, whatever she needed to do.

She sat inside an ambulance, an attendee beside her on the floor, rubbing his arm. *Probably trying to figure how he got shocked.* She looked behind him and saw Prince Philip standing just outside the ambulance bus.

*Where's Devon?*

She sat swung her legs over the edge of the stretcher and ignored the spinning room. Soft music played in the background. It was coming from the masquerade hall. "Is Sarah all right?" The needle, whatever had been in the shot the attendee had given her, must have been some counteractive agent to the entrophine Lenny had given. She needed to get out of this mobile prison and get back to work.

Philip turned at the mention of Sarah's name. "She's in the ambulance right beside you." He smiled. "She's going to be fine. Shaken, but basically unharmed."

"That's good to hear." She closed her eyes and inhaled a long breath, letting it out slowly. She stood slowly. "I need to find Devon."

Philip helped her down and signaled to the protesting attendee. "If she wants out, she's fine," he told her. He leaned close so only she would hear. "He brought you here and went back to help Alfie."

"And Lenny?"

A hard look crossed the Prince's eyes. "Taken care of."

"What about Maria?"

"Who?"

Rae swallowed and pretended to need a moment to catch her breath. If Devon hadn't said anything about Maria, she wasn't about to spill the beans. "May I talk to Sarah?"

"Of course."

She walked over on shaky legs, each step growing stronger. Philip cleared Sarah's ambulance so Rae could talk to her alone.

"You okay?" Sarah asked.

Rae smiled and rubbed her head. The bump was the size of a golf ball and still hurt to touch. "I need to see Charles. He's got such an awesome tatù."

"Charles?" Sarah repeated.

Rae sat on the edge of Sarah's stretcher and spoke quietly. "He's got this amazing healing tatù. It could fix me up in a jiffy. Sorry, it only works on the person carrying the tatù; it wouldn't fix you."

"I'm doing alright." Sarah fixed the emerald skirting of her dress.

"Did Devon come back with Maria?"

Sarah shook her head.

"She attacked me. I think she was working with Lenny."

Sarah signed. "I don't understand. Why would Lenny want to hurt me?"

"He told me it was because of your ability. Apparently there is some secret, unwritten law that King Henry created. He started the King's Guard to protect the throne. It's sworn that no tatù will ever sit on the throne of England." Rae sighed with the heavy news. "Others will continue to attack should you become the Queen of England."

The ambulance shifted as Philip stepped inside. "No one will ever hurt Sarah."

Rae watched as Philip squeezed by her to sit on the floor beside Sarah holding her hand. "I don't know if you can stop them." She glanced at Sarah, torn by the silent tears that coursed down Sarah's cheeks. "There are more, hidden in secret. You'll never be able to find them all. We wouldn't be able to find them."

"What has Sarah done?"

"Nothing." Rae pressed her lips together. "It's what she represents."

"I don't understand."

Sarah gently touched his cheek. "Let's not worry about it now."

Philip brought his hand to hers and kissed her fingers. "I'll worry about your safety always."

Sarah burst into tears. "It's complicated."

"If we married, you will always be in danger?"

She nodded. "So would you. I can't risk your life."

"What if I wasn't king? Would you be safe then?"

Rae needed to find Devon. This intimate conversation was meant for the two of them, not her. "I need to find Devon." If Sarah told Philip the truth, she wouldn't blame her. She was pretty sure she would do the same thing. "Will you be all right?"

Philip nodded. "There are guards Alfie selected to stay with us. We're fine."

Rae patted Sarah's leg and turned to go. She wished she didn't hear the word's Philip whispered to Sarah.

"I'd abdicate the throne for you, my love. If it meant protecting you, I would do it in a heartbeat. My brother can be king. No throne is worth your life."

Rae quickened her pace.

A man dressed in clothes similar to Alfie stopped her. "Ma'am?"

Rae hesitated, ready to blow the man with a gust of wind if he tried anything.

"Mister Wardell asked me to keep an eye out for you. He wanted to let you know he would be in the coat check room."

"The coat check?"

He nodded. "Yes."

"Okay, thanks." Rae didn't miss the smirk on the man's face as he turned his attention back to the ambulance. It pricked at her brain. Was he smirking because of the message he'd delivered to her, or because Sarah was in the ambulance? "Which part of the Queen's Guard are you with?"

He looked at her with raised eyebrows. "Excuse me?"

Rae turned a stony face and took up a firm stance as she faced the guard down. For reasons she didn't quite understand, she felt the need to confirm this guard's loyalty. "Lenny or Alfie?"

He blinked at her, completely caught off guard.

*He's team Alfie.* "Forget it." She hurried off to find the coat check - which has obviously been the reason for the guard's smirk, although she had no idea why.

Inside the building, she headed to the coat check, which happened to be before the security check. The masquerade continued like nothing had happened to disrupt it. No one knew, not even the media that had been there earlier madly snapping photos of the people in their costumes.

The coat room was empty except for the rows and rows of coats. She was about to leave when she noticed a small amount of light shining on the floor. *A partially hidden door.* She moved to it and stuck her ear against it to see if she heard Devon's voice.

"I don't know what happened, sir." Devon's voice portrayed the frustration he must have been feeling.

Rae opened the door and slipped inside. "Oh!" fell out of her mouth when she noticed Carter standing in the almost bare room, with Devon and a heavily bonded Maria, who glared and thrashed from her chair. Her eyes were wild.

"Rae!" Carter smiled and then frowned. "That's some bump."

"What's wrong with her?" Rae asked, ignoring the comment.

Carter glanced at Maria. "Brainwashed. Completely under the influence of your father's device."

"What?" It seemed she was saying that word a lot these days.

"We don't know how or when but the signs are all there." Carter turned to Maria. "Who did this to you?"

She spat at Carter, hitting him in the face. Carter pulled a handkerchief from his suit pocket and wiped his face. He shook his head. "She can't move her arms or legs but that head of hers won't stop." He closed his eyes and pressed his hands to his temple. "And she won't stop yelling at me inside my head."

Two could play at that game. *Where's Curtis?* Rae asked Maria. She repeated the question louder. *Where's Curtis? Is he in on this with you? Is he the one who brainwashed you MARIA! Look at me!!*

Maria's head swiveled toward Rae. She grinned wickedly, not looking like Maria at all.

Rae stepped back even though she knew Maria couldn't physically hurt her. "Has anyone been looking for Curtis?"

"Oh shit!" Devon pulled his tuxedo jacket off and came toward Rae. "Curtis helped dismantle the brainwashing machine. What if he's the one who put it back together?"

"He's a good guy," Carter said, not sounding entirely convinced

"So was Lanford," Rae added quietly. Brainwashing came in all different forms when her father was involved.

"He's gone. He stopped communicating back when Maria showed up inside the hall." Devon moved toward the door.

"He probably helped Maria get inside." Rae couldn't believe what was happening.

"Check the van. See if there's anything in there." Carter turned back to Maria. "I'm going to ask you one more time, who did this to you?"

"Do you want me to go with you?" Rae asked Devon. He hesitated a moment and the memory of him kissing her flooded Rae's thoughts. She touched her lips. How could she have forgotten?

"Stay with Carter. Try to get through to Maria."

Devon disappeared through the door.

Maria giggled and then burst out laughing. "You people are beyond stupid! Put the tazor back on me and let's settle this properly."

Carter loosened his tie. "That's not going to happen Maria."

"Then torture Curtis, see if he speaks."

The conversation went back and forth between the three of them with no progress. Carter jumped when Devon threw open the door, dragging a bound and gagged Curtis in behind him.

"What the hell?" Carter sighed. "How much more can we botch up this evening?"

"It's how I found him, sir." Devon pulled Curtis beside him.

Curtis began pointing and mumbling through the duct tape on his mouth. He grew more agitated by the moment.

"He's pointing at Maria." Rae stepped forward and ripped the tape off his face.

"Ow!!" he shouted as his face burned red where the tape had been. He barely drew in a breath before he was spewing words again. "She did this! She tied me up."

Maria rolled her eyes. "You planned everything, and then tied yourself up to make it look like you were a victim."

"I did not!"

"Liar!"

"Enough!" Carter bellowed. Then looked sheepishly at Rae and Devon. "The room's sound proof."

"We are wasting time here!" Rae rested her hand on the back of Curtis' neck. *Show me what happened.*

The skin to skin contacted set the memory in motion. An image appeared of Curtis working in the van. Rae peered in through the window to watch. Maria jumped up suddenly and told Curtis that Devon and Rae were in trouble. That they needed her inside the building. Curtis turned around to get Maria something, and she hit him with a needle similar to the one Lenny had injected in Rae. As he went down, Maria set to work on tying him up and gagging him. Rae jumped to hide by the tire of the van when Maria opened the back door and headed inside the building.

Rae let go of Curtis. "Untie him."

"Excuse me?" Carter asked.

"Untie him. He's not working with her. I saw it for myself. You can do the same thing, Carter. See for yourself."

Carter did. A moment later he too stepped back and shook his head. "She set him up."

Rae dropped into the only other chair in the room and rubbed her wrists. They burned from earlier, and her head hurt. She didn't have much energy left to fight this one out. She resisted the urge to put her head down on her knees.

Devon began to cut the ropes around Curtis.

Carter had other plans. He grabbed Maria's hands, only to slap them away a moment later. "I can't get through. She just keeps screaming at me and blocking anything I try to dig through."

Curtis walked around Maria. "Is she sedated?"

"Tazored. Can't move anything but her head until we figure this out." Devon sighed.

"I think I can stop the brainwashing."

Carter's head shot up. "Really?"

"I've been working on it back in my lab. It'll erase everything that happened while she was brainwashed. I've tried to search for the memories with my tatù, but they never come back."

"Do it." Carter ran his fingers through his hair. "Whatever it takes. She's dangerous like this."

"We won't be able to find out who brainwashed her."

Carter sighed. "I don't think we have a choice." He pulled his phone out of his suit pocket and checked it. "Curtis, you and I will take Maria back. Devon, can you take Rae outside? There's someone waiting to see her. You two need to be here another week. There's still too much going on, and it's unsafe to leave Sarah unprotected."

"Yes, sir."

"Who's here to see me?" Rae pushed herself up and held onto the chair to stop the room from spinning.

"Charles. I sent him up so you can get his tatù back."

*Thank goodness.* She didn't argue and let Devon lead her out of the room. She looked at Maria one last time, hoping her friend would be there the next time she saw her... If she ever saw her again. The odd comments and actions from Maria clicked into place. Rae stopped for a moment at the door. "Could this have happened when Maria was in the hospital?"

"It's possible." Carter picked up his phone and began ordering another ambulance, with PC members as its crew.

"Come on, Rae." Devon opened the door, and they stepped into the cloak room.

She let him lead her outside. She closed her eyes when the cool, fresh air hit her face, but only had a split second to enjoy it before a familiar voice intruded.

"Rae!"

*Molly. Do I have the energy for her right now?* Rae forced a smile on her face and turned to where the shout had come from.

Molly stood on the grass to their right with Charles. She beamed as they headed over. "Guess who I bumped into."

Charles nodded at Devon and reached for Rae's hand. "You look like crap."

Rae felt the zing of his tatù zip through her and the healing instantly began. Her headache lifted and when she touched her forehead; she could feel the big bump going down. The burning itch on her wrists went away. She smiled and twirled in her dress. Then swung around and hugged him tight. "I really missed you!"

Charles laughed. "Me, or my tatù?" He coughed. "Bit too tight, Rae."

She let go of him and stepped back, grinning. "Whoops. Sorry!"

Molly laughed. "Looks like your dress handled tonight's action better than you did."

Charles whistled. "No. I'd say she handled it pretty well." He shook Devon's hand. "I hear you have one hell of a story to tell us."

"We do! Maybe we should go back inside and make sure everything's alright. Sample the beer and drinks. I could use one." Devon gestured at his tuxedo. "I'm dressed for the occasion. You're in a suit, close enough for me."

Molly's phone rang from inside her purse. She fumbled through her purse trying to find it. The noise stopped when she finally pulled it out and handed it to Rae. "It's yours. It's been ringing all night. You forgot it at my place this afternoon when you changed."

Rae looked down at the list of missed calls and text messages. It began ringing again.

All the messages and calls were from Luke.

A memory of Devon's frantic words, before she passed out earlier, whispered in her head; *You are my heart. My whole heart.* Had he actually said that or had she just dreamed the words up?

She put the phone to her ear. "Hello?"

"Rae! Finally! You okay?" Luke's usual happy tone held a note of worry.

"I'm okay. Busy night."

"Tell me about it! You won't believe me if I told you."

She could say the same thing. "I'm, uh, kind of busy right now."

"You working?"

"Yes." She looked at Devon and quickly averted her eyes down to the grass. *Why did everything suddenly feel so complicated?* "What's up?"

"I found something out about your mother."

Rae straightened. "What? What did you find?"

"I think I may have just lost my job."

*Oh no.* What had she done, asking him to dig into something that was obviously meant to be hidden? If he got hurt, or worse, killed, it would be on her.

Luke gave a low chuckle. "Don't you worry. I can take care of myself. Plus, I think you're worth it."

Rae stole a glance at Devon again, but curiosity made her blurt out, "What did you find? What's so worth losing your job over?"

"A box."

"A box?"

"Let me back up a sec... So I started looking for stuff on your mom. Nothing in classified or places I shouldn't be. It didn't matter. After a few searches on the computer with your mom's name, I found a file on your mom. Just stuff about her connection with your dad. Not much else. So I went into the paper archives. Like a rolodex. Didn't know they even still existed. Okay, here is the interesting part. I found a note with a file number. The number refers to a serial code for items in the evidence locker."

Rae was scared to exhale. "What did you find?" she whispered.

"It took me two days to find the evidence box because it's in an old warehouse. Then it took longer because someone mislabelled the box.

Her heart thundered against her rib cage. Cops kept evidence boxes for murders and crimes. "Did it say my mom was dead?" She wanted to cry but bit her lip to hold it back.

"No. At least there is nothing inside the files to say so." Luke sounded surprised Rae would even jump to that conclusion. "I did find papers and a small container, like a chest."

"What was inside it?"

"That's why I've been calling you. I can't open it. I've tried and tried. It needs a key, but it's not in the evidence box."

The phone slipped from Rae's hand and fell onto the grass. She heard Luke calling, "Rae! Rae!" She watched Devon turn around and come back to her, saw him bend down to pick up her phone hold it out to her.

She stood frozen on the grass, dressed like a princess with two Prince Charmings wanting to rescue her.

She slowly took the phone from Devon's outstretched hand and pressed it to her ear. She couldn't speak, however inside her head, her inner voice screamed. *I have the key! I have the key!*

Whatever was inside that chest, her mother planted it there. She wanted Rae to find it. "I have the key. How fast can you get to London?"

# THE END!
## *Under Fire*
### Coming this Spring/Summer 2015

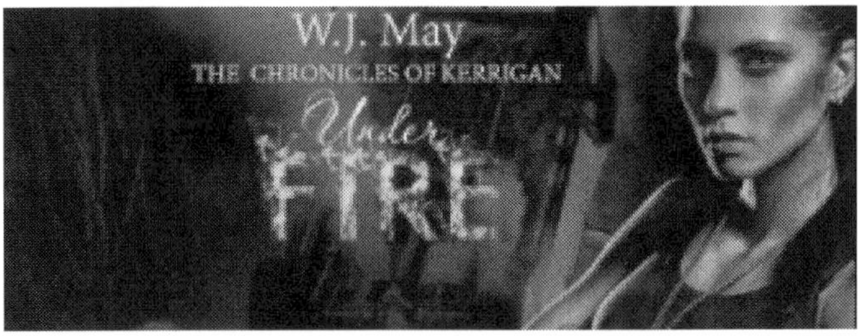
W.J. May
THE CHRONICLES OF KERRIGAN
Under
FIRE

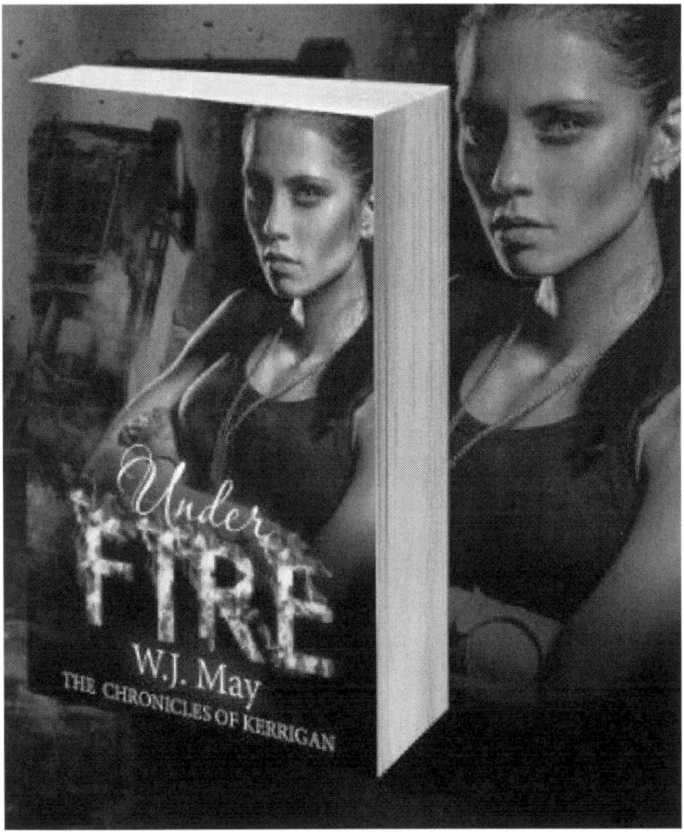
Under
FIRE
W.J. May
THE CHRONICLES OF KERRIGAN

**Note from Author;**

*I hope you enjoyed Royal Tea. If you have a moment to post a review to let others know about the story, I would greatly appreciate it! I love hearing from my fans so feel free to send me a message on Facebook or by email so we can chat!*

*All the best, W.J. May*

Newsletter: http://eepurl.com/97aYf
Website: http://www.wanitamay.yolasite.com
Facebook: https://www.facebook.com/pages/Author-WJ-May-FAN-PAGE/141170442608149

*The Chronicles of Kerrigan*
Book I - *Rae of Hope* is FREE!
**Book Trailer:** http://www.youtube.com/watch?v=gILAwXxx8MU
Book II - *Dark Nebula* is Now Available
**Book Trailer:** http://www.youtube.com/watch?v=Ca24STi_bFM
Book III - *House of Cards* is Now Available
Book IV - *Royal Tea* - Now Available
Book V - *Under Fire*, coming Spring/Summer 2015
Book VI - *End in Sight,* Coming Fall/Winter 2015

**More books by W.J. May**
**Hidden Secrets Saga:**
**Download Seventh Mark part 1 For FREE**
**Book Trailer:**
http://www.youtube.com/watch?v=Y- vVYC1gvo

Book Blurb:

Like most teenagers, Rouge is trying to figure out who she is and what she wants to be. With little knowledge about her past, she has questions but has never tried to find the answers. Everything changes when she befriends a strangely intoxicating family. Siblings Grace and Michael, appear to have secrets which seem connected to Rouge. Her hunch is confirmed when a horrible incident occurs at an outdoor party. Rouge may be the only one who can find the answer.

An ancient journal, a Sioghra necklace and a special mark force life-altering decisions for a girl who grew up unprepared to fight for her life or others.

All secrets have a cost and Rouge's determination to find the truth can only lead to trouble...or something even more sinister.

## RADIUM HALOS - THE SENSELESS SERIES
### Book 1 is FREE:

<u>Book Blurb:</u>
Everyone needs to be a hero at one point in their life.

The small town of Elliot Lake will never be the same again.

Caught in a sudden thunderstorm, Zoe, a high school senior from Elliot Lake, and five of her friends take shelter in an abandoned uranium mine. Over the next few days, Zoe's hearing sharpens drastically, beyond what any normal human being can detect. She tells her friends, only to learn that four others have an increased sense as well. Only Kieran, the new boy from Scotland, isn't affected.

Fashioning themselves into superheroes, the group tries to stop the strange occurrences happening in their little town. Muggings, break-ins, disappearances, and murder begin to hit too close to home. It leads the team to think someone knows about their secret - someone who wants them all dead.

An incredulous group of heroes. A traitor in the midst. Some dreams are written in blood.

### Shadow of Doubt
Part 1 is FREE!
Book Trailer:
http://www.youtube.com/watch?v=LZK09Fe7kgA

Book Blurb:

What happens when you fall for the one you are forbidden to love?

Erebus is a bit of a lost soul. He's a guy so he should be out to have fun but unlike the rest of his kind, he is solemn and withdrawn. That is, until he meets Aurora, a law student at Cornell University. His entire world is shaken. Feelings he's never had and urges he's never understood take over. These strange longings drive him to question everything about himself

When a jealous ex stalks back into his life, he must decide if he is willing to risk everything to be with Aurora. His desire for her could destroy her, or worse, erase his own existence forever.

**Free Books:**

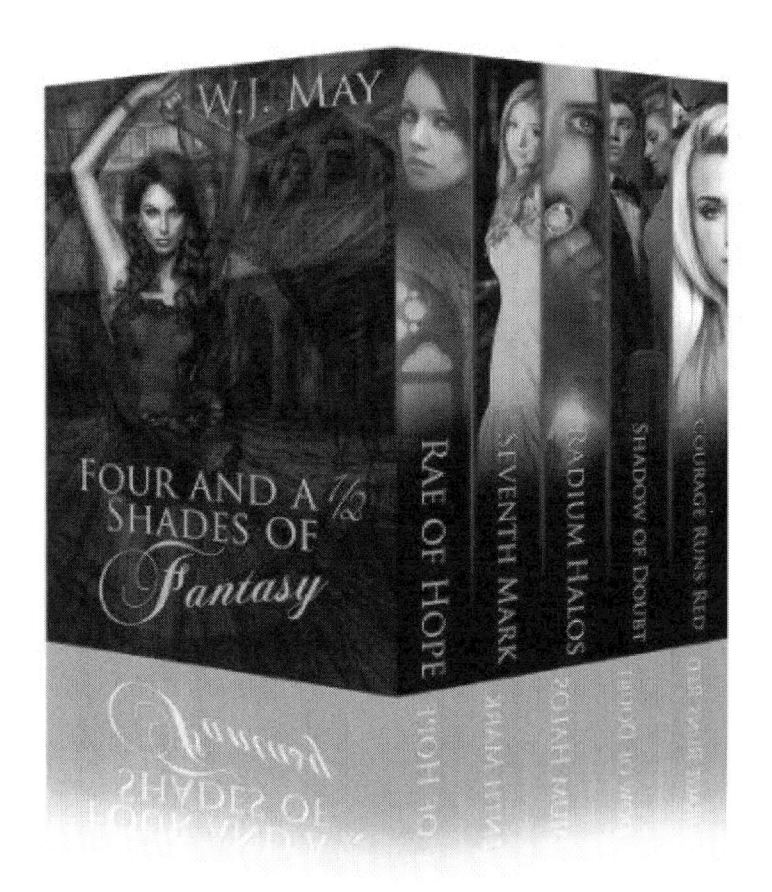

Four and a Half Shades of Fantasy

# COMING SOON:

**Book Blurb:**

What if courage was your only option?

When Kallie lands a college interview with the city's new hotshot police officer, she has no idea everything in her life is about to change. The detective is young, handsome and seems to have an unnatural ability to stop the increasing local crime rate. Detective Liam's particular interest in Kallie sends her heart and head stumbling over each other.

When a raging blood feud between vampires spills into her home, Kallie gets caught in the middle. Torn between love and family loyalty she must find the courage to fight what she fears the most and possibly risk everything, even if it means dying for those she loves.

## TUDOR COMPARISON:

**Aumbry House**——A recess to hold sacred vessels, often found in castle chapels.

Aumbry House was considered very special to hold the female students - their sacred vessels (especially Rae Kerrigan).

**Joist House**——A timber stretched from wall-to-wall to support floorboards.

Joist House was considered a building of support where the male students could support and help each other.

**Oratory**——A private chapel in a house.

Private education room in the school where the students were able to practice their gifting and improve their skills. Also used as a banquet - dance hall when needed.

**Oriel**——A projecting window in a wall; originally a form of porch, often of wood. The original bay windows of the Tudor period. Guilder College majority of windows were oriel.

Rae often felt her life was being watching through one of these windows. Hence the constant reference to them.

**Refectory**——A communal dining hall. Same termed used in Tudor times.

**Scriptorium**——A Medieval writing room in which scrolls were also housed.

Used for English classes and still store some of the older books from the Tudor reign (regarding tatùs).

**Privy Council**——Secret council and "arm of the government" similar to the CIA, etc... In Tudor times, the Privy Council was King Henry's board of advisors and helped run the country.

Coming to Audio Soon:

Did you love *Royal Tea*? Then you should read *Four and a Half Shades of Fantasy* by W.J. May!

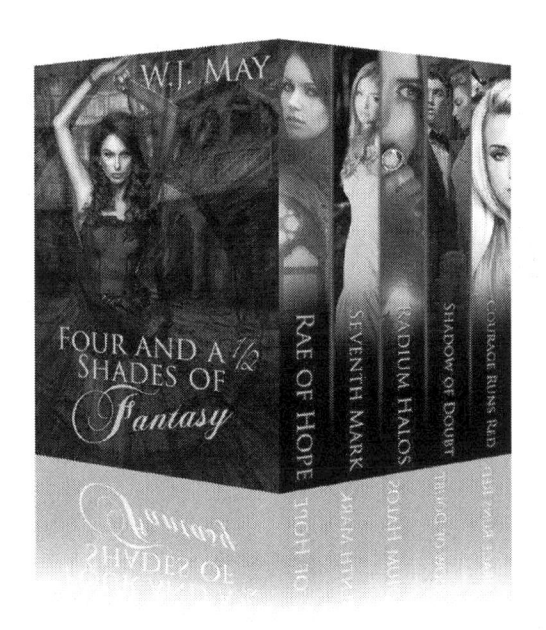

Four (and a half) Fantasy/Romance first Books from five different series! From best-selling author, W.J. May comes an anthology of five great fantasy, paranormal and romance stories. Books included: Rae of Hope from The Chronicles of Kerrigan Seventh Mark - Part 1 from the Hidden Secrets Saga Shadow of Doubt - Part 1 Radium Halos from the Senseless Series and an excerpt from Courage Runs Red from the Red Blood Series

Also by W.J. May

**Hidden Secrets Saga**
Seventh Mark - Part 1
Seventh Mark - Part 2
Marked By Destiny

**The Chronicles of Kerrigan**
Rae of Hope
Dark Nebula
House of Cards
Royal Tea

**The Hidden Secrets Saga**
Seventh Mark (part 1 & 2)

**The Senseless Series**
Radium Halos
Radium Halos - Part 2

**Standalone**
Shadow of Doubt (Part 1 & 2)
Five Shades of Fantasy

Glow - A Young Adult Fantasy Sampler
Shadow of Doubt - Part 1
Shadow of Doubt - Part 2
Four and a Half Shades of Fantasy
Full Moon
Dream Fighter
What Creeps in the Night
Forest of the Forbidden
HuNted